Flight of the Crow

by
Catherine Boyd

Copyright 2014

Montana, 1972

Chapter 1

Snowflakes the size of silver dollars. A chilling wind slicing wickedly through several layers of clothing. The sky soggy and turbulent with clouds in multiple shades of gray and off-white, with a tinge of navy blue. Four inches of snow covering the slowly awakening valley. Springtime in Montana.

Jesse Windchase reached down and switched off the ignition. He was lost, well, not lost actually. Jesse always knew where he was–he just didn't know for sure where he was going. The road had been clear enough before the freak snowstorm, so typical in Montana, but now it was completely obscured by the heavy, wet snow. He knew the general direction the road went, but being unable to tell for sure he decided to just wait until the storm was over. The snow would melt soon enough; after all it was April. The only disturbing aspect of the situation was the fact that he had told his new employer he would show up today, his first day of work on the C/6 ranch, before four o'clock this afternoon. He hated to break his word, but anyone who had lived in this state for more than six months realized how unpredictable Montana weather could be at any time of the year, and spring was the most unpredictable season of all. The Crow Indian part of him knew limitless patience, so he settled his six foot-four-inch frame back into the seat of the old Ford pickup, pulled his Resistol down over his thick salt and pepper hair, and relaxed into a state of vacuous rest.

He was later roused by nothing specific, just the instinctive knowledge that he was no longer alone. His eyelids flashed open, but he moved no other part of his body as he assessed his surroundings. Off to the left out of the north, a dark gray cloud seemed to hover near the ground, moving slowly in his direction but parallel at about three hundred feet. Having seen the sight many times during his forty-six years, he recognized it immediately as a small herd of cattle moving slowly through the lacy veil of large flakes, the wind at their backs. And behind them, thank the good Lord, a rider. He could get directions and perhaps make it to work on time after all.

***

Francine Larson shifted once in the saddle and pulled the collar of the duster a little higher around her neck. Her hat was pulled low on her face, and sunglasses protected her eyes from both the wind and the glaring snow. She rode with the easy grace of one who had spent years horseback, her body in perfect sync with the sway of the big bay leopard Appaloosa's rapid walk. She didn't mind the snow or the wind. Being outside was nearly always her preference, and being alone, for her peace of mind, a necessity. The big App mare trailed behind the Angus bulls, head down on a loose rein, headed for the home pasture. Directly behind her, his nose actually between her hocks, trotted a small blue heeler dog, his coat covered with a thick white mantle of snow. The path left in the wake of this entourage was a mixture of mud, water, and ice, as the snow melted furiously in the spring thaw and the pressure from the hooves of the animals aided in the process.

The old white pickup was a little hard to see amid the huge flakes, but Francine's sharp vision seldom missed anything. She saw the vehicle and the man in it, but gave no indication that she had. She turned neither her head nor her horse in the direction of the pickup, and continued with her task as if the vehicle and the man did not exist.

***

Jesse's eyes popped. He blinked, then blinked again. His jaw dropped. Unbelievable! The rider was not going to stop! He knew the man had seen him, knew it in his bones. He had seen the mare flick her ears in his direction, and by this alone he knew the rider realized he was there. It was the very worst of range manners not to acknowledge another soul encountered in the hills, not to mention the fact that this was a spring storm and a potentially dangerous one, but this man was actually going to ride right on past him! Jesse made his decision quickly. He sat up, grabbed the door handle, and jumped out. Where his boots made an imprint in the wet snow, the area immediately turned to slush and ice, making walking hazardous. Clutching his jacket together at the collar, he shouted and waved at the cowboy.

"Hey! Wait up!"

"*Damn!*" Francine thought, as she raised her rein hand a fraction. The slack in the reins remained visually unchanged, but the mare stopped dead in her tracks, her head up, ears alert. Francine hated talking to anyone, anytime, but even more she hated talking to dudes like this who were too stupid to stay home rather than go sightseeing in this kind of weather. Had the man not hailed her, she could have just ridden on by; now she had no choice. Well, she didn't have to make things easy for the fool. Francine never made things easy for anyone, and she wasn't about to start now. The bulls continued on at an even pace through the swirling snow, but Francine kept the mare steady in place. Snow enveloped both the rider and the horse, making them a ghostly apparition in the roiling grayness. She could have walked her horse over to the man, but instead, she made him struggle through the slippery snow to her. "*The stupid fool can just walk over to me,*" she thought. But even as the brazen words flashed through her mind, her heart began to beat a faster tempo, sweat beaded her temples and smooth upper lip, and the fear again settled upon her. A swift and silent prayer was sent heavenward as she dropped her chin to her chest only to raise it again slowly and continue her forward stare. She never turned her head in the man's direction.

Jesse waited only seconds before he realized the rider wasn't coming over to him- he would have to walk through the snow. Muttering under his breath, he slipped, slid and stumbled over the uneven, rocky ground and through the heavy, wet snow towards the rider. He couldn't remember ever taking so long to cover 300 feet, or being so angry as he did it. That cowboy was one rude hombre, and if he worked for the C/6 Jesse hoped he wasn't representative of the rest of the hands, or this new job was likely to last a record short period of time. Who was he kidding, anyway? He had to keep this job no matter what. There was a time though. . .

Jesse stopped about three feet from the rider as the heeler advanced from behind the horse, growling softly deep in his throat. He knew better than to push the dog; a blue heeler will heel a man as fast as he will a cow, and with no warning. Jesse was cautious, but fearless. He simply wanted to talk to the man, and he was no longer in a generous frame of mind. He could wait for the snow to melt and continue on his way, or he could ask this miserable cowboy for directions and start his new job off right- on time. So he asked.

"Howdy mister! Nice day for a walk, huh? Springtime in Montana, beautiful, just beautiful!"

Francine neither answered nor favored him with a glance, but kept her face pointed straight ahead, gazing off into the distance. The dog growled louder and began circling the man on foot.

Jesse's amiable intentions evaporated instantly. He had tried, and now he didn't care anymore. "If you want to keep your dog, call him off now" came the soft command.

Something in the big man's tone of voice made Francine glance at him, and she immediately recognized the fact that this man could, and would, kill her dog as easily as he breathed. She fixed her gaze on Jesse as if to memorize every feature, and instantly realized that classifying him as a "dude" was as far from accurate as one could get. This man was definitely no dude. He was tough, and a man not to tangle with. Self-confidence radiated from him, and Francine had a feeling that life meant no more to him than death. She registered the dark hair, gray at the temples, under the worn hat. The crooked nose, obviously broken in at least one fight. Large, dark brown, nearly black liquid eyes gave evidence of his heritage. Thin lips, even more thin now as they were compressed in obvious anger. But the most striking feature was the right eyebrow and outer half of the upper right eyelashes, where the normally coal black hairs were pure white. Scarred in a fight perhaps? At well over 200 pounds, Jesse was a formidable man.

Francine looked at the dog, snapped her fingers and pointed to the bulls up ahead. The dog raised his head questioningly at his mistress, then obediently trotted off after the herd.

"I'm looking for the C/6. Know where I can find it?"

Francine nodded her head affirmatively, slowly, and stared straight ahead again, but made no verbal response. Raising her right arm, she pointed in the direction of the bulls.

"Is this guy mute or what?" thought Jesse. And then he noticed the rider's face, what wasn't hidden behind the glasses and the hat. He saw the beads of sweat and knew them for what they were–fear. Raw, stark, fear. He dropped his head a moment, and inhaled slowly, deeply. He assumed his numerous unusual physical attributes had caused the normal response again. He thought he was used to it at forty-six, but he guessed maybe if he were honest with himself, he would have to admit that he never would really get used to it. Men usually took his looks fairly well in stride. Oh, they stared a lot, but it was the women that usually turned away in disgust or fear.

He sighed softly. "Do I just follow the bulls, then?"

The rider nodded and the mare instantly broke into a lope at some invisible cue, her sharp-shod hooves, secure in their footing, kicking up snowballs and leaving mud in their place.

Jesse stood in place, watching intently as the rider vanished into the veil of snow. The wind and the cold were forgotten, but not the rider's face. That man had been truly afraid of him, not disgusted. The water on his face had been the cold sweat of fear, not melted snow as he had first thought. Something about him made Jesse uneasy. Hopefully he'd never have to see him again.

He walked slowly back to the pick-up, thoughtful. After a few moments, he gunned the engine and slowly followed the wide path the bulls had tramped out of the snow, the gravel of the road visible through the mud. He had better things to do than worry about his looks and some nutty cowhand's response to them. He had a job, the first one in ten years, and he aimed to do his best to keep it. Not many folks would give an ex-con a job, but Glen Roberts had been willing to give him a chance, and Jesse would do anything to prove Glen's faith in him was justified. And he was never going back to jail. Never. He would die first.

Chapter 2

Jesse and Glen were seated in the manager's office, chatting casually about ranch work in general, and the C/6 in particular. Jesse had been born on the Crow Indian Reservation in Montana and had worked on different ranches throughout the state. Had it not been for his heritage and domestic troubles, he probably would have had his own ranch by now, or at least managing a spread like this one. But things hadn't turned out as he had planned. He was grateful to Glen for trusting him with this job. He and Glen went way back, and had known each other as kids on the Pitchfork ranch over near Glendive. That was a long time ago, but some friendships were made to last, and this was one.

Glen leaned his five-foot-ten-inch frame back in the oak captain's chair, splaying his legs out in front of him, his hands folded on his lap. He liked to rock back in his chairs when he sat, but his wife had finally cured him of the habit by making him replace them as he broke them down. Chairs were just too expensive, and besides, Glen truly loved his wife and would do whatever he could to make her happy. They had been married for thirty-four years, and he hoped they would make it another thirty-four. He had gray hair, brown eyes, and was all business. Sporting a small paunch, he walked with a slight limp related to a little accident with a rather protective cow during calving season some years back. Now he made the decisions and the money as best he could and left the harder work to the hands, of which there were three, now four with Jesse. A Bachelor's degree in Agricultural Business plus his years of ranching experience had landed him this job up Sixteen Mile Creek north of Bozeman, working for an absentee owner who paid well and came out to inspect the place only twice a year- branding time and hunting season.

The ranch ran about a thousand mother cows, divided up into the lower ranch down on the Gallatin River, and the upper place here on Sixteen Mile Creek, up in the Bridger Mountains northeast of Bozeman. The lush mountain grass yielded large claves in the fall, but the hard winters at that elevation made calving more difficult, so most of the cows were calved out at the lower ranch and trucked up to summer pasture in the spring with semi's.

Most of the help associated with the running of the overall operation were on the Gallatin River ranch; only a skeleton crew worked the upper ranch. Help rotated between the two ranches, with more men going up Sixteen Mile in the summer for haying, then heading back down country for shipping.

"Jess, I know how bad you wanted this job. I'm just sorry it has to be under these circumstances. Actually, it should be you doing my work, and I should be the one out there pounding posts and watching the south end of the cows heading north. You're a better man for this job than I ever thought of being, and you and I both know it."

"Yeah, well, that's life. You take what's dealt you. Only I really could have used a little better hand, my friend."

He looked Glen hard center in his eyes and whispered softly, "I didn't kill her, Glen. I didn't love her anymore, but I sure as hell didn't kill her. I don't know who did, and I really don't care anymore. I can't say she didn't deserve it, but honest to God, I didn't do it. I wanted to, that's for sure, but I didn't. Now, I just want to forget that whole period of my life and get on with what I do best. You know I can't go back to the reservation even if I wanted to. Sometimes I wish I could just fade away into the haze over these mountains. Guess this is about as far away as I can fade anymore. So, show me where I bunk and who I'll be working with. You're the boss, just tell me what to do and point me in the right direction."

Glen rose painfully to his feet. "Come on out to the bunkhouse and I'll show you around. The boys are a pretty good bunch for the most part, but we do have one strange fella here, and I do mean strange, if you get my drift. We pretty much leave him alone at all times. He doesn't talk much, and no one socializes with him at all; you'll understand why when you meet him. I didn't hire him, the owner, Adrian Miller, did. I don't know what the deal is, but I have my orders where he's concerned and he stays no matter what, unless he chooses to leave. He's different and that's an understatement, but he's exceptionally good with cattle and horses. The man is the only one with his own string, and the rest of the boys are pretty jealous of those horses of his. That's one rule here– your string is yours, and nobody touches one of your horses without your permission. You can pick three from the remuda in the morning when Franc brings them in. You'll have about twenty to choose from. There's a tack room in the barn; did you bring your own gear?"

"Yeah," Jesse answered as they walked through the front hall to the porch. The snow was already letting up and the sun was making a valiant effort to break through the heavy clouds. They went down the porch steps and headed across the yard to the bunkhouse. "I've got everything I need in the truck."

"Well, if you come up short anything essential, let me know. We have plenty of extra tack in the barn, and Peg goes into town once or twice a week for supplies. She'd be happy to pick up anything you need. Just let her know. I'm sorry I can't give you any days off until we're done calving, but when that's done, you can have every other Sunday, just like everyone else. I'm sorry I can't give you every weekend off, like folks in town get."

"Glen, don't apologize for doing your job, okay? Besides, what would I do with time off? I haven't lost anything in town, so there's no need to go. Hey, with this face I'm usually not real welcome anyway and it's not like the ladies are lining up to meet me, if you know what I mean? And if there's ever any trouble, I don't want to have been seen anywhere near it! I just want some peace and quiet."

Glen stopped and looked at his friend thoughtfully. "Yeah, Jess, I know. I just hope you can find some of that peace you need so badly up here in these mountains."

***

The bunkhouse was on the other side of the big barn. It was an older, rambling, one story building in fair repair, better than most Montana bunkhouses. Indoor plumbing made it a real palace.

The low porch roof leaked in a few places, but the three chairs on it, though now covered with rapidly melting snow, made one imagine cool summer evenings enjoying strong coffee and a smoke or just sharing wild tales with the boys. Glen led the way inside and held the door for Jesse. There was a main gathering room with an old pot-bellied stove in the corner. A couple of wooden straight chairs stood in front of the stove, and a long wooden table with benches on either side of it took up the center of the large room. Two decks of cards lay on the table, as if waiting for evening and the nightly poker game. The floor was bare pine, worn soft and smooth with the boot traffic of years. A broom, a mop, and a dustpan kept vigil in the far corner. To the right of the door, nails had been pounded into the soot-blackened wall, forming serviceable hooks for jackets, ropes and other miscellaneous ranch hand gear.

Three doors opened off the gathering room; a bedroom and bathroom on one side, and another bedroom opening off the other side. The bunkhouse had obviously been built specifically for its current purpose.

Glen walked over and opened the door to the isolated bedroom, motioning Jesse to take a look inside. Jesse poked his head in, noting nothing out of the ordinary. There were two cots, one on each side of the room, which was about nine by twelve, large for a bunkhouse. Two small dressers stood on opposite walls from each other, next to the cots. One cot was neatly made up with army blankets and two pillows. A pair of well-worn ropers stood next to the dresser. Along one wall someone had nailed up a long one-by-four board and pounded nails into it to serve as makeshift hooks. Two jackets and a pair of spurs hung there, waiting. A small window half covered with a torn window shade gave a dismal view of the outside, and a small wooden table with a folding chair served as a desk beneath it.

"I'm putting you in here with Franc. I know he's different, and I also know you'll probably hate his guts, but I somehow think you'll get along with him better than the others. He doesn't talk if he doesn't absolutely have to, so at least he won't bother you with incessant jabbering."

"Do the boys know about me, Glen? What have you told them?"

The older man sighed, and removing his hat, ran his fingers through his graying hair with his free hand. "No, Jess, I didn't tell them. But let's face it, you can't exactly hide that mug of yours forever. Bozeman isn't a real big town, but eventually someone is going to put two and two together and everyone is going to know who you are. That's one reason I think you ought to bunk in here with Franc. He couldn't care less if you were the Boston Strangler. He's an awful lot like you, really, just wants to be left alone. Hell, I'll just come right out and say it, and get the whole thing over with. Franc is as gay as they come, Jess. We all know it, and the boys sometimes give him a pretty rough time. But damn, he's the best man I have with the cattle and horses. He really does keep to himself, and he won't put any "moves" on you, I guarantee it. Besides, like I said, Franc comes with the ranch, boss's orders, and unless he chooses to leave of his own accord, he's here to stay."

"Glen, old buddy, old pal, you have to be joking!" Jesse looked positively apoplectic. "You're making me bunk with a man like that? Come on, man, you simply can't be serious! I put up with a lot of that in the pen, you can't expect me to put up with it here?"

"I can and I do, Jess. I have my reasons, one of which is I don't want any trouble in this bunkhouse. And I can feel in my gut that trouble is brewing. I'm depending on you to keep Franc alive, if it comes to that. Will you do it for me, Jess? Please?"

A shuttered look came over Jesse's whole countenance, as the Indian in him surfaced, forcing down his outward show of emotions. His affect became totally flat, and Glen could no longer read his friend. He was not surprised. Jesse was hard and complex, and ten years in the state penitentiary had molded him into an even harder, more inscrutable man. But he still had his pride, and Glen knew he was pushing Jesse to the limit. However, he also knew that there was no other way to bunk his men together. He just hoped that this arrangement hadn't cost him a precious friendship.

Glen dropped his head. He truly sympathized with Jesse's feelings, but he felt he had no other choice in this matter. Franc was an easy enough person to have around in that he never talked or socialized with anyone. But his sexual orientation made for real conflict with the other hands. Although in all fairness, Franc had never told anyone he was gay or approached anyone in the years Glen had known him, anybody could tell just by looking at him what he was. Sometimes a man had a gut feeling about something, and just had to go with it. In this case, he felt real trouble was right around the corner. One of the boys, Fred Beckett, was getting more and more vocal around Franc. He was not only saying more, but the language was getting rather vulgar and he thought he had overheard some threats. But he wasn't positive, and he knew that nothing overt had been done, and so had only his instincts to rely on. The other two men sharing the bunkhouse knew nothing about the fact that Franc "came with the ranch" so to speak. Glen knew that some teasing and lewd comments were going to be natural, but he was afraid things might go farther than that, and he hoped Jesse would be willing to be his eyes and ears in the bunkhouse. Glen rubbed his eyes with his left hand and let out a barely audible sigh.

There were only four beds in the bunkhouse, and Jesse was not only the newcomer, he was the only one Glen could trust not to cause any trouble. Jesse gave his friend a long, hard stare; Glen had a difficult time meeting his eyes without looking away, but somehow he accomplished the feat.

"Guess I'll just go get my gear and get settled in then. When will everyone be back?"

"Franc should show up anytime now, he was moving some bulls to the home pasture. Fred and Lucky are still feeding down at the lower place, but they should show up in about an hour or so. Just in time for supper, which, by the way, is over at the cookhouse. Sandy and Gene McIntosh live over there. Gene keeps up the grounds around the house and Sandy does the cooking. Hell of a cook too. Wait 'till you taste some of those homemade pies of hers. They'll really knock your socks off, let me tell you. Don't tell Peg, but I kind of wish she would take some pie making lessons from Sandy." Glen was valiantly trying to divert Jesse's thoughts away from his new bunkmate.

"Supper at six, breakfast at six. Cut out your horses after breakfast, then go with Franc. You and he will do all the calving from now on, and he can show you around. You two can work out your own schedule for night calving. He's been doing it all himself since we started, so I expect he'll be real grateful for any help he can get."

"What about Lucky and Fred? Don't they do any calving?"

"I'll tell you, Jesse, this had been a hard winter up here this year, and those two have been strung out just getting to the cows and bulls with all the hay and cake. Don't know why the boss won't let me hire some more help- maybe it was a bad year in the stock market!" Glen gave a wry laugh. "Well, got to go, Jesse. Any questions?"

"No, I guess not."

Glen turned and started back toward the foreman's house, slipping through the now muddy quagmire that was the driveway.

"Glen, thanks. I'll do my best for you."

"Jesse, I wonder if maybe I'm the one who needs to be thanking you. And I know you will. Take care, see you later."

Jesse stared off into the distance. The snow had stopped completely and water now ran in small rivulets everywhere. He had his freedom and a job doing what he had been born to do. He had one friend. He was in Montana. What more could a man ask for?

"*Just one more thing,*" he thought. "*Just one more thing. Why, in the name of all that's holy, am I saddled with this cowboy, and not just any man, but that clown I met on my way in to the ranch? That had to have been Frank- Glen said he was moving bulls.*" He wasn't sure how he was going to handle this situation, but he would give it his best shot. There was one condition though; if that Franc person ever looked at him funny just one time, there was going to be hell to pay. And Franc would be the one paying!

Chapter 3

Francine shut the wire gate behind the herd of black bulls and squatted on her haunches, fondling the dog's ears affectionately.

"Sammy, old friend, you did a great job, as usual. Don't know what I'd do without you, boy. You're the only one I can really be myself with, and I think I'd go stark raving mad without you. I love you, Sammy."

Sammy soaked up the affection ravenously, licking Francine's face with ardor. They were a real team, more than friends. Francine told Sammy all her dreams. She would have told him her hopes, but she really didn't have any. She expected her life would continue on as it had for the past five years here on the C/6, until she was too old to do the work, and just hoped she had enough money saved up by then to keep herself in modest comfort until she died. At forty, she figured if she was careful she would be able to keep ranching for about another fifteen or twenty years. Even though she was working for essentially peanuts, she spent nothing beyond what she needed for dog food and clothes, so most of her pay went into a special "retirement" account.

She gave Sammy one last pat on the head, then rose easily to her feet and rested her arm on the gatepost, looking off to the west toward the Spanish Peaks. The sun was just starting to set, and with the snowstorm over, the mountaintops were glistening a pale pink as the sun's rays reflected off the new snow in the distance. The colors were rapidly changing to various shades of lavender and rose. Francine never tired of these mountains. She never tired of the sagebrush, the rolling hills, or the vast emptiness of her self-imposed solitude. She was at peace when she was out in these hills, alone.

Occasionally she missed having someone to talk to who could return her conversation, but Sammy substituted pretty well over all. At least on the positive side, he never talked back to her! Of course, he never answered her, either. If she was careful, though, she just might be able to live out the rest of her life in some semblance of order and quiet. As long as everyone thought she was a man, she was safe. They all thought she was some sort of queer, and so far that had worked to her advantage. The other hands left her alone, rather than associate with someone like they perceived her to be. She worked alone, and seldom spoke other than a yes or a no. She had the act down pretty pat, but meeting that man today had really shaken her.

Something about him frightened her. He was obviously at least half Indian, and nobody's fool. He was a big man, and dangerous. She knew it in the deepest part of her being. It wasn't just his looks, either, although she had to admit she had never encountered anyone before with such an "interesting" countenance. The very essence of that man was vastly different from the average; he would take no pushing of any kind. Sammy was a pretty tough dog with anyone other than Francine, and most people backed away from him instinctively when he growled. But that Indian hadn't even hesitated, just essentially offered to kill her best friend for her. And he had asked directions to the ranch headquarters. Probably just passing through, maybe stopping to say "hi" to one of the other men. She sure hoped so, because if he was going to become a permanent fixture on the ranch she was going to have to work overtime to keep up her act. Well, as long as she didn't have to be around him except at mealtimes, she would probably be all right. No, he had to be just passing through.

"Well, passing through or not, it's nearly supper time. Come on my very best friend in the whole wide world, let's head for the barn."

She gathered the reins in her left hand, grabbed the pommel with her right, gave a small hop to plant her left foot in the stirrup, and swung up easily into the saddle. At five feet ten inches tall, she was not small, and her body was lean and toned from years of hard outdoor work. She adjusted the duster and resettled the well-worn, sweat-stained Bailey hat on her head, brushing her medium brown hair back from her face. It just reached the top of her collar; she had always meant to cut it shorter, thinking it might help with the deception, but so far no one in all these years had suspected her of being female. She told herself it was easier for her to cut, but the truth was, her hair was the one part of her femininity she had been able to hold on to.

Francine had perfect white teeth, straight, even brows, and clear blue eyes the color of a mountain lake high in the Crazy Mountains. A deep tan contrasted with the blue of her eyes, and slender white streaks fanned the corners of her eyes from squinting against the sun, giving evidence to a hard life lived almost exclusively outdoors. Those permanently etched lines around her eyes were the only ones a person noticed at first glance. Francine had no "laugh lines." She never laughed.

She had once. She had been a normal, healthy woman with normal desires. She had married a handsome rodeo bull rider. But that was a long time ago, and now she was a different person. She was Franc Larson, a gay cowboy, a loner.

The big Appaloosa mare knew the way to the barn, and headed there confidently, head down, moving at a slow, even jog. It was almost dark now. A few more months though, and the sun wouldn't set until nearly ten thirty at night. By then she would be at her favorite spot of all, the summer line camp. There she was always alone, and could be herself all she liked. She could talk and sing, and even smile occasionally at the antics of the abundant wildlife up in the hills. Three more months. But until then, a lot of calves to get on the ground.

Francine was getting tired, bone weary in fact. She had always enjoyed calving, but this year for some reason had been exceptionally tough all around. On top of an extra wet winter, it had been abnormally cold. And there had been more backward calves than she could remember in years. Every one of those had to be pulled. Then there were the heifers. Adrian had wanted to get some younger blood in the herd, so he had gone and told Glen to purchase two hundred head of two-year-old first calf heifers. She didn't know what kind of bull they had been bred to, but she had pulled every single calf out of those darn heifers. That meant less sleep than usual, which was very little this time of the year anyway, and now she was just plain tired. At least there were only about fifty head of cows left to calve up here, the majority being down at the lower ranch. Moving the bulls home today was a welcome break in the routine for her, but she really was just too tired to enjoy it as much as she normally would have. Right now food beckoned, and then sleep. She would check the cows again after supper, but didn't think she would have any calves tonight and could therefore, maybe, get a full six hours of uninterrupted sleep for the first time in three months.

After rubbing her mare down and putting her up for the night, Francine shuffled over to the cookhouse, Sammy trotting faithfully at her heels. Something smelled absolutely wonderful in there. One thing about this ranch, the food was top notch, the best she'd ever eaten aside from her mother's cooking when she was a child. She herself had been a pretty fair cook, at least she had thought so, but her husband had thought differently.

She left her hat and duster on the rack on the front porch, keeping her vest, chaps, and spurs on, and went in to take her customary seat at one end of the long wooden parson's table. Sammy wasn't allowed in the cookhouse, so waited patiently near Francine's outerwear on the porch. A bench on each side of the table seated Lucky, Fred, Gene, Sandy and herself. Glen and Peggy ate at their own house. She sat by herself at one end of the table, while the others grouped together at the other end. They would pass her the plates of food after they helped themselves, but she never acknowledged anyone other than Sandy, and to her she only nodded to show her appreciation.

Francine hadn't stayed alive this long without being observant, but even if she wasn't, it would have been hard to miss the big man seated next to Fred at the table. The same

Indian she had unexpectedly run across in the storm this afternoon. She moved as nonchalantly as she could, as if nothing was out of the ordinary, never deigning the newcomer with even a glance of curiosity. She sat down at her customary spot, alone, and waited for Sandy to pass her some steaming pot roast.

***

"Hey Franc! Got us a new hand here!" Fred cheerfully blurted out. He loved trying to get Franc to talk, and he had a feeling tonight he just might get the job done.

Jesse gazed steadily at the man he had met earlier today, waiting for some sort of response. There was none. Franc neither lifted his head nor acknowledged him in any way. He might just as well have been a fly on the wall for all the cowboy seemed to care.

"Hello, Franc, Glad to meet you." There was no reply. Franc obviously Franc did not want their earlier meeting revealed for whatever reason, and he would be happy to oblige him. He wasn't sure he wanted anyone to know of their meeting either. He hadn't mentioned it to Glen, and he really didn't know why he had kept silent; he just had.

"Jesse here is a kind of an old friend of the boss," said Lucky, always happy to contribute any little bits of information. "Where did you know Glen from, anyway?" he asked.

"I worked with him some over around Glendive," Jesse replied. He was not about to volunteer too much information, but on the other hand, he didn't want to antagonize anyone. He attempted to be cheerful, and steered the conversation on to the daily running of the ranch, and then to the backgrounds of each of the two other men.

Lucky was a ranch kid, born and bred, from over by Pony, Montana. There had been too many kids and not enough ranch, so he had been hiring out since he got out of college. He was thirty-five now, a likeable, friendly-faced young man of medium height with sandy hair and a winning, ready smile. Like many young ranch hands, his idea of a good time was a Saturday night in Bozeman, trying to pick up a good-looking woman. He hoped one day to get married, but so far he hadn't found that special someone. He was having a lot of fun looking though.

Fred was another story altogether. Born and raised up around the Browning area, he appeared to be the stereotypical tough guy, and seemed to want everyone to know it. His language was coarse, but he wasn't actually rude. He seemed to sense in Jesse a comrade of sorts, someone tough and mean. He also recognized Jesse as someone not to tangle with. Fred was six feet tall, about forty years old, and quick-witted. He laughed easily, but not always at things that were funny.

His sense of humor was at times rather distorted. For example, he had thought it was extremely funny the time his horse had moved too quickly after a cow and stepped on Sammy's back leg, snapping it cleanly. He laughed a long time over that one.

He had been married many years ago, but his numerous extramarital activities had been more than his patient wife was able to tolerate, and he had been single now for years. That was fine with him; it just meant he had more money to spend in Bozeman on his favorite women, of whom he had many to choose from. He was a good worker, and dependable. Though he usually got along well with most people, he was not especially liked by anyone.

Fred's pet project at the moment was Franc. He had despised the queer ever since he had first come to work on the ranch, about two years ago. Fred had wanted the riding position that Franc held, but Franc had already been there three years, so held seniority. He had to admit Franc was a genius with the animals. But just to watch Franc made him a little sick. The man walked liked a woman, he acted like a woman, and he never joked about women with the guys. He had to be as queer as they came, and Fred just couldn't stand a queer.

He had made some comments to Glen shortly after he started work, hoping maybe Glen would fire the little fairy. Not only would he not have to look at the wimp, but maybe he could have had Franc's job with the cows. Glen had put him in his place real fast, but politely, making it very clear that Franc was there for as long as he chose to remain, and to back off and leave the man alone.

He had never done anything overtly to Franc, but he had been pushing a little more all the time, trying to get some kind of response out of him. He would have loved to pick a fight with Franc, but he couldn't even get the man to say anything more than "yes" and "no", let alone rile him enough to get him to fight. Franc would just walk away whenever Fred tried to push him.

Well, Fred had a new button to push tonight, and he was sure going to enjoy it.

Francine was about half way through her meal when Fred casually dropped his first bomb.

"Hey Franc! You never said hello to our new cohort! He's a real nice fella, you're gonn'a really like him."

Jesse wasn't sure what was coming, but he didn't like what Fred had said so far. The words were harmless enough, but given what he had been told about Franc, he wasn't too happy about the possible insinuation.

"Yeah, looks like he's gonn'a be working here permanently. Guess he'll be working full time with you. Won't that be nice, a little help for you? Maybe you can finally get some sleep."

That got Francine's attention, and the fork stopped half way to her mouth. No, she couldn't have anyone working with her! Not once in a while, not part time, and dear God in heaven, for sure not on a daily basis! Especially not this Indian! It just couldn't be true! Glen wouldn't do this to her. But then, Glen didn't know. Good Lord, she was in deep, as in with no bottom, trouble. Her throat became tight, almost closed off with fear at the thought, and her mouth was dry as sand. She didn't think, in those few seconds, that her life could possibly get any worse.

And then Fred cleared his throat for his big announcement. His lips curved into a wide smile, as he cheerfully pushed that button for Franc. "And guess what Franc? He's gonn'a be bunking in with you!"

Chapter 4

The blood drained from Francine's face, and sweat instantly broke out there as well as on her chest and in her armpits. She actually thought for a moment that she might faint. She couldn't breathe, and knew she had to get outside. But how to do it in front of everyone without giving them an opportunity to see how distressed she was? She couldn't let anyone find out about her, she couldn't! How in the name of heaven was she going to keep her sex a secret if she had to share a room with a man? Hell, if she had to share a room with anyone! Maybe it wasn't true. She knew Fred had been trying to get a reaction out of her for months now, and maybe he was just joking. But in the silence following his announcement, no one corrected Fred's statement. Everyone was silent, watching her. Even Sandy, whom she thought of as somewhat of a friend, was watching her. Glances darted from Francine to Jesse and back again, waiting.

"*God, give me strength, please!*" She prayed silently. Keeping her eyes fixed and staring, she rose slowly to her feet, turned, and walked out of the communal dining room to the porch where she silently collected her things, and then walked out into the dark blanket of the Montana night, Sammy at her heels as usual. It was the longest walk of her life, and quite possibly the hardest.

Back at the table, the silence was all consuming and even somewhat oppressive for several moments after Francine left the room. Then Fred burst out laughing.

"Damn! Did you ever see anything so funny in all your born days as the look on that little queer's face when I told him he'd be rooming with old Jesse here?" He dove into his pot roast with renewed vigor, his shoulders heaving with mirth. "Should be a fun night tonight! Jesse, you gonn'a find out for us if the little fairy has any hair on his chest? How're you gonn'a sleep in the same room with that? Oh golly Miss Molly, I'd give a month's pay to hide in a corner of that room tonight when you boys settle down to bed. A month's pay, and maybe two! Jesse, you're gonn'a tell us all about it in the morning, right?"

Jesse glared at Fred, but made no response until it became obvious that Fred wasn't going to let up. He wasn't any happier about the arrangement than poor old Franc appeared to be, but there wasn't a thing he could do about it, and he really didn't appreciate the ribbing that seemed, at the moment, to be aimed as much at him as it was at Franc.

"Fred, do you mind if we change the subject for now so I can finish my meal in peace? Seems a shame to put a damper on what should be such a purely enjoyable time. I haven't had a meal like this in ten years, Mrs. McIntosh. I thank you for such a treat. Can I have a little more of that salad, and maybe another roll, please?"

"Why, thank you, Mr. Windchase." She shot a disdainful look at the other diners. "It's been a while since anyone seemed to notice whether I served roast beef or rawhide around here, and it's nice to know someone appreciates my culinary efforts!"

Lucky broke in with his usual wide grin. "Oh now Sandy, you know we'd all just up and fade into nothingness if you weren't cooking for us. Why, after eating this food of yours, anybody else's cooking would have to taste like shoe leather. Hell, it would actually *be* shoe leather to us. You've just got us spoiled, that's all."

The conversation veered to other subjects; tomorrow's weather, how much hay was left, how many cows were left to calve, the prices of cattle and hay this year. Fred's shoulders continued to shake with mirth occasionally, as if he couldn't help it. Jesse let the others do most of the talking, content to just listen. Then Lucky asked the question he had been dreading.

"Where have you been working the last few years, Jesse?"

An innocent enough question, if it had just been asked of someone else. He had thought about how he would reply to such an inquiry, knowing the odds were very high it would be asked eventually. Especially with his face. For some reason, as soon as people saw that half white eyebrow of his, they wanted to know his whole life's history. They seemed to know there was a good story there somewhere—nobody wound up with a face like his without a pretty good yarn behind it. But his life was his own, and his past belonged only to him, at least he hoped he could keep it to himself.

"Oh, I've worked pretty much all over the state. You name it, I've probably worked there. I'm just happy to be here, now. Thanks for the fine meal, Mrs. McIntosh. I'm so full I could bust, but I'm already looking forward to breakfast. If I can take a cup of that coffee with me, I think I'll go check out the barn."

"You just help yourself, Mr. Windchase. You take all the coffee you want, but there is a pot in the bunkhouse if you get thirsty later this evening." Sandy smiled happily. It had been a very long time since anyone had called her Mrs. McIntosh, and she kind of enjoyed the feeling of respect the term seemed to convey. That Mr. Windchase had the looks of the devil himself, but he sure had the manners! She wished some of those manners would rub off onto the other men, but she was nothing if not realistic. If wishes were quarters she would be rich.

"See you later, boys" said Jesse as he rose from his place at the table, stretched earnestly, and walked to the door with the panther-like grace that was inherent in him, a mug of steaming coffee in his hand. A walk before bed might help his frame of mind immensely. It was cold outside, but it was April after all, and the cold, now that the storm was over and the wind had died down to an almost perfect stillness, was almost pleasant. He thought he'd check out the barn before going to bed. With any luck Franc would have already turned in and they could do any necessary talking in the morning.

Franc had looked like death when Fred told him he had to share his room. He knew his looks were repulsive; he'd certainly been told that often enough over the years. But he was still a man, and he had some pride left. No, correction. He was a proud man, proud of his heritage and proud of the fact that he still had his sanity after all he'd been through in his life. He didn't want to sleep in the same room with Franc any more than Franc seemed to want to share a room with him. But that was life, and he guessed they'd both have to put up with it. But he'd thought he was done having to share a room with a queer. He'd had to do it in prison, and had to fight off a few of them, too. But he'd done it. He had no use for such men, if you could call them men. It was bad enough that he had to share a room with a sexual deviate, but with Franc Larson of all people? He was weird, obviously a coward, and rude beyond belief. Hell, he had some kind of night ahead of him!

***

Francine had carried off her exit well, until the porch door closed behind her and the cold night air hit her lungs. Then her body convulsed once, and she bent over at the waist, clutching her stomach as though in severe pain. Gasping for breath, she felt as if she were suffocating. Sammy jumped around her feet, aware that something was terribly wrong, but unable to help his mistress. Slow deep breaths, she told herself, and tried her utmost to do it. Slowly, her breathing became less frantic and labored, and her color began to return.

Oh my God! she thought. Oh my God! As her heart rate slowly returned to normal, she straightened, and began walking aimlessly, her mind unable to concentrate. Her first instinct was to flee, to simply pack up her things and leave the ranch. But where would she go? It was eight o'clock at night, for one thing, and at this time of the night, given where the ranch was, there was no place *to* go. And she couldn't leave her horses. If she left, wouldn't everyone be more suspicious than they already were? No one knew she was a woman. They hadn't figured it out in the past five years, so maybe, if she could just concentrate, she could think of something. *"Think Francie, think! You can do it, I know you can. Don't give up now. Oh Lord, help me!"*

Slowly, she began to collect her wits. Yes, maybe she could still pull it off, if she was careful. She could sleep in the barn, and say it was easier to check the cows during the night. She could say that with a new roommate she wouldn't be able to sleep as soundly between cow checks, so she would just save herself some trouble and stay out in the barn tonight. That would fix the problem for now, and tomorrow she might be able to think of something else. It would be a little cold out there, but she had slept through worse conditions. It could work. She resolutely headed for the bunkhouse to brush her teeth and collect a couple of blankets from her cot.

Francine had just finished fixing up a makeshift bed in an empty stall when she heard footsteps. Sammy growled softly about the same time. She knew who it was; no one else would have bothered to come out here. She realized when the soft padding continued her way that he had heard her moving in the stall, so was not surprised when he began speaking.

"Well Franc, looks like you're stuck with me. I don't like it any more than you do, but I guess that's life. I suppose we can make the best of it. If we can't be friends, can we at least agree not to be enemies?"

Silence permeated the stall area, as Francine pretended to finish up her bed, ignoring Jesse. Sammy continued his low warning.

"Look, Franc, can't you even acknowledge that I exist, for crying out loud? And call that dog off or you can plan on getting a new one!"

"Sammy." Spoken quietly, barely audible, but enough that Sammy took his place behind his mistress, his blue eyes never leaving Jesse. She supposed she would have to talk to the man. After all, it looked like they were going to be spending time together whether either one of them liked it or not.

"Okay. You exist. Now go away." Her voice was low, for a woman, and always had been. But she constantly feared that voice would give her away, since it sure wasn't as low as the average man's. But this guy didn't seem to notice anything out of the ordinary, thank goodness. One hurdle cleared.

"Turn around and face me, damn it! I'm not your dog, and I don't work for you, I work for Glen Richards." Jesse stared at the unyielding, rigid back presented to him. "I said turn around, or by God if you can't manage to turn around by yourself, I'll do it for you!"

Francine pulled her hat lower on her forehead, took a deep breath, raised her chin a fraction, and slowly turned to face him. Defiance emanated from her entire body. She raised her eyes to stare him fully in the face, and glared. *"Well,"* she thought, *"this is it. I either live or I die right here, right now. But if I have to go down, I'm going down with my head up."*

Jesse surveyed the man in front of him. He registered defiance, and pride, and yes, he was sure of it-fear. Franc Larson, for all his bravado, was terrified of him. He looked up toward the roof of the barn as he collected his thoughts. Was he that repulsive? He expected this reaction from the weaker sex, but not another man. Guess he'd just have to remember that Franc was no ordinary man, and chalk his reaction up to that. But it hurt, just the same, when someone reacted to him the way Franc was now.

"Have you checked the cows yet?"

"No."

"Let's go do it now. Show me where everything is, then I can split the checks with you, and maybe we can both get some sleep. And by the way, there's no need for you to sleep out here. I won't disturb you, I promise. And you won't disturb me. So why not pick up those blankets and move them back to your room?"

"I'll sleep out here."

From the look on his face, Jesse knew Franc meant every word he said, and that short of physically carrying him back to the bunkhouse, Franc would be spending the night in the barn.

"Okay. Let's go check those old girls and get it over with."

"I can check them my . . ."

"Mister," said Jesse in the same voice he had used when he offered to take care of her dog for her earlier, "I think it's time for *us* to go check those cows."

Francine grabbed her flashlight, and without a backward glance at Jesse, headed out the rear door of the barn to the pen that held the night drop. She didn't wait for him to follow, but knew he wouldn't be far behind. Sammy waited by her bed, knowing he was not allowed in the calving pen with her.

She wondered how much Jesse knew about cattle, and figured she would soon find out. Suddenly, he reached through the darkness and grabbed her arm to slow her down. She stopped, motionless, rigid. She was thankful that he couldn't see her face in the darkness, because she knew he would see her fear.

"Slow down and let me walk with you. I'm a stranger to them; they don't know me, and I don't want to upset them. If I stay right with you, they will relax again."

Softly, from out of the blackness, Jesse heard Franc's barely audible command.

"Take your hand off me right now, and don't you ever, *ever* touch me again. Do you hear me?"

Jesse dropped her arm as if he had been burned. He hadn't wanted to touch Franc, but he had done it out of necessity and for no other reason. Franc acted as if he were positively repulsed by the contact with him.

Francine drew a shallow breath, opened the gate, and began walking among the cows quietly, shining her flashlight in their faces and then at their tails, looking for any signs of agitation or impending birth. With only fifty cows to go, they were all in the pen tonight, and would be every night until they had all dropped their calves. She talked softly to them as she walked and occasionally stopped to stroke a special pet in the group. Jesse noted how the cows reacted to her presence, and had to agree with Glen; Franc was good with cattle. As a matter of fact, he was very good. Jesse was seldom impressed with cowhands; they were pretty much all alike. But Franc seemed to have a special affinity for the cattle, and it showed in their reactions to him.

Seeing nothing that looked like it would require attention during the night, they walked to the gate, then back to the barn. Francine switched off the flashlight and headed toward the stall. She neither looked at nor spoke to Jesse, but left him standing in the middle of the barn, between the box stalls.

"Doesn't look like anything's going to happen tonight. Why don't you just come on back over to the bunkhouse. I feel kind of bad, having you sleep out here just because I moved in."

"I'd better stay out here. Might get a calf tonight anyway."

They both knew it was a lie. There would be no calves tonight. But if that was the way Franc wanted it, that's the way he could have it. Jesse intended to get a good night's sleep regardless.

"Have it your way."

He walked over to the big main double sliding door, turned off the overhead lights, and shut the door. He then disappeared softly into the blackness of the night. Still fully dressed, Francine settled herself under the blankets with Sammy curled happily against her stomach. She was exhausted. The emotional strain of the evening had been almost too much for her, but so far, she had done it. Jesse had no idea she wasn't what she appeared to be. Tomorrow was another day, of course, with more worries for her, but maybe for now she could rest. Time enough to worry about tomorrow when tomorrow got here. She simply didn't have the strength to do it tonight. Somehow, she would handle Jesse Windchase. She had to. Sleep overcame her as she struggled with these thoughts, and her dreams were troubled that night for the first time in a very long while.

Chapter 5

It was chilly and damp in the old barn, even with Sammy curled up so close to her. She slept fitfully, unable to completely lose herself, as she had hoped, in a dreamless sleep. After months of nothing but pleasant dreams, she was suddenly cast backward in time. It was as if she was standing on the sidelines, watching the dream unfold, knowing what was going to happen next. But because it was a dream, she was powerless to stop its progression. Tears coursed silently down her cheeks as she turned fitfully on her bed of blankets and straw, watching her hopes for her future expire in her dream, as had her baby.

She was twenty-five again, and married to Todd. He had been such a handsome devil, and Francine had thought herself so fortunate that he had even looked at her, let alone asked her out. They had gone to a movie, something she seldom did, and it had been rather sexually explicit, too much so for a first date. But she had been with Todd, "the man," so even though she was uncomfortable with the movie's content, she was enjoying herself immensely. During one of the lovemaking scenes, he had started to kiss her and fondle her breasts, something no man had ever done before, and Francine really didn't know how to handle the new emotions his ministrations aroused. But she had enjoyed it. She couldn't deny that.

The dream shifted, and she had now been married for eight years. She had wanted a baby so badly in the beginning, before the beatings had started. When she realized what kind of man she had married, she knew she could never bring a child into this marriage, so gave up that dream. When she found herself pregnant by accident at the age of thirty-three, she was both overjoyed and terrified. She knew Todd wanted no children, and she knew that his reaction would be another beating. It was a severe one, landing her in the hospital with a broken arm and a concussion. Of course she had lied, as usual, and said her horse had fallen with her.

The tears came harder now, and she began breathing more rapidly as she slept. The baby was crying. Todd, yelling at her to "shut the brat up!" He was drunk, as usual. She tried to soothe the baby. She tried. But little Claire just kept sobbing.

"Oh Claire, baby, it's Okay. Mommy's here, don't cry! Please don't cry anymore! Mommy's here, baby, Mommy's here!"

"Oh Todd, no! Todd, no! Todd, please put her down! No, Todd! Don't shake her like that! Todd! Oh my God! Oh my God!"

She woke with a start, staring up into the blackness that was the loft of the barn. Her face was wet with tears, her breath shallow, and her pulse racing with her exertions during her dream. Seven years, and the dream still haunted her. She hadn't been able to save her little Claire. "Oh Claire, I'm so sorry! So very sorry." Claire had been only four months old. Her baby. And now?

She rose quickly, trying to put the dream out of her mind. She just couldn't think about it. She couldn't. Not turning the barn light on or using her flashlight, she slowly made her way out of the barn to the hydrant in the first corral, Sammy ever faithful at her heels. Inhaling deeply, she surveyed the night sky, with the myriad of dazzling stars and the brilliant display of northern lights flashing their splendor.

"Oh Claire, you would have loved this. But then, maybe you have a better view of it all than I do. I love you little girl. Mommy loves you with all her heart."

She raised the handle on the hydrant, and bent for a drink of cold spring water. Dashing some of the liquid on her face, she immediately felt refreshed, and more peaceful. There was no possibility of any more sleep tonight, so there was no point in going back to bed. The sky would be changing from velvet blue-black to deep purple as dawn prepared to arrive within about a half hour.

Francine settled herself down on the cement foundation that jutted out six inches from the barn, her back against the wall, her arm around Sammy's neck, and lost herself in the big sky that was Montana, waiting for the sun to make its appearance.

She sat there through breakfast. She would have enjoyed a cup of coffee, but after the dream, she just wanted to be alone. Instead, she checked the cows in the drop pen again where all was quiet, then went into the barn to saddle her mare, Mesa, in preparation for bringing in the remuda. Jesse needed to pick out his string, and Mesa would be exchanged for another of her horses. She had been ridden pretty hard the past three days and was due for a rest.

A quick rub down, and the mare was saddled. Francine led her out of the barn after arranging the gates for the incoming horses, swung herself effortlessly into the saddle, and left the yard at a slow jog. Sammy bounded along behind, cavorting like a young pup since he had no work to do other than keep his favorite human happy.

Jesse was just coming out of the cook house after a breakfast to remember, as Francine was heading out after the horses. They had all missed him at breakfast. When Franc hadn't shown up Fred had asked Jesse what he had done to the little queer, killed him? Franc seldom missed a meal, and it was almost unheard of for him to not at least grab a cup of coffee. They realized he hadn't slept in the bunkhouse, and Fred had laughed uproariously when he figured that out. Of course, as he reminded Jesse, he still didn't know whether Franc had any hair on his chest or not, so this would still need to be discovered.

Jesse had ignored the man, and lavished his attention on the pancakes and sausage that Sandy put on the table in abundance. Even if the pay wasn't the best on this ranch, a man would be a fool to leave food like this for no good reason. Boy Howdy, that

Sandy could cook! Franc had missed something special this morning. Well, he figured Franc knew where the food was, if he was too stubborn to come and eat it that was his own fault.

He assumed Franc had gone to bring the horses in, so he made his way across the frozen mud to the barn and prepared to wait a while. There wasn't much he could do until Franc got back, and he knew there was no point in checking the drop; Franc would have done it before he left.

***

Francine kicked her mare into a gentle lope once away from the barn area and headed for the hills to the north, where the horses wintered out on their own. There was plenty of old grass out here, and they were able to paw for their food without difficulty. Coming to the barn was a twice weekly treat, though, as they got to spend the day in the corral with hay in the bunks. The lucky ones even got a ration of grain.

The day was beautiful and sunny, with the promise of later warmth, and had things been normal for Francine, she would have had a slight lilt to her mouth. She loved to bring the horses in; she loved doing anything that allowed her to be horseback.

The north horse pasture was about two miles from the barn, and it took only a few moments to arrive at the gate. Dismounting, she opened the gate wide and hooked it back on the wire fence to prevent any hooves from catching in it as the horses came through. Mounting easily again, her gaze took in the closest part of the pasture, which was empty of horses. "Sammy, why don't you wait here, 'cause it's going to be fast and furious for a few moments, Okay?" Sammy obediently went over to sit near the fence, out of the way. He knew what was coming and where it was the safest to wait, but his gaze never left Francine as she kicked Mesa into a high lope and headed for the closest hill, then disappeared over the top.

In less than two minutes, after letting out one loud whoop, Francine had the twenty or so horses on the run toward the barn. They knew the way, so her purpose was just to bring up the rear.

The sun was chasing the frost from the mud left from yesterday's storm, and the footing was slippery, but the run was still exhilarating, as usual, and it helped to revive Francine's spirits. Sammy fell in behind her as the herd thundered through the gate, and the chase was on.

The horses rounded the barn at a slightly slower pace, the hardest running having been done across the meadow. They ran as one entity and entered the corral with no stragglers. Jesse was waiting and swung the gate shut after the last horse was in; he was anxious to see what kind of stock the C/6 had. It had been so long since he had been horseback, he felt like a kid at Christmas, and he could hardly stand the wait to pick out the three horses that would be his to use. He loved horses like he used to love his wife, damn her soul. It had been a long ten years, that's for sure.

Jesse leaned his crossed arms over the corral fence, watching the horses milling and jostling for the best places at the feed bunk where the hay waited. All colors and sizes, for Jesse it was like being a kid in a penny candy store with two dollars in his pocket, only better.

Francine sat motionless in the saddle, watching him. The man seemed genuinely excited about picking out his horses. He might be scary, but if he liked animals he couldn't be all bad. *"Stop it Francine,"* she told herself gruffly. *"He's still a man, and as such still your enemy. Don't be giving him any breaks. Todd had liked horses too."* She flinched at the quick memory, then focused her attention on the corral again.

"You can pick any three, your choice. But the two Appaloosas are mine, so forget them."

Jesse had already noted the Apps, and was eyeing them critically. They were splendid animals and the only mares in the bunch, with loud color and solid builds.

"Do you have any suggestions? Which ones are the best broke or the toughest?"

Francine did not acknowledge his questions, but seemed to concentrate on the horses. He could pick his own stock with no help from her. She would just see how well he knew horses. Reining the big mare toward the barn, Francine dismounted at the door and led Mesa into the barn to unsaddle her. It was time to change mounts.

"So, it's back to that, is it?" thought Jesse. *"Let's ignore old Jesse and maybe he'll go away. Can't answer a simple question, or make even the smallest effort to be civil. Fine, have it your way, Franc old boy."* But he had noticed the pallor under Franc's tan this morning, and the shadows under his eyes. He obviously hadn't slept much last night, and with no breakfast this morning, he was in pretty tough shape. Well, it sure wasn't his fault, he had tried to be friendly, no matter what kind of a guy Franc was. But it still kind of hurt that Franc would rather sleep in the barn with a dog than share a room with him.

He looked back toward the barn to see Francine leading her mare over to the corral. She opened the gate as Jesse stepped back to make room, led the mare inside, then removed the halter and patted the mare affectionately. He could hear Francine murmur to the horse, but couldn't distinguish what was said. Then Francine walked slowly over to another big mare, a dark sorrel with a blanket from the withers back to her tail, talked softly to her, haltered her, and led her back to the corral gate. Jesse opened the gate for her this time, but there was no acknowledgement from Francine, and she continued on into the barn with the horse following quietly behind.

Jesse opened the corral gate and went in, hoping he could do a halfway decent job of picking his string. Since Franc wasn't about to help him out in any way, he would have to rely on a little common sense and experience to pick these horses, and since a man couldn't possibly know without riding them how they were broke, he would have to observe how they handled themselves in the bunch and just go with that. He supposed he could exchange horses later if one or two just didn't work out for him, but he wasn't about to give Franc the satisfaction. He would try to choose wisely the first go 'round.

His presence in the corral disturbed the horses. He was a stranger, and his scent was new. They began milling, not in fright, but with slight unease. Jesse watched how they moved, and made his selections with careful consideration.

His first pick was a big bay gelding, tops on his list because of the way he handled his feet in the mud. He never missed a step, and good footing was essential. Next followed a sunrise dun, then a sorrel. They were all good-sized horses, and among the top in the pecking order; he didn't want a horse with no guts. And they all appeared to have better than average feet.

He left the corral to go find his new partner to tell him which horses he had picked, and ask what he was to do with them next. He found Francine in the barn, currying the sorrel mare she had led in earlier.

"I picked my horses. Thanks so much for all your help. Now what? Oh, and could you please give me an answer this time? It would be very much appreciated."

Francine was quiet for a moment, apparently thinking, but in reality getting her courage up to talk again. She had passed herself off last night and again a little while ago but this was another moment in time, and she was afraid. But she knew she would have to speak, and she had better just get used to the idea.

Jesse was getting very irritated. Was he so repulsive to be around that Franc would never even be civil? It was pretty hard on a man's ego and self-confidence.

"You'll find halters in the tack room. You can catch them all now and try them out this afternoon, or you can choose one to ride now and leave the others with the bunch until it's time to change horses again. Suit yourself."

She didn't realize she had been holding her breath after her long speech until she heard "Thanks," and he had walked away from her. Apparently, he still accepted her as being a man. She was safe for another day. "Thank you, Lord," she whispered, as she bowed her head briefly, then continued with her currying.

Jesse decided that one horse at a time was good enough, so caught the bay and took him to the barn. He led him to another stall, and then began cleaning his feet and brushing him down.

"What's the plan for this afternoon? I know, I know, you don't want me anywhere around. Well for your information, I don't especially want to be anywhere around you either, but Glen's the boss, and he said I'm to go with you. So, what's up, if you think you can bother yourself to talk to me a little?"

"We'll move some pairs out after lunch. And his name's Roger."

"Thank you for lowering yourself to speak. I do so appreciate your great effort on my behalf. Come on Roger, let's go see what you've got."

He led the big bay gelding into the alley, cross tied him, then slowly saddled him, learning the horses' individual traits as he proceeded. He might as well find out just what kind of horse he had here, before he attempted to do any real work on him later today.

Francine leaned back against an empty stall door, watching Jesse get acquainted with his new animal and gazing around the old barn. There were twenty stalls; ten tie stalls and ten box stalls. The tie stalls weren't used anymore; they had once been filled with teams every morning, but that was before tractors and pickups. There were days even now, though, in the winter, when a team would have worked far better than a tractor in the heavy snow. There were still a few ranchers in the country that used teams in the winter for feeding, but Adrian Miller wanted only the best new, modern equipment. Oh well, she was happy to have as much riding as she did in this day and age, when many ranchers had gone to four wheelers and motorcycles.

A wide alley ran the length of the barn, with doors leading amid the stalls to a large tack room, a feed room, and a sort of junk room. It was a barn seldom seen in Montana, and built solidly.

Jesse looked over at Francine. "Any special bit you recommend, Franc?"

Francine ignored him. A curb with a low port would work best on Roger, but she hadn't asked for any help with her work, she resented Jesse being here, and he would receive no help from her unless something drastic required it.

"Oh, right, I forgot. I don't exist. Thanks so much for your input." Jesse walked into the tack room, and spent a few minutes looking over the selection of bits. He had saddled the gelding with his own saddle, but there might be a better bit among the ranch's selection. He decided on his own gear, a medium port bit, and after bridling the gelding, led him out to the round corral to try him out. Francine followed at a distance. She wouldn't miss this possible show for the world.

But there was to be no show. Jesse realized immediately that the bit was too strong for the horse, when the gelding began throwing his head with the slightest pressure on the reins. He was heavy on his turns, also. Dismounting, Jesse removed the bridle and went to the barn to select another headstall.

Francine was impressed. Jesse knew his stuff, no doubt about it. The show was over. She figured Jesse didn't need her around anymore, and quietly slipped away.

When Jesse returned from the barn with a low port bit in another headstall, Francine was nowhere to be seen. "*Good riddance!*" he thought, and proceeded to get to know his new horse in private. It was so good to feel that horse between his legs and the sun on his back; he figured heaven couldn't be much better than this. It was going to be a good day, in spite of old Franc. He just knew it.

Chapter 6

Francine left the barn and headed for the cookhouse. She desperately needed a good strong cup of coffee. She needed a nap, too, but that would come later, she hoped. Eventually she would sleep, she knew.

Sandy looked up as Francine entered the main dining room.

"Coffee's hot, help yourself." She was used to Francine's silence. She didn't know why Franc never spoke, she supposed it had something to do with his being gay and the other hands, but she really didn't care.

"You want your lunch early? It's pretty much ready anyway."

Francine looked up in surprise. Sandy never broke the rules about meals. As much as she would have loved to eat by herself, she knew she would have to face the whole crew again eventually, and it might as well start with lunch. She shook her head, but Sandy could tell by the look in her eyes that she was grateful for the offer. Francine took her mug of coffee and went out to sit on the porch steps to nurse it until lunch was on the table for everyone.

At twelve o'clock sharp, the dinner bell rang and everyone filed in to eat. As they climbed the steps past her on their way in, Lucky glanced at her and bobbed his head, Jesse ignored her, and Fred beamed at her, then pounded her on the back hard enough to spill her coffee. He burst out laughing over his little joke and halfway skipped into the dining room.

Jesse realized what had happened almost immediately when he heard Fred's raucous laugh and saw the wet stain on Franc's vest. He knew the coffee had to have burned; Sandy made real hot coffee. But Franc just sat there and took it. Coward, he thought. Franc might be gay, but he was big enough that Jesse didn't understand why he didn't stand up even a little bit for himself.

Francine took a deep breath when the hot coffee scalded her chest through her vest and shirt, but said nothing. She would just accept it. She sure couldn't take her shirt off to get away from the searing heat of the hot liquid! She would have a first degree burn there later, but she figured it was a long way from her heart and she would live. Rising to her feet, she entered the dining room behind the others, taking her customary seat, and wondered what lewd comments would be coming her way this time.

Fred of course started things off with, "Hey Franc, I see you didn't sleep in the bunkhouse last night. What's the matter, old Jesse here not to your liking?" Then the sick laughter that was uniquely Fred's.

Jesse waited to see if Franc would have a reply, but he should have known the little wimp would keep his mouth shut. He decided maybe he would bail them both out of this embarrassing conversation.

"Fred, for your information, old Franc and I decided to take turns checking the cows, and he took the first watch. You probably just didn't hear him come in during the night, and he was gone again when you got up. And guess what, we both slept just fine. So you can knock it off 'cause I don't appreciate your comments any more than I'm sure Franc does."

Fred wasn't really buying Jesse's story, but he couldn't argue against it either. It was plausible, he didn't always hear Franc come and go during the night. Still, by the way Franc looked today, his night couldn't have gone too smoothly. But he didn't want to make this Indian mad, either. He was too big and ugly looking. He had obviously gotten that crooked nose and those white patches on his eye somehow, and he was willing to bet it wasn't because he was just passively letting someone go at him. There would be time enough to get at Franc; he could wait.

Francine never looked up from her meal. Jesse did think that maybe he would at least glance at him in acknowledgement, but he guessed he should have known better. Franc neither gave nor received.

Francine could hardly believe her ears! Jesse was actually defending her, in a way. No one had been that kind to her since she had left home and gotten married. As much as she hated to admit it, she owed him one. She couldn't do much, but she made up her mind to try and find some way to repay him.

***

After lunch, which passed with no further embarrassment to anyone, Francine and Jesse met in the barn by silent agreement. There were pairs to put out. They saddled their horses and exited the barn together, with no words exchanged between them. They mounted, and were riding side by side, though of course not too close, heading for the larger drop pen where about ten pairs were ready to go out with the main bunch already calved out.

"Well, Jesse, I just wanted to tell you how very much I appreciated your speaking up for me at lunch. What a prince of a guy! Why, you're welcome, Mr. Franc. It was my pleasure, believe me. After all, what are friends for, if not to help each other out from time to time!" Jesse rattled off the conversation with himself, knowing that Franc would say nothing in response.

Francine shot him a quick glance, and Jesse caught it. "*Well,*" he thought, "*old Franc **does** know I'm here after all. Whoopee!*"

Francine was impressed with Jesse's first choice in the horses. Roger was one of the better animals in the remuda. The Indian sure knew horses, he had proved that. The gelding was not one of the prettier horses, but was one of the best all-around working mounts on the ranch. Jesse obviously knew better than to pick a horse on looks alone.

***

The afternoon passed pleasantly. Francine saw that Jesse knew exactly what he was doing, and she could find no fault in his work or his handling of the stock. They sorted pairs and worked them out with the big bunch in perfect harmony, as if they had been trained together by the same master. Sammy waited patiently outside the corrals and pens, knowing when to stay out of the way. Cows with calves at side would not tolerate a dog anywhere near them. The job took most of the afternoon by the time they had moved the stock around to where they were supposed to be. The mud slowed them down some, but the sun was shining, and even though the air had a chill to it, the promise of spring hung heavy in the air. Altogether, it was one of the most pleasant afternoons either one of them had spent in years, and even though they weren't aware of it and no words were exchanged as they worked, a bond of sorts had formed between the two riders. They were almost friends by the end of the day, and they had each gained a deep respect for the abilities of the other, if not their personages.

Francine had spent the day trying to decide how to repay Jesse for his help at lunch, and she thought she had found a way. She would surprise him in the morning, if all went according to plan.

***

Supper passed without incident. Francine and Jesse came in to eat together, and Fred kept his distance this time. Conversation rattled around Francine as if she weren't there, which was just the way she liked it, and the atmosphere remained cheerful and friendly.

After supper, Jesse and Francine checked the drop together, and made an arrangement whereby Jesse would take first check, and two hours later Francine would take her turn. Thus each of them would get four hours of sleep at a time, rather than just two. Tonight there would probably be one or two calves, at least.

This system had been Jesse's idea, and Francine had jumped on it by nodding her head in agreement. It was perfect. She could get ready for bed while Jesse was at the barn, and he would be asleep when she got up to take her turn with the cows. She wouldn't have to worry about getting ready for bed in front of him, which of course was out of the question anyway, and for now, her biggest problem was solved. Thank God!

***

Francine waited that night until Jesse had gone out to check the cows before getting ready for bed. She showered and put on fresh clothes, then lay down on top of the bunk, covering herself with a blanket. It would be easier to get up and out when her turn came if she were already dressed, and besides, it would help to eliminate any chance for discovery just in case Jesse woke up while she was getting ready. Sammy took up watch on the floor at the foot of her bed, as usual. She was asleep within moments, exhausted after the night before, her alarm set for midnight.

When Jesse came in around ten thirty, he found Francine sound asleep on top of her bed. He watched her sleeping for a moment, Sammy keeping a watchful eye on the intruder, but not growling after the camaraderie of the afternoon.

"Franc really is an attractive man," Jesse thought, *"almost too pretty for a man"* It was just a damn shame, him being what he was. He was a hell of a hand, in spite of it. They could have even been friends, maybe, if he just wasn't gay. He turned away from his partner, whose face was relaxed and peaceful in sleep. Francine was resting dreamlessly tonight, a pleasant change from the stress and the sleepless night before.

She woke minutes before the alarm went off, and silencing it before it could wake her new partner, rose slowly and crept out the door, carrying her boots in her hand. She would put them on in the gathering room.

Jesse watched her leave in the darkness, the ever-faithful Sammy at her heels. Then he closed his eyes again and slept.

***

When she checked the cows, she found a four-year-old obviously in the early stages of calving. She knew she couldn't go back to bed, but had to wait to be sure there would be no trouble, and decided that now was as good a time as any to repay Jesse for his kindness to her at noon.

She went to the stall that quartered Roger, haltered and led him out into the alley of the barn, and then cross-tied him in place. The horse would need shoes if he was going to be ridden regularly now, and this was something she could do as a favor to Jesse. She had been shoeing horses ever since she was sixteen years old, and could do the job as well as any man. Her dad had taught her, and he had been one of the best. She had been shoeing her own horses ever since, but never touched anyone else's. The ranch paid for a horse shoer to come in twice a year. If she didn't shoe Roger now, he would have to go barefoot until the middle of May, and in this spring mud, his footing would be much more secure with calks on all four feet.

She went to the tack room and brought back her farrier's tools, an assortment of horseshoes in various sizes, and shoeing chaps. After visually inspecting Roger's stance, she began in earnest. Forty-five minutes later, Roger was sporting four new shoes with heel and toe calks, and a slight toe-out problem had been corrected. She patted him softly on the neck and fed him a cube, talking to him constantly.

"Well, Roger, old boy, it appears you have a new man in your life. Looks like he knows horses pretty good, too. After all, you were his first choice, you lucky thing. He rides like a hand, and I don't think you have a thing to worry about. Wish I could say the same thing! Can't believe I went and put shoes on you just for him. 'Course, he did kind of deserve something, after speaking up for me today with Fred. Can't believe he did that." The litany continued between Roger and herself, a one-sided conversation that filled a little of the emptiness deep within her. She unsnapped the horse from the crossties and led him back to his stall. She wondered how long it would take Jesse Windchase, super Indian, to notice his new horse also sported shiny new shoes.

She left Roger with his alfalfa and went back to check the cow that was calving, and was greatly relieved to find the calf on the ground, the mother cow frantically and carefully cleaning it off. A nice bull calf. Good. One less to lose sleep over during the night. She would go back to bed; it wasn't real cold out tonight, and the calf should have no trouble nursing by itself after it got around to getting up. Jesse would check them again within half an hour anyway. If she hurried, she could get back to bed and Jesse would never know how long she had been up.

She hurried back to the bunk house, took her overshoes off on the porch and her boots off in the gathering room, then padded as quietly as she could back to her bed, opening and closing the bedroom door as softly as possible. She was sure she hadn't disturbed Jesse, and sighed softly as she settled herself on her bed. She was instantly asleep.

Jesse watched the shadow that was Franc Larson glide across the room towards his bed. He wondered what had taken Franc so long–a cow having trouble? He marveled at Franc's litheness and grace. Too bad, again, to have it wasted on someone like him. Glen Richards had been right though; Franc was a genius with the stock. He could get a horse or a cow to do damned near anything he wanted them to. He had watched Franc carefully this afternoon, and the rapport between the man and his horse was phenomenal. Most ranches wouldn't allow a mare on the place, running only geldings. All three of Franc's horses were mares, and some of the best pieces of horseflesh he had ever seen. He just wished he could understand the man.

Franc was so reclusive; he had never met anyone like him before. A person would think Franc had been the one to spend ten years in prison, instead of him. The thought would not leave his mind though, of what a man Franc Larson might be if he weren't gay. People said that was something they couldn't help, and maybe they were right. He had never really thought about it before. But Franc never stepped out of line or made any insinuations of any kind to anyone, and Jesse knew, after spending the day with the man, that he never would. It was almost as if Franc were a different person, locked up inside that man's body, with no way to get out. And there was no happiness there, either. Franc appeared to be a man who just existed from day to day, taking what joy he could from his job, his horses, and his dog. He never thought, in all his wildest dreams, that he might someday actually feel sorry for someone like Franc, but he did. He couldn't help it. And in spite of everything, Jesse actually liked Franc. He didn't understand this feeling he had for the man; he wasn't sure he liked it much, either.

Running his fingers through his thick hair, Jesse shook his head once as if to clear the unwanted thoughts from his mind, then rose quietly to go take his turn with the cows.

Chapter 7

By morning, there were four new calves on the ground. Jesse had had his hands full the rest of the night, and had not gotten back to bed. There had been no trouble, but he felt he should stay with the new mothers to be sure there were no problems and that the new calves had nursed. Francine had awakened for her shift, but seeing that Jesse was still out, had gone back to sleep. She assumed that if he had needed help he would have had the good sense to come and get her. She had shown him, his first night, where the calf puller, snare, and various ropes and chains were kept. Besides, she was terribly exhausted, still, from the night before, and from the extra work of shoeing Roger.

Jesse popped his head into the bedroom at five forty-five and she was instantly awake.

"We got four new ones last night, they're all okay, and breakfast is ready in fifteen minutes. See you there." And he was gone again.

Francine lay quietly on the bed for a few moments, reflecting. She felt much better after about four hours of uninterrupted sleep. She was still tired, but it was, after all, calving time; a body was supposed to be tired this time of the year. A slow grin appeared on her face. She was glad she had gone ahead and put shoes on Jesse's horse. He really was trying to be nice to her, for whatever reason, and she did appreciate it, especially since so far her deception was still intact. She remembered how Jesse had deflected the conversation away from the other night yesterday at lunch. He hadn't had to do that. He could have told on her, and made her out to be just as strange as they thought she was, but he hadn't. Instead, for all that she had been downright nasty to him, he had been nothing but essentially kind to her. She hoped the shoeing job would partly make up for her rudeness.

"Well, Sammy, up and at 'em I guess. Another day." But it was the first day she had actually begun with a real smile on her face in years.

***

After breakfast, it was time to tag the new calves and put them, with their mothers, out with the big bunch, then check for scours, that potentially deadly condition that caused the calves to have uncontrolled diarrhea. Jesse opened the stall door, talking to Roger, and noticed the new shoes immediately. He whistled softly, staring. "How in the world?" He led the gelding out into the barn alley, and cross-tied him as usual in preparation for saddling. It was as good a job of shoeing as he had ever seen, and Jesse was very particular. He usually did all his own shoeing, because he was so fussy. He noticed that the little toe-out problem appeared to be corrected, and the gelding now traveled straight. He stood there, thinking, looking at those new shoes, trying to figure out how and when, and then it dawned on him. The only time it could have happened was during the night, and the only one who could have done it was Franc. He must have worked on it during his watch last night. That's why he was late coming back to bed.

Franc, he knew, had slept little the night before, out here in the barn. He hadn't gotten a nap, so he was even more exhausted last night. Still, he had taken the time to shoe his horse for him. Why? Franc hated his guts, didn't he? Hell, he wouldn't talk to him, or even look at him unless forced to, so what in the world was this all about?

Francine was a little slower getting to the barn. She was still kind of tired, and had to get one more cup of coffee down before she was ready to face the day. As she walked into the dark interior of the big barn, it took a moment for her eyes to adjust after the bright sunshine outside. She didn't see Jesse watching her intently, at first. When she did, she turned quickly away; she was very uncomfortable knowing he was observing her that closely. He had obviously spotted the new shoes, and now she was suddenly acutely embarrassed.

"Franc?"

There was no answer to his query.

"Franc, why?"

Again, silence.

"Franc Larson, you talk to me right now or by heaven I may just have to strangle you! Why did you shoe my horse? "

Francine swallowed hard. Here we go, she thought. What had she done! She thought at first maybe he was angry, but she knew she had done a top-notch job, even if she had been tired.

"It needed doing." She answered.

"It damn sure didn't need doing at midnight. And you were so tired you could hardly see straight, so let's hear the real reason, okay?"

"I . . ." Francine began, but was promptly cut off.

"And I'm sick and tired of talking to your back, so turn around and face me like a man. Anybody that can set shoes like you did sure ought to be man enough to talk to me face to face!"

Francine took a deep breath, and slowly turned around. She would have to be mending her ways around Jesse Windchase, and there were no two ways around that fact.

"Now, you can talk. Why?"

"Well," she began, hesitantly, "I realized I haven't been very friendly. It's true that I didn't want you here. But you've put up with me anyway. And then, yesterday," she paused briefly.

"What about yesterday? Go on."

"Well, you didn't have to tell Fred and Lucky that I had slept in the bunkhouse. You could have let them go on believing the truth. They probably didn't believe you anyway, but you tried, and that's what matters. Besides, like I said, it needed doing."

Jesse threw his head back and laughed! It was a fabulous day. He had a job, a horse, his horse had new shoes, his stomach was full with one the best breakfasts he had ever eaten, he was out of prison, the sun was shining, and the mute Franc Larson, gay cowboy prima donna of the C/6 had actually said more than three sentences to him, and to his face at that!

"Franc Larson, I don't have a clue what makes you tick, and I likely never will. But I'll give you this, you're one of the best hands with cattle and horses I've ever run across, and I've seen a few in my day. I should hate you, but I just can't seem to get the job done. And Franc, old boy, this is one pretty shoeing job. I don't know where you learned, but you must have learned from one of the best."

Francine turned away, before the smile that was trying hard to materialize actually made it to the surface. She turned toward the stall to get her horse.

"Franc?" The voice was soft, barely audible, "Thanks. I appreciate it."

Francine acknowledged his thanks and compliments with a slight nod of her head, then went to saddle Julie for the day's work.

***

The afternoon passed much like the one the day before. The weather was pleasant, the ground muddy, and the work was what they both loved doing. Again, they worked as a team, moving the pairs, then catching and doctoring sick calves. They could each rope equally well, and took turns whenever they spied a calf with the scours, that often-lethal diarrheal disease so prevalent in calves this time of the year. One would rope the calf, and the other would force the pills down its throat. They spent all afternoon at this, and by the end of the day had medicated about forty head of calves. By supper time, they were both pleasantly tired, and though Francine was still not speaking unless absolutely necessary, and then only in short sentences, talking was getting a little easier for her each time. She found herself starting to relax around Jesse, and she was beginning to think of him almost as a friend.

Jesse didn't seem to care anymore whether she was gay or not, or a man or not, he just seemed to see her now as a person. At least that's what she thought was happening. Because he wasn't sneering or laughing at her, she gradually began to relax around him. She was still afraid to let her guard down too far, but the days were beginning to fall into a comfortable routine.

Tonight, the pair walked in to supper together, side by side, actually. Fred was already seated at the table, and visibly gawked at Jesse. Why that Indian acted like he was friends with the little fairy! Even Lucky did a double take.

What was going on here? Nobody ever walked with Franc, for heaven's sake!

Francine split herself off from Jesse and took her regular seat. The food was passed to her as usual, and things seemed back to normal; Francine was ostracized once more. As she helped herself to roast beef with potatoes and vegetables, Fred started in again.

"Well, good day, today Jesse? I saw you cut yourself out a horse. Old Roger, wasn't it? He's one of the best, I think. I rode him some last fall, sure liked him, too."

"Yeah, Roger's a pretty good mount. He follows a cow pretty fair, and he's good on his feet. Sure felt good to be horseback again, let me tell you." Too late, he realized his slip. "You know, with winter and all, just not the best time of the year to be riding." He thought he had covered himself pretty well, no one seemed to question his remark about not riding for a while.

"How's the feeding going? This mud must kind of get to you sometimes. Don't you ever wish you were still feeding with a team up here?"

"Naw, give me the pickup cab and a good heater any day. Say, how you getting along with old Franc, here?"

"Okay. I got no complaints. He sure knows his job; he's a hard act to follow."

"Hey, you get the little sucker to talk yet? And what about that hair on his chest, I'm still waiting to find out you know? Us men, we got to stick together, right?"

Jesse never even looked at Fred, but glanced instead at Lucky, changing the topic of conversation to something more conventional and appropriate for the dinner table. Franc continued to eat in silence, trying to understand what had just happened. Jesse had essentially just stuck up for her again, and paid her a compliment to boot. She was glad now, more than ever, that she had put those shoes on for him.

The others continued visiting, and Francine rose, took a large mug of coffee with her and walked out into the night. At seven-thirty the sun had set, and the mud was freezing again, but it really wasn't that cold. Francine often enjoyed being out at night, watching the stars and the northern lights, so common this time of the year. She sat on the barn foundation again, as she had the other night, and just enjoyed the quiet. Since she couldn't be alone in her room anymore whenever she wanted, she figured this might become a habit real quick.

About fifteen minutes later, Jesse rounded the corner and came to sit beside her. Not too close, but close enough that the offer of friendship could not be mistaken.

They sat quietly together for several moments, watching the night sky. There was no need to speak for either one of them. They were beginning to understand each other, and words were unnecessary.

"Thanks."

The words were uttered softly, but they echoed in Jesse's ears like thunder. Franc had actually spoken to him, without being forced! What in heaven was going to happen next? He swallowed the lump that had suddenly seemed to form in his throat. He had no way of knowing exactly what it had cost Franc to talk without being forced to do so, but knowing Franc, even as little as he did, it had to have cost a lot. He felt almost as he supposed a father might feel, getting his son to accomplish something important. Good heavens, what was happening to him? He was actually happy a queer had talked to him! But again, there was just something about Franc he liked, he couldn't say what it was, and it scared him. It was as if Franc, tough Franc, needed him somehow.

"You're welcome." And he grinned in the dark, unseen. You want first cow check tonight, or do you want to run it like we did last night?"

"Like last night, if you don't mind, it worked good for me."

"Why don't you go on to bed, then, and get some sleep. I'll wake you if I need any help."

Francine slowly rose, tipped her hat to Jesse, and headed for bed, with Sammy close beside her. She was tired, and sleep sounded wonderful.

Jesse continued to sit there long after Franc had gone to bed. The night was beautiful, and the quiet had its own music to his ears, so long enclosed behind bars. He was thinking mostly about Franc, and tried to understand his feelings about the man. He hated himself for feeling this way about him. Trouble was, he really didn't know what he *was* feeling about Franc, and he thought maybe that's what was scaring him so badly. For him to be even civil to someone like Franc was bad enough, but he actually liked and respected the man. Well, at least in some areas.

How could he respect such a coward? Hell, he didn't know. Maybe he should just go to bed and worry about it later. He wished he knew where it was all headed, but he didn't have a clue.

He sighed, rose, stretched, and went to check on the cows.

Chapter 8

The next few days passed uneventfully. Spring continued to hover, tantalizing everyone with wisps of warmth. At six thousand feet, it took a little longer for that promised season to arrive, but it was no more welcomed anywhere else in the state.

Jesse and Francine spent most of their waking hours together, moving and doctoring cattle. They continued to split the cow checks at night, but now they only checked them every four hours, so each got eight consecutive hours of sleep. That's how they knew spring really was about here; they could sleep at last.

Glen left a message for Jesse with Sandy, requesting to meet with him after breakfast on Friday morning. As Jesse walked over to the foreman's house, he reflected on how his life had changed in less than a week. He had come here with unclear expectations, and then less than civil thoughts about his bunkmate. Now he was looking forward with such anticipation to summer he could hardly stand it. He didn't mind Franc anymore. Actually, though he hated to admit it, his respect for Franc was mounting daily. He didn't want to say he liked Franc, but that word pretty well described his feelings for the man. Franc had made absolutely no demands whatsoever on Jesse since they had met. He had thought that being around someone like Franc would turn his stomach on a regular basis, but so far it hadn't turned out that way at all. Franc was a "regular guy," so to speak. If he didn't look, act, and walk so much like a woman, he would have had no reservations at all about being his friend or spending time with him. True, Jesse preferred to be alone just as much as Franc appeared to, but the boss had specified otherwise, so that was that.

Glen opened the porch door just as Jesse mounted the last step. "Good morning! Come on in! How're things going for you, Jesse?"

"Pretty good so far, thanks."

"The boys give you any trouble about anything?" Glen reached out his hand and the two men shook vigorously, slapping each other on the back.

"Naw, Glen, they're not a bad bunch, really. That Lucky wouldn't hurt a flea, and Fred's all right. A little coarse, but nothing I can't handle. And you were right about the cooking–that Sandy is a cook second to none!"

"Ain't she something, though? I told you, didn't I? Her husband, Gene, is as much a wizard with the yards as Sandy is with the food. When the boss comes out the end of May for branding, just wait 'till you see the spread she puts on! It'll boggle your mind, boy, boggle your mind."

"Frankly, I don't see how it could get any better. Oh, I picked my horses out, like you said. I've only ridden the one so far, but I compliment you on your remuda. If the other two ride like old Roger, I'll be just plumb satisfied." They each picked a hardwood chair, sat down, and relaxed together as old friends will.

"I have to ask, Jesse, how're you getting along with Franc? Is he too hard on you in any way? Do you think you'll be able to stand being around him?"

"You know, Glen, I just can't figure the man out. Hell, maybe it's me I can't figure out. I started out hating his guts because of what he obviously is. Now, I kind of enjoy being around him. You were right, he doesn't care two hoots and a holler who I am or what I've done, he just does his job the best he can, and I can tag along or not. You were also right about the fact that he's a genius with the stock. Did you know he can shoe horses about as good as any man I've ever met? He stuck those shoes on old Roger one night, and I've never seen a prettier job in all my life. It was almost as pretty as the kind of work I do!" Jesse chuckled to himself, remembering the morning he confronted Franc with what he had done. Franc had actually talked to him, and had been talking, although somewhat reluctantly, ever since.

Glen's eyes opened wide. "Did you say Franc shoed your horse for you? Did I hear you right?"

"Yes sir, during the night while it was his turn to check the cows. I went to the barn the next morning, and there they were, just a shinin' in the sun like four new pennies."

"I suppose you're going to tell me he talks to you too, or some other such story!"

Jesse grinned. "Well, actually, yes, he does. Not often, mind you. To start with I had to threaten to beat it out of him, but he's coming around. He won't say a word to anyone else that I've noticed, but, yes, he will talk to me a little when we're alone."

"Well I'll be damned!" Glen voiced his genuine surprise. "That boy has never put a shoe on anyone's horse but his own since he started work here, and that's been five years this spring. And as for talking, I've never heard more than a 'yes' or a 'no' out of him in all that time. I tell him what to do, he does it, and that's the end of it. You must be some kind of miracle worker, Jesse."

"Naw, I just tend to treat him like a human, and it seems to go a long way with him. Did you know he eats at one end of the table by himself during meals? He won't even ask for anyone to pass the food to him; if someone doesn't pass it, he doesn't eat. Everyone else really shuns him. I kind of feel sorry for him, even if he is gay."

"He hasn't made any moves of any kind, well, you know what I mean . . ."

"Not at all, Glen. He's a perfect gentleman. If he didn't act like he does, nobody would know the difference. It might help if he cut his hair, but so many guys wear their hair long these days, I guess he has a right to wear it long if he wants to."

"Well, I hate making you bunk with him, but I really don't have any other choice right now. I figured it would be okay in the end, but I did think it might take a little longer. Any complaints or comments for me? Any changes I need to be making that you can see?"

Jesse thought for a moment, then replied, "Not really. I don't think anyone else could work with Franc. Lucky hates riding and Fred might kill poor Franc if he was to work with him. You know, that's the one thing that bothers me more than anything else about the man—why won't he stand up for himself? He's big enough to go one on one with Fred if it came to that, which, by the way, it might one day soon. You were right about that, too." He then described the incident with the coffee, and Fred's remarks at dinner.

"That's why I'm kind of counting on you Jesse. I don't want anything to happen to Franc. I kind of like him myself. But aside from that, I don't know what the relationship is between Franc and Adrian Miller, but I have my orders, and for the sake of my job if nothing else, I want to keep Franc happy."

"I'll do my best, Glen. Now tell me more about what's gone on in your life these past ten years."

They settled down with two cups of coffee and went to reminiscing. There was a lot to discuss, and they took the rest of the morning doing it.

***

It was Friday night, and Fred and Lucky had both gone to Bozeman to celebrate payday, each in their own vehicle. Lucky had found his favorite lady to spend the night with, and would not be back until breakfast. Fred, however, had not had such good fortune in finding female companionship, and showed up back at the ranch about two o'clock in the morning.

Francine had just come back from checking the cows, where everything was quiet. She was sitting at the table in the gathering room, having removed her boots, and was enjoying a cup of coffee before going back to bed, when the outside door opened quietly and Fred staggered in, dead drunk. She knew as soon as she saw him that she was in for trouble, and began to rise from the chair to go to her room. Fred moved faster than she would have thought possible in his condition, and shoved her roughly by the shoulders back onto the chair.

"Goin' somewhere Franc?"

Francine sat rigidly, silent, glaring at Fred with all the bravado she could muster. She lowered her eyes and made another attempt to get up, but Fred kept her pinned in the chair.

"No, Franc, I don't thin' so. Not yet. Maybe you can keep me company for a while, what d'ya say?" He kept her shoulders pinned with his huge hands, and the stale odor of alcohol was exhaled into her face.

She closed her eyes and fought the retching that was starting deep within her. It brought back too many memories, too many horrible memories. Oh, how she hated a drunk!

"Fred, please. Let me go." The words were barely whispered from her throat, which had nearly closed off from fear.

Fred gripped her tighter, leering into her face, his bloodshot eyes mere inches from hers.

"What's this? Franc's going to talk? What d'ya say, Franc? What d'ya want me to do?"

"Fred, let me go!" Again, the softly whispered plea.

"I got a better idea. Why don' you show me what you and that Indian do all night in that room together, how about that? I think that would be fun, don't you? You can just do whatever comes natural to you!" Fred leered and laughed drunkenly in her face.

Francine turned stark white as the blood drained. The fear gripped her again. Would she never escape her past? She suddenly became powerless, just as she had been when she was married and Todd would start in on her when he was drunk. She became limp and unable to move.

"You know little Franc, I ain't never kissed a fairy before. Always kind'a wondered what it would feel like. It must be okay, huh, if guys like you like to do it all the time. You and that Indian. Who'd a thought! And him being straight, too. You must have something Franc, and I think tonight, I want to find out what it is!"

She fixed her eyes into a blank stare over Fred's shoulder. It was over. If Fred continued, he would find out soon enough that she was a woman. If, by chance, she was lucky, she might escape without being raped by the drunk, but he would for sure tell everyone about her duplicity. Sammy started a low growling at Francine's feet. Fred began stroking the back of Francine's head and then the side of her smooth jaw.

"So smooth" he mumbled, "just like a woman!"

Sammy edged forward, growling louder, a warning.

Fred bent his whiskered face to hers and began a punishing kiss, grinding her lips against her teeth until she tasted blood. Her breathing had stopped, and she thought she was going to faint. She couldn't think and she couldn't pray; she was mindless.

Sammy took the moment to hone in, and with no further warning, in one swift movement lunged at Fred's ankle, gripping it in a deadly vise-like grip.

Fred's cowboy boots buffered the sharp teeth of the heeler, and as he lifted his mouth from Francine's, he bent to take care of the dog. Attempting at first to shake him loose, he soon saw that he would never dislodge the dog's fierce grip. He swiftly kicked Sammy in the ribs with his free boot toe, then bent and slammed the dog into the wall with the other. Stunned, Sammy lay on his side, breathing heavily but unable to move.

Turning his attention once again to his prey, his anger was doubled by Francine's obvious revulsion to him and the dog's quiet attack. He drew back, wiping his mouth with the back of his hand as if the taste of her was repugnant to him. She continued her vacant forward stare, unable to move in any way.

"What's a matter? You like Indians better? Why you little..."

Drawing back his right arm, he made a tight fist, then slammed it into Francine's right temple. Francine never saw it coming, but even if she had, there was no way to avoid it. She immediately sank limply to the floor, just as the door to her shared room flew open.

Jesse was across the room in three long strides. He wasn't sure where to start. Franc was out cold, Fred was staggering, barely able to stand, and Sammy was recovering and looked ready to attack anything that moved.

He shoved Fred into another chair, and began talking soothingly to Sammy. By now the dog trusted him, after all the time they had been spending together every day, and backed off as he bent over Francine.

"My God, what have you done, Fred!"

"Aw, the little fairy asked for it. Just sitting there trying to look purty for me. So I thought I'd just find out what it's like, you know, what you two are doing in that room at night."

That was all the excuse Jesse needed. He planted three punches in rapid-fire succession; one to Fred's gut, one to his eye, and one to his jaw. Fred slumped to the floor, out cold.

He then bent to see to Franc. He shouldn't have been out this long. Hell, Franc looked like death. A large bruise was forming on his right temple. What a place to hit a guy! From the looks of Fred, Franc hadn't even tried to protect himself. Then he noticed Franc's lips; they were swollen, and blood was clotted in places as if they had been mangled. Poor Franc! He picked him up carefully and carried him to his bed. Then he went for a cold washcloth to put on Franc's forehead. Sammy sat faithfully by the head of the bed, waiting.

While Jesse was getting the washcloth, Francine woke up, groggily. Her head was swimming, and she was having trouble remembering where she was and what had happened. Suddenly it all came back to her. Fred. He had kissed her. He had- oh, her head hurt! She had thought she was dying. How had she gotten to her bed? She sure didn't get here by herself! Jesse? Oh no! Had he found out? Did he know? Oh God, please don't let him have guessed! But if he had touched her, he would know! Francine was terrified.

Jesse strode back into the room, overwhelmingly relieved to find his roommate awake.

"Here, I brought you this for your head. You took quite a hit there." He approached the bed with the washcloth, and Francine shrank in mute fear. Jesse sighed. "It's okay, Franc. Fred's taking an unplanned nap for a while. He won't bother you again." He tried again to cover her forehead with the cloth, but Francine was nearly irrational, and squeezed herself tightly against the wall, trying to get away from him. It was a survival instinct, deeply instilled after years of physical abuse.

"Franc, it's me, Jesse. You know me. You know I won't hurt you. We're friends, remember?" Maybe that was pushing things just a little, but in that moment, he actually thought they were friends. "Come on Franc, it's okay. It's okay."

Jesse sat slowly and carefully on the edge of the bed. He looked intently at Franc, trying to see into the man. He noticed the wetness on Francine's cheeks. Why, the man was crying! Now what was he supposed to do? He reached out to gently put the cold, wet rag against the forming bruise, but Francine jumped as if she had been shot.

"Don't touch me!" came the panicked plea.

"Okay, okay. Here, you can put it on yourself." He handed her the cloth, and she reached out carefully to take it from his outstretched hand, then held it to the side of her head. Reality had returned for her. This was Jesse, not Todd or Fred. She knew instinctively that Jesse wouldn't hurt her.

"Thank you."

"You're most welcome."

"Jesse? I'm sorry. I couldn't help it. It has nothing to do with you, you know?" She realized she might have hurt his feelings when she refused his ministrations, but she couldn't help herself; it was all reflex on her part. And now that he apparently hadn't discovered her secret, she found herself relaxing in his company. His presence was somehow soothing to her.

Jesse looked away. He wanted to believe it had been reflex on Franc's part, but he was afraid it was his features that affected Franc that way. Most people hated for him to touch them in any way. He was simply a repugnant person. But again, it hurt that Franc thought he was so ugly he wouldn't even let him offer to help.

He used to have dreams, when he was in prison, that maybe someday he would marry again. Maybe he could find a good, honest woman to love, who would, miracle of miracles, even love him back. Lately, since he'd seen people's reactions to him, he had given up that dream. But it really hurt when someone like Franc, with whom he thought he was a friend of sorts, couldn't stand the touch of friendship.

"Forget it, Franc. I'm used to it."

But she knew, in that moment, that he wasn't used to it at all. And she realized how people must have treated Jesse, with him being half Indian and having a face like he did. When she thought about it, they pretty much made a pair. They were both unwelcome in society, each for their own reasons. And they were both loners. They obviously both had unpleasant pasts, which neither one chose to discuss.

"Well, I'm still sorry."

"Get some sleep, Franc. You're going to have quite a shiner in the morning, as well as a pretty fair headache. And you'd better be careful!" He grinned at her.

"Careful of what? Of Fred?"

"Of yourself. Do you realize you were talking again without me forcing you first? It might get to be a habit if you don't watch yourself!"

She might have smiled back at him, if her mouth hadn't been so sore. "Good night, Jesse Windchase." She turned over and faced the wall, willing herself to rest, but it was no use. It wasn't long before she began to feel claustrophobic. She had to get some air, and quickly. Sitting up abruptly, the accompanying sharp pain in her temple nearly forced her to the bed again.

"Jesse?"

"What is it Franc?" came the response from the other bed.

"Jesse, I have to get some air- I can't breathe! I'm going out to the barn."

"Okay. Be careful."

"Jess?"

"Yeah?"

"Would you come with me? I really don't want to be alone out there right now, but I do need to get out of here."

Jesse could hardly believe what he had just heard. Franc, the loner, actually didn't want to be alone.

"Sure Franc. I'll come with you."

They put their boots and jackets on, grabbed a cup of coffee each, and wandered out to their favorite spot by the barn. An hour later, no words had passed between them, but the coffee was drunk, Francine was breathing normally, and another bond of some sort seemed to have been forged between the two. By silent agreement they rose, and went back to their respective beds. The night was nearly gone, but they could still salvage enough of it for a short nap.

Chapter 9

It was a short night for Francine and Jesse. Their nap was exactly that- a nap. Five-thirty came all too soon, and as Francine rolled out of bed her head felt like it was going to split wide open with every move she made. It all came back to her- Fred, his fist coming at her, sitting out at the barn with Jesse. She wanted to crawl in a hole and just give up. Some days she wondered why she kept trying. So what if Todd found her? Did it really matter anymore, now that Claire was gone? Without Claire her life no longer had meaning, so why was she hiding? Who cared if she lived or died? Well, she knew her parents did, but since she couldn't communicate with them, they wouldn't know anyway. She had severed all friendships when Todd went to jail, so there was no one. Just Sammy. But Lord, it was getting so hard to go on, and sometimes she just wanted to quit. Let Todd find her, kill her, and get it over with. She threw her head back and stared up at the big sky that was Montana, the deep mesmerizing blue soothing her even as she thought of giving up. It had been nice of Jesse, though, to sit outside with her last night. She had needed someone, and she really couldn't think of anyone she had ever known that she would have preferred to have with her.

Jesse was good for her in some way she couldn't fathom. He asked for very little- mainly that she respond to him when spoken to, and that she look at him when they were conversing. She guessed that those two requests were pretty reasonable. She didn't really mind anymore, since he hadn't guessed her secret. And she was relaxing more and more around him. If he hadn't discovered her true identity by now, he probably wasn't going to. He had gotten used to her, she supposed. She did wonder what he thought about the little incident last night. Nothing had been said. When she and Jesse had gone outside to sit with their coffee, Fred had apparently gone to bed. Well, she was sure there would be some wise cracks made in the dining room. And Fred would undoubtedly have some choice words for everyone, like what a coward Franc was, and how the little fairy had come on to him last night. It had made her sick to her stomach. But what could she do? She couldn't very well say "Ah, sorry, Fred, but I'm really a woman, so would you please go away?" She didn't think so. If only she could get up some nerve to fight back, but when someone came at her that way, she was just too conditioned from past experiences to sit placidly and take anything that was dished out. She couldn't fight back. She didn't know how. Jesse must think she was a real wimp. Well, she guessed that's what she was.

Jesse came into the dining room just ahead of Francine. He had been out checking the drop, with no new calves during the night. But only a few head remained, thank goodness. He noticed the black eye Fred was sporting, then the purple on Franc's right temple. Wow, old Fred had really popped Franc. He was surprised Franc was even out of bed; his head must feel like it's about to bust wide open. *"Franc, old boy, when are you ever going to learn to fight back?"* Jesse thought to himself. Fred had been drunk, and he was pretty sure that Franc could have hit him first and stopped the whole thing. He just didn't understand that man.

Lucky took one look at Fred and burst out laughing. "Hey Fred" he gasped through his laughter, "where'd you get the shiner? Which one of your women did that to you?"

"Shut up Lucky!" growled Fred as he took his seat at the table. Then he noticed Franc's face, and he grinned. *"So,"* he thought, *"I hurt the little fairy, anyway. If that Indian hadn't come along..."*

Then Lucky caught site of Franc. "Gosh aw'mighty! Franc?"

Francine stared at her plate and ate her breakfast as usual. She figured they could stare all they wanted, she didn't care. It was nothing to her.

Even Sandy and Gene appeared concerned. They exchanged glances with each other, then Sandy offered, "Do you need anything to put on your head, Franc? I think I can find something back in the medicine cabinet that should help a little."

Francine shook her head, but said quietly, "Thanks, anyway Sandy."

That comment brought silence all around. The silent Franc had spoken! What was going to happen next around here? It certainly appeared that Franc and Fred had been in some kind of a fight last night, and no one at the table was about to offer any light on the subject. Francine hadn't looked at Fred, and she had been unconscious when Jesse had knocked him out, so she didn't realize he was sporting a black eye like hers. She wasn't sure what the fuss was about; she just wanted to eat her breakfast and get on with her work. She had a lot to do today.

Jesse said little, and let the rest at the table think what they would. Maybe it would be good for Franc's reputation if they all thought Franc had been the one to throw a punch at Fred. No one needed to know that he had done it, unless Fred decided to tell, which for some strange reason he wasn't doing.

Silence descended around the table, and breakfast was devoured with no further conversation. It was pretty obvious that no one was going to talk about what had happened last night, and from the look on Fred's face it was better to say nothing, at least for now.

Francine was the first to leave the table, as usual. She went straight to the barn and was saddling her mare, Julie, when she heard footsteps behind her; about the same time Sammy commenced his growling.

"Turn around Franc." It was Fred.

Francine didn't move.

"I said, turn around."

Francine turned. Then she saw his face for the first time. What the . . .? Then it dawned on her that Jesse must have punched him. But why hadn't Fred clarified things at the table? And when and why had Jesse hit him? She couldn't seem to put everything together, there was too much, too fast.

"Next time, Franc, that Indian won't be around to do your fighting for you. And there will be a next time, Franc, you can be sure. You won't know when it's coming, but it will come, mark my words. I have an excuse now, see, you hit me first, so I owe you one. That's the story I'll be telling. See how it works, boy?"

Francine stood silently before him, glaring at Fred steadily without blinking. Fred wasn't drunk now, and Francine wasn't nearly as terrified of a man if he wasn't drunk.

"Got'ya pretty good though, didn't I?" He laughed. "Maybe we'll just even up the colors on your face next time. I'll pretty up the other side for you!"

Sammy continued to growl, and began circling Fred uneasily. Fred knew when to back off, and he did so now.

"See you later, Franc, my boy. You be watching for me, you hear?" Laughing as he went, Fred left the barn.

Francine took a deep breath, and let it out slowly. So, Jesse must have taken a turn with Fred while she was out last night. Looked like he had done a good job of it too. She smiled softly to herself. It would seem that she owed him one, again.

***

It was later that afternoon before Francine brought up what had been on her mind since seeing Fred that morning. She had wanted to make sure they were alone when they talked. They had been moving more pairs around that afternoon, and had stopped for a short break while the cattle paired up through the gate.

"Jess?"

"Yeah?"

It seemed more and more of their conversations were beginning in this fashion. It still surprised Jesse, though, when Francine initiated a conversation.

"You did a good job on Fred's face."

"Well, he did a pretty fair job on yours first!"

"Why did you hit him, Jesse? He didn't do anything to you, did he? It wasn't your fight."

"Hell, Franc, it wasn't a fight at all! Why didn't you take a swing at him? He was drunk, you probably could have punched him out first and saved yourself a whale of a headache, not to mention that pretty purple face you're wearing today." Jesse shook his head in obvious disgust. Why he stuck up for Franc, he hadn't a clue.

Francine didn't really know how to proceed. It was pretty plain to her that Jesse was mad at her. She wasn't real sure why, though. Because she hadn't hit Fred first? She supposed that men probably thought along those lines. Kill or be killed.

"Well, I just wanted you to know that I appreciate everything you did for me last night. I mean, getting me to bed and all."

"Forget it, Franc."

"But Jesse, why did you punch him?" She really wanted to know what had set him off like that.

"Let's just say I didn't like the noises he was making, so I decided to keep him quiet, okay? Can we drop it now?"

He obviously wasn't going to tell her what had happened. But she was grateful to him for getting her back to bed, in any case.

"Hey Jess?" She was suddenly curious, wanting to know more about this quiet man with the craggy face.

"What now, Franc?"

"What kind of Indian are you, anyway?"

So, here came the questions. They always did, in the end. He debated whether to answer or not, then decided that if it kept Franc talking and maybe becoming a little more a member of the human race, he would oblige him with an answer or two. But he wouldn't let Franc dig too deep. Some things were too private.

"Crow," he answered, staring off into the distance. "I'm a half breed, it you want to know. My father was a full blood. I was born on the reservation down by Lodge Grass. Satisfied?"

"How'd you get the white eyebrow and eyelashes?" She couldn't help herself. She really was curious, having never seen anyone with a face even remotely like his.

"Not now, Franc." His face took on a shuttered look, and Francine knew the conversation was over, at least as far as it pertained to him. She could wait, though. They would have plenty of time. She wished she could understand why she was even interested in knowing these things about him. It wouldn't make any difference, in the end. She would still be alone. That was an unalterable fact. But the more time she spent with Jesse, the more she came to feel they were friends, of a sort. There seemed to be a mutual respect between them, and it was the first time in years that she had had a relationship with anyone like this. She was enjoying it, and Jesse.

Just watch it girl, she thought, Remember who and what you are, and don't get to thinking you might have any kind of a future with anyone, 'cause you know that's out of the question!

They finished up their afternoon's work, and each went their separate ways until dinner. Francine went to take a nap, as her head was still aching. Jesse made a visit to Glen's house.

***

Luckily, Glen was at home, and Jesse was ushered in without delay.

"Hi, Glen. Sorry to bother you, but I thought you might like to be kept informed of the events over at the bunkhouse." He proceeded to tell Glen his version of the fight last night between Fred, Franc, and himself. He tried to remain impartial and just relate the facts, but it was difficult for him. After what Fred had done to Franc, and then what he had said to Jesse, it was hard to remain unbiased.

Glen shook his head when Jesse had finished. "Why didn't Franc just punch him out first? If Fred was as drunk as you say he was, Franc could have decked him easily!"

"I don't know, Glen. I asked Franc the same question, but he never answered me. I think he just sat there and took it, but I'll be damned if I know why. I do like him, in spite of myself, but he is one strange cowhand, let me tell you!"

"I know, Jesse, I know." Glen ran his fingers though his hair, and then looked down at his feet, seemingly lost in thought. "Any suggestions, Jess? Do I fire Fred, or just let it pass and hope things cool down with him? You're right in the middle of things, what do you think?"

"Well," Jesse was thoughtful as he spoke. "I think old Fred will back off, at least for now. He never told anyone that it was me that hit him, and he let Lucky think it was Franc's work. We know Franc won't make any trouble, and will probably do everything he can to stay out of Fred's path from now on. Why don't we just let things go on as they have been for now. Fred's good help, you said, and we all know fights happen. Maybe we shouldn't make any more of this than we have to. You know, just chalk it up to a Friday night in the bunk house."

Glen gazed fondly at his friend. "I'll go with your instinct on this for now, then. Just keep me informed, okay?"

"Sure thing. No problem."

They visited about family and old times again until it was time for supper, when Jesse left for the cookhouse and some more of Sandy's world class cooking. It had been a long day, and he was looking forward to a good night's sleep. There were only about five cows left to calve now, and if he checked them at ten, he could go to bed and sleep until six, since Franc would check them at two. He was ready for some peace and quiet.

Chapter 10

Francine had already taken her shower and gone to bed when Jesse came back from checking the cows at about ten thirty. She was sleeping soundly as he entered the room. Sammy glanced up at him, but was used to his presence by now and was soon back to sleep, his head cradled on his paws, snoring softly. Jesse spent a few moments reflecting on Franc as the man lay sleeping.

He still couldn't figure out his reactions to Franc. He just wasn't like anyone he had ever known before. They seemed to be a lot alike, and yet they were vastly different. Franc continued to open up to him, although slowly, and even as Jesse was glad of that fact, he was also unsure just how close he wanted to get to Franc. He hated what Franc obviously was, and yet he respected the man. He despised Franc's weakness where Fred was concerned, yet he couldn't help feeling sorry for him at the same time. *"Poor Franc,"* he thought. *"To have to go through life like that. No friends, just a dog."* Then he smiled to himself. *"Hell, at least Franc has a dog! Who have I got, aside from Glen?"* He couldn't belittle his friendship with Glen; few friends were as close in this world as he and Glen. It was just that sometimes a man wanted more… He sighed softly, turned, and climbed into bed. Franc would check the cows at two. Jesse slept.

***

Francine woke easily and was up and out to the barn in moments when two o'clock rolled around. *"A quick check, and then back to bed,"* she thought as she walked among the few cows left to calve. Then she saw her. A six-year-old cow was in trouble; her calf was coming backwards. Instead of two front feet protruding from the birth canal, there was only a tail. *"Damn!"* she thought. The cow had obviously been straining for some time, and appeared to be very tired. Francine got her up and moved her out of the corral, down the alley, and into the barn. Once in the big barn, Francine switched on the lights and maneuvered the cow into an empty stall. Then she went for the calf puller and the snare, knowing she had a rough job ahead of her, and maybe an impossible one. She would have to reach inside the cow, push the calf forward, and turn the calf end for end. At the same time, the cow would be straining as hard as she could.

The cow was already lying on the straw, straining, when Francine came back with the equipment she needed.

"Okay, old girl, let's see if we can get this calf turned for you. Just relax, I'm here now." Her soothing tone of voice seemed to calm the cow somewhat, who knew instinctively that something was wrong. Having had several calves before, the cow sensed that this time something was very different.

Francine knelt near the cow's tail, took off her jacket, and rolled up her sleeves as far as they would go. Reaching carefully inside the birth canal, she began to work on the calf, trying to push it back in far enough so she could reach in with her other arm, grab its front legs, and flip it around. At the same time, the cow's muscles strained powerfully against her, and she tired rapidly. After about ten minutes, Francine realized there was no way she was going to be able to turn the calf by herself. She would have to get Jesse, and hoped the two of them would be able to do it. It was too far to a veterinarian, and the cow would die soon if they couldn't get the calf out. Not bothering with her jacket, Francine ran out of the barn and back to the bunkhouse for Jesse, her bloody arm held out and away from her body.

Jesse was instantly awake as the bedroom door flew open. Something was wrong, very wrong.

"Jesse! I need your help! I've got a tail-first calf coming!" Francine hesitated only long enough to grab a clean towel from her dresser before she was out the door and running back to the barn. Jesse was up and dressed in seconds, following close behind.

The cow hadn't moved when they arrived to help her. She was now so tired she could hardly raise her head, and gave the two humans no notice. She seemed to sense that she was dying, and was giving up.

"I can't push the calf back and turn it at the same time," Francine panted. "Do you think you can push it back while I try to grab its front feet?"

"Go for it!" Jesse positioned himself as best he could to push on the calf and still leave Francine enough room to reach in and grab its front feet. It took all the strength Jesse had in his upper torso, and all the dexterity Francine could muster, but after about five minutes of trying, their efforts meshed.

"Yes! I have his feet! Push one more time Jess!"

Jesse did, and the calf flopped end over end inside the cow's uterus. With the pain subsided for the moment, the cow rested wearily on her side.

"We did it. Jesse! We did it!" Francine was jubilant. She sat back on her haunches and grinned from ear to ear. The calf wasn't born yet, but the front feet were now protruding from the birth canal where the tail had been moments before. The cow would begin straining again within seconds, and the calf would be born, hopefully alive.

Jesse rested on the straw, lying on his side, waiting for the calf to be born. He too, had a grin on his face. They glanced at each other, beaming at the shared triumph.

"He's so handsome when he smiles!" Francine thought.

"He's almost too pretty to be a man, especially when he grins like that!" thought Jesse.

They quickly looked away from each other and back at the cow, which was beginning to strain again, and their happiness was shattered. The calf's head was turned back toward its shoulder. It could never be born in this position. Only the front feet were visible, where there should have been a nose also. They moved as a team, as if they had worked together all of their lives under conditions like these. Francine reached for the snare, and Jesse positioned himself to push again, this time on the calf's feet. They would have to push the calf back inside yet again, snare its head with the cable snare, then bring the head around to a forward position.

They worked patiently for over half an hour before Francine was able to secure the head. As soon as she did, the calf slipped out with only one push by its mother. Francine hadn't felt any movement by the calf when she was working on it, and was afraid it was dead, so was pleasantly surprised when the calf suddenly took a breath and began to shake. They pulled the newborn around to its mother's nose, gathered their equipment and left the pair alone to get acquainted.

They stood outside the stall for a moment, just looking at each other with mutual respect. Jesse was covered with dirty straw, and his hands were bloody, but he was smiling. That Franc sure knew how to work with cattle, he had to give the man credit.

Francine was glowing. She was so happy the calf had lived through the whole ordeal she was almost beside herself. Her arms were covered with blood, as was most of her shirt, but she didn't care. However, she was beginning to feel sleepy now that it was over.

"Wow! I'm sure glad those kinds of births only happen once in a blue moon! Thanks, Jess, I couldn't have done it without you." Francine couldn't thank him enough. She just hadn't been strong enough to push that calf back on her own.

"Yeah, I'm glad they don't happen too often myself. That was as tough a birth as I think I've ever attended. The cow's pretty tired, but I think she'll be okay, don't you?" Jesse was nearly light headed with relief.

"She should be. We can check on them again in the morning. Right now, I think I'm going to take another shower before I go back to bed. I'm kind of a mess, don't you think?"

Francine glanced down at her front, her arms out at her sides like a scarecrow.

"You go on ahead and take your shower. I'll wash up the snare and chains out here and be in shortly." Seeing Franc like that, all excited and smiling, made him suddenly very angry. He was a straight man, damn it, so why was he starting to have these feelings about Franc? He hated gay men! What was it about Franc? He was going to have to watch himself around the man. He couldn't seem to help genuinely liking Franc Larson, and that just wasn't right. He turned abruptly away, a scowl on his face, and the easy camaraderie was instantly gone.

She didn't know what had happened in those few moments. She had thought they were friends. Then Jesse had turned sour on her. Oh well, she would take a shower and get some more sleep. She was too tired to think about him now. The calf was the important thing, and he was all right, so nothing else mattered.

Francine rubbed her arms down with the towel she had brought as she headed back to the bunkhouse and a hot shower. It would feel awfully good after the night's exertions, and would also relax her and enable her to fall asleep more easily.

After her shower, she put on a pair of men's pajamas, large and loose fitting, instead of her clothes. She could dress in the morning when Jesse was out checking the cows, so it should be safe for her. It was always easier to fall asleep in nightclothes instead of work clothes.

Jesse had been faster at the barn than Francine expected, and as she entered the room after her shower, she found him getting ready for bed. She hesitated only a moment, suddenly fearful of being in the same room with him, then decided there was nothing for him to see after all, and relaxed. The pajamas covered her well, and she held her dirty clothes in front of her like a shield.

She turned to drop the clothes on the floor, on a pile of other dirty clothes, at the same time Jesse walked over to his dresser. They passed within inches of each other, not touching. Francine whirled and walked to her bed, settling in easily, then couldn't help watching Jesse as he strode around the room in his shorts, unaware of her scrutiny. My, but he was a well-built man! The muscles rippled under the smooth copper skin, and he moved with a natural grace reserved only for athletes. His wide shoulders melded into slim hips, and muscular thighs tapered into shapely calves. Jesse reached up to turn off the overhead light, then walked carefully through the darkness to his bed and crawled in. He sighed deeply, then lay quietly, reflecting on the night.

Francine smiled softly to herself, rolled over, and began drifting off.

***

Jesse was uneasy. Something was wrong, out of place, and he couldn't put his finger on it. Everything had been normal until he had walked over to his bed. Or at least he thought that was when things had somehow changed. He just didn't know. What could be different? He went back over the scene in his mind. Over and over he probed his brain for that nagging "something" that just didn't ring true. Was it Franc? There had been nothing different about the man, except that he was wearing pajamas, and it was the first time Jesse had seen him in nightclothes. Nothing strange about that.

Suddenly, in a flash, it hit him. "*Oh my God*!" he thought. "*Oh my God*!" He should have known instantly, but he guessed that ten years in prison had perhaps dulled his senses a little. When Franc walked past him, he had left a faint odor behind, lingering softly in the air. No perfumes, no added aromas, just the faint essence of a person. And the essence was that of a woman. Franc Larson was no man; he was a she, a woman! As sure as the sun would rise in the morning, Jesse knew he was right.

It had been ten years since he had smelled it, that smell that cannot be hidden from a man. Women have their own scent, and

Franc had it. He wondered for a moment if he could possibly be mistaken, then rejected the idea. He knew in his gut that he was right. But damn it, why had it taken him so long to catch on? Why hadn't he noticed her odor earlier? *"Well, dummy,"* he chastised himself, *"Cows and horses will tend to cover up anybody's personal smell. And she was always around the animals, just as you were."* But after a shower, she was clean, with clean nightclothes. And even though she could hide her body, she couldn't hide the fragrance of her womanhood from a man who had been too long denied the heady odor.

So, the next question was, why was Franc pretending to be a man? And obviously, Franc wasn't her real name, so who was she? And what was she hiding from? My God, the thought came to him, Fred could have killed her! No wonder she didn't fight back! He lay there, on his bed, trying to decide what to do with his new revelation. Confront her or not? And where would they go from here? He decided, after several moments of hard debating, to let Franc know that he knew the truth. Might as well get it out in the open and deal with it. Who knew where it would lead?

He took a deep breath, exhaled, then said quietly into the darkness, "Franc? You awake?"

Francine turned groggily over onto her back. What did the Indian want to talk about now? She just wanted to sleep!

"Yeah"

"Franc, I know."

Silence. There was no reply from Franc's bed.

"Did you hear me, Franc? I said I know."

Francine was wide-awake now. And terrified. Cold sweat suddenly broke out over her entire body, instantly drenching her pajamas and sheets. *"He couldn't know!"* she thought wildly. *"He just couldn't! I haven't done or said anything out of the ordinary, so how could he. . . ?"*

"You going to tell me what's going on? Or are you just going to lay there and pretend nothing is changed!"

She was frozen in place, suspended in time, unable to move or speak. For five years she had pulled off the deception. Five years, and now her life was over. A single tear lapped over her lower lid and trailed silently down her cheek. She struggled valiantly to maintain her composure, but it was useless. Another tear followed the first, and then another. Her heart was racing, her respirations shallow and labored, her body stiff, rigid. She couldn't let him find out she was crying. She had to be tough, somehow. But how? He was waiting for an answer, she knew. But what could she say? The truth? She wasn't even sure what that was anymore. And where could she start? Then Jesse helped her out.

"Why don't you start by telling me your real name? It obviously isn't Franc Larson."

She was trying so hard to compose herself; she knew she would have to say something. But she was sobbing silently, and the words wouldn't come, even though she tried.

"Look lady, you can start talking or I can come over there and make you talk to me! Get the picture? I want the truth out of you and I want it right now!"

She heard the springs creak as he began to roll out of the bed. That mobilized her into action.

"Francine!" She was able, finally, to get at least that much out. "My name is Francine. Okay?"

"That's a start. Get on with the rest of it." He settled himself back on the bed.

"Can we just leave it at that for tonight? Please? I can't talk now. I just can't."

"I don't think so. I think you owe me an explanation, and I want it tonight. So start talking."

"Look, Jesse, this whole thing has nothing to do with you, I want to be left alone. I just want to do my work and be left alone. I didn't want you here, I didn't want or need your help, and I don't want you now. Why don't you just go back to wherever you came from, and pretend you never met me?"

"Sorry, Francine is it? I think maybe I'm here to stay for a while. Keep talking."

She rose from her bed, shaking from head to toe, her body cold with fear. Dressing quickly in the dark, she headed for the door to leave. Jesse's arm shot out of the darkness in an iron grip, preventing her departure.

"Not so fast, Francine. You're not leaving now, are you?"

"Let me go!" she hissed at him. "Don't touch me!"

"Let go of you or what, you'll scream? I don't think so."

Reflexes took over, and before she even realized what she was doing, she kneed Jesse in the crotch, and as he doubled over in agony, she jerked free and was out the door, Sammy at her heels, heading for the barn. She couldn't think now, and she sure as hell couldn't do any talking. She needed time to collect herself, and to plan what she was going to do next. She had to come up with a plan. If Jesse told anyone, she was dead. Hell, she was probably dead anyway, after what she had just done to the man! The blackness of the night swallowed her up and she was gone.

Chapter 11

As Francine bolted out of the bunkhouse, she had no idea where to go or what to do, she just knew she had to get away. She had to get to a safe place. Her first instinct was to head for the barn, and her horse. She was too terrified to think clearly at this point. Five years of perfecting a role, of hiding, were all gone now. She had no idea what was in store for her, or how she would deal with the future.

She ran into the barn, and instinct still prevailed over her actions. She grabbed a bridle and headed for her horse's stall. Throwing open the stall door, she quickly bridled the mare, vaulted onto her back, and rode out of the stall and the barn as if the devil were on her heels. Feeling the terror of her rider, the big Appaloosa mare tore through the night with no urging, Sammy doing his very best to keep up.

As she rode bareback, Francine was still incapable of any clear and rational thought, but found herself heading unconsciously for the summer line camp. Instinct still prevailed; there was food and shelter at the camp, and no one would think to look for her there. Thank goodness it was early spring, since she had run out of the bunkhouse dressed only in a shirt, the ever-present vest, and pants. But the temperature was only about thirty degrees with a light breeze, and after about twenty minutes of riding, she was chilled clear through. The coldness that enveloped her heart spread from the inside out, and she began to shake as the mare continued to eat up the miles, heading into the higher hills.

What had she done? How had Jesse found her out? She kept going over the night in her mind but no matter how hard she tried, she couldn't find the answer to her downfall. Nothing had been different, except she had been wearing pajamas, but she was sure that nothing could be seen with them that would have given her away. So what was it? Had she said something? She was sure she hadn't. And now what? Well, she would get to the line camp first, and then try to formulate a plan. She was pretty sure Jesse hadn't tried to follow her, gosh, she really hadn't meant to hurt him, it was just reflex on her part. Survival. She had had to get away, and she just, well, she was sorry but it couldn't be helped. But she sure hated to think what might happen to her if Jesse ever caught up with her. He was going to be one mad Indian!

It was three hours of hard riding to the camp, and it was nearly dawn when she arrived. Her thigh muscles were sore from riding bareback that long and fast, and she was cold, her fingers nearly numb. There was still snow around the camp in places, where the drifts of winter hadn't yet melted, but it was isolated and quiet, which was what she now craved. She dismounted at the corral, a functional pen with an attached shed for protection. A small stream originated at the spring, where the springhouse still stood from many years ago, leaning heavily now with age. The spring gurgled slowly from its origination and meandered lazily downhill, through the corral, the adjacent pasture, and on down the hillside. Turning her horse loose in the corral, she looped the bridle over her arm and limped quickly back to the small cabin. Once inside, she sank heavily to the floor, numb with cold, fatigue, and heartache. The tears began to course silently down her cheeks unchecked and unnoticed. Francine unconsciously pulled herself into the fetal position, with her knees to her chest, her arms and hands entwined closely to her upper body, and began rocking in a parody of agony. Sammy lay as close to her as he could, offering what solace he was able.

How long she lay there, she didn't know. She was unable to think, and was only existing any way she could. Time passed unheeded, while she silently rocked herself and cried, and tried to retain her sanity. Eventually, she was exhausted, and slept fitfully.

Francine awoke sometime mid-morning, cold, stiff and sore, to find Sammy still curled up at her back. Faithful Sammy, whatever would she do without him? The events of the night came slowly back to her, and the tears began again. Wiping them away angrily with the back of her hand, she rose stiffly to her feet and began to assess her situation.

The line camp was composed of the horse shed and corral, a small pasture, the springhouse, and the cabin. The cabin was mainly used only by herself and then only during the summer months, but it was always kept stocked with supplies for any type of weather. There were canned goods on the shelf, blankets suspended from the rafters by baling twine, a plywood bunk bed in one corner, a wood cook stove, and various utensils. She could stay here for a week at least before she would run out of food. She quickly built a fire in the cook stove for warmth, then took down the blankets and wrapped herself in them, putting a chair in front of the stove and waiting there for the cabin to warm up. It didn't take long; the stove heated quickly and the cabin was small. There was a sink in one corner that simply drained out onto the grass, and a small square table with four chairs. The outhouse was out in the back. All the comforts of home, she thought, then settled herself for some serious thinking.

Staring at the stove, she began to mull over her options.

She wished she knew what Jesse planned to do with his new information. No one at the ranch, other than Jesse, knew she was a female. Even Adrian Miller, who had given her the job, didn't know. Adrian was her best friend's uncle, and when Clarisse had begged her uncle to give her friend a job, he had complied with no questions asked. Once the word was out, it would eventually get to town and from there only God knew how far it would spread, but eventually Todd was bound to find out. And he had sworn to kill her as soon as he got out of jail, which should have been about two years ago. Her parents didn't know where she was; they knew only that she was safe. Clarisse contacted them every few months with the old adage that no news was good news.

Clarisse was an old high school friend, the only one Francine had confided her story to. Todd hadn't known about Clarisse, so Francine had felt fairly safe in contacting her. Francine mailed her checks to her friend for deposit, and Clarisse sent her anything she needed when asked. But Todd knew a lot of people, and she realized that Todd's one burning ambition in life was to see her dead. She understood very well that he would not rest until he had found her and killed her. She had felt safe, here on the C/6 for a long time, but now it was all over.

Well, she would have to go back and get her other two horses and her gear, that much was for certain. But where could she go from there? There really wasn't any place to go. The neighboring ranches all knew about her as a gay cowboy, and she knew no one else would hire her. But that wouldn't solve anything anyway, because she would still have to invent a whole new identity. Not easily done.

It was beginning to look like she had two choices. She could stay here and take whatever came her way, or she could try to head for another state and another ranch. Maybe she should just start by staying here and seeing what developed. She knew she could hide out here for at least a week, maybe a little longer. *"Yes,"* she thought to herself, *"I'll just camp out here for a week until I can think more clearly, and then, when I have to, I'll think of something."* Her decision made, she took the blankets and fixed up the bunk for a bed, fed and watered Sammy, then crawled under the blankets and slept.

***

Jesse was mad. He was hurt too, but mostly he was just plain mad. He had done nothing to deserve what that woman had dished out to him. His balls hurt. And his pride hurt probably just as bad. What in the world was that woman trying to prove anyway? After he was able to stand and walk with some semblance of normalcy, he had gone to follow Francine, but she was thundering out of the barn on her horse as he was just stumbling out of the bunkhouse. She was gone, who knew for how long, but good riddance. He damn sure didn't need her kind of help to do his job. Lord, a man could die real young around a woman like that! He went back to bed to sleep off what was left of the night.

***

He was late for breakfast, but no one seemed to think anything about it. He guessed the night calvers kind of had their own schedule and routine anyway, after all, the cows didn't know that human meals were served at specific times.

Conversation was normal, not too lively at that hour of the morning. No one mentioned that Franc was missing. He guessed that no one really cared.

By ten o'clock Jesse started to have a twinge of conscience. It really was his fault that Franc, or Francine or whoever she was, hadn't had any breakfast. If he hadn't confronted her with his new-found knowledge, the two of them would be working in close harmony together right now, instead of him doing the work by himself, and Francine out there God only knew where, probably cold and hungry. The more he reflected on last night and his role in it, the worse he felt. She had been so happy after they had saved that calf! She had been talking to him more and more every day, and they had become friends of sorts. He guessed he should have known how she was bound to react when he confronted her with his discovery. He almost wished he hadn't figured it out. Life was much simpler before he knew he was a she, and he had sure felt better too. Boy, that woman had strong knees!

At lunch, when Francine didn't show up, Jesse was getting worried. Fred and Lucky asked where Franc was, and Jesse found himself actually making up some story about extra work he had to do. Why he didn't come out and tell everyone that

Franc was really Francine, he didn't really know. He just felt he couldn't do that, at least not until after he had talked things over with her. But where was she? He didn't have a clue. And yes, he admitted it, he was concerned. She had taken off without even a jacket, and with no food or clothing, how was she getting by out there in the hills? Damn woman, anyway!

After lunch, he went looking for Glen. He had to do something, even if it was wrong. He found Glen bent over the baler, even now thinking about summer and the work to come.

"Hey Glen!" He hailed his friend. "Can I talk to you for a minute? I kind of need to pick your brain if you don't mind."

Glen straightened from checking the bale knotters and smiled at Jesse. "Sure, Jess, anytime, you know that. What's on your mind?"

"Well, Glen, I have a slight problem. I got into a fight with Franc last night, and . . ."

"Jesse, you didn't hit him or anything did you?"

"No, no Glen, nothing like that. Just kind of a verbal disagreement. Anyway, Franc was more than a little bit mad at me, and, well, he took off early this morning and hasn't shown up either for breakfast or lunch. I feel kind'a bad, 'cause it really was all my fault. I shouldn't have pushed him, you know? I'm getting worried that I made him mad enough he just might not come back."

"What in the world did you say to him Jesse? I really thought you two were going to get on all right! What on earth happened?"

"I'd really rather not say, Glen, if you don't mind. It was kind of personal. I said some things I shouldn't have said, I guess. Anyway, I was wondering if you might have any idea where I might find him? So I can apologize? I just need to talk to him, and hopefully I can settle everything down. What do you think? Any ideas where he might have gone?"

Glen thought for a moment. "Did he take all his gear?"

"No, just one horse, as far as I can tell."

"Then he's probably somewhere on the ranch. My best guess is he's up at the summer line camp. He spends his summers up there by himself. Nobody else ever goes up there. Shoot, I don't know if the other boys even know where it is!"

"Can you tell me how to get there Glen? If you point me in the right direction, I can find it, I'm sure."

"Sure, Jess, I can do that." Glen thought for a moment to clarify the route in his mind, then drew a rough map in the mud with a stick, outlining the way to the line camp.

"It's a good three or four hour ride up there, maybe more. Probably close to ten miles one way, and the country is kind of rough in places."

"Thanks, friend. I'm sure I can find it. I just hope I can get him to come back."

"Jesse?"

"Yeah?"

"Why don't you figure on taking all the time you need up there. Maybe spend the night and come back down tomorrow. There are only a few cows left, right?"

"I think there's only about four left to calve, and they probably won't for another week yet."

"Well, I'll see to them while you're gone. Get Sandy to pack you up a sack of food for tonight. There's food up there, but we like to keep the cabin stocked, so anytime anyone goes up there he should take some provisions with him. Okay? See you both sometime tomorrow, I hope. I'll tell the boys you two are doing some checking up there so they won't be wondering what's going on."

"Thanks, Glen. I appreciate the help. See you tomorrow."

"Hey Jesse?"

"Yeah?"

"Treat Franc a little more careful next time, okay? He really is the best man I have with the cattle and I'd hate to lose him. Good luck."

They waved good-by to each other, and Jesse went to pack up what he thought he would need for the overnight trip. He was pretty sure he could find the cabin; he just hoped Francine would be there when he did.

***

Three hours later, Jesse was headed up country. He had caught an extra horse and put Francine's saddle on it, along with her jacket, a clean shirt, two cans of dog food for Sammy, extra provisions to help stock the cabin, and as an afterthought, Francine's kit with her toothbrush, comb and other essentials. He had found it in her top dresser drawer, and figured it was the least he could do for her. The directions to the cabin were committed to memory, and he was confident he could find his way. He wasn't at all sure, however, what his reception might be like when he got there; he would just have to chance it.

He talked to himself as he rode. "Damn woman. Tries to flatten my balls and here I am taking her a toothbrush. What's the matter with you Jesse? You lost every brain cell you ever thought you might have had somewhere back there in prison? Women are trouble and you know it. So what's the matter with you anyway?"

But he couldn't forget the times he had seen her cold with fear, or the times he had watched her work with the cattle and the rapport she had with them. The way she had shoed his horse when she could have been getting some much-needed sleep. The way she did a man's job and never asked for any special help or privileges. All she had really asked for was to be left alone to do her work and live her life in peace. And he, Jesse, had ruined all that for her. Maybe he hadn't meant to, but he had done it just the same.

He probably couldn't make it right with her, but he would try. Because the fact of the matter was, he missed her. He enjoyed working with her; hell, just being with her. He had enjoyed her company long before he had known she was a female. At least he didn't have to wonder about himself anymore- he wasn't abnormal or crazy!

He smelled the wood smoke before he saw the cabin. As he topped the last hill, he saw the cabin and corral nestled in a small grove of Aspen near the spring. It was a beautiful setting. Snow banks still filled the leeward gullies of the hills and the sagebrush, but spring was trying, even here, to get a grip on the land. He spotted her mare grazing in the small pasture.

"Well, Jesse, you might as well get it over with. Are you prepared to eat a little crow?" And with that said, he rode slowly up to the cabin, tied the horses to the hitching post in front, took a deep breath, and walked up to the door. He didn't knock; he just turned the latch and walked in. Francine was on the bunk, sleeping soundly. Sammy watched him enter, eyeing him closely. Closing the door softly behind him, he walked into the small room, not sure exactly what to expect. A board creaked loudly under his foot, and Francine was instantly awake. He stopped in mid stride, and waited for whatever was to come.

Chapter 12

Francine glared at Jesse with all the bravado she could muster, hate flashing from her blue eyes.

"Go away!" she spat at him, then rolled so her back was toward him and her face against the wall. Sammy, traitor that he had become, was actually wagging his tail.

"I think we need to talk."

There was no response from the bunk.

"Francine"

"Call me Franc, and I want you to leave. Now."

"Look, I just want to talk to you, okay?" Jesse was trying his level best to be civil to the woman, but it was becoming more difficult to hold his temper. Why couldn't she ever just be human?

"Okay. So we're back to that. You can either turn around and look at me so we can discuss this thing like two civilized people, or I can come over to that bunk and drag you out of it. What's it going to be?" Jesse meant every word he uttered, and Francine knew it.

Slowly, she rolled onto her back, then sat up and faced him. He got his first really good look at her, and was astonished. Her face was pale, with shadows under her eyes. The skin was parched and drawn across her cheekbones. She reminded him of some of the prisoners he had seen in solitary over at the prison in Deer Lodge. Good Lord, what had he done to her? He was suddenly more than glad he hadn't mentioned his discovery to anyone else. He had almost told Glen the truth, but Franc was his partner, and partners didn't rat on each other. Francine obviously hadn't been just playing at being a man, this had been very serious to her. She stared at him now, not willing to back down, but ready for the confrontation.

"Well, what do you want, Jesse?"

"I brought you something. Wait here a minute." Walking swiftly out the door, he returned in seconds with his arms full.

"Here, I brought your jacket, and this." He handed her the jacket and her kit with her personal items in it. She reached out and took them.

"I figured you might need these. You took off so quick"

"Okay, now you can leave."

"Look, we need to talk." He looked at her hesitantly, then lowered his body to one of the wooden chairs. "There're a few things we need to clear up, obviously."

"What's to clear up? You know I'm not a man, now so does the whole world. I no longer have a job or a place to live. I'll just stay here for a few days, then be on my way. You'll do fine here. Glen's easy to work for." She stood up and walked stiffly over to the stove, then began adding wood to the waning fire. That done, she filled the coffee pot with spring water from the water bucket, added the coffee, then put the pot on the stove to perk.

"What do you mean, you no longer have a job? I don't want your job! You still have a place to live and a job to do. Which, I might add, you do better than most men I've known!" Suddenly it dawned on him; she thought he had told everyone about her.

"I'm sure you and the boys had a good laugh over your big discovery. Well, I don't see any humor in it, so just leave me alone, will you?" She grabbed a mug from the shelf over the sink and slammed it onto the wooden counter.

"I didn't tell anyone, Francine", he spoke softly. "Nobody knows you're not who you pretend to be." He watched carefully for her reaction.

"Oh, right. Sure. You find out I'm a woman and you didn't run and tell all the guys? You expect me to believe that story? Give me a break! I'm not entirely stupid!" She turned away in disgust. "You must have told Glen or you couldn't have found me. You might be half Indian, but even you couldn't have tracked me up here. So don't tell me you didn't spill your guts to anyone!"

"I told Glen we had a fight, that you were upset and had taken off, and that I needed to find you and apologize to you. I didn't tell him anything more than that I had pushed you too far, and I didn't want you to quit. Honest, Francine, I didn't tell anyone you're a woman. I promise."

Something in his voice convinced her he was telling the truth. She wasn't sure she could trust him, but she didn't really have any reason not to. It had been so long since she had trusted anyone, it was hard to break the habit. But she wanted to believe him, she really wanted to believe him.

"You didn't tell anyone?"

"Not a soul. Scout's honor." He made an imaginary "X" across his chest with his right fore-finger, and then raised his palm, face out towards her. Then he smiled at her, not in fun, but in friendship, and the smile reached all the way to his eyes. He was sincere.

"Not Glen?"

"Not Glen. Not Fred, or Lucky or Sandy. Oh, I take it back, I did tell somebody." He was still smiling, and it disarmed her somewhat.

"I thought you said you didn't tell?"

"I guess I did mention it to Roger on the way up here, come to think of it. I might have muttered something about it to the wall last night as I was doubled over, too. Of course, I was in a little too much pain to have been thinking clearly at that time, so I can't be sure."

"Yeah, well, I'm sorry about that." She turned away again, somewhat sheepishly. "I couldn't help it. It wasn't personal, just instinct. I don't like to be touched."

"No kidding." Jesse gave a wry laugh. "I shouldn't have too much trouble remembering to stay plumb away from you in the future."

"You don't have to worry about it. I said I was leaving. You don't need me to help. I'll just move on, like I said."

"You can't leave. You need to stay and keep on like you have been. We can still work together, like before. We work well together, don't we? At least I thought we did. Look, I'm not about to tell anyone. Nobody else needs to know about you. If they should find out in the future, I can promise you they won't find out from me. What do you say, will you stay on?"

"Why would you want to keep my secret? What's in it for you?" She was skeptical, but she really did want to stay. She still had no place else to go.

"There's nothing in it for me. But I understand secrets and wanting them kept. You have your reasons, obviously, and I have mine. I'm a pretty private person too."

"Yeah, I noticed." The coffee was perked, and she poured herself a mug full, then went to sit opposite Jesse at the table.

"Is there enough for two?"

"What? Oh, sure, help yourself." She hoped he had more sense than to assume she might actually wait on him! If he wanted coffee, he could get up and get it himself.

He rose, grabbed another mug, poured himself some coffee, and sat down again. They sat quietly for a time, each lost in their own thoughts, warming their fingers around the mugs. They sipped their coffee slowly, and Francine finally began to relax.

Maybe it would be all right. Maybe he could be trusted to keep her secret. But could they really go back to the way things were before? She didn't know. If he was telling her the truth, no one else knew her secret yet, and maybe she could go back. She sure didn't have any better ideas at the moment. Lord, what a mess! Would her life ever be halfway normal again? She didn't have much hope at this point. Staying alive took precedence over normalcy.

Jesse finished his coffee and rose to his feet. "I'll just go put my horse up and bring in the supplies. Be right back. Don't go running off again, okay?" He walked to the door, preparing to leave the cabin.

"What do you mean, you'll just put your horse up? You're not staying up here with me! Forget it mister!"

"Yes, that's exactly what I mean. I'm staying up here with you tonight. Is that so awful?"

"You can't! No! You can just plan on going back to the bunkhouse tonight, but no way are you staying here!"

"Look, lady, we've been sharing the same room for weeks now, and I haven't done anything terrible to you yet, have I? It's too late to be going back down tonight. Besides, Glen told me to stay up here with you and bring you back down tomorrow. So just cool down. I'll be right back." And with that, he went out to tend to the horses.

Francine sat staring at the door as it closed behind Jesse. Now what? She guessed he was right; they had been sleeping in the same room for weeks now, before he knew. But somehow it didn't seem right, now that he did know. Could she really trust the man? Her head said no, but her heart said yes. Something told her that Jesse was an honorable man, and she had nothing to fear. She still didn't really understand why he hadn't told everyone about her. Anyone else would have shouted the news to the sky. Why hadn't Jesse? She sighed, shrugged her shoulders, and tried to think of something to have for supper. Maybe she should just let him cook. It would serve him right.

***

Jesse stepped out into the late afternoon sun. Well, one hurdle surmounted. She was going to let him stay the night. Gosh, was he really that detestable? Somehow, as long as she was passing herself off as a man, his looks hadn't seemed to matter so much. But now all of a sudden, when the situation became a man-woman thing, she couldn't stand to have him around. Hell, he just wanted to keep working with her like they had been. He wasn't after anything else from her, was he? He shook his head, and patting both horses kindly on their necks, led them over to the pasture and turned them out with Julie. What had he gotten himself into, anyway? And what was Francine hiding from? He figured it was going to be an interesting evening ahead of him.

***

Jesse ended up fixing supper with the supplies Sandy had sent up. He fed Sammy too, while Francine warily observed his every move. He felt like he was on display the whole evening. Supper was eaten in silence, and he was beginning to feel out of place. He washed up the dishes after they had eaten, then sat in front of the stove with his feet on a chair, a mug of coffee cradled in his hands. Francine settled herself in another chair a few feet away from him, sipping coffee from a similar mug. They sat in silence for some time, just staring at the stove and enjoying its warmth. Then Jesse decided it was time to get everything out in the open and get it dealt with. There was no easy way to begin, so he plunged right in.

"What are you hiding from, Francine?" he began softly.

"I told you to call me Franc. If I'm going to stay on, you can't go around calling me Francine half the time or you're going to forget and slip up one day."

He smiled to himself. So she had made up her mind to stay. Good. And he guessed she was right, he might slip if he called her Francine, so Franc it would be.

"Okay, Franc it is. Now, why are you posing as a man? And don't change the subject on me. You might as well tell me now and get it over with, 'cause I'm not going to let it rest until you do."

"I thought you said we all had secrets and I didn't have to tell mine? Going back on your word already?"

"I believe I said I understood secrets. I don't recall saying I was going to let you keep yours. So talk. Now."

Francine took a deep breath, and looked away at the other wall.

"And look at me when you talk to me. I'm hard to look at, I know, but I think you can handle it."

She turned to face him, then looked away. "I can't. I'll tell you, but I won't watch you while I do it."

He looked quickly at the ceiling, then down at his hands in his lap. There it was again. He would never get away from it.

"Okay. Go ahead. I'm listening."

"I was married for twelve years. When he drank, he beat me. That was in the beginning. Later, he beat me whether he was drunk or not, just worse when he drank. After we had been married for ten years, I found myself pregnant, an accident. He never wanted the baby. One day, he had been drinking heavily and the baby began to cry. I tried to keep her quiet, but I couldn't. He grabbed the baby and shook her, and shook her, and shook her. . . " Her voice faltered, and a tear slid unheeded down her cheek. "He just kept shaking her. I tried to stop him. I tried!" Her voice faded to a whisper, then stopped altogether.

Jesse couldn't believe what he was hearing. But he knew there was much more, and now he really wasn't sure whether or not he wanted to hear it. He saw the tear, which was soon followed by another, and then another. She couldn't help herself; the tears had a life of their own. He handed her his handkerchief.

"Go on", he said softly.

She took a deep breath, coughed once and began again.

"I took her to the hospital, but it was no use. She was dead. He had shaken her to death. She was only four months old! Just a baby! How could he do that? He told the doctors she had fallen off the couch when we weren't looking. They probably would have believed him, but I couldn't let him get away with it. I told them the truth, and he went to jail. Five years. That's all he got for killing my baby. Five measly years." She blew her nose, and her voice was stronger now.

"He did promise me one thing before they took him off to the state prison. He told me that when he got out, he was going to find me and kill me for ruining his life like that. He told me there was no place I could hide that he couldn't find me, and I believed him. So, I did what I had to do. I ran, and I hid the only way I could think of. The only kind of work I know is ranch work, and besides, I couldn't stand to live in town. So, here I am. And now you know. Are you happy, now?"

Jesse didn't know what to say. It had never entered his mind that she might be hiding out to stay alive. He thought it might have been a macho thing, or even a bet or a dare of some kind. But this? Her husband wanted to kill her?

"Are you still married to him?"

"I divorced him as soon as he went to prison."

"Can't the authorities do anything to help you?"

"No. They say they can't do anything until he breaks parole. He's too smart for that. He'll just wait until he thinks no one suspects anything, and when he finds me, it will probably look like an accident. Sometimes I don't know why I just don't let him find me and get it all over with. I don't have much to live for anymore anyway."

"Are you sure he really means to kill you? Are you sure it wasn't all a bluff, you know, just to scare you?" He couldn't believe a man would hold that kind of a grudge against a woman, a grudge strong enough to kill her!

"Oh, he'll kill me all right. When he finds me. He'll take his time about it, he won't be in any hurry. But I have no doubt that he will do it. I was married to him a long time, and I think I know him pretty well."

"Francine, why on earth didn't you leave him when he started to beat you? Why did you stay all those years?" He was trying hard to understand, with little success.

"Simple. He threatened to kill my parents if I left. I did leave one time, and of course I went to my folks. He came over one night and killed my dog. Then he fixed the brakes on my mom's car. It was after he threatened me. Mom was driving in town and the brakes failed on a hill. She was able to avoid hitting anyone else, but she was hospitalized with several broken bones. The police said it looked like an accident, and nothing was done. They couldn't prove that Todd had anything to do with it, and besides, he had a perfect alibi for the previous night. I went back to him, and he told me it was lucky for my parents that I had because they would have both died if I hadn't. He admitted to me that he had rigged her car. So what else could I do? I had no money and no job. I couldn't let him harm my parents, so I stayed. But after he killed Claire, I just disappeared. And I hope to God he never finds me." She shuddered with the thought.

"He knew all my friends, and I couldn't endanger them, so I called an old friend from high school that he didn't know about. She was able to get me this job through her uncle, and I've been here ever since. I send her my checks, and she has set up a bank account for me. I go by the name of Franc Larson, and so far, the ruse has worked. I never go to town, I don't write to anyone, and I keep to myself. Clarisse has called my folks for me, so they know I'm all right. But I don't write to her, I call from the phone in the cookhouse if I need anything, and she sends it to me. It's worked out alright so far. As long as he's looking for a woman and I can pass myself off as a man, I'm okay." She wiped a stray tear with the back of her hand, and turned to look at Jesse. "Have you heard enough now? I sure hope so, 'cause there isn't anything left to tell."

"Yeah," Jesse replied, "I think I've heard plenty. Why don't you get ready for bed? I think I'll just sit here for a while."

Francine rose and went to prepare for bed. She was exhausted from last night as well as from telling her story. It wore her out every time she even thought about her past with Todd.

***

Jesse sat motionless, reflecting on all she had told him. He had heard some stories about battered women before, but had never, to his knowledge, known a woman who had been beaten. Poor Francine! And her baby! It was all pretty hard to take in. But he had no reason to doubt what she had told him. At least now he understood why she was impersonating a man. It all made sense, now that he knew the whole story. And it made him feel very protective of her. No one would ever find out from him that she wasn't a man, that was for sure. And he would do all he could in the future to protect and help her. She deserved that much. He rose and stretched. It was late, time to get some sleep.

He made up a bed for himself on the floor, and was soon settled for the night. Francine went to her bunk and was resting quietly. The kerosene lamp was extinguished, and darkness pervaded the cabin.

"Francine?"

"Yeah?"

"Thanks for telling me. I won't betray you, you have my word."

"Thanks, Jess. Good night."

It wasn't long before Jesse heard Francine's deep, even breathing, signifying sleep. He lay quietly, his hands folded behind his head, wild thoughts running rampant through his brain. Sleep was the last thing on his mind.

Chapter 13

Sometime during the night Jesse got up, put on his heavy jacket, and went out for a walk. As the cold night air hit him, he thought about Francine's wild ride up to the cabin two nights ago without any outerwear, and decided he probably didn't even know what cold was. Though his jacket held in his body's warmth, as he turned Francine's story over and over in his mind, he became chilled from the inside out. It was pretty hard to believe that in this day and age, something like what Francine had told him could actually happen. That a woman would have to live in constant fear of being murdered by her own husband. Unbelievable! And to think that she was forced to charade as a man just to stay alive, doing a man's work. Why, that woman should be happily married with a passel of kids and a good husband to take care of her. If he could he would… He caught himself on that thought. He refused to allow himself to think about what he would do with her if he could. But those eyes of hers! A man could literally get lost in them. They were so blue and direct, and honest. At least he could quit beating himself up about the fact that he had been somewhat attracted to her when he thought she was a man. He remembered thinking that Franc Larson was just about too pretty to be a man. No wonder. He was a she. Good Lord, what a mess! Life was supposed to get simpler for him, now that he was out of prison and back in society.

At least now he understood a lot more about her. For instance, when they had first met in the snowstorm, why she had tried so hard to avoid him. Why she couldn't look at him. Why she had been literally sweating with fear. She probably reacted that way with every new man she ran across, never knowing if they would recognize her as a woman, or perhaps actually knew her former husband and might tell him where she was hiding. What a pathetic way to have to live. At least in prison he was still allowed to be himself. No wonder she wouldn't talk. She was terrified her voice might give her away.

A lot of things in their relationship had changed over the past couple of days, he reflected, but one thing had not. She still couldn't stand to look at him. He remembered when she had been telling him her story, and how even when specifically asked to look at him while she talked, she had turned away. She had even said she couldn't look at him. And the other times when he had tried to be helpful and she had turned away from him. Well, he couldn't help what his face looked like. He knew he was ugly, but he would live with it. Hell, he didn't have any choice about that! He hoped that he and Francine could at least be friends, if she could stand to stay around him when they went back to work. It was going to be hard not to treat her with deference to her sex, now that he knew. But he would have to try, for her sake. He couldn't give her away. If for no other reason, if Fred ever found out about her, she probably wouldn't be safe in the bunkhouse. He was bad enough drunk when he thought she was gay, what on earth might he do to her if he knew she was a woman? Those thoughts snapped his mind back to the night Fred had punched her. He hadn't really had time to reflect on that night until now.

"My God!'" he said out loud, "he might have killed her!" When he thought of the severity of the punch that had knocked her cold, he got physically sick in the pit of his stomach. To hit a woman that hard! And she had never said a word. She had just sat there and taken it. No wonder she never stood up for herself. If for no other reason, she had been avoiding calling any attention whatsoever to herself. If she had tried to fend him off, he would simply have gotten more aggressive. She really hadn't had any choice. She sure had a strong knee, though! He hoped he never made her mad enough again to take it out on him like that. Boy Howdy, but she had hurt him that night! What was he going to do with her? He didn't have a clue.

***

When Francine woke up early the next morning, it was to the smell of freshly brewed coffee on the small wood stove. Nothing, to her mind, smelled better than fresh coffee perked over a wood stove or made in a tin can over an outdoor fire. Not much tasted better, either. She turned over in her bunk, sighed, and remembered the events of yesterday. It had been nice of Jesse to bring her things up to her. She really didn't expect anything nice from him, especially after the way she had kneed him in the crotch the other night. It honestly had been a reflex action on her part, but she had thought at the time that he deserved it. But now she had to admit that she felt badly about it. Maybe she would apologize again later today. But for now, coffee!

Jesse was nowhere around, so she helped herself to a mug and went to sit out on the small front porch of the cabin. The sun was just coming up, and even though it was still cold outside, the day was promising to be beautiful. She sat on the top step, nursing her mug with both hands, thinking.

What was she going to do about Jesse? She had never told anyone the whole story before, and she hadn't wanted to talk about it last night, but the whole experience had been strangely cathartic for her. Her thoughts were far less troubled than they had been in years. Something about Jesse was calming to her. She found that she was actually enjoying having him around. For a man, he wasn't half bad! She wondered where he had slept last night, as there had been no signs of him in the cabin when she got up. She hoped he hadn't stayed out in the shed or something just because of her mouth. On the other hand, the thought occurred to her that maybe he wouldn't want anything more to do with her, now that he knew what a spineless wimp she had been. What kind of a mother would have let her husband kill her own baby, anyway? It was a question she asked herself almost daily, with no good answer. She was worthless, both as a woman and as a mother. She was good at her job, she knew that. She knew cattle and horses, but as a wife and mother, she was worthless. She sighed deeply, looking out over the hills that made up the Sixteen Mile area. It was so beautiful up here. Too bad she couldn't just stay at the cabin all year 'round. Life could be so peaceful.

The sun was shining fully on her face, her eyes closed, when Jesse approached the cabin from the east side. He stopped a moment, staring at her upturned face, then continued toward the steps. Francine's eyes snapped open as he walked up to her, and their gazes met briefly, before they each looked rapidly away. Jesse entered the cabin, and Francine rose to her feet, following close behind. It was time to get on with their lives, and whatever the future might hold for them, but first they would have to surmount the acute embarrassment they both seemed to be feeling.

"Jesse," she began, taking a deep breath. "I want to apologize to you..."

"For what?" He kept his back to her, and began taking some breakfast items out of his pack.

"For lots of things. Look, this isn't easy for me, okay? But I really am sorry I hurt you the other night, you know? What I said, about it being just reflex, that was true. I didn't stop to think, I just had to get away from you." Suddenly, she was angry. Here she was, trying to apologize to him, and thank him also, and he wouldn't even look at her! Okay, so she should have done something to save her child, but she was still a human being, and the least he could do was look at her when she was trying to talk to him.

"Jesse Windchase, I'm trying to talk to you here, do you think you could at least turn around and give me the courtesy of looking at me while I'm attempting to give you an apology? You always make me face you when you're talking to me, so how about returning the courtesy for a change?" "*Men!*" she thought to herself.

Jesse turned around instantly, and leaning against the crude wooden counter, crossed his arms across his chest.

"Go ahead, then Francine. If you're going to say something nice to me, I'm damn sure going to listen!"

"I told you, don't call me Francine! The name is Franc, remember?"

"Okay, okay. Franc it is. Now, what was it you were saying? Something about apologizing?"

"I can't believe I'm doing this," she muttered under her breath, shaking her head from side to side. "I would like to tell you that I am truly sorry for, uh, what I did to you the other night. I know I must have hurt you, and after all you had done to try to help me earlier, it really wasn't very nice of me. I…"

Jesse let out a snort of derision. "Well, that's one thing for sure we can agree on, sweetheart, it damn sure wasn't very nice of you!"

"Don't call me that! Not now, not ever! Understand? I am not now, nor will I ever be your sweetheart! I don't use words lightly and I won't be around you if you are going to be calling me stupid names. Jeez, why am I even trying, anyway?" She threw her hands in the air in a gesture of exasperation. "You don't want to listen, you just want to give me a hard time. I don't know why you came up here, and I sure as hell don't know why I'm standing here like a fool! Forget it, just forget the whole thing. Just stay away from me, okay? Just stay away!" She whirled lightly on her feet and started to leave the cabin.

Jesse instinctively reached out, grabbing her arm to prevent her from walking away from him. Too late, he realized his mistake, and reflex began to take over in Francine's brain again. She twisted in his grasp and her right knee came up in a flash. Jesse instantly released her and threw both hands across his privates.

"Damn, woman! Okay, okay, I give up!"

Francine realized at the last moment what she had been about to do, and her knee came back down.

"I'm sorry, I forgot for a moment that you don't like to be touched. You must have the fastest knee in Montana, lady!"

Francine put both hands to either side of her face, and lowered her gaze to the floor, her breath coming fast. She just couldn't seem to help it; when someone touched her, she had to get away in whatever manner it took to accomplish the feat. Here she had been trying to apologize to Jesse for kneeing him in the crotch, and she had almost done it again. What was wrong with her, anyway?

Jesse slowly let out the breath he had unknowingly been holding, and his hands relaxed at his side. He had very nearly gotten himself killed again, or so it would have felt. She had warned him she didn't like to be touched, and he had gone and grabbed her again. He could understand now, though, why she reacted the way she did. He would just have to remember that little item about her and be sure he never did it again. His hands came up in front of him, as if to ward her off.

"Look, Francine," At the look in her eyes as he used her given name, he knew he was in trouble yet again. "Sorry, I momentarily forgot. It won't happen again. Franc." He would try again and maybe this time he could get it right.

"Franc. I'm sorry I grabbed you. You had already told me you didn't like to be grabbed, and I went and did it anyway. Call it a momentary lapse on my part. I'm sure it won't happen again, okay? And I'm sorry I called you sweetheart. I didn't mean anything by it. I won't do that again, either. I accept the apology you were trying to make to me. Now, do you think you could do me a favor?"

She lowered her hands and looked frankly into his face. "What?"

"Do you think you could maybe make a special effort to keep both feet on the ground when you're around me? Even if I do screw up, I promise it won't be on purpose, okay?" Then he smiled at her, because at her woeful expression, he simply couldn't help himself.

She watched the smile spread clear across his face, like a little boy's smile after finding a huge snake. She couldn't stop her smile that responded to his. And Jesse thought it was probably the most beautiful sight he had ever seen in his life. Francine Larson had the most awesome smile, and a perfect set of glistening white teeth. In that moment, he realized how truly beautiful Francine was, even without a good haircut or a clean face. How could he ever have thought she was actually a man, no matter how hard she had tried to convince the world otherwise? Francine was all woman, no doubt about it. He thought his heart would melt at the sight of her. And in that instant, he knew he loved her beyond all reason.

Her smile faded as he continued to stare at her. What was wrong now? Why was he staring at her like that? She had said she was sorry, he had said he was sorry, so why couldn't things get back to normal now?

"Jesse, what's wrong? Now what have I done, for heaven's sake?"

He turned his face quickly away, before she had a chance to recognize the love and admiration that must surely be radiating from his eyes. He would have to watch it, she wouldn't like the thoughts he found himself thinking. He didn't have a chance in hell with her, and he knew it. But he couldn't help himself; there wasn't a thing he could do about his feelings. One thing was certain, she could never find out how he felt about her. She would either kill him, or run so far and fast he would never see her again. And if she did that, her ex might find her, and he couldn't stand to think what might happen then, if what she had said last night was even a little bit true.

"Nothing." He looked back at her, his emotions again under control. "It's just that you smiled and I don't recall ever seeing you actually, I mean like you really mean it, smile."

"I smiled when we pulled that calf and it was alive, remember?"

"Yeah, Franc, but it wasn't the same. That was a 'I'm happy' smile, and this was a kind of 'let's be friends' smile. Or did I read you wrong?" He didn't know what he would do if she said she couldn't or wouldn't be friends with him. Friends. That's all he could ever hope for, but he wanted that right now more than he had ever wanted anything in his life.

She actually had to think about her answer. Being friends with a man was, for her, a commitment of sorts. She didn't take friendship lightly, since she only had one. Being friends with Jesse would make two, but he would be the only one she could talk to on a daily basis. Could she trust him? Really trust him? In a split second, she made her decision. She knew, somehow, that if she couldn't trust Jesse Windchase, half Crow Indian, she could never trust anyone ever again. She would risk it.

She gazed solemnly at his closed face, his half white eyebrow and eyelashes standing out in stark contrast against his jet-streaked hair, and held out her right hand.

"Friends?" she queried.

"Friends." He slowly let out the breath he had been holding while waiting for her answer and reached out to take her hand. They shook, very formally, and the pact was sealed. At the touch of her warm flesh, a jolt shot through his hand and up his arm, straight to his gut. He felt as though he had been electrocuted, after a fashion, the sensation was that sharp.

"Now can we eat breakfast, please? I'm starving Jesse! What did you bring with you?" She turned briskly away from him to rummage through the supplies he had brought.

The tense moment passed, and he had survived, in more ways than one. He knew he would never be the same again, and he wasn't sure at this point how he felt about that. But for now, breakfast called.

"Are you going to cook or am I?"

"You just go right ahead, cowboy. I don't much like my own cooking." She wasn't about to bare her soul any farther and relate to him how many of her meals had ended up on the kitchen floor or on the walls because Todd had hated her cooking. She could cook if she had to, but she wasn't about to have another man belittling her culinary efforts.

"You got it. Bacon and eggs coming right up! Why don't you pour yourself another cup of coffee while you wait?"

So she did. She even broke one of her rules and set another mug out for Jesse. She didn't pour it though. There was a limit after all!

Chapter 14

Breakfast filled the hollow spot in Jesse's stomach, and he began to get very sleepy, having slept very little the night before. A hot cup of coffee pretty well finished him off, and he began to nod in his chair. Francine smiled softly to herself as she watched him valiantly trying to stay awake.

"Hey Jesse, why don't you crawl over onto that bunk and take a nap? I'll go take a ride along the north fence on section 8 and see how badly the snow took it down. Get an idea how much fencing will have to be done before we turn the cows out in that pasture. It will take me a couple of hours and you can get a good rest in. Okay with you?"

"Fine. I should go with you, but I honestly don't know if I could stay awake that long. I guess I didn't sleep much last night."

"Yeah, you really don't look too chipper right about now. You're a pretty fair cook, though, thanks for breakfast." She reached for her hat, chaps, and spurs and headed for the door. "What time do you want to leave today?"

"We need to be back in time for supper, so how about sometime around two o'clock? Will that give us enough time so we don't have to hurry? Maybe we can enjoy a little of the scenery this time?"

"Two it is. See you later."

Jesse watched her exit the cabin, then half stumbled over to the bunk, settled himself, and was instantly asleep. He didn't wake up until he heard Francine come back into the cabin around two that afternoon.

***

Francine took her time checking the fence, in no hurry to get back to either the cabin or the main headquarters. She loved it up here, and with Sammy trotting along for company, she felt she lacked for nothing. She hoped Jesse was getting some much-needed sleep; he looked like he hadn't slept in a week. She rode carefully, mindful of the muddy terrain resulting from the melting snow, emptying her mind as she went. She found one stretch of fence that would need some new posts and wire, and would require at least an afternoon's work, but there was plenty of time. The grass didn't really come in up here until June, but she would keep a mental note so as to bring plenty of supplies when she came up for the summer.

When she returned to the cabin, the two of them packed up everything that needed to be returned to the cookhouse for Sandy, caught their horses and started back to the ranch headquarters. Francine had to admit she was grateful to Jesse for bringing her saddle up for her. She was an excellent bareback rider, but a saddle was a lot more comfortable. They rode in silence for a couple of miles, enjoying the sounds of nature and spring around them, the afternoon sun warm on their backs. Finally, Francine broke the silence.

"Jesse?"

"Yeah."

"I just have one question for you."

"What is it Franc?" He remembered not to call her Francine, at least. He knew he had to make it a habit not to call her by her given name.

"How did you figure out about, well, you know?" She was embarrassed. Had he somehow seen her body when she didn't realize it? How had she given herself away? She thought she had been so careful. She had, after all, pulled off the deception for five years, so how had she finally slipped up?

Jesse smiled to himself. She would probably never understand. If he hadn't spent all those years in prison, with no women around him, he might not have found her out. But to a man that long deprived, well, a woman's fragrance is a pretty heady odor. One thing for sure, he couldn't remember ever smelling anything so sweet. Francine would never need perfume, like some women did, to smell exquisite to him. She had her own perfume, unique to her.

"You probably wouldn't understand, Franc. Shall we just leave it alone for now?"

Francine reined in her mare. "No, Jess, we definitely will not leave it alone! If I did something specific to give myself away to you, I need to know about it so I don't make the same mistake again, you know what I mean? I sure wouldn't want Fred to find out! So spill it, how did you know? Where did I mess up?"

Jesse halted Roger, trying to figure out a way to tell her she simply smelled more than good. He sat quietly for a moment, then looked at her and said, "You smell like a woman, Francine. That's all."

She stared at him in confusion. "What do you mean, 'I smell like a woman'? What kind of a statement is that? I don't use perfume, hell, I don't even use a scented shampoo! I use a man's deodorant, for heaven's sake! You want to try again?"

"You smell like a woman. And don't use profanity. It doesn't become a woman."

"You don't have a damn thing to say about my language, Jesse Windchase, and don't you forget it. I'll swear if I want to! Now tell me!"

"I did. You have a unique odor, all women do. I just haven't been around a woman in a very long time, and after your shower the other night, when you walked past me in our room, it suddenly dawned on me that you smelled more than just clean. It did take me awhile to figure it out, but then it just suddenly hit me. That's all. Apparently no one else has noticed it, or maybe they just haven't been near you after you've cleaned up. I don't know."

Francine mulled this over in her mind. He seemed to be telling the truth, since she couldn't figure out any other way he could have guessed. But why had he said he hadn't been around a woman in a long time? Where had he been that there were no women around? She would ask him about that later. She had never thought about a woman's scent before. Although now that she did, she realized that men have a distinct odor about them, too. Each man had his own individual scent, upon reflection. Gosh, such a simple thing!

"I understand it, Jess. You have your own individual scent about you, too. I guess I just never thought about it before." She nudged her mare into a walk again.

Jesse followed, shaking his head. It somehow surprised him that she had noticed him enough that she identified his scent as he had hers.

They continued with their journey back to headquarters, with no further conversation between them. They each became lost in their own thoughts, just enjoying the companionship and the fresh mountain air. Sammy bounded along sniffing the sagebrush for the occasional jackrabbit, with little success, but like the riders, enjoying the balmy spring air.

***

Glen Richards looked up from his desk just as the riders were leading their horses into the barn. He smiled to himself. Good, he thought. Jesse got the job done. I wonder whatever he said to Franc, though, to make him take off like that? Must have been something pretty bad. Guess it really doesn't matter, as long as he got Franc to come back. He went back to his accounts, and thought no more about the pair.

***

As Franc and Jesse walked in together for supper, no one even glanced at them. It was as though they had never left. Francine took her customary place at the table, and Jesse, though he desperately wanted to sit next to or across from her, sat where he normally did. The conversation was as usual, the weather, the prices of cattle, grain and hay, and weekend plans. It was May now, and the cattle were nearly ready to go out on grass with only a little supplemental feed. The hard winter work was about to ease up.

Jesse and Franc checked the cows together after supper, and it was obvious there would be no calves tonight. Actually, the last four stragglers probably would end up calving out on the range as they would be so late. That was okay with them; they could start sleeping regularly through the night, and get more work done during the day. Branding would be starting any day, and there were corrals and fences to go over before turning the stock out.

There was not much conversation between them now. They each felt somewhat embarrassed, for no reasons they could fathom. Bedtime approached, and Jesse suddenly became uneasy. Now that he knew Franc was a woman, how was he going to spend his nights in the same room with her? Not only because she was a woman, but loving her as he did, how was he going to handle the situation? To be in the same room, night after night, unable to touch her, to hold her, was going to be a torture he was dreading. Hell, any woman was going to arouse him after ten years, but Francine wasn't just any woman! She had unwittingly become nearly his very life's blood, as necessary to him as breathing.

She had taken a shower, but of course it never occurred to her that her very presence was disrupting to Jesse, let alone the fresh, womanly smell of her after her shower. She moved about their shared room easily now, with the need for subterfuge gone. Careful to keep herself covered at all times, she nonetheless was now able to again brush her hair at length in her room, and in general, able to be herself as she normally behaved only in strict privacy. She had to admit, it was truly a relief to have the pressure gone while she was with Jesse. To not have to be constantly worrying with every sound she uttered and every move she made, that Jesse was going to discover her secret, was a great burden of worry off her mind.

Jesse, on the other hand, was having a far from easy time of it. As Francine walked casually around the room in her pajamas, he found himself trying not to stare, yet his eyes followed her furtively, unable to get enough of the very sight of her. Occasionally, the fabric would tighten across her chest as she was brushing her hair, and it was obvious why she was never seen without a vest on. Her breasts were full and high, even at her age, no doubt due to the strenuous lifestyle she led. He lay in his bed, under the covers, in physical agony. His body would betray him, even if his actions would not. He had been with no other woman since his wife, over ten years ago, long before her murder, a long time for any healthy man. But to be in the same room with Francine, whom he loved desperately, was a sweet torture indeed. He thought he might go mad with the wanting of her. How was he going to endure night after night in the same room with this woman, whom he wanted so badly? How could he not spend night after night with her, when his soul might die without her? His agony was all too real. Even if he hadn't spent time in the state prison, even if he had an at least passable appearance, even if he wasn't half Indian, he was passionately in love with a woman who had no use for any man, and had made it abundantly clear that she would never have any sort of feelings for him. It was hell to be with her, but it would be an even worse hell to leave her. He was trapped in a hell of his own making, and there wasn't a damn thing he could do about it.

Sleep was more than difficult for him that first night back, and it didn't get any better. Each night the struggle within him continued, unabated. And each night he fought his impulses. Francine remained oblivious to his true feelings about her, falling immediately to sleep and sleeping soundly until dawn.

***

The four remaining cows left to calve were turned out with the main herd, and spring work began in earnest. Calves were medicated for scours daily, corrals needed to be repaired before branding, stalls needed cleaning, and fences had to be checked for snow damage. Fred and Lucky were still feeding, even though it was May, as spring grass was late at 5600 feet elevation. Jesse and Francine worked as a well-oiled team, as if they had been working in tandem for years. The barriers were down between them now, and they conversed easily. Francine still did not laugh or smile often, but it was becoming easier for her to do so. Jesse had difficulty letting her do her share of the work, but she had made it plain that she could and would do her share, and to back off, so he had. He worried about her constantly, and his love for her grew daily, if it was possible for him to love her any more than he already did.

***

Francine had forgotten about Fred's promise to even the score with her. The days stretched into weeks, and she found herself enjoying working with Jesse, a lot. Sometimes it scared her how much she liked being around him. And as she relaxed around Jesse, she began to relax more around the rest of the men. She still wasn't speaking to them, but she seldom thought of them as a threat any more. She felt safe with Jesse, a dangerous state for her to be in since now she had to remind herself to be cautious when not around him.

Fred had not forgotten. He hated Franc. He had been plotting ways to get back at him, biding his time. He wanted nothing more than to beat Franc until his face was pulverized, but realized that he might never get the opportunity. There were other things he could do to Franc, though. Like his horses, for instance. Franc was pretty proud of those Appaloosas of his. Maybe Fred could borrow one of those mares one day.

It was time to switch horses again, and Francine had run the remuda into the corral before breakfast. She went to the cookhouse to eat, and enjoy her morning coffee. She noticed that Fred wasn't there, but thought nothing of it. Maybe he had a bad night last night and had to sleep a little more of it off this morning. She really didn't care. She and Jesse sat on the porch steps after breakfast, enjoying a companionable cup of coffee before cutting out their fresh mounts, then walked casually over to the barn to begin the day's work in earnest.

As they approached the corral, Francine's heart rose to her throat. Fred was riding Julie. The mare was sweating profusely, foam coating her chest and flanks. Spur marks raked her flanks and shoulders. Fred was wearing a grin as wide as Montana, thoroughly enjoying himself. Jesse glanced at Francine, and was sick at what he saw on her face.

"Let me, Franc," he said to her quietly.

"No, Jesse, she's my horse, and I'll take care of it."

"Franc. . ."

"I said I'd take care of it. Stay out of my way, Jesse." Her face set, she opened the gate and entered the corral.

"Get down Fred. Now."

"What's a matter Franc? Don't like to share? Haven't been horseback in a while, and I just figured you wouldn't mind sharing. After all it's just a horse. No big deal, right? Right nice kind of a mare, here, too. You got good taste, Franc!" And then he laughed, as if enjoying a really good joke.

Francine walked calmly over to her horse, and before Fred thought to ride out of reach, grabbed the reins just under the mare's chin. "I said, get down, now, Fred."

"You think you're gonn'a stop me, Franc? Think again!" With that his right foot came out of the stirrup, and his toe caught Francine just under her chin with the full force of his kick. She sank to her knees without a sound, still conscious, but dazed and in pain. Fred laughed uproariously at the sight.

Jesse was instantly at her side, helping her to her feet. "Franc, please. . ."

She brushed him aside, and before Fred or Jesse realized what she was about to do, she had whipped out her pocketknife and slashed both reins just below the shanks of the bit. Fred was still laughing, not realizing what had happened.

"Sammy!" she called softly. Then she pointed at the mare.

That was all the instruction Sammy needed, and he went about doing what he did best. He heeled the horse, hard. Julie wasn't sure what had hit her, after all that had gone on before, but she did know she wasn't going to stand there and take any more abuse. Her head dropped, she let out a bellow as only a thoroughly angry horse can do, and went to bucking in a fashion worthy of any pro rodeo horse. Fred didn't have a chance. He grabbed for the saddle horn when he realized he didn't have any reins, and instinctively clasped his legs around the mare's girth, unwittingly digging his spurs in deeper. The harder he tried to hold on, the harder the big horse bucked. Jesse and Francine stood off to one corner of the corral, watching the action, Jesse with a grim smile on his face at the poetic justice of the scene before him, while Francine's face was rigid as stone, impassive.

When Fred finally went spinning through the air, it seemed justice had been done. He hit his head against a corral rail as he landed, and appeared to be out cold. Blood ran down his right temple, and he didn't move. Neither Jesse nor Francine bothered to see if he was all right. If he was dead, so be it. Otherwise, he could just wake up on his own.

Francine walked slowly over to the heaving mare, talking softly to her. She ran her hands lightly over the mare, taking in all cuts and scratches. Then she slipped off the saddle and bridle, leaving them in the mud and dirt of the corral. Jesse watched her from across the corral, sick at heart for her. He could kill Fred himself, if the horse hadn't already done it. But he noticed the rise and fall of Fred's chest, so knew his wishes were in vain.

"Catch your horse, Jess, if you're going to, 'cause these horses are going back to the hills right now." With that, she turned away before he could see the tears in her eyes, then spat blood on the ground before her. She caught Julie, and led her to the barn, never looking back. Jesse quickly caught his fresh horse and Mesa, and then followed her to the barn.

"Franc, are you all right?"

"Yeah."

But he knew she wasn't. Leaving the horses cross-tied in the alley, he went over to her. She tried to turn away, but this time he caught her by the shoulders and held on tight. She was too upset and hurt to even think about kneeing him again, and found herself unable to move.

"Look at me Francine," Jesse said softly. When she tried to turn away, he caught her face with his hand and brought it around so he could assess the damage. Her beautiful face was streaked with tears, and blood flecked the corners of her mouth. "Ah, Francine," he sighed, then because he didn't know what else to do, gathered her close to his chest, offering the only kind of help he knew how to give.

At first, she tried to pull away from the unfamiliar position and warmth, but Jesse held her fast.

"Don't, Francine. Don't. Let me, please?"

At his insistence and in her weakness, she stayed in his protective arms for a moment, and then suddenly pulled away.

"I have to get out of here, Jesse." And wrenching herself away from him, stifled the sob that threatened to escape with every breath. "Thank you for bringing Mesa." She saddled and bridled the fresh mare, and leading Julie, left the barn. Jesse was right behind her, leading the dun gelding.

They went to the corral, where Fred was just trying to get himself up out of the mud, swung open the gate, and had the horses moving at a lope for the hills within moments. She had to get away, out in the hills, maybe back up to the cabin for a while.

***

The remuda was back in their pasture in record time, Francine having ridden like the devil was on her heels. Poor Sammy had all he could do to keep up, taking known short cuts whenever possible, and Jesse was riding like he hadn't done in years. He got off to shut the gate after the last horse was through, but Francine never even slowed down. She swerved her horse at the last moment and headed up into the hills, the mare's feet still flying. By the time Jesse had the gate shut and was back in the saddle, Francine had a large lead on him, and it was all he could do to keep her in sight, let alone gain on her. That horse of hers was fast! He knew she was hurting, though, and there was no way he was going to let her go anywhere without him, not in her present frame of mind.

Francine was running on adrenaline and nerves. No rational thought was possible for her right now, and if she allowed herself to think, she would hurt even worse, so she rode. Hard. After ten minutes or so, it finally penetrated her mind that Mesa was breathing hard, and she could feel the mare laboring between her legs. Realizing what she was doing, she finally reined the mare in, guilt overcoming her at what she had almost done to her horse. She slid quickly to the ground, grasped Mesa around her neck, and began sobbing into her mane, great, heart-wrenching sobs that seemed to have no end. Sammy finally caught up with her, and lay down at her feet, exhausted.

Jesse saw her stop, and reined in accordingly, approaching her slowly. He was at a loss as to what to do for her. The loud sobbing was almost more than he could bear, loving her as he did, but he knew she found him physically repulsive so was hesitant to try to hold her again. Yet, he knew of nothing else he could possibly do that might somewhat ease the pain he knew she was feeling, both mentally and physically, and so, even at the risk of being rebuffed, he dropped his horse's reins and carefully approached her from behind. Placing his hands firmly on her shoulders, he spoke softly. "Francine, it's okay. I'm here. I won't let him hurt you again, I promise."

Immediately, her back stiffened. In anger? Fear? Repulsion? He didn't know. All he knew was that even though it hurt him terribly that she would react to his touch this way, he couldn't *not* touch her. He sighed deeply, then turned her around to face him, attempting to hold her close for comfort. She immediately began flailing his chest with both fists, screaming even as she fought him. At that, Jesse nearly cried himself, but refused to give up or let go. He tightened his hold, and suddenly unable to fight any longer, she collapsed against him, sobbing uncontrollably. One of Jesse's hands slipped to her waist, and the other found her head, cradling it softly. Her hat fell to the ground, unheeded, and she finally relaxed against him, no longer fighting the close physical contact.

The sobbing continued for what seemed like hours, but was in reality probably only minutes, then receded into soft gasps. Somewhere in the process, Jesse had begun to softly rock her back and forth, back and forth. The feel of her in his arms was almost more than his starved soul could take; it was beyond heaven, and suddenly he couldn't help himself. He knew he would never have the opportunity to kiss her soft lips, but he couldn't resist tasting her hair. His lips seemed to have a will of their own, and he couldn't have stopped them if he had tried. One feather light kiss touched the side of her head, and then another, and another. He found himself inhaling deeply the scent of her, and recording in his brain for the future the exquisite feel of her softness. Her breasts were pressed to his chest, and he wanted nothing more than to never have to move again. If he could die right now, he would die a happy man.

***

Slowly, Francine's wearied mind began its way back to reality, and suddenly she realized just what was going on. She was in a man's arms, and she was actually enjoying the comfort those arms were giving her. It took several seconds to notice that not only was Jesse holding her, but he was softly kissing her head over and over again. And it felt good. It had been so long since she had allowed any kind of human closeness—over five years. She had forgotten what close human contact was like, and how good it could feel. But this was Jesse, her work partner. What on earth must he think of her! Suddenly she broke the spell and the physical hold he had on her, stepping quickly away and turning to look anywhere but at him.

"I'm sorry. I don't know what came over me."

"No, Francine, it's okay. I just thought, well, . . ."

"Don't worry, I won't break down like that again. I was just so upset . . . Fred."

"Look Hon, I told you, Fred won't ever hurt you again. I'll see to it." Suddenly he realized what had slipped out of his mouth, and was horrified at what he had nearly given away. And he knew he was in trouble with her yet again when her head came up and her eyes grew bright.

"Look, cowboy, I appreciate what you were trying to do for me. I'm not totally insensitive. But I told you once before, don't go using words like that around me, ever. I'm sorry if I led you on just now. I was upset, I admit, but I had no reason to lean on you like that. It didn't mean anything. Nothing. So don't go getting any ideas. I am not your "honey" now, and I never will be, so forget it. Message understood?"

"Understood." He sighed deeply, looked at the horizon for a moment, then back at his love, hoping that what he felt didn't reflect in his eyes for her and the rest of the world to see. He couldn't bear the humiliation that would bring him.

"Could I please take a little better look at your chin and mouth for a moment, if you've settled down enough? How badly did he hurt you? Don't worry, I'll behave myself."

She glanced at him, then looked quickly away, finding it hard to maintain eye contact with this big man who had just given her such comfort. She was embarrassed. What must he think of her! Leading him on like that! It never occurred to her that Jesse was doing the things he was doing because he wanted to; she assumed that she had somehow coerced him into holding and kissing her. She was too worthless as a human being for any man to willingly console, let alone kiss tenderly like that. She knew exactly what she was, and thus she knew that she was totally unattractive and unlovable to any man. Dear God, how would she ever be able to work with him again, let alone share a room with him? She wanted nothing more than to have a huge hole in the ground just come along suddenly and swallow her up. But now he wanted to check her over to see how badly she was injured from Fred's kick. Her hand went to her jaw as she remembered, and rubbed it softly.

"I think I'm all right. I was so upset about what he did to my horse, I forgot what he did to me. I'm a little sore, but I'm okay."

"Here, let me see." His hand came out to gently grasp her chin, and he turned her head first to one side, then the other. "Nothing showing on the outside except a bruise right under your jaw. How are your teeth?" He remembered the blood on her mouth in the barn.

Francine gave her full attention to the inside of her mouth now, and winced as she felt the abrasions on her tongue and the looseness of about three lower teeth.

"I guess I won't be eating any steak for a while. Seems he managed to loosen up a few teeth for me. But at least they are all still there."

"If they are just loose, they should tighten up again within a few days. Just watch what you eat. Drink lots of coffee." And then he smiled at her. She smiled back, and for him, it was like the sun bursting out after a hard rain. It was going to be all right. She was going to forgive him. They could at least still be friends.

***

"Look, Jesse, I'm sorry about what went on just now. It was all my fault. I shouldn't have reacted to Fred's prank as hard as I did, but I'm alright now. Thanks for putting up with me, and for trying to help. I know I imposed upon you, and I'll try not to do it again."

Good grief, she thought holding her was a hardship for him! Either that, or she was trying not to hurt his feelings by voicing how she really felt about him as a man. How she found his looks more repulsive than she could stand on anything beyond a friendship level.

"The pleasure was all mine, ma'am. Hey, don't worry about it, okay? It's all over and done with."

"Okay." She stuck her hand out at him, and waited to see what he would do. He grasped it firmly, and they shook, friends once again. It really was going to be all right. Now she just had to keep from killing Fred, somehow.

"What do you say we kind of take the rest of the afternoon and maybe check a little fence? It's still a beautiful day, and there's nothing more important we have to do today. How about it? So what if we miss lunch, we can make it back for supper and fill up then to make up for lost time, so to speak."

"I don't know if I can ever go back and face Fred again, Jesse. I just don't know. I was thinking about going to the line shack for a week or so. There's enough food up there, and maybe you would bring me more supplies?"

He understood what she was saying. She didn't want to go back around any of them at headquarters, ever. But he also knew that was no solution for her. She had a reputation to uphold, and so far she had done a great job all around. Now was no time for her to quit, and Jesse would be there to back her up any time she needed him.

"Francine, I . . ."

"It's Franc, remember?"

"Yeah, right. Franc. Okay. Look, I think you should go back with me this afternoon. Pretend like nothing happened. Fred was way out of line, and I can get him fired for that. He will be gone tomorrow; all I have to do is tell Glen what went on this morning. Glen doesn't hold with that kind of behavior, you know that."

"I don't know. I don't know if I can go back and face that man. Or whatever he is."

"If you don't, Franc, he wins, don't you see? Don't let him run you off, girl. You're worth more than that, a lot more. Don't let him win, please."

She raised her head to look Jesse firmly in the eye. "*Gosh, he is a handsome man,*" she thought. And he was right–she couldn't let Fred win, and run her off.

"Okay, you win, I stay. But I don't want you telling Glen anything about this morning. I don't want Fred leaving the ranch because I told on him. I wouldn't want someone ratting on me, and I won't rat on him- and neither will you. Fred stays. Agreed?"

Jesse considered what she was saying. He knew she was right, but he was afraid for her, just the same. As long as Fred was around, things would probably only get worse for Francine. All he could hope to do was to look out for her as best he could. So far, it seemed he had done a pretty poor job of it, though.

"Agreed. We do it your way."

She smiled at him, and again, his heart melted. "Let's go check some fence, cowboy."

***

The rest of the miles they put on their horses that day were considerably easier than the first ones, and by the time they headed back to the barn, the easy rapport between them had been reestablished.

As they entered the dining room for a well-anticipated supper, they both stole a glance at Fred, who as usual was there ahead of them. He was looking pretty tough, with several bruises to his face in various locations. Francine stifled a chuckle, but Jesse out and out grinned like the proverbial Cheshire cat. Fred ignored them both. It hadn't occurred to Francine that Fred might be the most embarrassed about the whole incident; she had just expected more ribbing and jeering from Fred as usual. But it was looking as if Fred just wanted to forget the whole thing, and pretend that it never happened. Francine couldn't help herself, and she finally allowed a small smile to tickle the corners of her mouth. She had a feeling that Fred wouldn't be trying to ride any more of her horses again any time soon. Maybe she hadn't lost anything after all. She really owed Jesse big time, though, for taking care of her today. She would have to at least thank him properly later. But in the meantime, she was hungry! Her teeth were still loose, so it looked like it was going to be lots of mashed potatoes tonight for her. She was just happy she could eat at all!

***

That night, after her shower, she finally got enough courage up to thank Jesse properly. She was still embarrassed that she had actually encouraged his embrace after she relaxed, and it bothered her that she still remembered how good it felt to be held. She would have to be careful; Jesse was a good friend, nothing more. She couldn't ever trust another man any farther than that. Besides, Jesse wouldn't ever see anything in her that he might want. She was a failure at everything but cattle and horses. She had been a failure as a mother and had been unable to even protect her own child. She couldn't cook. And she was beyond poor in bed. Todd had told her that often enough. Jesse was a man in every sense of the word, and he would want a real woman, not some useless thing like her. She would have to be careful to keep the lines firmly drawn, lest she be tempted to hope for something more.

She was in her bunk, dressed warmly in her nightclothes, when Jesse came in to get ready for bed. He tried to be careful when in the same room with her, turning out the lights before he undressed. He usually slept in the nude, but since becoming aware of the fact that Franc was really Francine, he had started sleeping in his shorts. He didn't own any pajamas.

She heard him slide under the covers in the dark, took a deep breath for courage, and began. "Jesse?"

"Yeah?"

"I want to thank you. Again."

"For what?"

"For being my friend." There. She has said it.

"Anytime, Francine."

He lay on his back with his arms cradling his head, remembering how she had felt in his arms, how she had tasted. He ached for her now, and could do nothing about it. What was that old saying? *"Life's a bitch, and then you die."* Unrequited love. He had read about that somewhere, but never in his wildest dreams did he think it might ever happen to him. Yet here he was, loving a woman for the first time in his life to such an extreme he thought he might explode, and he couldn't even tell her how he felt. He had loved his wife, at least when they were first married, but not like this. It was almost unbearable. He was lost in his thoughts, thinking her asleep, when her barely audible voice carried softly through the darkness to him.

"You're the best friend I've ever had, Jesse. And right now, besides Sammy, you're really my only friend. Thank you." Francine turned over in her bunk and went instantly to sleep.

For Jesse, once again it would be awhile before sleep visited him. He drew his hands down to his sides, and found his fists clenching and unclenching seemingly of their own accord. Yeah, it would be awhile before he slept.

Chapter 15

Life on the ranch went on day to day, much as it had been. Spring arrived in earnest, and the temperature warmed daily. Robins returned, the grass began sprouting and greening up, and the cattle ceased consuming the vast quantities of hay in search for green sprigs. The last four cows would be really late dropping their calves, and had been turned out with the rest of the pairs. They would calve out in the hills without assistance, and hopefully with no trouble. It was May in Montana, that month when people finally believed that winter was at last exhausted.

Fred and Lucky were still feeding, and starting to work on haying equipment, readying it for the upcoming haying season which would start in earnest around the Fourth of July. Francine and Jesse rode every day, checking calves for the ever-present scours. They took turns; one would rope and the other would push the large oblong shaped pills down the calf's throat. With the next calf to be doctored, they would switch duties, so each was able to keep up their roping skills. When not doctoring calves, there were miles of fences to check and begin repairing before the cows could be turned out in summer pastures when the grass really came on in earnest. They continued to work as a well-matched team, which made the work more pleasant for both of them.

Jesse was in such a constant state of euphoria just being next to Francine, that he simply couldn't imagine life taking any other turns for him. He wanted nothing else but to be able to stay close to the woman he loved beyond even his life. Conversation was now easy between them, and Jesse was grateful that he no longer had to coerce Francine into speaking more than three sentences at a time. But he remained extremely careful around her, never touching her unless it could be passed off as an accident in close quarters. He knew that even though he loved Francine to distraction, Francine felt nothing more for him than friendship.

He would have to be grateful for what she allowed herself to give, and knew he had no right to ever ask for more. But just being around her on a daily basis was so much more than he felt he deserved, given his looks and his history, that he was content with what he had of her.

***

Francine couldn't remember being happier than she was right now, spending time with Jesse. He was easy to be around, with a ready smile for her and a constant sense of humor that kept her smiling until some days her face actually ached with the unaccustomed effort of it. He had made no further effort to touch her, for which she was grateful. There were times when she caught herself daydreaming about him, wondering what it would be like to have someone like Jesse love her the way every woman dreams of being loved. At those times, she would soon jerk herself back to reality, and mentally scold herself for even daring to dream of such things. Jesse was a "man's man", and he would never look at her the way a man looks at the woman he loves. She was, after all, unlovable, wasn't she? She was tall, and plain, and getting old with a face that blatantly displayed every hard mile she had ridden. She had absolutely nothing to offer any man, especially a man like Jesse. But, oh, some days the wanting in her became so intense it was like a vise around her heart!

Earlier in their relationship, she had questioned him about his unusual white eyebrow and eyelashes. He had declined to answer as to how he acquired them, and she had not asked again. At first she had a little difficulty keeping herself from staring at his unusual features, but now she never noticed the differences. He was just Jesse, her friend. And to her, he was the most handsome man she had ever met. Now, she only wanted everything to stay just as it was. She had a friend she could work and be herself with. She didn't have to pretend with Jesse that she was a man, and that in itself was such a relief that she began to feel years younger on a daily basis.

Fred had left the two of them entirely alone since the episode with Julie in the corral. Apparently, he had received a message that he could read with no chance of misinterpretation, and seemed to have no desire to repeat the mistake he had made. What went on in his mind, no one knew, but as long as he made no outward displays toward Francine, no one cared. But the more Fred was around Jesse, the more respect he came to have for the Indian, and decided if Jesse enjoyed the company of a queer, more power to him. He really wasn't interested in fighting him, and he seemed to realize that if he began picking on Franc again, he would have to deal with Jesse also at some point in time. It was very clear to all around that Franc and Jesse were a team, and as such, it was probably wiser to leave the pair to themselves. Besides, work was starting to pick up, and there just wasn't the time or the energy now for anything extra.

**

Around the middle of May, irrigating started in earnest in the hay meadows. Fred and Lucky did most of the irrigating, with Glen helping out here and there. Getting water to saturate the meadows at just the right time to promote optimal hay growth was crucial for a good hay crop, and changing the sets began at 5:30 in the morning, with the last change usually around 10:30 at night. In Montana, it seldom rains enough to ensure a hay crop without extra water, and with the winters being as rough as they usually are, plenty of hay is critical for winter survival of the stock. The only relaxation the hands had now, for sure, were their Friday or Saturday nights in Bozeman, and at those times, the relaxing was done in earnest.

It was on one of those visits to Bozeman that Fred stumbled, completely by accident, upon a juicy tidbit of information. While soothing his throat with some good Canadian whiskey at the Mint Bar, he became engaged in conversation with a couple of hands from a ranch over on the Gallatin. One thing led to another, and the subject of jailbirds somehow came up. When they began talking about a big Indian with a half white eyebrow and white eyelashes, he knew they couldn't be talking about anybody other than that Indian he was working with. He couldn't believe his luck in hearing about Jesse Windchase, former inmate at the Deer Lodge State Prison for ten years or so. And the charge? Murder. That Indian had spent time in the pen for murdering his wife! Brother, was he ever glad now that he hadn't provoked Jesse any further than he had; who knew what might have happened to him? He could have been maimed or killed, thrown out on the bone pile—you just never knew what an Indian might do anyway, and one that had been convicted of murder? He wondered if Glen knew about Jesse's record, and made it his designated duty to inform him, which he did the next day, as soon as he was able to get his head in working order again.

After breakfast and his first water change, he tracked Glen down where he was getting the sickle bar in shape on the swather. He admitted to himself that he owed Jesse one for not turning him in to Glen for his escapade in the corral with Franc's horse, but for heaven's sake, this was murder they were talking about! Glen must be told!

"Glen, can I have a word with you? You got a minute?"

Glen straightened up, stretched his back, and gave Fred his full attention. "Sure. What's on your mind, Fred? I sure hope you don't need an extra day off- we really can't spare the time right now."

"No, Glen, nothing like that." He looked at the ground and kicked at the grass with the toe of his boot, unsure as to how to approach his boss with the topic at hand. "I, uh, well, I sort'a stumbled across something last night that sure surprised me, and I, uh, well, I just figured maybe you should know about it."

"Well, spit it out man!"

"I, uh, I don't like to go around spreadin' tales about anybody, but darn it all, Glen, I just figured you ought to know about this."

"Fred, will you just say it and get it over with, please? I've got work to do here!"

"Okay, okay. Well, it's about that Indian you hired. Jesse Windchase."

Glen braced himself—he felt sure he knew what was coming. Fred had finally found out about Jesse's jail time. He had hoped that no one would ever know, but it seemed he could forget about that.

"Are you gonn'a warn me that Jesse is a jailbird, Fred?"

"You knew?"

"Yeah, I knew."

"And you didn't warn any of us? What's the matter with you?"

"Didn't figure it was anyone's business but his. As long as he does his work and stays out of trouble, it's nothing to do with me- or you either, for that matter. For what it's worth, he told me he was innocent of that murder, and I for one believe him. I've known Jesse for years, long before he ever went to jail, and I'm plumb sure he never killed anybody."

Fred wasn't sure what to say next. He couldn't believe there was a jailbird working among them, and his boss didn't think it was worth mentioning!

"But Glen . . ."

"And don't 'but Glen' me, Fred. Jesse doesn't do his work, you come to me. Otherwise, leave it alone. It's nobody else's business about his past, any more than your past is anybody else's business, okay? I don't want you repeating this to anybody, understood? Did you tell Lucky?"

"No. Thought I should run it past you first, you bein' the boss and all."

"Good. Let's keep it that way. Just keep your mouth shut, and everything will be fine."

"Boss, don't you think that Franc, at least, should know about this?" Even though he had no use for Franc, he really felt that he of all people should know who he was working with.

Glen looked Fred right in the eye with a no-nonsense stare, and Fred didn't need to be told again.

"Right, boss. My lips are sealed. Promise. Won't mention it again." And with that, Fred turned on his heels and headed back to work, shaking his head and mumbling to himself as he went. He just couldn't figure what this world was coming to, that's all. *"Decent folk having to work with Indians, and jailbirds to boot."* Nope. Just couldn't figure it.

***

With May also came spring branding, a ritual celebrated on every ranch in the west with brand laws. On the C/6, it was a weeklong process, with the cattle on the lower ranch being worked first, then the rest up Sixteen Mile. Rather than take the hands away from their regular work, a specialized branding crew was hired every year, which made the rounds of all the bigger ranches. These crews were often made up of rodeo cowboys, looking to keep in practice and make some extra money on the side. They provided everything but the branding irons, and were fast and efficient. Fred and Lucky spent several days getting the chute, alleyway, and corrals in shape for the stress of working the cattle through them, while Franc and Jesse made sure the cattle were accessible and that all were accounted for. It could really make for discord when branding is over with, and several pairs are found later that had sneaked through the fence and remained "slick."

Glen hired the same crew each year. It was run by a son of one of Glen's best friends, a young bronc rider with a good reputation for doing a clean, fast job. Garth ran a crew of six, with new kids in the crew every year as others went on to other work or went home to help run the family ranch. This year was no exception. There were two new men on the crew; one of them went by the name of TJ Newton.

Today was Friday. The branding crew would show up Monday afternoon sometime, set up camp, and be ready to start branding Tuesday morning. They would eat supper with the crew of the C/6 Monday evening; everyone would get acquainted then.

Chapter 16

The branding crew traveled with all their own gear, including tents, propane torches for the branding fires, ropes, horses and tack. They considered themselves to be professionals in the branding business, and they were fast and efficient at what they did. The only thing the ranch had to provide was the stock for them to work, necessary vaccines, and a good spread of food, three times a day. Otherwise, point them in the right direction, and they just went to work. It would take three to five days to brand all the calves at the upper C/6 ranch, depending on the weather. Wet hides don't brand well, so if it rained or snowed on any given day, all branding work would cease until the weather cleared up.

It was up to Jesse and Francine to drive the cattle into the corrals in the morning. Then all hands would help in the sorting, putting calves in one pen, and mother cows in another. When the sorting was done, the branding crew went to work.

Monday evening saw the table in the cookhouse laid out with what looked like enough food for twenty teenage boys. As the men filed in for dinner, their eyes were glued to the feast before them, as men tend to do when home cooked foods in abundant amounts are displayed.

Francine was never up to crowds, and especially crowds of men, so waited in the bunkhouse until after dinner. Sandy was used to that- Francine never ate with the men at branding time. Sandy fixed her a plate, and set it in the oven to keep warm. Francine would show up after the crew had left the cookhouse.

Jesse ate with the crew, enjoying the camaraderie. The plans for the morning were discussed, and then the wild stories began. But Jesse had begun to grow a little uneasy during the meal. He was almost certain he recognized TJ Newton from somewhere, but he couldn't quite place where. And he found TJ staring at him frequently also.

***

    Todd saw Jesse right away, upon entering the cookhouse. After all, with Jesse's size and that half white eyebrow and eyelashes, Jesse was unforgettable. His was a one-in-a-million face, that was for sure. He had never had any confrontations with Jesse in prison, but he recognized him, and remembered the reputation Jesse had in prison as a murderer and a big man you didn't want to tangle with. It surprised him to see him working here, on the C/6, but since he was a jailbird himself, he didn't hold it against the man. After all, everyone had to earn a living, and Jesse had just as much right to work as he did. Todd shrugged, and joined in the lively conversation. There was work to do in the morning, the kind Todd loved best.

***

    Tuesday morning, the rising sun found Jesse and Francine mounted and gathering cattle. They would work one bunch of roughly five hundred pairs every day until the work was finished. Francine had always hated branding time. While the men seemed to enjoy wrestling with the calves, and the smoke and noise that went with it, she considered the whole process to be nothing less than necessary torture. It had to be done, but she didn't have to like it.

    As the cattle filed into the large corral, Fred and Lucky moved in to shut the gate firmly behind the last cow. The branding crew had a good fire going in a small barrel stove, heating the three sets of irons all at one time. The calf table was anchored firmly to the posts at the end of the alley, and soon the calves were sorted and ready to be worked. Jesse and Francine took one last look to be sure their assistance wasn't needed, and then headed over for their breakfast. They would eat, down some well-deserved coffee, then head out to bring in the next bunch of pairs. Due to potential disease problems, while the calves were still small, they tried to run no more than seventy-five pairs in a bunch, so they would be moving herds of cattle all day long, keeping a constant supply of fresh calves for the crew to work. Five hundred calves a day was considered a day's work, if everything went well.

***

They had just brought in the second bunch of pairs when something about one of the branding crew caught Francine's eye. Reining Julie around so she could get a better look, Francine's gaze was riveted on the man in the dark blue shirt. She couldn't place it at first, but there was something about the way the man walked that really unnerved her. There was something... Why, he walked like Todd used to walk, with a distinctive swagger to his step. "*It couldn't be,*" she thought. Todd just couldn't be here. He couldn't.

Pulling the brim of her hat lower on her face, she readjusted her sunglasses, trying to eye the man out of the corner of her eye. When he finally turned his face toward her, and she was able to get a good look, she thought her heart would stop. It was Todd. Here. Now. And there was no way out for her. He hadn't seen her yet, but it was only a matter of time. And he would kill her this time, as he had promised. Her shoulders slumped as she realized that her days were now numbered. It was almost a relief, in a sense, to know that it was finally over. She wouldn't need to hide any longer.

***

Jesse knew when he rode up behind Francine that something was wrong. He could see it in the way she was sitting in the saddle. Where she was normally at ease and one with the horse, now she was rigid, with slumped shoulders, and her head was down. He reined Roger around so the horses were head to tail, trying to get a good look at her face, but the sunglasses and the lowered hat prevented that. "Franc- what's wrong?"

"Whatever makes you think something is wrong?" Her head came up with this, but she stared out into the far pasture, refusing to look at him.

"It's written all over your body, Franc. Something is really bothering you, and I would like you to tell me what it is. Maybe I can help. Or is it something I did or said? Is that it? Did I screw up again?" He hoped not, golly he hoped not. It tore him up inside to think he might have inadvertently hurt her in some way.

"There's nothing you can do, Jesse. And don't worry, it's nothing even related to you. It's just all over, that's all."

Nudging Julie into a walk, she started toward the barn just as Todd looked her way and stared.

**

Even with the sunglasses and the hat, he recognized her. He smiled to himself. He had found her, finally. Now she would pay, as he had promised. From the way she was sitting that big mare, he knew she had seen him, too. Good. Now she could stew about it for a while before he did anything. He would, after all, have to make plans. This had to be done properly, and that would mean she should sweat a little first. And maybe he could find some ways to stretch the whole thing out. After all, anything worth doing was worth doing well, and seeing Francine suffer was definitely something worth doing! She was trapped, and he knew it as well as she did. But it did surprise him that Glen would have a woman working for him.

Turning to Fred, who was running a gate next to him, Todd pointed toward Francine and pointedly asked, "Who the hell is that? Since when does Glen hire women around here?"

"Hell, that's no woman, that's Franc. He's one of those limp-wrist fellas, know what I mean? A queer. A fairy. We just stay away from him, and he pretty well keeps to himself. He's damn good with the cattle, and Glen keeps him on because of that. That's pretty much all he does, just works with the cattle and horses. That big Indian is his partner, and I figure he's kind'a lookin' out for Franc these days. Don't pay to get too close to them fellas. Jesse probably don't want to be sharing anyway, if you know what I mean!" With that, Fred winked at Todd, and laughed raucously.

Todd nodded solemnly but smiled inwardly. So that's the way she had been hiding out all these years! Posing as a man. He never would have guessed. He debated whether or not to spill the secret and tell Fred who Franc really was, but then thought better of it. It might suit his purpose even better if he just played along with her scam. After all, if she was a man, he could treat her as one whenever he got the chance. And he aimed to get all the chances he could!

***

The thought of running seared itself across Francine's brain, and she very nearly acted on it, until she saw Todd look at her knowingly across the corral. One look told her all she needed to know. He had recognized her, and would not allow her to escape this time. If she ran, he would follow, and she would never get a large enough lead on him to escape. She didn't want Jesse mixed up in any of this. They were friends, that's all, even though she wished it could have been more, and he didn't need to get hurt because of what was between her and Todd. Reining to a stop, Francine pivoted the mare and headed out to gather another bunch of pairs. She still had a job to do, and she would do it. What would be, would be.

Jesse followed a few paces behind until they were well away from the corrals and all the activity. Then he urged Roger ahead until he was parallel with Francine.

"Hold up, Franc. We need to talk."

"No, we don't, Jesse. There's nothing to talk about".

"Franc, if you don't stop and talk to me, I am going to have to stop your horse for you, and I know how you hate anybody touching your horses, so just hold up like I asked you to."

Francine reined the big mare to a halt, all her defenses up. She didn't want any trouble. She didn't want anything.

"Talk to me, Franc. What's going on? And don't give me that 'nothing' crap. You and I both know something big came down back there at the barn, and I want to know what it is."

"Jesse, it's nothing to do with you. I told you. Now just lea..."

"Francine, I thought we were friends. Actually, I thought we were just a little bit more than your average friends. If you can't trust me, who can you trust? I promise, I won't spread it around, whatever it is. I just want to help you, if I can. But I have to know what's going on before I can help. You know that. So quit the clam job and spill it!"

Pushing the brim of her hat back from her forehead, she stared into the distance. She supposed she might as well tell Jesse what was going on- he was bound to find out in the end anyway. She thought about it; she wanted to tell him. It would be so nice to share this burden with someone she could trust.

Turning her gaze to confront him, she studied the creases in his brow, that half white eyebrow glistening in the sunlight. And she knew in that moment that she loved him.

She smiled at him, and his heart melted. At least she wasn't mad at him for any reason, or she wouldn't have been smiling at him. He began to relax a little, and smiled back. Lord, but he loved that woman! If only he dared tell her how he felt; if only there was some hope she might someday return his feelings. But he knew that was impossible. She had made that plain enough in the past weeks.

***

I do, Francine thought. "*I love this big homely man. I love him like I have never loved anybody in my life. And I can't tell him. For sure not now. I might be dead tomorrow, and what purpose would my telling him how I feel serve? No purpose whatsoever. Besides, Jesse needs a real woman to love him, not some emotional cripple and failure like myself.*" And she knew she couldn't tell him about Todd. She just couldn't do that to him.

"Jesse, now hear me. You are my friend. My best friend. You know that, I think, don't you?"

"Yes, Francine, I do. So why…?"

"If you think anything of our friendship at all, I want you to drop it. Don't ask me again, because I'm not going to tell you. Believe me when I say it's nothing to do with you, and that there's nothing you can do about it. Just respect my privacy on this one, and let it go. Can you do that?"

Jesse could see by the set of her jaw and the look in her eyes that she meant what she said. She wasn't going to trust him with whatever her problem was. Suddenly he was more worried than ever.

"You aren't gonn'a take off on me, are you? Like, sneak away and never come back or anything like that?" If she left him now, he doubted he would ever be able to breathe again. But he couldn't think of anything else that would throw her like this, only that she might be planning to run away for some reason.

Francine sighed deeply. "No, I'm not going anywhere, Jesse. You can rest easy." She was going, but nowhere he could follow. She just didn't know when it would come. And in the meantime, she would have to find a way to keep Jesse away, so he wouldn't be involved. She had to protect him, if she could. And she didn't want him seeing her around Todd, and how much of a coward she was around him. Loving him as she now knew she did, she couldn't bear the thought of him seeing her that way, beaten and cowed.

"Promise?"

"Promise. Now can we get on with our work? I want to get this branding over with for this year. We've got cows to move, so let's get to it!"

Jesse didn't like her answer, but knowing her as he did, he knew she wasn't lying to him. She wasn't going to leave. But what on earth was bothering her? He couldn't figure it out. And why couldn't she trust him? Maybe they weren't such good friends as he thought they were. But she was right, there was work to be done.

***

Francine rode the rest of the afternoon with such mixed emotions in her heart that it was almost unbearable. Todd was here, and he was going to kill her in a way that would look like an accident, she knew that. He would never risk going back to prison. And now, just when he shows up again in her life, she discovers she is in love with Jesse Windchase, a Crow Indian. Life was so screwed up! It just wasn't fair! But even if Todd hadn't come back into her life, she could never act on her feelings for Jesse. He would never want her as a man wants a woman. All she could do was embarrass herself around him.

What on earth was she going to do? Somehow, she had to keep Jesse away from her and Todd. She didn't want Jesse getting killed as an innocent bystander. She was just going to get what she probably deserved, after all, but Jesse didn't deserve any of it. This had nothing to do with him. But how was she going to keep him away? They worked together daily. There had to be a way.

Chapter 17

That evening, it began.

She had gone into the cookhouse as usual when the crew was there, to get her plate of food, and was heading out the back door with it to eat on the steps. Being weary from the day's exertions, her instincts probably weren't as keen as they normally were, especially since she knew Todd was in the area. She was sure that Todd was off somewhere with the other men; it never occurred to her that he would be watching her at that moment.

Starting down the back steps with her dinner plate in one hand and a cup of coffee in the other, she tripped as a foot came suddenly out of the darkness, and she fell down the remaining three steps, spilling her plate and coffee, and landing on her face in the food. She knew without looking up what had happened, and heard the rough laughter as if through a fog. Todd.

"Well hello, Francine, my love! Long time no see! Did you miss me? Huh?" Todd baited her with his smooth, soft voice.

Francine lay where she had fallen, frozen in place. Her knee ached where she had smashed it on a step as she fell, and hot gravy stained the front of her shirt. A sharp pain in her right cheek told her it was bruised also; she had fallen hard, totally unprepared. At least she didn't think anything was broken- yet. But she couldn't face him, this man whom she hated and feared more than anything on this earth.

When she refused to answer or look at him, he was pleased beyond measure. She was obviously back in her old subservient mode, and he could do as he pleased with her, anytime he wanted. She wasn't going to fight or scream. Good. Her hat had fallen off when she fell, and he quickly reached down, grabbing her by her hair, and pulled her roughly back to face him, the soft darkness enveloping the tableau.

"I asked you a question, sweetheart. Aren't you gonn'a answer like a good girl?" Todd smiled into her terror-stricken face, his handsome, boyish good looks masking the evil beneath. "What's the matter, didn't expect to see me? I told you I'd find you, didn't I? And I never lied to you before, so you should have known it was only a matter of time." He yanked her head back mercilessly, leering at her, his face only inches away from hers as he squatted next to her in the dirt. At that gesture, the ever-faithful Sammy began a low growl, in warning.

"Answer me!" he rasped. "And call the dog off or I'll kill him where he stands! Now!"

"Sammy, it's okay, boy. Go lay down," she managed to whisper.

"That's better. Now tell me how much you missed me, Francine. And look me in the eye when you say it."

Francine reluctantly made eye contact as requested, and whispered, "It's good to see you again."

"I asked you if you missed me. Please answer the question correctly like a good girl."

"I missed you. Now please let me go, Todd."

The hatred in Todd's eyes, even in the dark, was frightening. He leered at her again, and then let his gaze drop to her chest, leaving her imagination to guess what he was thinking. "I told you what I would do when I found you. But I want you to think about it some first. Want you to be looking forward to it. Maybe dream about it at night. And I don't know what's been going on with that Indian, but I can tell you right now it's gonn'a stop, tonight, or you're both gonn'a be sorry you were ever born."

"Todd, leave Jesse out of this. We aren't doing anything- we're just friends, that's all. He doesn't want anything to do with me, in that way. We're just friends. I swear it. Please, Todd, leave Jesse alone."

"Well, we'll see how good you are to me, and then I'll decide, how's that sound?" With that, still holding her painfully by her hair, Todd pulled her roughly up against him. "You're mine, Francine, and nobody else's. Here's a little reminder for you, so you won't go and forget. Wouldn't want you letting anybody else handle what belongs to me." With that said, he pushed her face into the food and dirt, then released her hair and stood up. Laughing softly, he kicked her viciously in the ribs before walking off soundlessly into the night.

Francine rose slowly to a sitting position, tears sliding silently, unheeded down her cheeks. Sammy sat faithfully at her side, trying to lick her stained face. She hugged the dog to her chest, grateful for his presence. It had begun. She knew this was only the beginning. Todd would play with her until he was tired of the game, and then it would all be over. Somehow, she had to get through this without any harm coming to her beloved Sammy or to Jesse. Somehow.

Painfully, she pulled herself to her feet. Her cheek hurt, and her left knee ached. Her right side protested with every breath and movement where he had kicked her. He had hurt her, but not any worse than he had before. She knew Jesse would notice, but she would simply tell the truth- she had tripped on the back stairs of the cookhouse, and had fallen hard. But she would be all right; nothing to worry about.

She wouldn't be having any dinner that night, however, and she was awfully hungry after the hard day's work. But there was nothing to be done about it. She gave what was left of her dinner to Sammy, who gratefully gorged himself on the "people food", then headed for the bunkhouse and a shower, after a slight detour to the horse trough to rinse her face.

She was in luck- the men were all still out drinking coffee and spreading tales. Francine was able to get to the shower, and then to bed before Jesse came in for the night, for which she was grateful. She knew she would never be able to hide much from Jesse, but he was sure to notice the bruise on her cheek, anyway. No way to hide that from anybody. She just hoped he wouldn't notice the slight limp from her other injuries.

***

By the time Jesse came to bed, Francine was already sound asleep. A hard day's work, lack of food at supper, and her encounter with Todd had left her exhausted, and she never heard him enter the shared room. He was quiet when he came in, in order not to wake her, but it was obvious that she was sleeping very soundly. He took a chance, and walked silently to her bedside, standing a moment to watch her in sleep. God, but he loved that woman! If only there was some way to tell her, some way that maybe she could come to at least not be repulsed by him. He would give anything, anything at all. Being friends with her was good, but he wanted so very much more.

Suddenly she turned over onto her other side, but didn't awaken. Jesse stared, bewildered, then clenched his jaw tightly in sudden anger. There was a large bruise on her cheek, with some minor scratches and clotted blood. If Fred had hit her again, he would kill the bastard! His hands clenched at his sides, but he stood motionless. He didn't want to awaken her, but he wanted to know who had done this to her. They were going to pay, and pay dearly for this, whoever it was.

In the end, he decided to let her sleep. She obviously needed the rest. But in the morning, she was going to tell him what had happened, whether she wanted to or not.

***

Morning came so soon, it seemed. Francine awoke slowly, letting reality sift into her foggy head in slow increments. She didn't want to remember. She didn't want to face another day. But life went on, and she still had a job to do, whether Todd was here or not.

Jesse was already up and dressed, and was sitting in a chair near her bed holding a cup of coffee for her when she finally came fully back to life.

"Here." Holding the mug of steaming coffee out to her, he said, "Looks like you need this pretty bad. Gonn'a tell me what happened last night, or do I have to beat it out of you?" As soon as the words were out, he realized his mistake. She instantly shrank from him.

"Hell, I'm sorry, Francine, I didn't mean that. You know I didn't mean it. It just sort of slipped out. Take the coffee. You know I would never touch you like that, don't you? We're friends, remember? Friends don't beat each other, for any reason."

Francine sat cautiously up in bed, wincing with the pain in her ribs before she realized what she had done, but gratefully accepted the mug of coffee. She knew Jesse didn't mean what he had said, but reflexes were just that- reflexes, and uncontrollable.

"I know you didn't mean that, Jesse. Thanks for the coffee. I needed it."

"Well?"

"I tripped and fell down the back stairs of the cookhouse last night. That's all. Managed to hit my head and my knee on the way down, but I'm okay." She wasn't going to mention her ribs. He didn't need to know anything about them being bruised and sore.

"Before or after you ate?"

"Before. But I didn't want to let Sandy know what had happened, so I just gave what was left to Sammy, took a shower, and went to bed. I left the plate on the back porch."

"You must be famished! Why didn't you get another plate of food? Sandy would have gladly dished you up another plate full."

"Didn't want to bother her again. Besides, I was just so tired that all I could think of was a hot shower and getting myself to bed. I was more tired than hungry. I'll eat today, okay?"

He knew there was no arguing with her, so didn't press the matter. He wanted to blame her injuries on a person, but he was sure she wasn't lying to him. He was convinced she really had fallen down the stairs. Besides, he was with Fred last night, so he couldn't have done it to her. But it hurt his soul to see her in pain.

"I'll be right back. You enjoy that coffee." And he was gone.

He returned in five minutes with two pancakes, buttered and jellied, rolled up like cigars.

"Here- this should hold you until it's our turn for breakfast. I'll go get the horses ready while you eat and dress, and I'll meet you at the barn, okay?"

"Thanks, Jesse, this is just perfect. You go ahead and I'll be right there."

***

Jesse left her, and she chewed the pancakes gratefully, washing them down with black coffee. She couldn't remember a better breakfast, or a more charming waiter. What would she ever do without Jesse? She hoped she wouldn't have to find out before it was all over. And that thought brought her back to reality, hard. Would she die today? Probably not. Todd would prefer to drag things out for a little while. Make her worry and suffer. She would rather he just got it over with, but her wishes had never mattered to him before, so she knew they for sure wouldn't matter now. He had hurt her last night, but he had hurt her much worse in the past. She knew what was coming, and just hoped she was still strong enough to take it. If she showed any weakness, he would be more brutal with her.

Well, for now, there were cows to bring in, and calves to work. She was probably going to be allowed to live at least until branding was over with, which meant that she had a few more days. It helped to have a time frame for her death. Maybe she couldn't get rid of Jesse while the branding was still going on, but after that, she would have to figure something out.

Francine pulled her vest and chaps on, then buckled on her spurs. Anchoring her hat firmly on her head, she grabbed the ever-present sunglasses, and headed for the barn. At least she could spend her final days doing what she loved best- riding.

Chapter 18

The interior of the barn was entombed in darkness. Francine entered the little walk-through door, groping in the dark for the light switch, while Sammy played near a stray hay bale outside, trying to catch one of the mice that had taken up residence beneath it. Suddenly a brutal fist to her mid-section doubled her over, and she fell hard to her knees, groaning in pain and unable to catch her breath. Todd sneered at her in the darkness above her.

"Mornin' Francine, my dear. Have a nice day." Chuckling, he disappeared into the dark shadows.

Francine gave a low moan, and a single tear edged its way down her cheek. She bit her lip to keep from crying out until she tasted blood. Still clutching her middle, she rose slowly and painfully to her feet, staggering just a little. Leaning against the wall for support, she waited until she was able to breath normally again, then found the switch and went to saddle Julie for the day's work.

"Just like the old days", she thought. He always did know how to hurt her where it wouldn't show to the casual observer. She just wished he would go ahead and get it over with. This cat and mouse game was going to hurt her more than the actual beatings, never knowing when they were coming.

She was just cinching up when Jesse entered the barn. One look at her face, and he knew something was wrong, again. Or was it still?

"Franc, you okay?" he asked quietly.

Francine only nodded. She gathered up her reins, and heading out the big sliding barn door, said "I'll meet you out in the big corral." She left.

***

Jesse was dumbfounded. Something was wrong, that was for sure. His heart seemed to clench in his chest. Was she tired of his company? She was certainly avoiding him, starting with last night. For the first time in his life, he was nearly ashamed of his heritage. Was that what was putting her off? Had she finally decided she didn't want anything to do with Indians? It didn't seem possible, but what else could it be? Was it his face? That half white eyebrow and eyelashes? His crooked nose? He tentatively rubbed his hand over the offending hairs, ruefully remembering the terrible fight that had been the cause of them. He had very nearly died in that fight, but so had his antagonist. It hadn't seemed to bother Francine before, but was she now tired of looking at him? His eyes misted over at the thought that she might want nothing more to do with him, for whatever reason. He knew he would ride to hell and back for her, and never ask the reason why, if that was what she wanted from him.

"Please, God, let it be something else. Please don't let her not want me around her anymore. I survived prison, but I don't know if I could survive this life anymore without her." The cavernous barn absorbed his pleas.

He groomed and saddled his horse, then met her just outside the big corral. They headed off to gather the first bunch for the day, Francine just staring straight ahead, offering no opening for conversation.

When they came to the pasture gate, Jesse dismounted, opened the gate, and then leaned against the side of his horse. Francine glanced briefly at him, wondering what he was doing.

"Francine, are you gonn'a speak to me at all? Or are we just gonn'a spend the day like strangers?"

"Like strangers." And she rode on through the gate.

***

She had to keep her distance from him, she knew. Loving him as she did, she couldn't let him know what was going on, or

Todd might just kill him, and that she couldn't bear. He could do as he liked with her, but if something happened to Jesse? Even if he would never return her feelings, she had to protect him any way that she could, and right now, the only way she knew how to do that was to keep him away from her as much as possible. She knew she might be hurting him, but she just didn't know what else to do. But oh! It hurt so to not laugh with him; to have that camaraderie back! She felt so very alone again, and she missed the easy way that was between them.

Once inside the gate, they went their separate ways. Having worked together this long, they had the routine down pat. Jesse rode off to the north, and Francine to the south. They would make a big circle in the pasture, riding up the fence lines on each side, then meeting in the middle and pushing everything they found back down to the gate. Sammy went with Francine, of course, and was invaluable at getting the pairs to mother up. Nothing promoted that activity like a coyote or a dog. Often, the mother cows hid their babies in the sagebrush, pretending they didn't even have a calf; a good dog changed their minds in a hurry.

Francine had about thirty-five pairs pushed toward the center of the pasture, when one cow decided to take her calf and head for the hills. She reined the mare hard after the cow, jumping Julie into a fast lope as she did so.

Suddenly, without warning, Francine was astonished to find herself hitting the ground, her left foot still in the stirrup.

It took her a second to understand- she had lost the saddle right off of her horse, and it was hanging under Julie's belly by only the flank cinch! Fortunately, she had managed to hold onto one rein, so she wasn't going to be afoot. Gingerly, she got back on her feet, still sore from last night's fall and this morning's brutal punch. Now she would have more sore spots from hitting the ground.

She grabbed the saddle blanket and after calming Julie, smoothed it over her back. Hefting the saddle, she positioned it on the mare, and began looking for what had gone wrong. It didn't take her long to find it. The off billet had been sliced nearly through, and when she had jumped the mare out after the cow, the sudden twist was all that was needed to finish the break. She was just thankful that Julie was as dead broke as she was; a less level-headed horse would have come unglued with a saddle hanging under her belly, catching her feet.

Francine quickly punched three holes in both ends of the leather strap with her pocketknife, then spliced it with a section of leather lace she always carried on the flank cinch ring. They often came in handy for range repairs of all kinds. She didn't want Jesse finding out about this. He would want to know who was responsible, and she was afraid of what he might do if he found out.

***

Jesse had just climbed to the top of a small rise about three hundred feet away, and saw Francine working on her saddle. Something was wrong. He could tell she was doing some kind of repair work, and Francine always kept her tack in excellent repair. Obviously, she was okay, but he would check her saddle over later. He rode off back the way he had come, and continued gathering the herd. He could wait, for a while. But he would find out what was going on, one way or another.

***

After supper that evening, Jesse slipped out to the barn to get a good look at Francine's gear. It took only a few moments to discover the new off billet that had replaced the spliced one. The leather had not yet formed to the cinch ring. Francine had put this new one on while Jesse was eating, but where was the old one? And why was there a new one? He soon found his answer in one of the trash barrels in the barn. Pulling out the old billet, it was immediately obvious that it had been cut. Reality was somewhat slow to dawn on him, but when it did, he was livid.

If Fred did this, he's a dead man. Jesse had served time in prison for a murder he didn't commit, but right now he was more than ready to go back for one that he did, if it meant protecting Francine. He was sure that she knew who was responsible. Her body language was more resignation than fear. If she didn't know, she would be afraid. She wasn't afraid, so she knew, and he was going to find out. Tonight.

***

Francine was already in bed when Jesse entered their shared room. She was pretending to be asleep, but he knew she was faking it. Probably didn't want to talk to him, but that was just too bad.

"Francine", he said softly as he stood over her bed, "I know you're not asleep. You need to answer a few questions. Now"

She remained with her face turned to the wall, saying only "Go to bed, Jesse. There's nothing to talk about."

"You're not getting off that easy, my girl. I saw you fixing your saddle out there in the pasture today. I suspected something was up, and I just came from checking your saddle over. You put a new off billet on this evening, and I found the reason why in the trash barrel."

Francine went rigid. He knew someone had sliced her leather. He knew someone wanted to hurt her. Hopefully, he hadn't guessed who it was.

"Leave it Jess. It's nothing to do with you."

"Nothing to do with me? That's supposed to be the end of it? Someone tries to hurt you, maybe get you killed, and you want me to 'leave it'? You've got to be kidding! I thought we were friends, Franc. You and me. I thought we were friends."

"We are friends, Jesse, but . . ."

"No buts about it, Francine! Friends tell friends what's going on. What's bothering them. They share, you know? Maybe you don't know. Maybe it's been so long since you had a friend that you can't remember, but I'm reminding you now. And I think you know who did it, don't you? I know you do."

"Jesse, I asked you to leave it alone. It's my problem, not yours. I'll handle it in my own way, in my own time, okay?"

"No, Francie, it's *not* okay! You could have been killed. If you had been riding a colt, you might well have." He couldn't help himself. "I couldn't stand it if something happened to you, you know." The words came out softly, as he sat ever so easily on the edge of the bunk. He reached out a hand, tentatively, to lightly stroke her hair. It was still wet from her shower, and damp to his touch. His nostrils breathed in the fresh, womanly scent of her. Lord, but he loved this woman!

***

At his soft stroking, Francine felt the tears starting. She tried to hold them back- oh, how hard she tried. But that simple act of kindness was her undoing. One by one, the tears slid slowly down her cheeks. His hand reached out to brush them away, and she didn't try to stop him. She couldn't. She loved him so much! She knew he was just being kind, but she was so terribly starved for any human comfort, she felt herself leaning, against her will, into the warmth of his hand.

Tears formed in Jesse's eyes at the sight of hers, and with a groan, he gathered her into his arms. For once, Francine didn't resist. It was heavenly to be held! She sighed softly, and leaned into him, resting her head on his shoulder, the tears spilling silently into his shirt. She didn't return the embrace, only snuggled deeper into the masculine warmth and strength of him, this big homely man who had become her only reason for living. She knew she shouldn't allow this to be happening, but something stronger than her will kept her in the safety that he offered. She would resist, eventually, but for now, she was safe.

***

How long they stayed that way, they had no idea. Jesse was afraid to move or say a word, in case the spell would be broken, and the last thing he wanted was her moving away from him. So he held her, for what seemed like only seconds, softly stroking her hair, saying nothing, almost afraid to breathe in case that small act might break the magic of the moment. Finally, the tears stopped. Francine sighed deeply, and pulled away.

"Thank you, Jesse. I guess I needed that after all. I'm okay now. You don't have to hold me anymore. I'm sorry about all of that. The last thing you need is some sniveling woman crying on your shoulder. I'll try not to let it happen again." She looked up at him and managed a weak smile that didn't reach her eyes, then turned away and settled back into the bed.

"Glad to be of help, ma'am." She seemed to think it was a burden for him to hold her! If she only knew! What was he going to do with her? He would give anything if once, just once, she would look at him with something more than friendship or gratitude, but he knew he would settle for whatever she gave him. At least she wasn't mad at him, and she didn't seem repulsed by him. Thank God!

"Now, about that billet…"

"No, Jesse. The subject is closed."

"Francine! I am going to find out who did it. Believe it. Was it Fred? I think you know. Was it him? I'll kill the son of a bitch whoever it was!"

That was exactly the reaction she was afraid of. She couldn't tell him. Maybe he wouldn't find out after all.

"No, not Fred and that's all you need to know. I said I would take care of it. Now leave it, please, Jesse. Do this for me, I'm begging you. Leave it alone."

"No, I can't."

"Jesse, I have never asked you to do anything for me, but I'm asking you now. Drop it."

He looked at her long and hard, debating whether or not to reveal his feelings for her, but now it seemed there was no way to avoid it.

"I love you, Francine, and because I do, I can't stay out of it. I won't. I'd rather die than see you hurt again. If you won't tell me, I'll go find out for myself. It stops, and it stops here, tonight. Now, are you going to tell me who did it?"

"No. I can't."

She stared at him through misty eyes. He had said that he loved her. As a woman? Or as a friend? She didn't know. It was enough that he cared about her enough to use that word "love." Her vision clouded somewhat as she watched him rise and walk slowly to the door. Heaven only knew what was going to happen next!

Chapter 19

Jesse sat quietly in the gathering room of the bunkhouse, waiting for Fred to come in for the night. The Crow in him took over, and he sat motionless, waiting. He was so quiet that when Fred finally did come in, he almost didn't see him sitting there.

"Hello, Fred. Had a busy day today?" The words were spoken so quietly, Fred had to strain to hear them.

"Yeah, okay I guess. Getting those calves worked right on schedule. How 'bout yourself?" He was a little leery of Jesse. Something was up, and Fred didn't like it. He could feel the hatred emanating from Jesse clear across the room. Hell, what had he done now? He hadn't touched Franc ever since that last go 'round, and he didn't intend to, but Jesse obviously had a burr under his saddle about something.

"Had a little fun on the side, did you?"

"What are you talking about, Jesse? I haven't done anything and you know it! So back off!"

"Haven't done anything you say? You really gonn'a sit there all innocent like and tell me you didn't slice the off billet on Franc's saddle today? You're really gonn'a try to convince me you didn't do that? Think very carefully before you speak, Fred. Be very, very careful!"

Fred's face blanched. Someone had cut the off billet on Franc's saddle, and Jesse obviously thought that he had done it.

"Honest to God, Jesse, I don't know what you're talking about. I didn't cut anything. I haven't even been near the barn today! I swear to you, I didn't!"

Jesse rose slowly out of his chair, and rounding the table, came to within a foot of Fred. Suddenly he reached out and grabbed Fred by the front of his shirt, shoving his fist under the man's chin, and slamming him up against the wall. Fred winced.

"Jesse, calm down. I didn't do anything I tell you!"

Their voices were coming through the walls, louder and louder. Francine couldn't help but hear them, and was suddenly terrified that Jesse might really hurt Fred. She had to stop him before he did something really terrible. Stumbling out of bed, she raced to the door in her pajamas and bare feet.

Jesse's right hand came slowly around Fred's throat, while his left held him pinned to the wall. Slowly, he began to squeeze.

"You might have killed him, Fred. Now it's your turn. You aren't going to hurt anyone ever again, I promise." He squeezed a little harder.

"Jesse! Stop it!" He managed to gasp, "You're choking me! Stop it! You don't want to go back to jail for another murder, do you? Wasn't murdering your wife enough for you? She probably didn't do anything to deserve it either!"

The gasp from the now open door caused Jesse to turn around. Francine stood there, her fist in her mouth, and the look of horror on her face made Jesse sick to his stomach. She hadn't known.

"Franc-I…"

Francine turned, and shut the door slowly behind her as she retreated back into her room.

Jesse looked long and hard at Fred, then slowly released him.

"You had better be telling me the truth, Fred. That's all I have to say to you right now. But I will find out who did it. Trust me. I will find out if it's the last thing I do." He turned and went to confront Francine, alone.

Murder! Jesse was a murderer! She couldn't believe it. It just couldn't be true! She had finally found a friend, someone she thought she could trust, and he was a murderer? Shock made her shiver uncontrollably.

"Francine…"

She quickly turned her back to him, but not before he saw the look of disgust and horror on her face.

"Francine, I didn't do it- I swear to you, I didn't do it."

"Did you spend time in jail for murder? Was Fred telling the truth?"

"Yes, but I was innocent, I swear."

"For murdering your wife?"

"Yes."

"How long?"

"Ten years."

"Does Glen know?"

"Yes."

"Were you ever going to tell me?"

"No."

"Why not?"

"Look at me, Francine."

She remained standing with her back to him.

"Francine, look at me, please."

"I can't. Not right now." How could she look at him? One minute she had been nestled in his arms, taking comfort that she so desperately needed, and the next she finds out the man is a convicted murderer! He had murdered his own wife, for heaven's sake! She felt betrayed all over again. Numbly, in the back of her mind, the question popped into her mind- had he beaten his wife as well? Was he really no better than Todd after all? Had she been suckered all over again? She couldn't think. Her mind was on overload. Her hands flew to frame her face, her skin chalky white. Her head began to shake from side to side, and low moans escaped her lips, unintelligible sounds.

***

Jesse was devastated. He had truthfully hoped she would never find out, knowing that if and when she did, her reaction would be exactly as it was now that she knew. She found it almost impossible to trust men, and just when she was finally able to trust him completely, his past was thrown up in her face.

If he could have just prepared her somehow, but then he'd had no idea that Fred was going to come out with it. Or that she would hear it.

What had he done! If only he had listened to her, and left Fred alone. But he couldn't have done that either. It wasn't in him to leave what he considered attempted murder, and do nothing about it. Especially when it concerned someone he cared about more than his very life.

"I'll explain it all, if you'll let me. Please."

She stood silently for several seconds, then spoke quietly from across the room.

"If you will leave me alone, I would like to get dressed now. I'll sleep in the barn tonight."

He stared at her back, uncomprehending.

"You won't stay in the same room with me?" He strode silently across the room, reaching out a hand to touch her shoulder, and then thought better of it. It was obvious she couldn't stand for him to touch her. Not now.

"Francine. Please. I meant what I said. I love you. Please don't do this. Let me explain."

"Maybe tomorrow, Jesse. Not now. I just can't handle it now, okay?"

"Then I'll leave. I'll sleep in the barn tonight. You stay here."

"I can't. I can't stay here tonight. I'm sorry. We'll talk about it tomorrow." She pivoted quickly and began to gather up her clothes. Stuffing everything into a big plastic bag, she pulled her boots and her jacket on, jammed her hat low over her eyes, and without a backward glance, left the bunkhouse.

Once in the barn, Francine quickly dressed, and noting that it wasn't that late, trotted over to the main house to talk to Glen. Fifteen minutes later she was back in the barn, saddling Julie. Closing the big barn door after her, she mounted quietly in the moonlight, and with Sammy at the mare's heels, disappeared into the indigo blanket that was the night.

***

Jesse, hidden in the shadows, watched impassively as she left, his heart numb in his chest, his spirit nearly broken. And there was not a thing he could do to stop her.

Chapter 20

Francine rode slowly, Julie and Sammy grateful for the slower pace after the hard day's work. Julie picked her way carefully, her muzzle occasionally sifting the wind for any unusual scents, her ears constantly focusing on various night sounds. Sammy pulled into his favorite place just behind Julie's hocks. Something was definitely wrong with their owner, and they sensed it the way animals do.

An overwhelming sadness pervaded Francine's entire being. She was essentially numb. Jesse was a murderer! He had spent time in Montana State Prison. Ten years, for heaven's sake. And he was never going to tell her. He had said he was innocent. Did she believe him? How could she? By not telling her, he had essentially lied by omission. And yet, he had been the best friend she had ever had. How could she reconcile the two Jesse's? One was a devoted friend and confidant, and the other a murderer?

His own wife! Had he beaten her first? Or had he just strangled her slowly. Maybe he had shot her. Stabbed her? It was beyond comprehension. Had she almost made another tragic mistake by trusting him? If Todd hadn't found her, would Jesse eventually have turned on her, and beaten her just as Todd would do? She didn't know. She just didn't know.

She felt more alone now than she had ever felt in her life. She had loved Jesse. Years ago, she had thought she was in love with Todd, but realized over time that it hadn't been love at all. She had been infatuated with Todd. He had stroked her ego, told her all the things every woman longs to hear from a man, and she had been led along like a lamb to the slaughter. But Jesse! Jesse she had truly loved! The betrayal was almost more than she could bear.

Glen had been very understanding. He hadn't asked any questions, taking at face value her explanation that she needed to take some time off. Francine had never asked for any favors since coming to work for Glen, and even though he was a little upset that she would choose branding time to leave, he also recognized that it was urgent. He had told her to go, and they would get along without her somehow.

Francine had nowhere to go but the line cabin. She wasn't running from Todd this time, she was running from Jesse. Hopefully he would be kept so busy that he wouldn't have time to come looking for her. She was pretty sure she would have a few days before anyone came for her, if they came at all. Todd would find her eventually, she knew, but right now it didn't seem to matter anymore. She no longer cared whether she lived or died. Her trust was shattered, her heart broken. The pieces of her that were left didn't matter. Jesse! How she had loved him! Another man had betrayed her- what was the point of living now? She almost hoped Todd would come for her soon, and end her torment. Then she could finally be at peace.

***

Jesse lay awake all night. The occasional tear managed to find its way from one eye, then the other. He never bothered to wipe any of them away. Francine was gone, and it was his fault she had left. If he had only kept his nose out of her business- but how could he? Someone had tried to hurt her, bad, and loving her as he did, he couldn't stay out of it. He just couldn't. But by not listening to her, through his own actions, she had found out about his prison sentence, and the fact that he had been convicted of murdering his wife. It had taken him months to get her to trust him, and now it was all for nothing.

He knew she never wanted to see him again. He doubted that anything he could say to her, if she would ever even allow him that close, would change her mind. After all she had gone through with her husband, and the life she had been forced to lead as a result, trust was such a fragile thing with her that once destroyed, it would never come back. He loved her as he had never loved anyone in his life before, and he had lost her. How would he live? How would he even draw his next breath? He didn't know. He was pretty sure where she had gone. For an instant, the overwhelming urge to follow her almost had him on his feet. But he held his breath, and the feeling passed. It would do no good to follow her. If she wouldn't talk to him here, she wouldn't talk to him anywhere. He choked back a sob as the full reality of his loss hit him.

***

The next day, Todd was one of the first to notice that Francine was nowhere around. Since she was his prime interest at the moment, her conspicuous absence threatened to unleash his simmering temper. But he held his composure- he would find out what was going on in due time. She wouldn't get away from him this time, no matter what she thought.

With only two days of branding left, as long as the weather held, even though they were now short-handed, the work progressed uneventfully. The usual jokes were told, the food was inhaled on breaks, and one by one the calves were sorted, branded, castrated, and vaccinated.

On the last day of branding, Todd managed to engage Fred in conversation over coffee on the porch, and casually questioned what had happened to that "fairy cowboy" that was doing most of the riding at the start of the roundup.

"Oh, he's probably up at the line camp. Don't know where else he would go. Funny he would leave before the work was done, but something must have come up or he never would have left like that. Maybe he was sick. Maybe he was love sick!" Fred laughed uproariously at his puny joke.

Todd seethed inwardly. So she thought she could run away from him, did she? Thought maybe she could hide where he wouldn't find her. He would fix her, all right. He would show her what happened to women that crossed him. He really thought she had learned a long time ago that it didn't pay to rile him. Just showed you how wrong you can be. Well, she would find out that she couldn't run from old Todd. He felt a warmth beginning in his groin as he began to contemplate what he would do to her when he found her. Fred said maybe she was lovesick. He could fix that for her. And he would.

Fred had mentioned the line camp. "Is that a pretty good ride from here? If he was sick, would it be too far for him to get to, you know, in that condition?"

"Naw, just a few hour's ride up north a ways. Why, you wann'a go see if you can help him out?" And Fred laughed again. "Maybe it had something to do with that fight last night."

"What fight?"

"Well, it wasn't a fist fight or anything like that. Just, well, I guess somebody sliced the off billet on Franc's saddle, and Jesse found out about it. He was looking at me- had me shoved up against the wall, choking me, and I managed somehow to get the question out, did he want to go back to jail for another murder just as Franc came out of the bedroom. He heard the whole thing. Jesse let me go right away and took off after Franc. I always did kind of wonder if those two were having a little "thing," you know what I mean? Anyway, guess old Franc didn't take too kindly to hearing that his bunkmate was a convicted murderer. I've been steering clear of that Indian for a long time now anyway, but after I heard about his record, I've been extra careful around him. Don't want to be next on his list, you know? He's pretty big, and he's mean, too. He's somebody you want to stay away from, believe me."

"Well, well. I sure never thought about the two of them together. That Indian just didn't look the type."

"See, you just never can tell about them, can you! Maybe he likes it both ways. After all, he was married. Maybe that's why he offed his wife- maybe she found out about his liking for men!"

"Yeah, maybe. Talk to you later, Fred." And Todd ambled off. Sleeping with that Indian, was she? The thought of him touching his wife sent his brain into overload. "Your days are really numbered now, Francine. You're gonn'a be sorry, girl. Real sorry."

Todd had planned numerous other little "events" for Francine, but now his plans would have to change since she had left the headquarters. But that was okay. In the end, it didn't matter because the final result would be the same. It just meant he would have a little less preliminary fun. But he could manage. Yeah, he would make do.

That night, it started to rain. The crew had finished their work on the C/6 just in time. There would be no more branding anywhere for a few days, as the storm system was forecast to hang on for most of the rest of the week. Three to five days of rain.

The next morning, they loaded their horses and gear, and after setting up the next branding appointment and where to meet, each went their separate way. Waving good-by, Todd watched his friends leave, and then pulled out on his own mission. The line camp was north, within a few hours ride from the main headquarters. Shouldn't be too hard to find.

He drove carefully until he was well out of sight of the main ranch house and yards. Then he pulled off onto one of the ranch service roads and followed it for about a mile. Parking on the side of the road, he donned his slicker, unloaded his horse from the trailer, and headed off to find Francine. It might take him a while, but he would find her. He smiled to himself again as he began to plan what exactly he would do to her when he finally found that camp. He felt safe enough. His vehicle was parked well out of sight, and no one would be out in this rain for days, anyway. And when they did venture out, they would be checking cattle almost exclusively, looking for any sick calves after the stress of branding. Everyone had seen him leave, and no one suspected anything between Franc and himself. This was going to be fun!

Chapter 21

Francine lay on the bunk, listening to the rain patter steadily on the roof. She loved the sound of the rain. She felt secure, and safe here. She missed Jesse terribly, but she had Sammy for company, and that would have to be enough.

Thinking about Jesse was all she had been able to do for the past two days. She was finally starting to wonder if maybe she should have given him a chance to explain. He had sworn to her that he hadn't done it. He said he was innocent. Maybe she should trust him one last time.

"Oh, Francine, you are crazy, girl! Are you sure you even want to consider working with him again? A convicted murderer?" But then she remembered his kindness to her, and the way he had held her when she had needed it so badly. He had told her he loved her. Maybe he really did. In the end, it didn't matter, because no matter how hard she tried to banish him from her thoughts and her heart, he wouldn't go. She loved him too much.

She realized that she loved him no matter what he had supposedly done. If he had murdered his wife, so be it. He had paid the price with ten years of his life, and if he would eventually murder her as well, what difference did it make whether it was Jesse or Todd that did the job?

In the morning, she thought. I'll ride out in the morning, and hopefully set things right again. With a small smile on her beautiful mouth, she drifted off to sleep.

***

At first, she couldn't place where she was. Or what had awakened her. A loud noise... And then she saw him, and her eyes first went wide with fear, then clouded over to stare vacantly straight ahead. Todd stood leaning against the closed and bolted door, a smirk on his face.

"Did you think I wouldn't find you, Francine? Did you really think you could get away with it? I thought you knew me better than that, girl; well, now you do." He sauntered over to one of the chairs and sat on it with a loud sigh.

"I think I need some coffee to warm me up, Francine. These Montana spring rains are sure cold!"

As if in a daze, Francine struggled to her feet, and headed for the coffee pot. She filled it with fresh cold water, added the grounds, and set it on the stove to perk, then went back to the bunk, sitting on the edge, her eyes never leaving Todd's face.

Todd sat casually, smiling at her the whole time. Oh, this was going to be fun, all right. Lots of fun. Again, the warmth seeped into his groin in anticipation.

When the coffee was perked, Francine poured him a cup and placed it carefully in front of him on the table.

Todd sipped carefully. It tasted so good after his long ride in the rain! But of course, he couldn't let her know that.

"It's too weak, Francine. Make a fresh pot. You know how I like my coffee. Why didn't you make it right? You never did do anything right the first time. I always had to teach you, didn't I! Come here."

It was said softly, but the hardness underneath wasn't lost on Francine. She came to get the mug, intending to toss the coffee and make a new pot for him. As she reached out to grab the handle, Todd backhanded her across the side of her head. She spun to the floor, dazed for a moment, then attempted to stand again. This was all part of the ritual, and she had been through it many times before.

"Never mind. I think I'll just drink it the way it is. Can't take the time to make more right now, can we? We have too many things to do, don't we Francine?"

She stood before him, eyes downcast, waiting for whatever was to come next from his crazed brain. She just hoped it would be quick.

"Take your shirt off."

At this, her head came up, and her eyes met his. "What?"

"Didn't you hear me the first time, my dear little wife? I said, take your shirt off."

"Todd . . ."

His fist to her stomach broke off her utterance. She doubled over, and sank to her knees. Slowly, her hands came up, trembling, and began to unbutton her shirt. She felt degraded, and shamed. But she complied. What choice did she have? But it looked like he wasn't going to kill her quickly. She had hoped for too much this time.

"Hurry it up, Francine! I see you aren't any better to look at now than you were years ago. Still don't have anything a real man would want, do you? Probably satisfied that Indian, though. Indians aren't too choosy, I hear. But, if that's all you've got, I guess it will have to do for now. I don't see anything better around! Come closer my dear."

"Todd, please, don't."

"I said, come closer, Francine."

She obeyed, despair and resignation written all over her face. Tears seeped from the corners of her eyes, unheeded.

Todd hadn't had a woman in more than two weeks. Branding had taken up too much time lately. Now he had to settle for this pitiful excuse for a female, but then, he could do things to this woman he couldn't dream of doing to any other. Good! He could still make her cry! This was fun!

Todd wiped his mouth with the back of his hand, and saw the trace of blood he had left when he hit her. This was really good- he was leaving his mark already.

"Get over on the bed."

She sank to her knees. She honestly didn't think she could manage to walk to the bunk, no matter what he threatened her with. And she wasn't sure that it mattered anymore, anyway.

Todd, losing his patience, grabbed her by her hair and dragged her the short distance to the bunk, then threw her bodily upon it. He rolled her onto her back and began. But the blood had crazed him, and he wanted more.

Francine screamed with pain, and then suddenly fainted.

When he was finished, he discarded her like a rag doll. Blood began to seep from her, and he smiled in unforeseen pleasure. He hadn't known it could be this good, or he would have done it years ago. He pushed Francine to the floor and gave her no more thought for the moment. It was getting dark now. He would take a short nap, recover himself, then have a little more fun with her before he finished her off for good.

Chapter 22

Francine woke to a reality that was a nightmare. She hurt all over, she was cold, and her nemesis lay sleeping soundly on her bunk. She slowly flexed all her limbs, and found nothing broken. Dully, her brain began to dwell on survival, and she wondered if she could crawl to the door and escape without waking Todd. It was worth a chance. She gingerly got to her feet, then headed for the door, softly, weaving from the pain throughout her body.

"Ready for the next go 'round already, are you, Francine?"

Francine froze in place. He was awake. She should have known. Slowly, she turned around to face him. Suddenly, she remembered Sammy, and wondered what Todd had done with him. She couldn't help herself; she had to know.

"What did you do with my dog?"

"Worried about your dog, are you? Well, I couldn't shoot him, because the noise would have alerted you. And I wanted you to be surprised, Francine. Actually, he must have been off somewhere, maybe hunting gophers or something. Lucky for him. I would have clubbed him to death if he had gotten in my way. But he wasn't here."

"Thank God," she thought to herself. Sammy did that sometimes, went off by himself to hunt. At least she didn't have to worry about her faithful dog. She could let it all happen, now. She had nothing else to worry about.

As he stared at her in her nakedness, dried blood streaking her thighs, he felt himself stirring again. It was time for a little more "activity".

"Come back over here, Francine. It's time for a little more fun!" And he laughed.

***

Francine lost track of time, and everything became a blur. Her eyes no longer focused, and pain blinded her to her surroundings. She knew she was bleeding again, but ceased to care. She became totally unresponsive and catatonic.

Todd used her over and over until he was totally spent. He was hungry after his exertions, and told Francine to get up and fix him some supper, becoming enraged when she didn't respond. Her eyes remained open, but she was simply unable to move. She couldn't help it. She could hear him telling her to get up, but it was as if he was speaking to someone else, not to her.

His anger at her insubordination knew no bounds now, and he began using his fists on her. Her abdomen, her face, her chest, anywhere he could aim a blow, he did. And when he finally sat back to draw a deep breath from his exertions, he seemed content at the damage he had done to her. He left her to fix himself something to eat while Francine curled her body into the fetal position.

When it was time for bed, Todd rolled her onto the floor again, and crawled under the covers on the bunk for a much-needed rest. Tomorrow, he would have some more fun.

In the morning when he was rested, he used Francine again and again, leaving her on the floor rather than going to the effort of moving her to the bunk. And after each time, he beat her.

Floating in and out of consciousness, she was barely aware of what was happening, but knew that the end must surely come soon now. The human body could only take so much, after all. Her only regret was the fact that she was unable to tell Jesse that she had forgiven him for not telling her about his murder charge and prison sentence. She wished she had given him the chance to explain the whole thing. Maybe he really was innocent, after all, although she didn't care if he was or not. She loved him, for better or for worse. And whatever had happened in the past, it was in the past. He had been nothing but good to her for as long as she had known him, and that was all that mattered. But he would never know now. Ah, well, there was nothing she could do about it. But in her heart, she murmured, *"I love you, Jesse. Thank you for all you have given me. I'm sorry. Forgive me, please."*

***

For two days, Todd used Francine in any fashion he could imagine, and after each time, he beat her. When he could no longer perform, it was time to quit and end it all. In his perverted mind, it was all her fault that he could no longer get an erection, and he beat her for that. He beat her because she didn't respond to him. He beat her because her limbs were cold, and he didn't like touching cold things. He beat her because she didn't get up and fix him his meals, so he had to cook for himself. He beat her because she had sent him to prison. He beat her because she was there, alive. At one point he became so enraged he took his belt off and used the buckle end on her. His anger simply knew no limits anymore, and since he knew he was going to get away with the whole thing, he took his time, used his imagination, and did his worst.

***

It was time for him to leave. The rain would be stopping soon, after three days, and he didn't want to leave any tracks. Without tracks, when she was finally found, it would be assumed a drifter had attacked her. There was nothing linking him to the crime scene. And he would be sure she wouldn't be able to talk. He would kill her, just as he had promised he would. She was nearly dead now, anyway.

He glanced over at her where she lay on the floor. Blood covered most of her body, and she lay with her eyes closed, her breathing labored. The sight of her disgusted him. No, it wouldn't take much to finish her off

He cleaned himself up, dressed, and prepared to leave. It was time.

Walking over to her, he kicked her viciously in the ribs- he thought he heard something crack, and smiled. It was just too bad she had played out so soon. There were a few more things he might have enjoyed doing to her, but she would have needed to participate. Oh well. He had fun while it lasted.

Straddling Francine, he set to her in earnest. This time, he meant to kill her, and his fists carried all the power he could muster. He beat her, and beat her, and beat her- and when he saw that she was still breathing, he beat her some more.

Francine had lost consciousness, permanently, some time ago. She was totally limp, each blow driving her deeper, if it was possible, into oblivion.

Finally, Todd was tired. He felt for a pulse, and found none. He watched her chest for the rise and fall that would betray the fact that she was breathing, but there was no movement. Finally, she was dead. Good. He landed one last blow to her face, now unrecognizable, for good measure, then began carefully wiping the cabin down for possible fingerprints. When he was satisfied, he strode to the door and opened it to the steady drizzle, raised his face to the sky, then slammed the door hard behind him and went to saddle his horse. It had been his finest work, he knew, but it was time to leave now. There would be more calves to brand in a few days.

For some unknown reason, the slamming of the door permeated Francine's brain. Maybe the loudness came as a shock to her system, or maybe it was the vibration from the slamming of the door, but suddenly, her body shuddered slightly, and she drew a faint breath. Francine was alive. She was unconscious, but she was alive.

Chapter 23

They had finished the branding before the rain set in. The branding crew had been gone for several days now, and Jesse was kept busy riding in the drizzle and the mud, checking for sick calves, doctoring those that needed it. But always, in the back of his mind, was Francine.

She had been gone for four days now. He couldn't believe she was never coming back, and finally began to worry about her. Maybe something had happened to her out there in the hills. Even the gentlest horse could take a fall, or spook at a bear. Any number of things could happen to her, and whether she ever wanted to see him again or not, he was becoming convinced that he needed to find her, just to be sure she was all right. And maybe when he did, just maybe, she would let him explain, and forgive him. All he knew was that these last four days were the most miserable days of his life. Without Francine, there seemed no reason to get up in the morning. He would talk to Glen. Maybe, if nothing else, he could take some supplies up to her. That would be a good excuse.

***

He did talk to Glen that morning, and by midafternoon, he was on his way to the line camp, mounted on Roger and leading a packhorse laden with supplies. Whether she hated him or not, she would be needing food. If nothing else, Sammy would be running out of dog food. He knew Francine had taken nothing with her when she left. It was the least he could do.

When he reached the cabin, he noticed Julie grazing contentedly in the small pasture near the cabin. Sammy greeted him with a wagging tail, looking gaunt and hollow. Something was wrong; Sammy looked like he hadn't eaten in days. That wasn't like Francine- she would never let Sammy go hungry, no matter what her personal feelings were.

He went up the steps to the cabin, and knocked on the door.

"Francine, are you in there? It's me, Jesse. I know you probably don't want to talk to me, but I brought supplies. Francine?" He stood, frowning, but only silence greeted him. There was no sound from inside the cabin.

He tried one more time. "Francine! Open up!"

Again, silence was his only answer.

"I'm coming in. You'd better be decent!" And he opened the cabin door.

***

For a moment, he couldn't move. He saw what appeared to be a body on the floor, but it was covered with blood. There was even blood on the walls and the floor. It took a moment to comprehend what he was seeing, and even then, he wasn't sure that his eyes weren't deceiving him. Finally, it registered.

"Francine!" He sprinted the few steps to the body, then sank to his knees beside her. "Dear God, please let her be alive. Please." Oh God! What had happened here? It looked like someone had put her through a meat grinder!

Bending low over her face, he felt for breath and a pulse. His shaking fingers found a weak, thready pulse, and when he put his lips to hers, he was able to feel a slight breath as she exhaled.

"Thank you, God! She's alive!"

But he hadn't the faintest idea where to begin. He was afraid to move her, but somehow, he had to get her off the floor and onto the bed. Ever so carefully, he gathered her into his arms and placed her gently on the bunk. Grabbing a blanket, he covered her, trying to figure some way to warm her frigid body. She was so cold! A fire. That should come first. The cabin was cold and dark, even though it was spring.

In what seemed like hours, but was in reality only minutes, Jesse had a fire going in the cook stove, and could feel the warmth almost immediately. But it would take more than a wood fire to warm Francine up. Briefly, he considered heading back to the ranch and calling for help. But he didn't dare leave her for the hours it would take him to get to Glen. Besides, he couldn't leave her like this. No way.

Taking his boots off, then his clothes, he slipped under the blanket with her and gathered her close, trying to warm her with his own body heat. He could think of nothing else at the moment.

How often had he dreamed of holding her this way, close, intimate, their naked bodies entwined. But he had never imagined this. He knew that any movement would be causing searing pain for her, but he supposed she was beyond feeling anything at the moment, and warmth was more important than anything else right now. It was painfully obvious that she was holding onto life by a mere thread, and he was terrified. If his will alone could save her, she would live. He couldn't lose her, not now.

They lay together, entwined, for hours. Jesse never noticed, and Francine never woke up. But slowly, he could feel the warmth seeping back into her, and he thanked God repeatedly. As he held her, he talked to her. Whispered to her. Told her of his love for her, and his deep need for her. He kissed her face tenderly, just little feather kisses. He stroked her blood-matted hair. And all the time, the tears flowed from his eyes, and he was powerless to stop them.

As he felt her warmth returning, another thought came to his mind. It seemed to start deep within his gut somewhere, and it inched up and throughout his body until it consumed him. He would find whoever had done this to her. He would find that man or men and kill them with his bare hands. He had no fear of prison or retribution of any kind. But whoever had done this to his love would pay with their lives.

As Francine warmed up, her breathing became more regular, and her pulse stronger. Jesse hated to move from the bed, but he needed to tend to the fire, and get her cleaned up. She wasn't home free yet, not by a long shot, but at least now he had hope.

He carefully eased himself out from under the blanket, washed her blood from his body, then quickly dressed, fed the fire, and put some water on to heat. He would clean her up as best he could, then wait and hope she regained consciousness. If she didn't, he wasn't sure what he would do. She had to come around, she just had to. If she still hated him when she recovered, so be it, but he wanted her to be able to at least tell him who was responsible for this. He had to know!

The water finally heated, and Jesse set about trying to wash the blood from Francine's body. He couldn't believe it! Her body was covered from head to toe with caked, dried blood. He started at her face, tenderly sponging until the blood loosened and came away, soaking into the cloth. There was so much blood that it seemed he was constantly changing the water in the basin he had found. He had never seen so much blood on one person, with the person still alive. He glanced at the floor where he had found her, and the walls where the blood had splattered, and shook his head in disbelief. That she was still alive was nothing short of a miracle.

It seemed like hours before he had her body washed. With the blood gone, now the bruises and cuts were obvious. Her nose was broken. Several teeth were gone. Those beautiful teeth! That beautiful face! He wept again for her, for what she had suffered at the hands of some unknown assailant.

He tenderly felt her nose. It was terribly swollen and obviously broken, but maybe there was something he could do to try to lessen the deformity. Working deftly, he found the shattered bone near her left eye. Inserting his finger carefully into the left nostril, he worked the flesh until he found the crepitation, then attempted to remold the bone working from both inside and outside of her nose. When he was finished, he could only hope that he had been successful. It would take several days for the swelling to go down, and then he would be able to tell better whether or not he had been able to reset the fragmented bone.

Leaving her at last, he went outside long enough to bring the supplies in and take care of the horses. Poor Sammy only waited on the small porch, wagging his tail each time Jesse passed. When all the supplies were in, Jesse opened a can of dog food and smiled sadly as Sammy wolfed its contents in two fast gulps. He could get water from the creek. At least the dog would feel better now.

There were numerous cans of soup in the supplies he had brought, and he picked out the old favorite, chicken soup. His mom had told him once that chicken soup was the very best when you were sick, and he had nearly always believed his mom. He wasn't sure she would be able to swallow anything, but he also knew that if she didn't, her chances were not good. If he left her to get help, she would probably die while he was gone. If he stayed, she would die if he couldn't get any nourishment into her. All he could do was try.

When the soup was warmed, he carefully strained the broth into a mug. Then, cradling her head with his left arm, he attempted to pour some of the warm liquid into her mouth. With the first few tries, it simply ran down the corners of her once beautiful mouth. But finally, she swallowed. Little by little, he was able to get small sips into her, until he figured half the mug's contents had made it into her stomach. The other half had dribbled out the sides of her mouth. But he was content with half a mug's worth inside of her; it was something, a start. If he could keep her warm, and keep her swallowing broth, she just might make it.

Jesse finished the solid parts of the soup himself, made and drank two cups of coffee, then shed his clothes again and crawled back under the blanket with Francine. He would keep her warm. He didn't know what else he could do for now. At least he would be there for her if and when she woke up. Sighing deeply, he kissed her gently again on her forehead, and settled in for the night, his love cradled tenderly in his arms.

Chapter 24

It was morning. Jesse had been dozing off and on all night, afraid to move in case it might disturb Francine. The sun was just topping the hills to the east, the rain gone at last for several more days.

He looked closely again at Francine. He couldn't believe that anyone had been able to survive a beating like that. In all his days on this earth, he had never seen anyone beaten to this extent, and he had seen a lot in his day. But she was warm, and her breathing was regular, though still shallow. He felt for a pulse, and found it steady, and definitely stronger than last night when he had first found her. For the first time, he began to really have hope that she might live.

That day was spent much like the one before. Keeping Francine warm, cleansing the wounds that seeped with any movement, forcing sips of broth at regular intervals, slipping under the blanket with her to keep her warm. She remained unconscious through it all. Swallowing the broth was simply a reflex action caused by liquid on her throat.

Jesse kept up the routine for three days before Francine finally opened her eyes.

He was pouring hot soup into a mug, and when he turned around he found her staring at the ceiling. Just staring, out of the one eye that was able to open to a mere slit; the other remained swollen shut. When he moved toward her, she sensed there was someone else with her, and tried to turn her head toward the sound he made. It was too much for her, and her eye closed again. She let out a faint sigh.

Sitting the mug on the table, Jesse was at her side in an instant. "Francine? Can you hear me? It's me, Jesse. If you can hear me, just squeeze my hand, okay?"

Ever so softly, her index finger curled faintly around his hand. It was the most minimal of movements.

"Oh, thank God!" Jesse sobbed, and clasped her hand to his chest. He was crying, and tears, once started, had a will of their own, unstoppable. Careful not to crush her hand, Jesse sat on the bunk next to her, and rocked, gently holding her hand. She was going to live!

***

Francine was dazed, barely able to comprehend anything. She wasn't sure where she was, but she hurt everywhere. Someone was with her. Todd? Was he still here? Had he discovered that she wasn't dead after all? No, the voice had said it was Jesse. Jesse? Oh, yes, now she remembered. She worked with someone named Jesse, didn't she? She thought she was dead. But no, you couldn't feel or hear anything if you were dead, so she really must be alive. But it hurt so! Just to breathe hurt! She wished she were dead. At least then it wouldn't hurt anymore. And she slipped into a deep sleep.

The next morning, Jesse decided he could leave her long enough to go for help. He could ride back to headquarters, tell Glen to send a helicopter, and be back at the cabin with Francine within six hours or so. He was sure he could leave her that long. She needed to be in the hospital just as soon as he could get her there.

Francine was awake for longer periods at a time now, and was consciously swallowing the broth. Her face was unrecognizable, and he swore under his breath every time he looked closely at her. He was going to find whoever did this, just as soon as she was in the hospital, and he would kill them. It was just a fact, now.

He sat on the edge of the bunk, Francine watching him out of her one eye again. The other would probably open tomorrow. It was a miracle the madman hadn't blinded her in his rage.

"Hon, I have to leave you for a few hours. I…"

She cut him off with a groan. Painfully, she was able to articulate "No!"

"Francine, I have to. You need help. You've got to get to a hospital where they can take care of you properly. I'll only be gone for a few hours."

"No."

"Please, hon., I have to go."

"No. Don't want to go. Here. Got to stay here. With you." She was thinking much more clearly now, and there was no way she was going to a hospital. She knew she was going to live, and she realized it was going to take her a long time to heal. She would heal much quicker in a hospital, but as soon as she was admitted, the police would be involved, and it would probably be in the papers. Montana was a big state, but there weren't that many people in it, and it would be only a matter of time before Todd found out that he hadn't killed her after all. And in the end, she would just have to go through this all over again. She would surely die the next time.

Jesse was perplexed. Why didn't she want to go to a hospital? It didn't make any sense!

She coughed a little, wrapping her arms around herself, guarding and wincing with the pain. But her voice was clearer when she spoke again

"Jesse, trust me, will you? I can't go to the hospital. I won't go. Please don't make me!"

He knew he could force the issue. She was in no condition to object to anything, physically. He tried one more time.

"Francine, you need to go to the hospital. Let me get you there. I won't be gone long, I promise."

"No."

"Francine, I'm sorry, but I'm going now. I'll be back as soon as I can."

As he rose to leave, her voice followed him as if from a great distance.

"Do you love me, Jesse?"

How could she even question his love for her? Hadn't he made it plain enough?

"Francine, I told you I loved you, and I meant it. With every fiber of my being. I love you so much it hurts. I never knew a man could love this much and live. Answer your question?"

"If you love me even a little, you won't make me go." A tear slid down one cheek.

He groaned. He couldn't leave her like this. If this was what she wanted, he would abide by her wishes. He was pretty sure she was out of danger, but she would probably need cosmetic surgery, and that was best done as soon as possible. Maybe she didn't realize how much damage had been done to her face?

"Francine, I don't know how to tell you this, but your face... You are going to need cosmetic surgery to try to repair the damage. Without it, you may well be disfigured for life. You're so beautiful, Francine, please go. If you wait, it will be more difficult if not impossible to repair to any extent. Please..."

"No. I know what I'm doing. And if you love me, you won't make me go. If I go he'll find me."

Sighing deeply, he gave in. He worried for her, how she would feel when she looked in a mirror years from now, though it made no difference to him how she looked. He would love her no matter what she looked like. They would stay at the cabin until she was well enough to travel, at least. Then, it would be her decision, what she would do next. He only hoped that she would forgive him at last, and allow him to stay with her, whatever she decided to do.

"Francine, I'm going to have to go back and tell Glen something. I can't be gone any longer, or someone is going to come looking for me. If you won't go to the hospital, I'm still going to have to leave you long enough to check in at headquarters. I can make up some kind of excuse and get back this afternoon. You'll be all right until then, I'm sure. I'm make the trip as fast as I can.

"But no hospital, promise?"

"Promise. But I still don't like it."

"And you don't tell Glen or anyone else?"

"I won't tell a soul. I'll bring back some more supplies while I'm at it. If I have to, I'll just quit. Whatever it takes, okay?"

"Okay."

He rose to leave. If he hurried, he could still make it back before dark. He would have to come up with a pretty good story to explain his absence, and his reason for taking off again. He knew they could get along without him down below, at least for a while, but they would soon have to be moving cattle to the higher pastures as the grass came on. As he opened the door to leave, he heard her faintly calling to him.

"Jesse? Hurry back, will you?"

He smiled at her.

"I'll be back before dark. Rest easy while I'm gone. Sammy's right outside." And he left, quietly, careful not to slam the door.

He stewed all the way down about what he was going to tell Glen, and in the end, thought he had a pretty good story. He would tell him that Franc had taken a spill; his horse had tripped in a gopher hole. He was okay, but had severely sprained his knee and was unable to get around very well. When Jesse had first gotten to the cabin, Franc had been unable to walk at all, which was why Jesse had stayed. Didn't want to leave a man down like that, after all. Anyway, there was a lot of fence that needed fixing before they could turn the cattle into the higher pastures, so Jesse was going to take another pack horse up with supplies for a couple of weeks. They would both head down when Franc was better, and the fences were all fixed.

He recited his story and Glen had just looked at him kind of strangely, then nodded his head in agreement. Jesse breathed a sigh of relief, and set to gathering supplies.

In the end, he made his way back up with two pack horses laden with enough human and dog food for several weeks. He had surreptitiously gathered most of Francine's clothing and toiletries, and anything else he could find that he thought she might want during her convalescence. And he made it back before dark.

Glen was no fool. Something was up, and Jesse wasn't talking. But Glen also knew Jesse, and he knew that if it weren't important, Jesse wouldn't have asked to go up with Franc. He knew there was no "funny business" going on between the two- Jesse was totally straight. But something was not quite right. If Jesse or Franc needed or wanted his help, he would be there for them, and if they didn't, well, so be it. He would see them when they came back down. Whenever that would be!

Chapter 25

They managed to set up a routine, of sorts, and the days passed. When she was finally able to sit up, Jesse would wrap her in blankets to keep her warm. He still slept with her at night, naked, for warmth, but Francine had never pulled away from him, or expressed any emotion at all, for that matter. He never touched her inappropriately, or gave her any cause for alarm. It was as if she were dead inside. She made no response to him at all. She just didn't care.

He had finally managed to get all the blood washed out of her beautiful hair. There were cuts, some gaping though scabbed over, covering most of her scalp. Head wounds always bled copiously anyway, and at last he was satisfied with his results. Her hair wasn't shiny anymore, but at least it was clean, and swung freely now.

He thought about getting her dressed in some of the clean clothing he had brought, but she was too sore to be getting dressed. It was all she could do just to sit up on the side of the bed. If she had owned a nightgown, she could probably have worn that, but posing as a man for so many years, she had no feminine clothing at all.

Jesse kept up a rambling monologue in the small cabin when Francine was awake. If she needed anything, she would ask, but otherwise she was silent. It was still too much work to talk, and she needed her strength to heal.

Jesse wondered if she still hated him for not telling her about his murder conviction and prison sentence. They would have to talk about that one of these days. He supposed that for now, even *he* was better than anyone else to have around, if she wanted to keep her injuries a secret. But he longed so much to be not just tolerated but loved in return, the way he loved her. If only! But she was allowing him to take care of her, and for now, that was enough.

***

For her part, just staying alive and healing was taking top priority in her life right now. She felt empty. She knew she was imposing on Jesse, but he had said that he loved her. He kept calling her "hon", and she didn't stop him. Somehow, it felt kind of good, like when he wrapped her up in the blanket. Secure, sort of.

She knew he had only told her he loved her because he felt sorry for her. No decent man could possibly love her, especially now, after what had happened. No man wanted another man's leavings, let alone one that now looked like she did- a freak. She hadn't looked in a mirror; she didn't need to. She could imagine what she looked like. If she had been homely before, she would be downright frightening to look at now, on top of being useless. Jesse was just being kind to her, that's all. But she was grateful to him for that. She didn't want to be alone right now. There was a constant fear, at the back of her mind, that Todd would come for her again if Jesse weren't there. That he must know, somehow, that she was still alive. If he found her once, he would find her again.

She realized that they were sleeping together, naked. Jesse usually didn't climb into the bunk with her until after he thought she was asleep. She would lie so quietly on the bunk, her breathing so shallow, that he couldn't tell the difference. But she didn't flinch when she felt his nakedness against her own, and after several nights, she began to look forward to the time when he would come to bed. His warmth was welcome.

And often, during the night, she would come awake with a start. Her eyes would fly open while she remained totally motionless. She would hear Todd coming for her; she could almost feel the vibration of the floor as he walked to her bunk. Then she would feel the warmth of Jesse's body next to hers, and she would realize that it was just a dream. Todd wasn't here–

Jesse was. And he wouldn't let anything hurt her; she was safe with Jesse.

Francine had a lot of time to think. Sure, she slept a large portion of each day, but there were more and more hours of wakefulness, too. She remembered finding out about Jesse being a murderer, about her fear and disgust of him. But somehow, it didn't seem to matter anymore. After what Todd had done to her, nothing Jesse could do meant anything. Had he really killed his wife? If that was true he had paid for the crime with ten years of his life. Right now she really didn't care one way or the other. With the care and gentleness he was bestowing on her daily, hourly, it didn't seem possible that he could have done such a thing. She was convinced now that he would never do anything remotely harmful to her, at any rate. But she wanted to know. She just wanted to know. And so, one afternoon, she surprised him by initiating conversation.

***

They were sitting out on the porch. Jesse would carry her out there to sit in the sunshine in the afternoons now, when the sun was at its warmest. Sitting quietly together, Sammy curled up beside her feet, they would sip strong coffee while watching spring come to life in the high country.

"Jesse?"

The sudden unexpected sound startled him.

"What?"

"Did you kill your wife like Fred said you did?"

"No, Francine, I didn't. I swear to you I never laid a hand on her. There were times, I'll admit, when I…"

"I don't want to know any more, Jesse. I just wanted you to tell me the truth. Is it the truth? Can I believe you?"

"I have never openly lied to you, Francine. I didn't kill her. I did time for it, but I didn't do it. Do you want to know the whole story?"

"No." She paused for a few moments, considering. "If you say you didn't kill her, then I will believe you. But I really don't want to know any more about it. It doesn't matter to me."

Was he so unimportant in her life that the truth of what had happened didn't even matter to her? The pain in his heart was sharp, and brutally piercing. Somehow, he felt he had to reach her, to make her understand what she meant to him.

Wasn't it possible for her to see past his face to the person within, to the man that loved her to distraction? He had already told her that he loved her, and had been committing that little sin of using words of endearment with her. She had made no comment, one way or the other about it. It was as if there was a high, thick wall around her. He wanted to break through it, somehow. He had to. He knew that he was never going to let her go again. No way on God's green earth. He had almost lost her once, and somehow, he had to find a way to keep her in his life. Right now, the only way he could think to do that was to somehow convince her that he really, truly loved her. Maybe, even if she couldn't love him back, she would accept his love and the protection it offered from the world. He didn't care. He would take whatever he could get, if it meant keeping her in his life.

There was time, though. He didn't have to explain everything today. She wasn't going anywhere for a couple of weeks yet, he was pretty sure. In the meantime, he would just continue to try to show her, in every way he could think of, that she was his love, and always would be, no matter how she looked, no matter what she said to him. There was nothing she could do to shake what he felt for her.

Chapter 26

The swelling was gone now, for the most part. Her body remained mottled with purple and pale yellow from the massive bruising, but it seemed that only one or two ribs had been cracked in the attack, and other than her broken nose, that was the extent of the skeletal injuries. For days, her urine had been rust-colored, indicating kidney damage, and Jesse had worried constantly. But now, she was able to take herself to the outhouse, with Jesse's help, and she told him that at least that part of her injuries had also healed. She wouldn't need surgery to repair her kidneys.

Her nose remained swollen, but it didn't appear to be disfigured. Jesse began to be hopeful that his emergency realignment nose job had been successful. The teeth she had lost were molars, and the loss wasn't evident upon casual observation. She would have scars on her face, as she would over the rest of her body, but neither of them seemed to care.

Speaking was still an effort for her, as was any activity, so she rarely did. What was there for her to say, anyway? She had no future, no hope, and nothing to look forward to. She was sure that Jesse would be leaving her as soon as he was sure that she was self- sufficient. She wished she didn't love Jesse. If she didn't, her future wouldn't look quite so bleak to her. But life without Jesse, now that she had been allowed to be near him for so long, was unthinkable.

***

They were out on the porch again, enjoying the sun, sipping coffee, each of them quietly enjoying the company of the other. No words needed to be said. The robins were back, and the gold finches and chick-a-dees carried on their lively, exclusive conversations. Even Sammy seemed to be entertained by them.

Jesse sighed deeply. He hated to even bring the subject up, but the time had come- he had to know who had done this to her.

"Francine, I have to ask you a question, and I hope you can answer me. okay?" The question was raised softly on the light spring breeze.

Without looking at him, she replied. "What do you want to know, Jesse?"

"Can you tell me who did this to you? Did you know him? Or them? How many of them were there?"

She thought about lying to him, but decided it would serve no real purpose. She hadn't lied to him before, and she wasn't about to start now.

"Todd. Todd did it. Just like he said he would. That's why I wouldn't let you take me to the hospital. Word was bound to get out about me, and when it did, he would know he hadn't finished what he set out to do, and he would eventually come for me again. At the moment he thinks I'm dead, and that's the way I want it to stay. As long as he believes he killed me, I'm safe. Although right now, I'm not too sure that I care too much one way or the other, to tell you the truth." She smiled, a slight, sad, little smile. "At least I'm getting a paid vacation- how's that for a little humor?"

"How did he find you? How…?"

"He was one of the branding crew. TJ. Remember?"

Jesse swore softly under his breath. TJ. He felt so stupid! The man was right under his nose, and he hadn't put two and two together. Now upon reflection, he did remember seeing him at Deer Lodge. That was why the he had seemed familiar that first day on the ranch.

"Well, Francine, I want you to know that he is now a dead man. I promise you he will never bother you again. I'll see to it."

"No, Jess! I don't want you to do anything, you hear me? Leave it alone! It isn't your fight, and as long as he doesn't know I'm alive, it doesn't matter anyway. Forget about him, okay?"

"Forget about him? Are you out of your mind? I know he beat you pretty bad, but I didn't think it had affected your brain that much! Oh, no, Francine, he's a dead man; he just doesn't know it yet."

"Jess, you can't! You listen to me, now! If what you told me is true, you already spent enough time in prison for something you didn't do. If you go after Todd, it will only be a matter of time before the authorities figure out it was you, and this time it will be prison for something you *did* do! I know you, Jesse, and being locked up like that had to have just about killed you. You aren't going back there because of me. No way. Let it be."

"Tell me something, Francie. If it were the other way around, if you were me, would you let it drop? Would you walk away and figure that what's done is done, and not make that man pay for what he did? Could you do that?"

Could she? Impossible! If he had nearly killed Jesse, she would have shot him herself, she knew. "No, I guess I wouldn't. But Jesse, you'll go back to prison, I know you will. There's no way you can get away with it. In the end, they will find me, and it will be so easy for them to figure out you did it, why, it won't take them any time at all. He isn't worth it, Jess, he just isn't worth it. I can't let you go after him. Forget about him, please. Just stay here with me and forget he even exists."

Jesse stared at her, willing her to look back at him, which she finally did. Their gazes locked for what seemed like an eternity, and each knew the other's mind. She knew he would soon leave her, and the thought terrified her. She also knew she wouldn't be able to stop him, no matter what she did or said. She had lost him, no matter how it turned out, and she would soon be alone again. She had no idea how she would survive without him.

***

That night, Jesse decided that she was well enough she didn't need him for warmth anymore. Rather than make an issue of it, he just went ahead and made up a bed for himself on the floor after he was sure she was asleep.

Francine waited for him to come to her as he had been doing, but finally drifted off to sleep, unable to stay awake any longer. She missed him, but felt secure in the knowledge that he would come to her later, as he had been doing.

Sometime during the night, she awoke in a drenching sweat. She was cold, she was alone, and she was terrified. Her shriek pierced the blackness of the cabin and echoed through the night outside.

Jesse was at her side in an instant, also terrified.

"It's okay, Francie, I'm here. It's okay." He reached out to stroke her damp forehead; she was ice cold, and shaking all over.

"Jess, where were you? I couldn't find you! I was so scared... You weren't here!" She bolted upright in bed and grabbed him, hugging him to herself desperately.

"I'm right here, Francie. I'm right here. I'm not going anywhere tonight. Now go back to sleep. Everything's okay, I promise."

"Jesse, come to bed with me, please?"

"Sure." He laid himself down on top of the blanket next to her, one arm tenderly across her waist. How he loved her! How he yearned to lie naked again beside her, under the blanket. But he was sure she wouldn't want him that close to her, in that way.

"Jess- please- like you have been. I want you here, with me, like before. Please?"

He had been careful to only come to her after he was sure she was asleep, and had risen before she awakened every morning. He had been so sure she didn't know he had been sleeping with her. But she was asking him to come to her again, as he had been doing every night since he had found her.

"Are you sure, Francie?"

"I'm sure. I won't sleep without you, Jess. Please."

Quickly, he shed his jeans and underwear, and slid under the blanket next to her. His whole body was trembling slightly at the nearness of her naked flesh, and the fact that she had asked him to join her. He knew there was nothing sexual about it, and probably never would be on her part. But just to lie next to her- at her request! His throat nearly closed off with the emotion he felt.

Francine turned then, to fit spoon-like against him, her back to his stomach. She reached for his arm and drew it across herself, around her waist.

"This time, don't leave me in the morning, okay? You can stay until I wake up. That is, if you don't mind?"

"Mind? Woman, haven't you figured out yet that I love you?"

"I'm not worth much, Jesse. Maybe a little before this, but now…"

Jesse groaned and pulled her even closer, if that was possible. He breathed in the scent of her, that fragrance that had so early on beguiled him. Taking the chance, he buried his face in her hair, then softly kissed her neck, then her shoulder. He couldn't help it- his body's response was instantaneous, and he felt like dirt. But he couldn't let her go, either.

"Jess…!"

"Don't worry, Francie, nothing's going to happen. I can't help my reaction to you, but I promise you, on my life, nothing more is going to happen. I love you so much! I would never do anything to hurt you, you know that. You can trust me, Love. I promise." He stroked her hair gently, waiting for her to settle down again. He meant what he said to her- he couldn't help how his body reacted to her, but he would never act on it. He would never hurt her in any way, if he could help it.

Francine finally became accustomed to the hardness at her back, and when he made no move to act on it, relaxed and drifted off to a peaceful sleep, but Jesse was awake long into the night. He wanted to prolong his joy as long as he could, and sleep would only shorten it for him. Finally, though, he couldn't help himself, and he slept.

Several times, barely wakening, he softly kissed her back or her shoulder, his arm never leaving her waist. And in his dreams, Todd was dying over and over again, at Jesse's hand. A smile lingered on Jesse's face as he slept on.

The next two days and nights were spent much the same way. He continued to sleep with Francine at night, naked, as close to her as he could get. His erections were actually painful, but he couldn't control them, and he certainly couldn't act on them, so he tried his very best to ignore them. Francine became used to the fact that whenever he was close to her, this was his reaction. But he never frightened her in any way, and in the end, it just seemed natural.

***

It was strange, in a way, Francine thought. She should be terrified of being so close to Jesse, yet it was as though what Todd had done to her, he had actually done to someone else. She had learned while she was married to him to compartmentalize, in a way, her life. She would shut down emotionally, and even though he was able to hurt her physically, she was able to function because she could black out the beatings in her mind. Oh, she would hurt, sometimes for days after one of his rages, but he never touched her soul. And this time, also- it was as if the beating had happened to someone else. Not to her.

***

One night, Jesse seemed to be holding her especially close. He couldn't get enough of her, the feel of her, the smell of her. She was almost ready to complain that she couldn't breathe, when suddenly it hit her.

"You're leaving tomorrow, aren't you." It was a statement, not a question.

"Yes."

Her blood ran cold, and she stopped breathing. She knew there was nothing she could say or do to prevent his leaving her. He was going to hunt Todd down and kill him, no matter what she said. Then they would find him, and lock him up. He might not get the death penalty, given the circumstances, but he would never be free again. He would never be hers. They would never have a future of any kind. Her hopes were eliminated at that moment.

"I'll admit it, Francine. There's nothing in this world I want more than to make love to you, here, now, tonight. I love you so much, it defies description. I want to make you mine. I want to leave here tomorrow knowing that you belong to me, in every sense of the word. I want to mark you somehow, as my own, for all eternity. I want to leave you with all the memories of the bad times you have known, all memories of Todd, to be gone forever from your mind. I want to leave you with no room in your mind for any thoughts other than ones of me. But I know that I can't do that, not right now. It's too soon. And I know that you might never be able to let me love you like a man wants to make love to his woman. That's just one more reason why I'm going to kill him. Hurting you is hurting me, and he's taken something from both of us. We don't have a future as long as he's alive, always wondering if he has found out that he didn't kill you after all. And if I do find him and kill him, I know where I will end up. Either way, I lose. Well, frankly, I'd rather go to my grave knowing that he isn't ever going to hurt you or any other woman ever again. It's just the way it has to be. Can you understand?"

And she did understand, because she realized that if the situation were reversed, she would feel the same way. She wept softly for what might have been, and turning over, buried her face against his chest, pulling him to her with her eager arms. It was nearly his undoing.

The stroking began almost unconsciously. He really wasn't even aware that his hands were roving over her softly, caressing as they moved. Francine felt the love in them, and made no move to stop him when she found her own hands mimicking his. It felt so good! So good to be held and loved! She was afraid, but she was more afraid of losing him forever, of never having this time together. She knew it would hurt her, but she was prepared to let this man do anything he wanted with her, just this once. She needed him as much as he needed her.

His mouth found hers in the darkness, and she made no effort to draw away from him. He kissed her softly at first, not wanting to hurt or frighten her. But when she responded so willingly, he moaned, and the pressure of his lips increased even as his tongue began moving of its own accord. He couldn't help himself; he was lost. He was touching her as he had longed to do, in places he had only dreamed of. His mouth found and tasted parts of her body he had thought never to have access to. And Francine was kissing and tasting him in return, moving against him rhythmically, instinctively. She wanted him, as she had never wanted another man in her life, and the realization surprised her. After what she had gone through, she had been sure that she could never respond to any man, ever again.

Suddenly Jesse let out a moan, and attempted to draw away from her. Francine pulled him back to her.

"No!"

Then it was too late for him, and he spilled himself against her, mortified.

Feeling the moist heat, she realized what had happened, and gathered him as close to herself as she could, kissing his head tenderly, loving him.

"I'm sorry, Francine. I'm sorry. I didn't mean for that to happen."

"It's okay, Jesse. I wanted you to make love to me. I wanted you. I just wish you...."

"No! Francine, I can't do that with you- I would hurt you too badly. You must know how much I want to, but I can't. I'm just sorry that what just happened, well, happened- you know what I mean. I'm embarrassed, and I'm sorry."

"Don't be embarrassed, Jesse, it was only natural. I wanted you too, you know. I love you Jesse. I have loved you for a very long time."

His heart skipped a beat as her words sank in. She had told him that she loved him. Pulling away from her, he searched her face in the darkness.

"Francine, are you telling me the truth? Do you love me? Or are you just trying to be nice to me, to maybe thank me for taking care of you?"

"Oh, Jess! Do you honestly think I could have allowed what just went on between us if I didn't really, deeply, love you?"

"But what about…."

"Jess, nothing that has gone on before matters to me. Nothing. I don't care about your wife, or what you did or didn't do to her. I don't care about your prison time. I don't care about anything but you. Can you understand that?"

"What about my face, Francie? Doesn't that repulse you? My nose, my scars?"

She laughed softly. Men could be so very dense sometimes! As if his looks made any difference to her at all, other than to make him more attractive to her!

"Jess, I love you. Just accept that, okay? Don't question it, don't – oh- just- I love you. That's all you need to know. Good enough?"

"Woman, you have no idea…!"

"Oh yes I do. I most certainly do. Now if you don't mind, would you please hold me again, at least for a little while?"

And he did.

Chapter 27

Too soon, it was dawn. Francine knew that nothing she could say would change Jesse's mind; he was leaving. This morning. Terrified that she might never see him again, it was all she could do not to cling to him, to beg. But she knew it would not alter his proposed course, and would serve no purpose but to upset them both, so she refrained.

She watched him from the bunk as he began gathering his things. Tears glistened unshed in her eyes. Finally, when it looked as though he was through with his rough packing, she rose, and dressed for the first time since her ordeal with Todd. She remained stiff and sore, but was able to get around fairly well now.

"I'm ready."

"Yes. I'll walk you to your horse."

"There's no need..."

"I'll walk you to your horse." She rose and led the way out of the cabin.

He saddled his gelding, and turned to her.

"Francine, I'll be back. I promise."

"Don't be making promises you can't keep, Jesse."

"This one I'll keep. I'll be back."

"Jess..."

"I don't know for sure what I'm going to tell Glen yet, but I'll come up with something before I head out. I'll fix it so that no one will be up here bothering you while I'm gone, so you don't have to worry about that. I don't know how long I'll be away, but I'll be back when I've finished what I have to do. I probably won't be able to stay with you, Francine, but I *will* come back, at least for a while. I can't live without you, you know. Not anymore."

"I'll be here, Jess. Whenever you make it back, I'll be waiting. I love you. It feels like I've known you and loved you forever. Please be careful."

As he turned to mount, he heard the sob catch in her throat. He had thought that maybe it might be easier for both of them if he didn't touch her, but at the sound, his resolve was lost. Dropping the reins, he turned and gathered her in his arms. Holding her tightly, he began kissing her softly anywhere his mouth could touch her. He stood there, inhaling the scent of her, storing it into his memory, that fragrance that was hers alone, that had initially started them on this journey together. He loved this woman so much! It was really beyond comprehension. He knew that he would return to her; nothing short of death could keep him from her.

Francine clung to him frantically, terrified of the impending loss and emptiness his departure would ensure. What Todd had done- it was if he had done it to someone else. That was in another lifetime, in the past. All that mattered now was Jesse, and the life she desperately wanted to have together with him. And it was possible, if only Jesse would forget about Todd and let the whole thing go. But she knew that she might as well wish for the Missouri to stop flowing, because stopping Jesse would require the same kind of force.

Francine tried with all that she had not to cry, knowing her tears made it more difficult for him to leave her, but it was no use, and they coursed down her cheeks. She pulled her head away from him, and gazing into his eyes, lifted her face to his.

Even after what had transpired between them last night, Jesse was afraid to push, to kiss her as he longed to do. But Francine did it for him. As her lips tentatively touched his, he groaned and took what she was offering as a parting gift. He kissed her soundly, then his lips left hers to plant feathery kisses all over her upturned face before homing in to her mouth once more. This kiss was going to have to last him for a long time.

At last, as if by mutual consent, they pulled apart. Holding her by her upper arms, Jesse stared hard into her beautiful eyes.

"I love you, Francine. With everything that I have, with all that I am. And I will be back. Wait for me?"

She nodded, kissed him one last time, then turned and walked back to the cabin.

Jesse watched her until she reached the porch steps, then swung into the saddle and kicking Roger into a fast lope, left his love, his jaw firmly set, his mind already beginning to plan the death of Todd Larson.

***

By the time he reached the ranch headquarters, he had made up his mind what he was going to tell Glen- he was going to tell him the truth. If he couldn't trust Glen, he couldn't trust anyone, and there was no way he was going to lie to his best friend.

***

Jesse had been in the foreman's home for over an hour, explaining all that had gone on. Glen listened with a look of pure awe on his face- he couldn't believe what he had just heard. Franc was really Francine? He was a she? Todd had beaten her nearly to death?

"Damn!" Glen was essentially speechless.

"Yeah, I know, pretty hard to believe, huh? But it's all true, I swear. I'm just sorry you have to find out this way, but then, I guess there really isn't any good way to tell this story. But Glen, I love that woman like I've never loved anyone in my life before. I can't let Todd get away with it, and I can't live without her. It's a real mess, and I'm sorry, but I have to leave."

"You're going after Todd, aren't you, Jess." It was a statement, not a question. He knew Jesse too well. Besides, Glen would have done the same thing if he was in Jesse's shoes, and there would have been no stopping him, either.

"You do know where it will probably get you in the end, don't you? Are you sure it's worth going back to prison for?"

"I have to do this, Glen, you know that. If you could have seen her, when I found her…" Jesse choked up, and had to look away for a moment. "Glen, she was more dead than alive. I've never seen anyone beaten that badly and live. What kind of man can do that to a woman?"

"I don't understand it any more than you do, Jesse. I don't know what I'd call him, but he sure isn't a man!"

"Well, I can promise you one thing, Glen, he isn't ever going to beat another woman like that. Ever."

Glen studied his friend thoughtfully. "No," he said softly, "I don't suppose he will."

"I'll be back when I'm finished with what I have to do, if that's okay with you. Then, I don't know what will happen. I'd like to stay here with Francine until they find me, if you don't mind. I could just stay up at the cabin with her. I wouldn't expect you to be paying me, or anything, but I'll do what I can up there to help her out for as long as I can. If it's a problem for you, I won't let you know when I'm back. I can just head up there, and that way, if anyone comes asking about me, you can honestly tell them you haven't any idea where I am. How does that sound to you?"

"That's fine with me, Jesse. After today, I haven't seen you, and I don't know a thing. Nothing. And I will personally take supplies up to Franc- or Francine- every couple of weeks, so she won't have to come down for the summer. We can get the cattle moved up, and she can just take over from there like she does every summer. You're sure she's going to be all right? No permanent damage?"

"I wouldn't have left her if I thought that. No, I think she's going to be okay. I didn't tell her that I was going to let you in on everything, so you might want to let her know I told you. But be sure to let her know that you aren't going to tell anybody else about her secret. At least when I get finished with Mr. Todd Larson, she won't have to hide out anymore. She can go back to being a woman, and living a normal life if she wants. The nightmare will finally be over for her."

"While yours will be just beginning, won't it, Jesse? I'm sorry, friend. I wish there was something I could do to help you." Glen shook his head sadly. He too realized what was ahead of Jesse. He would be caught eventually, and with his record, he didn't stand a chance. If they didn't hang him, he would for sure spend the rest of his life in prison. For Jesse, that was the same as a death sentence. Glen sighed deeply.

"So, you'll sort of watch out for her while I'm gone?"

"Sure, Jess, as best I can. Don't worry about her. You just go do what you have to do, and I'll take care of things here."

"Thanks, Glen. I appreciate it, more than you will ever know." He reached out his hand, and Glen clasped it firmly with his own then pulled Jesse to him in a great bear hug.

"Take care of yourself, Jesse. Be careful."

"I will, Glen. And thanks."

Rising to his feet, he strode quietly from the room and on outside. He was packed and driving out of the yard within minutes, his jaw set, his mind already working on a plan to find and kill Todd Larson.

Chapter 28

It didn't take Jesse long to find Todd Larson. There weren't that many branding crews in the country, and a few simple questions soon led Jesse to his quarry. Within four days, he was following Todd everywhere he went. He tried to decide whether or not to let Todd know he was being followed, and in the end, decided it might help to make Todd suffer a little more. When Todd came into town, Jesse could be seen leaning up against the outside wall of the bar, or against the hood of his pickup. It only took one appearance to put Todd on the alert.

Something was up. Todd could feel Jesse's eyes on his back before he could search him out. What was that Indian doing following him? He was sure he was being followed, no doubt about it. But why? He couldn't have figured out that it was he who had killed Francine. She was dead. And dead people tell no tales! If Jesse had known who Todd was during branding, there might possibly have been some trouble then. But Jesse hadn't known. Francine obviously hadn't told him. So what was going on? Did he just suspect something? He had covered his tracks too well, he was sure that not even an Indian like Jesse Windchase could have followed them. But everywhere he turned, Jesse was there, staring at him. He began to get nervous.

Jesse was taking his time. His hatred knew no bounds, but he was nothing if not careful. He would take his time, and Todd would suffer appropriately for what he had done to Francine. And as he watched, he planned. Todd's death would be long and painful, as painful as Jesse could make it, which was requiring a little creative thinking on his part. He knew he would pay with his life for what he was going to do to the man. Well, if he was going to go back to prison, or be hanged, it might as well be for taking his full revenge. He wasn't going to endure the punishment for just shooting someone. This was going to be well worth his time. And Francine's suffering.

For two weeks, whenever Todd left a ranch and went to town, Jesse was there. He would appear seemingly out of nowhere, and just as suddenly, he would be gone. Todd never knew when or where he would spot him, but he realized that there was no way he would ever escape him.

Finally, while picking up some supplies in Big Timber one day, he couldn't take it anymore. He decided to approach Jesse and have it all out with him. Seeing Jesse lounging against a pickup as he came out of the hardware store, he headed straight for him, rage in his eyes.

"What the hell do you think you're doing, Jesse? Following me around like this? What's with you, anyway?"

Jesse glared at Todd from under his hat, then relaxed his countenance, gave a soft smile, and very casually walked away. In seconds he had vanished, and Todd never saw where he had gone. He had simply melted into the crowd. Sweat glistened on Todd's handsome brow. He was marked, and he knew it.

Finally, it was time. Jesse had followed Todd for three weeks. It was the end of June. It was time to end it.

Branding was finished throughout the country. Todd was back on the home place, over north of Ennis, ranching with his parents again for the summer. At least he felt safe at home, since he had only seen Jesse whenever he was in town. It never even occurred to him to be looking for Jesse out in the hills.

It was early morning, and he was heading out to check some fence. He never had time to realize what had happened- the rope sailed out, the slack was jerked up, and suddenly he was on the ground. He hit hard, landing on his right hip, and a sharp pain surged through him.

"What the...?!"

"Hello, Todd. It's time." Jesse stared impassively down at Todd from the boulder that supported him, the rope taught in his hands.

"Time for what? What are you stalking me for? I'm gonn'a send you back to jail so fast, your head will be spinning in the breeze. Now let me go!"

"I don't care what happens to me, cowboy. But today, you will die."

"Jesse, have you lost your mind? Listen to yourself, man! I don't know what's going on inside that thick head of yours, but you've got no reason to be after me." He struggled to his feet, the rope around his chest, and just as he was able to get his balance, Jesse jerked him to the ground again.

"Francine, Todd. For Francine."

"What are you talking about? I don't know what you're talking about, damn it! Now let me go!" Francine was dead. He couldn't know who had beaten her to death. It could have been anybody, and Jesse wasn't going to pin the deed on him. No way!

"She's not dead, Todd."

"What? What did you say?" Todd went white, and sudden terror gripped him. Was the Indian telling the truth? But it couldn't be possible- he had made sure before he left her- she was dead all right. "Are you trying to tell me something has happened to my ex-wife?" He would bluff and stall as long as he could, his brain racing frantically for some way out of this mess.

"I said she's not dead. And she told me everything. So, now, it's your turn."

Todd nearly fainted. Looking into Jesse's impassive face, he knew his time was limited. He knew that Jesse was going to impart some sort of justice before the day was over. He was going to die.

Jesse quickly rolled Todd over onto his stomach, and tied him securely. Then he mounted Todd's horse, and rode him back to the pasture gate, where he unsaddled the gelding and turned him loose in the section. He didn't want the horse heading home, riderless, and alerting Todd's parents; he couldn't be interrupted before he was finished.

Walking back to Todd, he deftly tied a leather thong around the man's neck, and keeping his hands securely tied behind his back, allowed Todd to get to his feet. Keeping him on the leather tether, Jesse began the trek into the higher country, picking his way carefully through the rocks, Todd stumbling along behind. They were heading into rattlesnake country, now, and there were numerous rocks and boulders of all sizes, making walking difficult. Todd was having trouble, his cowboy boots not conducive to hiking in rocks, but noticed that Jesse never missed a step. And he was wearing moccasins.

Jesse led Todd northwest into the hills for over three hours, until they finally arrived at what seemed to be Jesse's camp. His pickup was there, and the remains of a camp fire, as well as some other camp gear.

"How long have you been up here, Jesse, watching and waiting for me?"

Jesse ignored him, and began his preparations.

"Jesse? I asked you a question!"

Jesse whirled upon the unsuspecting man, and with one swift movement of his leg, had toppled Todd to the rocks. He tied the end of the leather leash to a stake securely pounded into the ground, then turned his back on Todd and began to strip.

Todd stared at him in total fascination and horror. Jesse was powerfully built, and big. He moved with grace and purpose, wasting no movements. For Todd, it reminded him of a pet wolf he once had. He had thought the wolf to be his friend when it was a pup, but when it reached maturity, one day it had looked at him, then trotted off. It had returned to the wild, to its heritage, just as Jesse seemed to be doing now. Terror poured through him.

Jesse was ready. He stood above Todd, totally impassive. Todd had become nothing more than an evil insect to him something to be trampled and eliminated, slowly and painfully.

Squatting down next to Todd, he untied the leather tether from the stake, then slowly tightened the noose around Todd's neck in increments, strangling him with a determined slowness. Todd's terror knew no limits. He couldn't breathe! Jesse was strangling him! He tried to struggle, but it was no use. And that big Indian just stared into his eyes, showing no emotion whatsoever.

Jesse prolonged the torture. It took Todd a long time to pass out. Jesse felt nothing as he looked at Todd's limp body.

***

When Todd awoke again, he found himself totally naked, each of his limbs spread and tied with leather thongs to stakes in the ground. He lay on his back, spread-eagled, waiting for what would happen next. He shuddered as he felt ants and other insects crawling over him. Sweat began dripping off his face. He stared into that Montana sky, where only the deep blue spread above him. Not even a cloud to cover his nakedness, or cool the heat that was beginning to build, reflecting and shimmering off the rocks.

He had heard stories about what the Indians used to do. How they would tie their victims up like this, then leave them for the ants to devour slowly, or heat and thirst to do their work. He couldn't believe, in this day and age, that this was happening to him. This was supposed to be a civilized country!

"Jesse! They'll get you, you know. There's no way you'll get away with this. Why don't you quit now, while there's still a chance for you? I won't press charges if you just let me go now. How about it? Untie me, and we forget we ever saw each other. Deal?" His plea was ignored.

Jesse sat on his haunches, sharpening a large knife on a whetstone. Finally, he tested the blade by scraping the hairs on his right forearm. It was sharp. It was time.

"First, I am going to make sure you never rape another woman. After that, I haven't decided for sure how to finish you off. Just like cutting a calf, Todd. No difference."

As the full import of Jesse's intent pierced Todd's brain, the horror of it implanted itself, and he yelled out. "Nooooo-o-o-o!"

He could have done it quickly. It could have been over in seconds. But Jesse was all Indian now, with blood lust running high in his veins. Whatever he did to Todd, it would be too good for him.

He squatted over Todd for several minutes, before he went to work. Todd screamed in pain, and writhed in agony. When it was over, Jesse laid the testicles on Todd's chest, and then turned away from him. The flies were already swarming at the desecrated flesh.

***

Something was wrong. Jesse had planned so long and so hard to kill this vermin, and now that it was time to finish it, he found himself nearly sick to his stomach. He had thought that the castration would inflame him to continue, but instead, he found himself disgusted. Oh, he still wanted Todd dead, he wanted to avenge Francine and all that she had suffered, but he had never taken a life before. And now that the act was before him, he was afraid he just couldn't do it; he didn't think he could kill another human being. The very thought of it was making him ill. Maybe what he had done was enough.

Keeping his back to Todd, who was sobbing like a baby, Jesse stared up into the deep mesmerizing blue Montana sky. The spring sun warmed his naked skin that took on a glow with the rays. Thoughts ricocheted through his brain, firing nearly too fast for him to focus on any of them. Finally, he sighed deeply, and bowed his head. He couldn't do it. He couldn't kill anyone, not even the filth that was Todd Larson. It nearly shamed him, and yet, he felt more of a man that he had felt in weeks. It was settled now. It was finished.

He turned back to Todd, who was still sobbing uncontrollably. There was a bucket of cold spring water nearby, and Jesse washed his hands carefully, then doused the man thoroughly. It was as close as he could come to washing the wound for him. The very sight of Todd made him want to vomit, not because of the mutilation, but because of what a disgusting creature he was.

"Shut up."

Todd started to moan again, and Jesse kicked him savagely in the ribs.

"I said, shut up, Todd."

Todd went quiet.

Jesse quickly dressed himself, and this time, the moccasins went into the cab of the pickup. He would wear his boots again. He was through with this game of revenge.

"I have decided to let you live. I'm not sure why, Lord knows you don't deserve it, but that's the way it's going to be. If you come after me, try to file any charges or have any contact with either Francine or myself in the future at all, I'll hunt you down and finish what I started here today. You can count on that. I will also see to it that if for some reason I don't kill you first, you will go to prison for the rest of your life for what you did to Francine. Understood?"

Todd could only nod affirmatively, his body shuddering in pain and shock.

Jesse slashed the tethers holding Todd to the four stakes, and he was free. He was broken, but he was alive.

"You know where you are, and you know where your horse is. You should make it home okay. Although, you might prefer to walk rather than ride, I suppose." Jesse had to smile to himself. He was feeling better now, since he had decided not to kill the man. He had fixed it so Todd would never forget him, and he would never harm another woman, he was sure. It was a good day. Maybe he and Francine could have a future together after all. Todd would never bother either of them again, and since he hadn't killed the man, there was no death sentence looming over his head anymore. His eyes danced. He could go back to Francine, and they could begin to plan. Yes, it was a good day, and it was good to be alive!

He gathered what gear was on the ground, climbed into the pickup, and without a backward glance at Todd, drove away. He was heading home, to Francine.

***

Todd remained at the campsite for what seemed like an eternity. He couldn't believe what had transpired that day. He was now a eunuch, but he was alive. Under the circumstances, he figured he'd better not do much complaining.

He began to dress, but found that he couldn't stand any underwear or pants due to the pain. He put his socks and boots on, and carrying his pants, began the long hike back home. Since it was all downhill and he was on foot, he figured he could cut across country and make it home by dark. Beyond that, he couldn't think. He would get his horse and gear another time. Jesse was right- he wouldn't be doing any riding for a while.

Shock, heat, lack of water, and pain were taking their toll. After three hours of hiking, Todd stumbled on a loose rock and went down hard, hitting his head on a boulder as he fell. Blood poured from the gash in his temple as his body tumbled down the hill. He never regained consciousness. They found his body three days later.

Chapter 29

Jesse stopped at the ranch headquarters to let Glen know he was back. He would gather more supplies, then head up to Francine. He related, though not in any detail, what he had done to Todd Larson, but made it plain he hadn't killed the man. Glen was proud of him; he knew what it had taken for Jesse to control himself. He was genuinely happy for his friend.

***

Francine was nearly back to normal. She had been checking cattle and fences daily, the others having moved the cattle up to the higher pastures for her. Glen had been up to see her, and now that her secret was out in the open, there was more of an easy friendship between the two. She waited every day for Jesse to come back. She prayed that he wouldn't be killed, and that even if they couldn't be together in the end, that he would be okay. Each evening, she sat on the little cabin's porch with a cup of coffee, watching the sun go down, and waiting. Hoping. Praying.

And then one day, she came in from her day's work, and there was Roger in the pasture. He was back!

She couldn't wait to see him. She was terrified. She was shy. She was nervous. She was embarrassed. She was afraid he might have changed his mind about loving her. She was like a bride on her wedding night.

He was pouring a cup of coffee for himself as she entered the cabin. Sammy bounded over, wagging his tail, Jesse now his second favorite person. Uncertain, he squatted to fondle Sammy, then rose and turned to stare at her, drinking her in with his eyes, afraid that perhaps with his absence and the passage of time she might not want him around anymore.

Francine could see the uncertainty in his eyes as he gazed hungrily at her. Suddenly, her insecurities fell away–they were nothing compared to the love she felt for this man. Crossing the short distance to him, she stopped before him, and then reached out with both arms.

Jesse took her offering. With a moan, he gathered her close, and held her as if he would never let her go. Lord, but he loved this woman! She owned his soul. Tears began trickling down his cheeks, but he didn't care. He was back, and Francine still wanted him. That was all that mattered.

"You still want me." It was a statement, muffled against her neck.

"I told you I loved you. Don't you know how it nearly killed me to have you away from me all those weeks? Jesse, I nearly went out of my mind, worrying about you. You are okay, aren't you?"

"Yeah, I'm fine. Lord but it feels so good to hold you again. Francine, I can't leave you again. I can't. You're my whole life now."

"As you are mine, Jess."

He had thought about what he wanted to ask her all the way back. He didn't know if it was too soon, or what she would say, but he needed to ask just the same. Before coming back, he had stopped in Bozeman at the jewelers and bought a ring, a small, plain gold band. He was praying that she wouldn't reject him, but the very idea that she might terrified him.

"Francine, I have a question for you."

"Ask away, Jess."

"Francine, will you . . .uh . . .well . . ."

"Spit it out Jess. What do you want?"

He took a deep breath. Still holding her close, he finally blurted out, "Will you marry me?" Then he was deathly still, waiting for her answer. If she said no, he thought he might die.

"Jesse, I don't know if…"

Pushing her away a little, he stared deeply into her eyes. "Francine, I'm not asking you to make love with me. Not now. I just want to marry you. I want to sleep with you every night, and not feel guilty about it. I want to know that you are mine, and you won't ever leave me. I just want to love you, and protect you, if you'll have me. Will you? I don't care about anything else. The physical part of it doesn't matter to me right now. Whenever you're ready. What do you say? Will you? Marry me?"

She reached up and kissed him full on the mouth.

"When? Today? Tomorrow? Right now? Whenever you want to, Jesse. I'm yours. Just say the word."

He crushed her to himself so hard she cried out in pain.

"Gosh, I'm sorry, Francine. I'm sorry. Did I hurt you? Are you okay?"

She laughed. "I'm fine, Jess. You just don't know how strong you are sometimes!"

He picked her up and twirled around the small space with her in his arms. The world was a glorious place! Glorious! They had a future, a life. He felt like a king. Putting her down, finally, he pulled the small box out of his pocket and handed it to her. Inside was the small gold band.

"I'm sorry, I didn't get you a diamond or anything. I was hoping that if you said yes, you wouldn't want to wait too long, so this was all we would need. Was I wrong? Did you want an engagement ring?

"No, Jess. This is all I want. I've had the other, and I don't need it. Really, all I want is you. Shall I wait until it's official, or should I put it on now?"

"Maybe we should wait. You know, do it up right. But only for a few days. I don't want to wait any longer than I absolutely have to. I love you, woman. I love you so much!"

"I love you too, Jesse. With all my heart. You and Sammy." She laughed at the look that crossed his face with that remark. Then, she became very serious.

"Jesse, I have to ask, did you...?"

"When it came right down to it, Francine, I couldn't. I'm sorry, but he wasn't worth it, and I just couldn't do it. He won't ever be bothering any women ever again, though. I did see to that."

She searched his face, questioning.

Seeing the unspoken question, he answered it for her. "I castrated him. That's probably all you need to know, okay? That's enough. Anyway, I promise you he won't be attacking anybody else, ever again. It's settled."

Her eyes went wide, and then she couldn't help herself. She smiled, ever so slightly.

"Good for you Jesse. Good for you. I'm proud of you, you know? And I'm so thankful you didn't kill him. So thankful. Come here and let me hold you again. I can't get enough of you!"

That night, when it was bedtime, each was embarrassed as to the sleeping arrangements. Jesse wanted to sleep with her as he had been before he left, but was afraid to ask. Francine wanted the same thing, but was also afraid for various reasons.

"Francine, I know we aren't married yet, but...?"

"Jesse, would you mind...?"

They laughed together, then stripped, and crawled under the blanket, clasping each other, tasting, inhaling the scents, loving. Jesse had vowed there would be no more than this until they were married, and he was going to stick to it. Even what had happened before, would not happen again. He had himself under control this time. He couldn't help his erection- that was instantaneous whenever he got close to this woman that he loved so desperately, but he was careful to control his movements. There would be no more accidents. Fleetingly, the thought of Todd flashed through his brain, and he smiled to himself. He could now enjoy what Todd never would again. It felt good.

Chapter 30

They were fixing breakfast when they heard the sound of an engine. Opening the cabin door, they saw the ranch jeep just pulling up to the porch, Glen at the wheel. All smiles, Jesse came down the porch steps to greet his friend.

"Glen! Glad to see you! Come on in, we're just about to eat. Have some coffee, at least. And wait until you hear the news!"

Glen never said a word. A scowl on his face, he climbed out of the jeep, walked past Francine and Jesse without looking at them, entered the cabin, and slammed the Bozeman paper down on the small table.

"You told me you didn't kill him, Jesse. I never thought you would lie to me. Pack your things and get out. I can't abide a liar!"

"What …"

Jesse looked from Glen to the headlines on the paper. "Ennis Man Found Mutilated, Dead."

"You lied to me, Jesse."

Francine was staring at first one man, then the other. Jesse had lied? He had told her also that he hadn't killed Todd. What was going on?

"Hold up, Glen. I told you I didn't kill him, and I didn't. I didn't lie to you. I don't know what killed him, but I sure as hell didn't."

Glen stared hard at his friend. He wanted to believe Jesse, but the paper….

"Glen," Jesse returned his friend's hard gaze, "I'm telling you I didn't kill him. I swear on all that's holy, I'm telling you the truth. He was sitting up, talking coherently to me when I left him. He had his clothes, and all he had to do was walk on home. You know and God knows that I wanted to kill that man, but I didn't do it. I don't know what happened later, but he was most definitely alive when I left him. I am not lying to you; I never have, and I never will." He turned to Francine.

"The same goes for you, Francine. I have never lied to you, and I never will. On my honor, and my love for you, I swear it."

"Well, Jesse, I think you have a major problem. Todd is definitely dead, and you were obviously the last person to see him alive, that we know of. Chances are, the law will be on your trail in no time, if they aren't already. Right about now, I'm not sure whether or not it makes a bit of difference whether you're guilty of murder or not. Your chances are pretty slim, having a record for murder like you already do. Now mind you, if you killed him, I don't much care one way or the other. I think he had it coming. But what I can't take is you lying to me. I think, however, that you're telling me the truth about this. I can see it in your eyes."

"Oh, Jesse! What are we going to do?"

Jesse noticed that Francine asked what 'we' were going to do, not just him, bless her heart. He didn't know. He couldn't think clearly right now. He had thought everything was okay. He was innocent, and hadn't killed anyone. But would he ever be able to convince the authorities? He doubted it, he really doubted it. There was too much against him, and time was already running out. He had been seen following Todd in various towns for weeks. With his face, it wouldn't be hard to identify him.

"Well, Glen, I guess I have to thank you for coming up here and letting me know about this. I don't know what I'm going to do yet. I need to think. If you don't mind, I need to be alone for a while. Thanks again for coming." And he opened the cabin door for his friend to leave.

"Sure. You take care, Jesse. If you need anything, just let me know. I'll do whatever I can to help you, as long as it doesn't mean breaking the law, but don't ask me to lie for you. That's one thing I can't do. Sorry."

"Wouldn't expect you to, Glen. Thanks for all your help. I know I don't have much time. I have to think. Talk to you later."

Glen left, and they were alone in the cabin. Jesse sat down hard in one of the chairs, his head in his hands, his world crashing down around him as he sat. What was he going to do? Was there any way out? He didn't know. He had tried so hard! He was innocent! It was just like before, with his wife. He hadn't committed that crime either. But he knew that no one would ever believe him. Francine! How could he leave her now?

Francine walked up quietly behind him, and gently wrapped her arms around his shoulders. Whatever he had or hadn't done, she loved this man, and she vowed that nothing was going to take him away from her now that she had him back.

"Whatever you decide to do, wherever you go, I'm going with you." She whispered quietly into his soft, thick hair. "I won't lose you again, Jess. And I'm not willing to let you just give up and go to jail. We'll think of something, between us. I know we will. We just have to think."

"Yeah. Well, I'm thinking, and short of skipping the country fast, I haven't any other ideas. But I don't have a passport, and I doubt that I could get one even if I had the time and tried. I don't know, Francine. I don't know what to do."

But his comment had started her brain thinking. Leave the country. That's what they could do!

"Jesse, you've got it! We'll leave the country!"

"Francine, how? I told you, I can't get a passport. How am I going to leave the country?" He swiveled in his chair to look at her, and the light dawned. "Canada? Do you really think we could make it? The two of us?"

"Damn right, Jesse. If we really mean to do it."

The idea took hold, and each processed the possibilities and all the implications. Could they really do it? But how?

"Horseback. Through the backcountry. We take our saddle horses, and several packhorses, and we could make it, I'm sure. We are only a few hundred miles from the border, and if we cross at night, through ranchland, we just might do it. Hell, Chief Joseph did it, only he quit too soon. If he could do it, we can!

We'll need to travel at night, but if we can get started before they start looking for me, we have a chance. Once there, I have other friends on reservations and farther north. If we can cross the border Francine, we just might be home free." Jesse's eyes began to glow with the possibility of it.

"We'll need a map, so we can avoid any towns, and maybe even stick to forest all the way to the border. And enough supplies for at least a month. It's summer, so there's feed and water all the way for the horses. But Francine," Jesse looked sadly at her, "It will mean leaving everything you know. You are just now able to get your life back, and I can't ask you to leave it again for heaven only knows what lies ahead. It will be a rough life, woman. We can't ever live in a town again, probably even up there. We will be outcasts for the rest of our lives. And it will take us all summer and fall, maybe even the first part of winter to get to the North Country. It's going to be hard, real hard. I can't ask you to do that."

"Jesse, what kind of life have I been living the past seven years? You think it hasn't been hard? And remember, I've been alone the whole time. I'm used to a rough life." She smiled fondly at him, at his eagerness. "Besides, I don't have a life if I don't have you. So what's to think about? When can we leave?"

"We can't go for a few days yet. I just hope we have enough time to pack up before they get here. I think we do, but it's going to be close. And we will need money, or gold, something even up there."

"We'll make it, Jesse, I know we will."

For the next three hours, they planned what they would need, the route they would take, and when they would leave. It would take them several days to get organized–this was a big undertaking. But the alternative didn't bear thinking about. They had to make the run for the border, and they knew they would never make it in a vehicle. Besides, the one thing she couldn't think of doing was leaving her horses or her dog. They needed to get back to the ranch headquarters to get the horses they would need, as well as supplies. And Francine had some calls to make.

They rode down right after lunch.
Glen was nowhere around when they got there. Francine headed for the cookhouse and the phone as soon as she left the barn. The first call was to her mother.
"Mom, it's me, Francine. It's okay now, Mom, everything is fine. I can't tell you anything more than that right now, but I'll be getting back to you soon, okay? I just wanted you to know that I'm all right. Did you read about Todd in the papers? You did? Then you know I'm safe from him. I have some other things going on at the moment, and I can't tell you any more than that, but I just wanted you to know that I'm okay, and I love you, Mom. And Dad, too. Now don't worry about me, and you'll be hearing from me. Take care, Mom. Say hi to Dad for me. Love you." And she hung up. She couldn't let her parents know what she was planning; it wouldn't be fair. The police could possibly find and be talking to them before the week was out.
The next call was to her old friend, Clarisse, to whom she told the whole story, and left nothing out.
"Clarisse, I need a couple more favors from you, old friend. I am sorry to bother you, but this is really important. Please close my account for me, convert it into Canadian gold and silver coins, and Fed-Ex the whole amount to me here at the ranch tomorrow. Got that?"
"Francine, are you sure you want it all? You've got five year's worth of wages saved up–you want the whole thing in gold coins?"
"Yup. You got it right. The whole thing. All of it. Tomorrow."
"You leaving the country or something Francine?"
"Yeah, or something. Look, I'll send you a letter explaining everything, but for right now, I need the coins. You probably won't get the letter for a month or two, but I promise, I will

answer all your questions then. And Clarisse, thanks for being such a good friend all these years. I don't know what I would have done without you . . ."

"No problem. The gold will be there tomorrow. Don't forget to write!"

"I won't. Bye. Take care of yourself!" And the connection was broken.

After completing her calls, she went to the bunk house and started writing, one very long letter to Clarisse, and another longer one to be forwarded by her friend to her parents at a later date. She didn't want either letter to be mailed for at least a month though, giving her and Jesse plenty of time to put some distance between them and her friends. Then she began packing what was left of her things at the bunkhouse. There wasn't much. They would have to take their belongings up along with the packhorses during the night. They didn't want anyone seeing them leaving with a string of horses- it would lead to numerous questions. They couldn't afford to have anyone but Glen knowing they were heading out on horseback.

Francine could easily take one packhorse, or even two. It wasn't unusual to take a couple of horses, packed, up for the summer to the line shack. She did that every year. But extra horses could cause a lot of talk. They would take two horses up during the night, and two the next morning. The four packhorses could carry several months' worth of supplies, plus all their clothing and extras.

After organizing everything that they could at the bunkhouse, they went to Glen's house to await his return. He had to know they were leaving, and they would need bills of sale for some of the horses, as well as permission for extra supplies.

While they were waiting, they talked softly between themselves, going over plans again and again.

After about an hour, Glen returned, and the meeting began.

"Glen, I'm going to let Francine do all the talking, and that way you will be able to honestly say that I never told you anything. I'm trying to keep you out of this, but as friends, I can't just up and leave you without some explanations. Does that sound fair? Can you deal with this mess that way? I realize we are just talking semantics here, but at least this way you won't have to actually, literally, lie for me. Fair enough?"

"Fair enough, Jesse. You know I want to help you in any way I can, and I will. But I can't out and out break the law, either."

"Okay, Glen, here's what we want to do, but we do need your help." Francine took a deep breath, then continued. "We need to buy a couple of horses from you for pack animals. I have my three, and I can pack two of them, but we are going to need three more, the way we figure it, one to ride and two to pack. I'll pay you in gold tomorrow, after the Fed-Ex man comes. Also, we could sure use some supplies from the cookhouse, if that's all right. We'll be happy to pay you for anything we take, just name your price. Oh, and one more thing, could we borrow a pick-up later this evening? Jesse's white pick-up will have to be found in Bozeman, I guess. We can't leave it here."

Glen looked from Francine to Jesse and then back to Francine again. "Do I dare ask just what you two plan on doing? Or will I be happier if I don't know?"

"Let me answer you this way, Glen. Chief Joseph once made quite a run with his tribe on horseback. Clear enough?"

Surprise glimmered in Glen's eyes as he took in the implication of what Francine had just said. Then a big smile permeated his whole face as he reached out to Jesse and gave him a big bear hug.

"Take anything you need, Jesse. Anything. Count it as wages for both of you. I'll write out a bill of sale for the horses- just pick out whichever ones you want. After all, Franc is one of the best hands that I ever had the pleasure of working for me, and I would sell him anything he wanted." Turning again to Francine, he said with great sincerity, "Franc, or Francine, you really are one of the good ones. You gave me more than an honest day's work for a day's pay, and never complained. You did a good job, and I hate to see you go, but I understand, and I wish you only the best. I know you have one of the best men I ever had the pleasure to meet. He'll take good care of you." Glen turned away from them as a tear threatened, then turned back again. "Aw hell," he said, and hugged first one, then the other. "You two take care. Now get out of here before I start bawling like a baby."

***

"Jesse, I think maybe you had better head out of here tonight, just in case." They were absently nursing cups of coffee out behind the barn again, thinking, and planning, the ever-present Sammy napping at their feet. "We don't know how close the cops are on your trail, and any time we can buy, we had better take. It should take them a while to figure out about me, and with luck, they never will. At any rate, they shouldn't have any reason to be after me, or to even know I actually exist, although these days, they may be able to track me down eventually. If they manage to put the two of us together, then I'm in trouble, but until then, I can move about." She took a slow sip of the dark liquid, mindless of the flavor. "Why don't I get a couple of geldings in, we can pack them up, and you can take them up to the cabin tonight. I'll follow tomorrow after the gold arrives, and bring all my horses, and we can maybe head out the following morning. What do you think?" Francine's brain was working double time, trying to sort it all out.

"I don't want to be away from you for even that long, but I think you're probably right. I'll head up tonight, and plan on seeing you up there tomorrow sometime."

Within just a couple of hours, the horses were caught, saddled with packsaddles, and loaded with various supplies. Francine's horses were left in the corral rather than turned out, to be easily caught the following day. Leaving the three in the barn that Jesse would take, they went about the evening routine as if nothing had changed, barely talking, sitting at their regular places in the cook-house, Jesse making normal conversation with Fred and Sandy. Francine ate her meal in silence once more, her heart racing in anticipation and fear at what lay before her.

The meal was over, and while Fred and Lucky sat on the bunkhouse porch sipping coffee, Jesse and Francine were busy in the barn shoeing the two horses Jesse would take up that night. They were careful to pack extra shoes and shoeing equipment for the trip, also. Francine's Appaloosas had excellent hard, black feet, and really didn't need shoeing, but she would shoe them tomorrow, anyway. She was going to use any insurance she could!

After seeing that the horses were ready to travel, they ran Jesse's pick-up over to Bozeman and left it in one of the University parking lots. They hoped it would take the authorities a while before they found it among all the other parked vehicles belonging to students. While in Bozeman Jesse wanted desperately to find a pastor or Justice of the Peace to marry them, but realized that it might only lead the authorities to them even faster. His face would be on the front page of the Bozeman Daily Chronicle soon enough, and there was no sense in giving the police any information about him at all. There would be no marriage. Three hours later, they were back at the ranch.

It was time for bed. Francine and Jesse lay on their respective bunks, afraid to touch with others so close, afraid to talk, waiting for the opportunity to leave.

Finally, it was time. Jesse rose from his bunk, smoothed the blankets, and then went quietly to Francine.

"You be careful, Francine. I'll see you tomorrow. Remember I love you." He reached down and kissed her lightly on the mouth, stroked her hair softly, then turned and strode quietly from the room.

In minutes, he was mounted, leaving the barn riding Roger and leading two sorrel packhorses. No one saw or heard him leave, and the darkness swallowed him up in seconds.

***

The next day, Francine spent most of her time checking her gear, shoeing the remaining two Appaloosas, and trying to act normal while waiting for the Fed-Ex truck to arrive, which it did around 3 PM. She signed for her packages, marveling at the weight of them. The gold and silver coins didn't take up much space, but golly, were they ever heavy!

She was just heading over to tell Glen good-by and thanks one more time, when a Montana State Police car pulled up in front of the main house. Francine halted in mid stride, trying to decide what to do. They were on to Jesse already, just as they all had feared. Two men in uniform got out of the car, just as Glen came out onto the porch to greet them. Glancing up, he spied Francine gathering the reins and ropes of the horses as she mounted slowly. She looked carefully at her boss, then tipping her hat casually in salute, turned and rode slowly out of the yard, Sammy bringing up the rear behind the last pack-horse. The policemen watched her ride off with no particular interest.

"Act natural, Francine, old girl, just act natural. Don't get in a hurry. Don't draw their attention in any way. Just act like normal. Like you're doing your regular job." And she did.

Chapter 31

Francine savored the ride up to the line camp, knowing it was probably the last time she would ever make it. She rode slowly, letting her eyes feast on the colors, shapes, and sounds that were the C/6 and the Bridger Mountains. It had been her home for the past five years, and she was going to miss it. She had loved her job and all the riding it entailed. She had been able to be herself most of the time, away from everyone. Now Jesse Windchase was in her life, and the future lay ahead, unknown, uncharted.

When she topped Hatfield Mountain, she reined in her horse and sat for a moment, resting the horses and just soaking up the countryside. Thinking back to previous rides in this country, she smiled to herself as she remembered her astonishment at spotting a huge grizzly last summer. It was right here on Hatfield, and the bear had just looked at her, then ambled on its way.

She could see for miles in all directions, and it was more than heaven on earth to her. Montana sang a special song to all her children, and Francine knew every verse. She would miss it. Raising her head, she breathed in that clear mountain air, unique to the Big Sky Country; it was so tangy she could almost taste it. Home. Montana was home.

The sun began its decent in the southwest, and shadows began competing with each other to earn the title of longest. It was time to go to Jesse, and her new life.

"It's time to go, Sammy." It was said quietly, and wistfully. She lifted her rein hand slightly, and the mare walked on. Her face set, she began the last few miles to Jesse.

***

He was waiting on the small porch for her as she rode up that evening. Seeing him, she dropped the reins and dismounted before the mare had come to a full stop. Instantly, she was in his arms.

"Oh, Jesse! The police are at the ranch already! I was so scared. I wanted to say good-by one more time to Glen, but they came, and I had to just ride away." She hugged him tightly. "Gosh, I'm glad to see you. But they're too close already, Jess. Too close!"

Talking softly, as if to a frightened colt, Jesse held her close and soothed her. "It's going to be okay, Francine. They shouldn't have any reason to put the two of us together yet, and they won't be up here for at least a day, if then."

"Jesse, I can't talk to them. You know I don't talk to anybody anyway, and especially not to them. I wouldn't be able to pull it off. I'm too scared. I can't be here when they come up here!"

He had hoped that maybe she could play the part just a little longer, and that would buy them some more time, but realized how impossible that would be for her. Besides, if something did go wrong, and they did catch him, she would be forever convinced in her mind that it was somehow her fault, and she would never forgive herself.

"How tired are you Francine? Can you ride for a few more hours? I'm thinking, maybe we should be traveling at night and sleeping during the day. At least for a while. Are you up to it?"

Her response was a kiss. "Lead on, my love. Whither thou goest, and all of that."

They were organized and heading into the higher country within an hour, Francine leading the way. Having been riding this country for years, she knew where all the gates were, as well as stream crossings and the shortest way to get off the C/6 land. It would take them all night.

They pressed on in the darkness, the horses picking their way carefully, making little noise in the soft spring grass, enjoying the cool night air. Francine became exhausted, but said nothing, and continued making the trail. Jesse knew she had to be tired, but he also knew they couldn't afford to stop and rest, not even for her, not now. They needed to make as much time as they could, as fast as they could, before the authorities had any idea where to begin searching.

It was well after dawn when Jesse called to her to stop. They would make camp here for the better part of the day, and then continue on later in the afternoon. There would be no campfires at night; they could cook only during the day, when the fires would not be as easily noticed.

In a small clearing, Jesse went about setting up a make-shift camp. The horses were unsaddled and hobbled nearby, and the sleeping bags were spread out under some Ponderosa Pines, for shade and also to hide them from any passing aircraft. The horses would look like anybody's ranch horses out to pasture, at least for now. Knowing that Francine must be exhausted, Jesse made the fire and cooked a wonderful smelling breakfast of eggs and bacon, with strong camp coffee. Pleased with his efforts, he turned to bring a plate to Francine, but found her fast asleep on her sleeping bag, her hat at her side, her head cradled on her arm. He thought he had never seen a more beautiful sight in his life, and probably never would again. He hated to wake her up, but she needed to eat; she could sleep afterwards.

He woke her gently, and they ate, talked, planned, sipped their coffee, then slept soundly on their sleeping bags during the heat of the day, nestled together in exhausted repose, Sammy curled up at their feet. It was the pattern they would follow for weeks.

***

It would be nearly four hundred miles to the Canadian border by the route they would have to take. It would take them about two months, maybe three to make the trip, if the weather didn't slow them down too much. They would have to keep to the mountains, where there were trees for cover, which meant they would have to detour to the west. Heading north would take them out of the forested areas eventually, and they couldn't take a chance on riding the plains, even at night. Although the first night they had ridden pretty much straight north, the next afternoon when they started out, they turned west, toward Helena. They could get lost in the Big Belt Mountains, and would head for Lolo National Forest and the Bob Marshall Wilderness area northwest of Helena. Then they could turn north again. The only big obstacle would be Interstate 15, which would have to be crossed at night, with great care. If they could make it to the Whitefish Range, they could make it across the border, they were sure.

For the next three days, the routine was the same. Francine soon became accustomed to it, as did the horses and Sammy, who thought this all a truly great adventure! It was peaceful, the weather held, and they saw no signs of any police or anything at all out of the ordinary. Francine nearly forgot that they were on the run. Life was good. She was with Jesse, and she lacked for nothing when she was in his arms.

Then one day, shortly after noon, they were awakened by the sound of a motor. Jesse was instantly awake, and quickly grabbed Francine close to him, reaching at the same time for Sammy's collar. Francine was having trouble recognizing the sound, but Jesse knew it for what it was instantly. A helicopter. They were perhaps not really on his actual trail, but they were looking. They must have found his pick-up by now, he thought, and the search had begun.

"Jesse?" Francine was struggling to move, but Jesse held her close. They were well under the pines, and he was confident they were completely hidden from the air. The horses might be visible, but they should draw no attention, at least not this early in the game. As long as they didn't move, he was sure they wouldn't be seen. Eventually, after what seemed like hours, the craft flew away. They hadn't been seen, but the chase was definitely on.

Jesse let out the breath he hadn't been aware he was holding, then kissed his love soundly.

Francine was terrified. She had been seduced into forgetting what was at stake with the peacefulness that had pervaded their days in the hills. Now it all came back to her in full force, and suddenly she was sobbing, and clinging to him with all that she had. If she had moved she might have drawn their attention! How could she have been so stupid! She had actually wanted to crawl out into the open to see what was making all that noise! What Jesse must think of her! She was so ashamed.

"Don't worry about it, Francine. You didn't." He was reading her mind. "Everything is all right, and they're gone. They won't be back at least until tomorrow. And they won't even try at night, I'm sure. So you can relax now." He held her close.

The full impact finally hit her. She now truly understood what was at stake, and she didn't much like it. It struck her that the one thing that bothered her most was the fact that they couldn't get married, and she decided that was totally unacceptable. When she was calm again, she sat up and stared him hard in the eyes.

"Jesse, I want to do something. Here, right now."

"What, Francine? Whatever you want, you know that."

"I want us to get married. Now. Before God. I want to know that I am really yours, and I want to wear that ring you bought for me from now on. Can we do that Jess?"

He smiled, loving her with all his heart. "Sure we can, Francie. I think God will understand."

Holding hands, they drew each other to their feet, never letting go. Staring into each other's eyes, Francine said, "Do you want me to go first, or do you want to?"

Jesse kissed her lightly, softly on her mouth, then pulled away from her, still holding her hands. His heart was full with the knowledge that Francine wanted him as badly as he wanted her.

"Francine, I want to tell you here and now, before God and on my honor as a man and a Crow, that I love you above all else in my life and on this earth. You are my woman, now and forever. I promise to love you, through the good times and the bad times, for the rest of my life. I promise to protect you with all that I am, as long as I am able, from any evil that might ever befall us, to the best of my ability. And God, I promise you that I will love this woman you gave me more than my life, for as long as you give me breath. Thank you, Lord, for Francine, and for the kindness You have shown me in giving her to me. She is more than I deserve; I will honor her always."

Francine gazed up at Jesse, all the love in her heart reflected in her eyes. A light breeze feathered her hair around her face, framing it as she spoke.

"Jesse, I likewise promise before you and God to love you and respect you always, as long as God sees fit to keep me with you. You are my husband in every way. Where you go, I go. I will do my best to be a good wife to you, now and always. I love you. Thank you, God, for this man, and for restoring my life to me."

Jesse took the gold band out of his pocket, and slipped it on her finger. As far as he was concerned, they were just as married now as if they had done the whole thing in a church. They had made their vows before God, and that was what counted. Holding her close, he slowly lowered his head to hers and kissed her in a way he had never kissed any woman before in his life. She was his, now. His. He could hardly believe it, and tears clouded his vision as he lifted his head contemplating the miracle that had just taken place.

Francine was crying openly, tears coursing down her cheeks, unheeded. This man was now her husband. And oh! How she loved him! Nothing else mattered, and the world fell away as all they saw was each other, their love.

Suddenly, Jesse wanted his new wife, as a man wants a woman. He felt himself stirring, unable to control the reaction to his thoughts, and Francine saw it in his face. Glancing down, she saw the physical evidence of his desire. Smiling softly to herself, she reached for his belt.

"Francine, no, you don't have to. It's okay, really..."

"Jesse, you dummy, I want to. I'm your wife now. I want to *be* your wife in every way. Understand?"

"But I don't want to hurt you- I don't want you do to anything you don't want to. Todd..."

"Jesse, that was another life. It happened to another woman, not to me. That part of my life is over, and I love you so much if you don't let me show you how much right here and now, I just might explode!" She looked coyly at the ground and muttered, "Unless of course, you don't want me..."

He needed no further urging. Lowering her to the sleeping bags, he began to slowly undress his new bride, kissing, fondling, worshipping every inch he uncovered. Going slowly so as not to frighten her, he explored every inch of her body, licking, tasting, loving, her hands and mouth urging him on in his exploration. Jesse made her feel beautiful, and for the first time in her life, she believed that she was.

He was unable to hold himself in check any longer. Staring deeply into her eyes, questioning, he waited for her answer, and when her arms pulled him to her, he sighed, closed his eyes, and the mating began. The sun freckled its pattern on their bodies, glistening on the sweat that coated them as their vows were sealed between them. They were one, now, at last.

Francine hadn't known that lovemaking could be like that. She had had no idea it could be anything but painful, and she felt like she supposed a bride should feel. She loved this man. And they would make it to Canada. She knew it.

Jesse lay with his arm over Francine's waist. He couldn't believe the depth of his feelings for this woman. He hadn't known it was possible to feel this way about another human being. Recognizing the fact that God had truly given him a priceless gift, he thanked Him once again. He knew he didn't deserve her, but he would do his best to keep her safe and happy, always, for as long as she would have him.

***

They slept, woke, made love, reveling in each other and their love, then repeated the cycle until they were spent. Finally, they slept until it was time to saddle up and head out again into the night. Canada was still a long hard ride away from them.

Chapter 32

It took nearly two weeks to make it to Helena and Interstate 15. They camped in a spot with only one hill between them and the highway, trying to think of some way to get across. It would have to be after dark, obviously, but even then, how to do it? They had spotted patrol cars in every little town they had passed, observing carefully from high vantage points as they traveled. Even little Maudlow, where only a handful of people lived, sported an MHP car as they passed by through the trees.

Jesse spent an extra day, resting the horses, figuring a way to get across the highway. He left Francine and took Roger to check further up and down the road. Finally, he found a place where he thought they could make it. The road widened on both sides of the highway where a small stream flowed under it. There were trees and good cover within a short distance of the fences on either side of the highway, and they could see traffic coming for miles in either direction. In the dark, it would be easy to spot any headlights long before they were near. If they timed everything just right, it could work. They would cross that night.

***

They waited until nearly two o'clock in the morning; traffic was almost nonexistent at that hour. Few local people in Montana travel at night if they can help it because of the deer. Tourists don't always realize what a road hazard they can be, and manage to hit their fair share of them during the summer, but it was the best chance they had. Jesse's biggest worry was those horses of Francine's. The white blankets on the Appaloosas seemed to almost glow in the dark; they would have to be very careful not to be seen in the moonlight.

Jesse slipped down on foot, crawling along the fence line on his belly, the fence pliers in his back pocket. Every time a car passed, he flattened himself against the ground as near to the fence as he could get without getting himself caught in the barbed wire. No one was looking for him here, and in the dark he was practically invisible.

When he reached the spot he had determined was the best place to cross, he began with the bottom wire and quickly cut all five wires, then pulled them back against the fence to form a wide opening. Waiting for a break in the traffic, he then sprinted across the highway and cut the fence in the same way on the other side. When it was safe, he ran back across the highway and over the hill where Francine waited with the horses and Sammy. He nodded to her in the darkness, and she understood.

Mounting Roger, Jesse rode slightly ahead toward the Interstate, waiting for just the right moment. After about ten minutes, his chance came. He signaled Francine, and the horses began a lope for the highway through the gap he had cut in the fence. They had only a few moments to make it across before another car would surely be along.

Jesse led the way, leading two pack horses, Francine following leading her two horses and Sammy at their heels. Jesse's horses led across the first two lanes, the median, and the final two lanes without incident, and he crossed thankfully through the opening on the other side of the highway. Turning, he suddenly saw that Francine was in trouble. The first horse was refusing to step onto the pavement! She had never seen a paved road before and was having none of it. He quickly tied his two packhorses to a wooden fence post, and then raced back to help Francine, uncoiling his rope as he rode. The lights of an oncoming vehicle registered in the corner of one eye, and adrenaline began to course through his body.

Francine was nearly in tears, unable to move the obstinate mare. Julie was pulling for all she was worth on the recalcitrant packhorse, but the pavement offered no traction. Jesse raced Roger across the road and in behind the reluctant mare, then brought the knotted end of his rope down hard across her hindquarters. The mare jumped, slipped, and almost went down, then gained her footing and lunged across the pavement, hooves flying in seemingly every direction, trying for purchase. Jesse stayed behind her, popping her with his rope every time she showed any signs of hesitating, and soon had them racing for the hole in the other side of the fence.

"Keep going–head for the trees!" he shouted to Francine as they cleared the fence. I'll be right behind you!" But the headlights were close now, and he knew he wouldn't have time to get his own string out of sight before the car was on them. He could only be as still as he could, and pray. He jumped to the ground, holding Roger close, and watched Francine and her horses disappear over the small rise into the nearby trees. His horses were all sorrels, and he would just have to hope that they blended into the darkness well enough to remain unseen.

He was lucky. The car coming at them was going so fast the driver was doing good to see the road, let alone anything off to the side. Jesse figured he must have been doing at least 90. *"Crazy fool,"* he thought to himself. *"Going to get himself killed, driving like that."* He shook his head at the driver's stupidity, then mounted Roger, gathered up the lead ropes from the other two horses, and followed Francine over into the trees.

After he caught up to her, they rode a little further into the cover the trees afforded them before they dismounted. Jesse gave Francine a quick hug, then pulled out his fence stretcher and a coil of smooth wire from one of the packs.

"I'll see you in a little while. Hang tight!" Mounting Roger, he drifted off into the darkness to repair the gaps he had made in the fences. He was fixing them with smooth wire instead of barbed wire, but he figured no one would notice–at least for a very long time and maybe never.

As he approached the fence, he saw the blinking lights from a Montana Highway Patrol car. The patrolman had pulled the speeding car over, about a mile from where they had crossed the highway. Thanking God for watching over them, he went about repairing the holes he had made. He knew they had been lucky- that patrolman could just have easily stopped the speeder here as a mile down the road. If he had stopped him here, they would have been seen for sure, with no way out. But they had made it. They had crossed the Interstate and were in the Helena area. Now there was nothing but wilderness in front of them for weeks. It would be hard riding, but it should be fairly safe. If they made it to the Bob Marshall, they were just about home free. Not many hardy souls would try to follow them in there, if they even thought to look for them in that area, which he doubted. He was counting on the fact that if anyone thought they had headed to Canada, that they would look mostly straight north, not northwest. Actually, he was figuring that no one would even suspect he had headed this way at all- and especially not on horseback. That was his ace in the hole.

Working quickly, as much by feel in the darkness as by limited sight, Jesse soon had the broken fence wires spliced; the fence stretched into the distance in both directions as far as he could see in the dark. Gathering his fence pliers and stretcher, he mounted and rode off to join Francine. He wanted to make a few more miles before dawn, and put some country between them and the highway.

Francine was waiting patiently in the darkness. Mesa nickered softly at the approaching horses, and Francine raised her head, watching for Jesse's appearance in the velvet softness of night. She heard the horse's footsteps before she saw him. As he dismounted, she ran to him and gathered him close in her arms.

"Have I told you lately that I love you, Jess?"

"No, woman, I don't believe you have at that. It's been at least a few hours, I'm sure. Do you? Still love me?"

"You know I do. You just have no idea how much, cowboy."

Jesse buried his face in Francine's hair, drawing deeply on the scent of her. This was what made his life worth living. Lord, but he loved this woman!

"Francine, I'm so very sorry to have gotten you mixed up in all of this. I mean, if I hadn't gone after Todd, he probably wouldn't have died, the cops wouldn't be after me, and I wouldn't have you out here in the middle of nowhere, running for your life and living like a damn Indian. I wanted so very much more for you- you deserve the best out of life. Certainly more than I can ever give you now!"

"Jess, I don't care. Don't you get it yet? I just don't care. As long as I'm with you, nothing else matters. And as far as being on the run like this, well, I have to admit I'm not crazy about hiding from the police, but golly, who could ask for more out of life than getting to cross the Big Sky Country on good horses with someone you love more than your life? Frankly, I feel sorry for other folks. They haven't any idea what they're missing." She paused, and made a wry face. "Now, I do admit that I might not feel quite the same way if it was winter, but it's not. And I also confess to wanting a hot shower desperately! But what have I got to complain about? I'm not punching any time clock, and there's nowhere I have to be. So just lead me on, fearless leader, and let me enjoy you. I love having you all to myself!" And with that, she freed her head, reached up to frame his rugged face with her hands, and planted a big kiss right where Jesse needed it most.

"Francie, I want you right here, right now. I don't even want to wait to make camp. But that's not right for you, so cut it out, please!"

With a small laugh, Francine, enjoying her power over this big man, began to slowly unbutton her shirt. It was hard for him to tell what she was doing, in the darkness, but when she reached for his hand and placed it over her breast, he was lost.

"Francine…"

"Yes, Jesse?" Her hand found his groin, and with a moan, he began loving his new bride again, unable to stop himself even if he had wanted to. And it was obvious that Francine wanted him as badly as he wanted her. They were married now, and there was no need to stop. So he didn't.

Their lovemaking took on a new kind of urgency, there, in the dark. And it was over in just a few minutes. Sated, Jesse fought to regain his breath.

"I'm sorry, love." It was the first time since their union that he hadn't taken the time to satisfy his wife's needs as well as his own, and he felt terrible, as if he had failed her somehow.

"Jesse, it's okay. Really. I'm just going to make sure that you pay for that little omission later. Oh, baby, are you ever going to pay!" And she smiled to herself in the darkness, as she began dreaming up ways to make him suffer with agonizing anticipation at a later date.

"Francie, I hate to end this here and now, but we really do have to make a few more miles before dawn. I want to be well away from this highway. Just in case. Shall we ride?" One more quick kiss on her forehead, and they broke apart to head out once more into the cover of darkness.

They were able to travel nearly six more miles in the few remaining hours until dawn, but when Jesse hobbled the horses to graze, he noticed one of the packhorses had lost a shoe during the night. He would tack another one on before they left later that afternoon. Right now there were more pressing things at hand- and when they had made camp and satisfied themselves with a hearty breakfast of bacon and the remaining eggs they had packed, Jesse set about making love properly to his new wife.

***

It was four days later that a Montana Highway Patrolman just happened to stop for a break at the exact spot they had crossed the Interstate. Seeing something shiny on the edge of the pavement, Jack Thomas got out of his patrol car to check it out. It was a horseshoe. Now what in the world was a horseshoe doing along the edge of the highway? Didn't make any sense. This was a controlled access highway, and no one rode along here. As he stared at the shoe in his hand, then let his gaze wander easily around him, he suddenly realized that something was not quite right with the scenery. He knew something was wrong, but couldn't quite put his finger on what was out of place. Shaking his head, he tossed the horseshoe onto the floor of the cruiser, and proceeded on down the highway.

    He was several miles away before it hit him- the fence. The fence wasn't right. He made a U-turn at the next highway crossing and sped back to where he had found the horseshoe. Looking to his left, then his right, he suddenly realized what was wrong. There were splices on the fence on both sides of the road, all five wires on each side. An accident might have resulted in the wires being cut and spliced again on one side, but not on both. "Holy shit!" he muttered under his breath. In seconds he was on the radio, and in twenty minutes there were investigators joining him in the Helena countryside along Interstate 15.

    Jesse and Francine were sleeping peacefully in the shade, resting from the long night of riding, unaware that their trail had been picked up.

Chapter 33

It was over 200 miles as the crow flies to the Canadian border from the Helena area. A man on a good horse could expect to make about eighteen to twenty miles a day over fairly easy terrain. Two people with six horses between them, four of them heavily packed and traveling through the Bob Marshall Wilderness area, could expect to make ten miles on a good day, and substantially fewer on an average day. And no animal could keep up that kind of pace in the mountains day after day without rest, so they would have to stop for a day of two every so often. Reaching Canada would for sure take two months, perhaps longer.

It was the first part of July now, and they were in the high country very near the continental divide, the elevation averaging between 6500 and 7000 feet. Snow came early up here, and often arrived for short periods every month of the year; it came to stay in September, lightly at first, then with increasing vengeance.

Jesse knew they could be facing some tough going towards the end of their journey. And getting across the border undetected was only part of the problem; he still wanted to get them to the north country of Canada before the dead of winter, when travel would become essentially impossible. He didn't know if he could do it, but he was going to give it his best shot.

***

When they first heard the helicopter in the late afternoon, they weren't too concerned. Heading for denser forest where they knew they were hidden, they waited calmly for the machine to pass. The Forest Service used helicopters up here all summer, watching for small fires breaking out, and general survey work. It never dawned on them that their trail had been discovered, and that the authorities had an idea where they were heading. Having ridden for days with no sign of humanity, they had become lulled into thinking that their path and destination was unknown.

When the second helicopter flew over within a few hours, Jesse knew they were being trailed, and his worry increased.

How had they found them? Well, they hadn't been caught yet, and they weren't about to be. They would simply have to head for the higher, even rougher country nearer the divide. If they were to be caught, someone on horseback would have to do it. Where he and Francine were making their trail, no vehicles would ever come close.

***

Detective Evan Smazick had grown up on the eastern Montana plains. After graduating from Yale at the head of his class, he had predicted a bright future for himself in a prestigious law firm, but after only a few years of practice became painfully disillusioned and went into another field of endeavor. The problem was, Evan was just too honest. He saw everything in black and white, with no gray areas. A person was either innocent or guilty- motives didn't enter into any equations. Evan couldn't be bought or swayed at any price, and when he saw his fellow lawyers throwing justice out the window in favor of a win at any cost, Evan was done. Law enforcement had always appealed to him, and now he was back in his home state doing something he really enjoyed. When Todd Larson was discovered, and the main suspect easily identified, Evan was called in only when Jesse had seemingly disappeared from the face of the earth. With the discovery of the thrown horseshoe, it hadn't taken Evan long to surmise where Jesse was headed. The problem before him now was how to actually find and capture Jesse Windchase up in that wilderness.

He had to admit that his heart really wasn't in this chase. He had had a long talk with Glen Richards at the C/6, and after hearing about the beating Todd had given Francine, his ex-wife, he had to admit that if he were Jesse, he probably would have done the same thing. But murder was murder, and this was Jesse who had done it before. The state probably should have hung him when they had the chance after what he had done to his wife, but the evidence just hadn't been quite substantial enough for a first-degree verdict. But if they had hung him then, Evan wouldn't be chasing all over the country now, and Todd Larson would still be alive. Although, given what he had heard, he had to admit that Jesse had probably done society a favor.

Evan was an honest and fair man. He did his job, and he did it well. His main sin was that of pride; he was painfully proud. As long as everyone played fair with him, he was pleasant to work with. But if he was crossed in any way, he could turn ugly in a second.

Thin and wiry, being horseback was second nature to him. In a way, this seemed to be almost a vacation for him- spending a few days in the hills, horseback. And he was a good tracker also, one of the best in fact. However, it hadn't taken him very many days to concede that he would need help in tracking the pair. He was good, but it seemed that Jesse was even better at covering his tracks.

Samuel Three Irons, a full-blooded Flathead tracker, had been called in to assist him. Of course, they had lost several days when Evan had to back track out of the mountains to pick up Samuel, but so far Samuel had been well worth the wait. The man could track a butterfly across the prairie, and by traveling lighter than the fugitives, they were now slowly gaining on them.

***

Francine was bone tired, and sick. She thought she might actually throw up her toenails, and was unable to hold even a cup of coffee down. Sammy was hovering continually, trying to lick her face every chance he got, knowing his mistress was distressed. Jesse was worried, not only because his love was ill, but also because her illness was costing them valuable time. But Francine obviously couldn't travel in this condition. It was morning, and she hadn't become ill until it was time to eat breakfast, right before settling down for the day.

"Jess, I'm so sorry! I don't know what's wrong! I must have the flu. Just let me rest for the day, and maybe by tonight I will feel better."

"Don't worry about it, Love. You go right ahead and rest. If you can't travel for a day or two, I'll find some place to hole up. You just get to feeling better." He kissed her softly on her forehead, and covered her with a blanket, trying to make her comfortable.

She slept soundly, and when she awoke late that afternoon, she felt wonderful. She couldn't understand why she had been so ill that morning, but decided it must have been a short-lived virus, and was just grateful she was okay now.

They packed up their gear again and set off in the cool late afternoon air, heading north and west as the terrain allowed. Traveling after dark as they had been doing slowed them down a little due to decreased visibility and poor footing with the evening dew, but it was still safer than trying to travel by day. They made fair time that night, covering nearly ten miles, and Jesse was grateful for the distance. Every mile behind them was a mile closer to Canada, and freedom.

The next morning, Francine was ill again. And again, after an hour's rest, she felt fine. In fact, she was ravenous by suppertime, and Jesse laughed as he watched her consuming copious amounts of food. He loved to see a woman with a healthy appetite, and he loved this one in particular.

"Francine, you are beautiful! And I love you."

"If I don't stop inhaling this food, you won't have anything more to do with me, with the gut I'm going to put on at this rate."

"Yeah, right. Like I could ever get tired of just looking at you, woman. I love you, remember that. And that means I love you whether you are fat or skinny, or old and gray... It doesn't matter to me, Francie. Just don't ever leave me."

"Fat chance of that, cowboy. You're stuck with me now, for better or worse, remember? That means even when I'm old and fat! But since I have a lifetime guarantee here, I think I'll have another biscuit, thank you very much. You're a great cook, Jess. For a man, I mean." And she smiled broadly at him.

***

Later that night, as they were horseback again, it came to her. The nausea and the voracious appetite. It had happened to her once before, and then there was Claire. Oh my goodness! It couldn't be, but it was-she was pregnant!

Her first thought was of pure joy, and then dismay as she remembered what had gone on just a short time ago. Whose baby was it? If it was Todd's child growing within her, how would she feel about it? What would Jesse feel? Would he accept her if the baby was Todd's, or would he leave her if she was carrying another man's child? Knowing Jesse as she did, she felt confident that he would stay with her, no matter what. But could he love this baby if it wasn't his? And her baby needed to be loved by both of them.

The more she thought about the situation, the less it mattered who the father was. This baby was hers, and she loved it with all of her heart and soul already. She hoped, desperately, that Jesse was the father, but in the end, it really didn't matter to her. She was the child's mother, and she would love it no matter who was the father. She wished she could figure out how far along the pregnancy was, but so much was a blur shortly before and after Todd's beating that she had no idea when she had cycled last. She could be more than two months pregnant, or only a few weeks.

She desperately wanted to tell Jesse about the baby, but was afraid that he might treat her differently if he knew the truth. And she knew that she was slowing him down now as it was in his dash for Canada. Oh, she kept up well enough, but the fact remained that if she were a man, he would probably be farther along on his journey. If nothing else, if she were a man, there would be no romantic interludes along the way, and she realized that in the end, even those few stolen moments might count for something. She decided that there was plenty of time to tell Jesse later, so kept her secret to herself, but vowed to conquer that dreaded morning sickness if it was the last thing she ever did. If it kept up, it wouldn't take Jesse long to figure out what was up!

The next morning, she opted for a piece of plain bread and a cup of water, telling Jesse she was just too tired to eat right then. It worked, and by taking slow, deep breaths, the nausea soon passed, and she was able to fall asleep. She made this a routine for several days, until finally the nausea relinquished its hold on her, and she was able to eat regularly again. Her appetite definitely increased, and Jesse enjoyed watching her shovel it in, never suspecting a thing.

Chapter 34

Storm clouds covered the moon, and thunder boomed periodically, echoing off the rocky walls of canyons as the summer storm moved across the mountains. Silver shards of twisted lightning flashed, beacons in the darkness, too bright to see clearly. A cold drizzle began, turning soon to steady rain, saturating the ground and the riders within minutes. Francine and Jesse had put their rain gear on, which gave them some protection, but the wind sapped the warmth from the cores of their bodies, weakened now by short rations and fatigue. Storms in the high country, whether in the summer or in the dead of winter, were always hard on man and beast. The only relief they offered were from the deer and horse flies during the day, and they had no benefit at night. The steady rain made the footing slippery and treacherous for the horses, and they made little progress. Their only consolation was the knowledge that if someone actually was tracking them, not only would they be slowed in this also, but the rain would help to obliterate any tracks.

Jesse was leading the way, picking a trail carefully across a steep shale slide. He was very uncomfortable about crossing these rocks, especially in the rain, but couldn't see any other way across the face of the hill. The small shale rock shifted dangerously under the horses' hooves, and sure-footed though they were, it was precarious going, with each hoof starting a miniature rockslide.

Suddenly, Julie's front foot hit a particularly loose section, and she panicked. Unable to get her footing, she began sliding, fighting to stay upright. Francine gave the mare her head, trying for all she was worth to help her regain her balance. The packhorses she was leading became panicked at the scene in front of them, so Francine quickly loosed the dally on the lead rope of the first horse and dropped it. If Julie went down, she didn't want the other two horses pulled over with her.

Suddenly, Francine knew Julie wasn't going to make it- she was going down.

"Jess!" The cry was frantic over the rain and thunder.

Jesse reined in and turned in the saddle just in time to see Julie sliding and tumbling down the face of the hill, her footing gone, Francine's yellow slicker a blur in the murky darkness as the mare tumbled over the rocks.

The horse slid feet first for a hundred feet or so, then hit a large boulder sticking out of the slide, and began to roll over. Francine was thrown clear, and tumbled next to her horse all the way to the bottom of the hill where a small stream had begun flowing from the rain.

Jesse dismounted on the uphill side, quickly hobbled his horse, and slid all the way down to where Francine lay unmoving, Sammy frantically licking her rain streaked face. Julie lay several feet away, kicking futilely, unable to get up.

"Francie?" he bent over her pale face, willing her to be alive.

"Jess?" Her voice came softly, the breath knocked out of her. "Jess- what?"

"Julie lost her footing and you both went down. You okay Darlin'? Anything broken do you think?"

She couldn't remember, but she moved all her extremities, and nothing seemed broken. She was sore and would be stiff as a board tomorrow, but she would live.

Suddenly, she was terrified. "Jess- the baby? Will I lose the baby?"

The blood left Jesse's face at her words. Baby! Francine was pregnant? And she hadn't told him?

"It's okay, Francie, you're okay."

"The baby, Jess, will I lose the baby?"

"No, Darlin', everything's fine. Let me help you up and see how you do."

Leaning heavily on him, Francine was able to slowly stand. Again she moved all extremities, and nothing was broken. Bruised, but okay. But she was terrified about the baby. She couldn't lose the baby! She wouldn't!

Jesse stared at her in the darkness, through the now pouring rain. She was pale, but seemed otherwise unharmed. A baby? He still couldn't quite take that one in, and they would have to do some talking, soon.

Holding her close, he whispered comforting words and soothing sounds into her ear until he felt the shaking leave her body.

"Will you be okay for a minute? I need to check on Julie."

"Yeah, I'm alright now. Go help her up; she must have a foot caught or something."

He left her standing, trembling ever so slightly, and went to check Julie. What he saw sickened him; she had obviously broken a hind leg in the fall. There was nothing to be done for the mare, and Jesse would have to put her down. He didn't dare use his pistol, afraid that even with the cover of the storm, a tracker might hear the shot. He had no idea where or how close his followers were, and he couldn't afford to take any chances.

Walking slowly, hindered by a heavy heart as well as by the treacherous footing of the shale rock, he made his way back to Francine.

"Francie, hon, Julie didn't make it. Her leg is broken. I'm sorry, Love, but I'm going to have to put her down. We can't leave her like that; she can't even get up. If I don't put her down, the wolves will get her, and you don't want that, I know."

"Oh Jess! NO! Not Julie! Oh God, not Julie!" Sobbing, she collapsed against his chest, and he held her tightly for a few moments as she sobbed her heart out over the loss of her horse. Then, slowly, she sniffled and backed away from him.

"You go do what you have to do, Jess. I'll be okay. Just go do it. I'm going back up with the other horses, and I'll meet you up there when you're done."

"You go on up. Can you make it or do you need me to help you?"

"I can make it. Just take care of my horse, please." She turned away and began the difficult climb back up the steep, slippery hill, Sammy at her heels. She loved all of her horses, but the big Appaloosa mare had been her favorite. She would feel her loss for a long time.

At the bottom of the hill, Jesse squatted in the rain next to the mare's head, stroking her softly. "Easy girl, easy there. I know it hurts. I'm going to make it better for you. I'm sorry, girl. I am so sorry." Julie sighed and relaxed under his stroking and soft tones, knowing this human would help her, somehow.

She never felt the knife at her throat, and Jesse continued stroking and caressing her with his hands and voice as she bled out and died. The last time he had felt this sick to his stomach was when he had found Francine on the cabin floor.

He continued stroking the horse for a moment after she was gone, then rose slowly and began removing the gear and packs she was carrying. Francine would need the saddle, probably for Mesa, and they would have to ditch one of the packsaddles. It was hard work, getting a saddle and packs off of a dead horse, but he finally accomplished the feat, and struggled with what he could carry up the hill to where Francine and the other horses were waiting.

It was a precarious place for a rest and conversation, but some decisions had to be made, and he couldn't carry the saddle and gear across that shale hillside. They would have to shed some supplies and saddle Mesa right here before they could go on.

Jesse walked up and put his arms around Francine from behind, cradling her to his chest. He knew she was hurting emotionally as well as physically, and he gave her what comfort he could.

"You okay?" He bent, and brushing her damp hair aside, gently kissed the nape of her neck.

"I'm all right. Thanks, Jess. Seems I have to tell you that a lot, don't I?"

"Don't worry about it. For you, anything, anytime." He gave her a gentle squeeze.

"Francine, it seems we have a problem here. Something is going to have to be left behind, you know? If you ride Mesa, and you certainly have to ride one of these horses, we have to ditch something. We're short a horse now. Any ideas?"

"You're the boss, Jess. What do you advise?"

"Well, we have food, dishes, pans, etc., clothing, blankets, and gold. Seems to me the most expendable item we have is the gold. We can't live up here without food, we can't cook too well without the pots, and we could freeze without the blankets if we don't make it out of the mountains by winter. We're a little short of shopping opportunities up here. I think the gold is of the least amount of use to us. But Francine, that's your wages for several year's worth of hard work. True, it doesn't take up a lot of room, but it is pretty heavy. I think we can keep probably half of it, but I think some will have to go, if you agree."

"What is it they say, Jess? It's only money? Well, they're right. It *is* only money. And you can't eat gold. I'm with you. Throw out whatever you need to. As long as I have you, I really don't give a damn about anything else. Do whatever you have to do."

They stripped Mesa's packsaddle together, and put Francine's saddle on in its place. Trying to make as much space as possible with their limited resources, Jesse began trying to lighten the load. He decided that any extra pans or pots could go, so kept only one saucepan. The frying pan would go. The coffee can for making camp coffee went. He couldn't throw out the coffee itself, however. That would have been like throwing Francine out- well, not quite that bad, but almost! Some clothing was set aside to be tossed. He didn't dare throw out any food; they had little enough as it was and would soon have to be living on wild game if he could snare it along the way.

In the end, he had a neat little pile of items that he felt were non-essential, but the question remained-what to do with it? And the gold. He figured they could keep about half of it by tucking the coins in loops and folds of the canvas covering the packs. But on this hillside, they couldn't even bury anything. They would just have to toss things, and leave them. The trackers were going to find the dead horse anyway, he supposed, so he guessed it didn't really matter if they found the supplies they tossed. But he didn't want anyone to have Francine's hard-earned gold.

Smiling at her in the dark, he held both hands out full of gold coins. "Shall we?"

"Go for it. Let's see who can throw the farthest, what do you say?"

"Aw, Francine, no contest. I'm the man here, remember? You haven't got a prayer!"

"Give it your best, cowboy! Beat this!" And she threw a coin as high and as far as she could.

Jesse laughed out loud. He couldn't believe he was throwing gold away like this! He gave a coin his best throw.

They took turns several times, then got serious about it, and just threw the coins as fast, hard, and far as they were able. When it was gone, she turned to Jesse, grabbed him around the waist, and kissed him hard.

"I love you, Jesse Windchase. Now let's head for Canada before I change my mind!"

He kissed her back soundly, loving her for her courage, then held Mesa while she mounted safely.

"Be careful, Darlin'." He didn't have to say that, he knew, but he couldn't help himself. It was automatic. And he had, after all, nearly lost her a second time, tonight, here on this blasted hill. What had he gotten her into?

Chapter 35

Evan and Samuel found Julie three days later. They had lost the trail after the storm, the tracks having been washed away by the rain, but by eyeballing the terrain, they were able to make pretty good guesses which way Jesse and Francine were traveling.

Samuel spotted the horse first. They were riding ever so carefully across the shale face of the hill, when he thought he saw something flashing in the sunlight. Trying to follow the shine, his eyes roamed over the horse. Leaving his mount with Evan, he slid his way down the slope to where Julie lay, and whistled softly under his breath. What a shame, a big, beautiful animal like that. He took in the whole scene at a glance; the broken leg, the throat neatly slit. Yup, just a damn shame. But now they were down one horse, and the supplies that horse had carried.

The tracker shaded his eyes with his hand, and again noticed something shining in the sun. Walking toward whatever it, he soon discovered a solid gold coin. "What the he…?" What was a gold coin doing out here in the Bob Marshall?

He turned and began his trek back up the hill when he spotted another one.

"Mr. Smazick, there's gold coins out here! Come see for yourself!"

"Leave them Samuel. We're after people, not gold, remember? Let's go!"

But Samuel had the fever instantly, and wasn't about to go anywhere until he had found all the coins he could. Evan could sit up there and fume, or he could hobble his horse and come down here with him and find some gold, it was his choice. But Samuel wasn't about to walk away from a possible fortune for any man, and was soon on his hands and knees, digging through the rock for the coins that hid impishly there.

Evan made his choice; he sat, waited, and fumed.

***

Jesse and Francine gained about four hours on their pursuers that afternoon.

Jesse hadn't brought up the subject of the baby for another day. They couldn't talk during the storm, while they were trying to move and make time, and when they stopped at daybreak to rest Francine was in no shape to talk about anything. She was tired, sore, and miserable over the loss of her horse, and definitely not in a talking mood. He waited until after they had slept, and he had a fire going for supper before he broached the subject to her.

"Francie?"

"What?"

"I want to know about the baby."

"Yes. I thought you might."

"Are you pregnant, for sure?"

"Yup. I sure am."

Jesse let out a whoop, grabbed his woman, and danced around with her tightly in his arms hollering "Halleluiah! I'm gonn'a be a father! Can you beat that! A father!" Then he stopped whirling her around to kiss her soundly.

As he kissed her, his passion rose again. He hadn't known it was possible to love her more than he already did, but now it overwhelmed him once more, in an even different way. And he wanted her again, right here, right now. His kisses became more demanding, his hands roaming over her body suggestively, until she pushed him away.

"Jesse, don't. We have to talk."

"It won't hurt the baby, will it? What's wrong?"

"No, it won't hurt the baby at all. But Jess, I have to tell you…" She paused to take a deep breath, holding him at arm's length away from her.

"Jess, the baby might be Todd's. You know? It might not be yours. I'm sorry to have to tell you that Jess, but that's how it is. You might not be the father."

"Oh Darlin,' I'm the father all right. Don't you have any doubt about that! And frankly, I wouldn't care if Todd *was* the father, because he's not here, and I am. I'm the daddy, and that's the end of it!"

"But Jesse, think! It could be Todd's! How are you really going to feel about possibly raising Todd's child? Can you do it? Can you love this baby I'm carrying no matter who the father is?"

"Francine, come here, Love. Come here." He gathered her close once more, his cheek against her hair, and feathered light kisses wherever his lips touched her.

"Francie, trust me on this. Todd is not the father. After what he did to you, there's no way you could have been pregnant. Your body could not have sustained a pregnancy at that time. You were so nearly dead, that body of yours had all it could do to keep YOU alive, let alone nurture a baby. No way."

"But, Jess, I haven't cycled since Todd. It could be him."

"Francine, you almost died. Nothing was working right then, or for a while afterward. You and I are going to have a baby, Francine. A baby! I'm so excited I can't stand it! I just wish we were somewhere, anywhere else but here, on the run. I'm so very sorry about that. But damn! A baby! Is it a boy or a girl?" Immediately he realized what a dumb question that had been, when he saw her stifling a laugh.

"Oh, Jesse, I do love you so!" And it was her turn to kiss him.

When they were sated, they ate, then curled up in each other's arms to spend the day sleeping. Jesse was instantly asleep, tired from the exertions of the day and the emotional news. Francine lay awake for a time, contemplating what he had said about his paternity. Could he be right? Would it be nearly impossible for this baby to be Todd's?

In the end, it didn't really matter after all. Jesse loved her, and he obviously loved this baby she was carrying. And Jesse would be the father, regardless. She smiled and drifted off.

Sometime during the afternoon, Jesse woke, aroused again. He couldn't help it, and he woke her in his desire, desperate to possess her once more. He couldn't seem to get enough of her, and while he had seemed to be tireless before, now he was insatiable. He was alive, in the wilderness, with the love of his life, and he was going to be a father. If he weren't a hunted man, life would be just about perfect.

Francine, recognizing his need, pulled his face to hers, kissed him soundly, then began stroking and loving the father of her baby.

***

Jess was awakened during the day several times by the helicopters, and he realized that the authorities must be closing in. Somehow, they had to increase their lead, but how to do it? They were traveling as fast as they dared already. And the horses were starting to show the frantic pace they had been keeping; the three sacks of oats that had been packed when they began their trek were long gone now. Jesse had reset several lost shoes during the past month on various horses, and he was running low on shoes. One of the sorrel geldings had much smaller feet, and Jesse had no more shoes in his size. If he lost another shoe, he would go lame and they would be forced to leave him.

He considered lightening their packs, if it were possible, and then discarded the idea. If they absolutely were forced to throw some of their supplies out, then of course they would. But they had packed only what they considered to be essentials in the first place, and when Julie died, they had discarded everything they thought they could get by without at that time. Probably the bulkiest items were clothing, but he certainly didn't want to discard any of that. Matches, ammunition, his guns, Sammy's dog food (which was running dangerously low now), flour, sugar, coffee, the ever-essential cooking pot; he couldn't think of a single thing he could afford to discard.

He worried about Francine, in her condition. He didn't really know much about pregnant women; his wife had never wanted any children. But he knew this constant, frantic, hard pace couldn't be good for his wife or the baby she was carrying. Francine was holding up well, but she was tiring. He noticed that she was sleeping harder and longer whenever she had the opportunity. He was so very proud of her! And he was so happy at the prospect of being a father, of having the love they shared becoming so much a living part of themselves.

Jesse had hoped to make the Canadian border sometime in August, but now he had to rethink his plans. If the helicopters were hovering more frequently in this area, even though they had not been spotted, their presence meant that someone knew roughly where they were. And if they knew where they were, they wouldn't have too much difficulty projecting their line of travel and objective. That meant Jesse had only one choice, if he meant to stay free–they would have to reverse direction, circle around, and head south for a while in order to either completely lose their trackers or at least confuse them and perhaps gain some more time. He didn't know how he would tell Francine what he was planning. It meant that Canada was going to be probably another month away at the earliest, and winter would be close on their heels. And Francine would be at least four months pregnant by then. He sighed deeply, worry continuing to crease his brow. There was no alternative. They would have to head south.

***

When Francine awoke that afternoon, she could tell at once that Jesse was troubled. She had been sleeping so soundly she never heard the three helicopters that floated overhead during the heat of the day; she had no idea how close the police were to finding and apprehending them.

"Jesse, love, what's wrong?" She came up behind him as he stirred up the fire for their dinner, wrapping her arms lovingly around his upper torso, kissing the back of his neck.

"Francie, we have a problem," he began.

Francine laughed at this pronouncement, a light, almost musical laugh. Sammy's ears perked up at the unfamiliar sound coming from his mistress, and he began jumping around like a puppy with the joy of it. "Jess, please, can't you come up with something I don't already know? Were you trying to be funny, or did it happen naturally?" By now she was laughing so hard the tears were streaming from both eyes, and she was unable to stop. They had a problem! The understatement of the year! She grabbed Sammy and hugged him close in a fond embrace.

"Francine, it isn't funny. We really have a problem. 'Another' problem. And trust me, there is no humor in it at all."

"Oh, Jess, what on earth could be worse than the problems we already have? Unless the cops are just over the next hill with their rifles pointed, ready to fire. Relax, Cowboy!" And she continued laughing, trying valiantly to stop before Jesse got angry with her.

"Well, woman, see how this tickles your funny bone." He rose to his feet, then turned to face her. "We have to turn around and head south, and forget Canada for a while."

The laughter died on her lips. South? Was he joking?

"Jess, no! Why in heaven's name would we head south? Canada is north, for goodness sakes. Have you lost your mind?" She stared at him in bewilderment.

"No, Francie, I haven't. They're close. Too close. There were three helicopters that flew over us this afternoon while you were sleeping, and that means they know at least the general area we're in. We have to lose them, somehow, if we can. And the only way I can think of to do that is to head the opposite direction from where they think we are going, which means, we go south. It also means probably another month on the trail. Can you handle it, Darlin'?"

"Oh Jess! Much as I hate it, I'll handle it, don't worry. Me and Junior here will be just fine. Hey, cowboy, as long as I'm with you, that's all that matters, and we both know what happens if they catch up to us, so lead on. I trust your judgment."

"I haven't the foggiest idea how they ever figured we were here in the Bob Marshall. Just can't figure it." He began to pace softly as he thought out loud. "But obviously, they know- three helicopters a day doesn't add up to just a guess. They're right on our tail- just wish I knew for sure how close they really are. Anyway, we have to figure they're nearly right around the bend, and we can't afford to let up any. If anything, Francie, we're going to have to travel longer and sleep less. I'm sure whoever is tracking us is traveling lighter than we are, and therefore making better time. So, either we lighten up, which I don't see how we can, or we travel longer. We can't travel much faster or we're gonn'a end up on foot. These horses are getting plumb worn out already. I just hope they make it. And poor old Sammy must have footpads like shoe leather by now, with all the miles that fellow has put on." He reached down and fondly scratched Sammy's ears as he spoke.

When they broke camp that evening, they reined their horses due east, and after about five hours of hard riding, turned south.

Chapter 36

Samuel and Evan came across one of their deserted campsites two days later. It amazed both men that five horses, a dog, and two humans could camp for hours and leave so little behind to show they were ever there. Jesse was adept at burying waste and covering old fires; he even scattered the horse's manure so there were no telltale piles. But Samuel was nothing if not a tracker, and it was the shoe prints of the horses that led him to the spot. He had actually stumbled across it by accident. He knew which way the fugitives were heading, but had not really come across any tracks since finding the dead horse. He would follow the trail for a few miles, then lose it again either in thick brush or when Jesse and Francine crossed a creek and came out the other side either upstream or downstream, depending on Jesse's whim.

But it was obvious now, the pair was for sure heading north, and from the remains of the camp, they were only about two days ride ahead.

Samuel smiled and looked at Evan. "We got'em, boss. Not far now."

Evan shaded his eyes with his hand, surveying the mountainous terrain before him. Personally, he had thought to apprehend the pair long before now, and was surprised it had taken this long to even find a camp. He had been trailing them for weeks, and he was getting weary. He missed his wife and kids. He missed a hot bath and a shave, and a good steak. They had ample supplies, with two pack mules, but he was getting pretty tired of camp food.

He stood, pondering, for a moment.

"You know, Samuel, sometimes I don't much like my job. I know Jesse killed that cowboy, but from what I hear, the man deserved everything he got. Murder is still murder, but the thought of locking up a man that can survive in the wilderness like this man can, well, obviously he belongs outside. It will probably kill him if he gets life in prison."

Samuel only grunted in response. He was good at his job, and he thought he understood his quarry; the man would do anything he could to stay out of jail. Anything, rather than give up the freedom of the wilderness. He was alive out here, with the Montana sky and the mountain wind that sang a steady if unknown song to all that would listen. Personally, he didn't much care one way or the other about Jesse Windchase. He understood the man, and his job was to track and find him. What happened after that was up to the law. His job ended when Jesse was caught.

"Let's go, Samuel. What is it the cowboys say? We're burn'in daylight!"

***

Jesse and Francine circled carefully that night, wary of encountering their pursuers as they backtracked. Jesse knew he would have to go probably ten miles south, at least, to throw them off. If he could just get them trailing him south, once he felt they were certain he wasn't headed for Canada, he could turn and with his wife, make a straight run north.

He left a clear trail for a while. Staying out of the trees, carefully leaving prints in dirt, breaking branches from bushes as they passed through. He couldn't be too obvious, or the tracker would suspect, but he wanted to make certain they were followed, at least for several miles.

Heading downhill for the most part, they made their way through the now cold Montana night. The temperatures hovered in the mid-thirties every night, all summer long in the high country, but at least the flies abated after dark, and riding was pleasant. After four nights of hard riding, they hit the North Fork of the Sun River, and Jesse breathed a small sigh of relief.

"Francine, now we start to give them a run for their money. We stay in the water for as long as we can. It will be slow going, but we're going to stay in the river for as long as possible before we come out and leave any tracks. We want them to have to look for us, hard. We might have to carry Sammy, though. I don't know if he can take that much water; he would probably have to swim quite a little. We can take turns carrying him, okay?"

"Whatever you say, Jess. I'm with you, you know that." Francine gazed lovingly at him. "Jess, we are going to make it, aren't we?" The question was uttered softly. The immensity of their journey was finally becoming a reality to her. What had looked merely interesting on paper was far different in reality. Her pregnancy was taking more out of her than she had expected, and each day her weariness seemed to increase.

"Francine, I promise you, we will make it. Don't worry, now, just try to hang in there, and think about a new life in Canada with a baby. Hell, maybe we can have about five of the little rascals, what do you think about that? Too many for you?"

"Jesse, I can't imagine anything more wonderful than having your children. As many as you want- well, at least a couple. But I really would like to finish this pregnancy first, before we plan on any more, okay? I think one at a time is enough!"

"Then let's go, woman. Got to get you to Canada! Can't be having babies out here on the run like this." He leaned across his horse to give her a big kiss, smiled broadly at her, and turned his horse into the river.

Three hours later, they came out of the river onto a bank covered with small rocks. They might chip a rock or two, but there would be no tracks. Dismounting, Jesse dug out some hardtack from the packs, and they chewed hungrily. Sammy had the luxury of a handful of dry dog food; the horses would have to wait. Blowing hard, they hung their heads from the past exertion; they were tired. Walking through the river was much more strenuous than traveling over any kind of dry ground. They were unsure of their footing, and water made the going slower and harder.

Needing to make time and distance, Jesse decided to risk the helicopters, and continued traveling the following morning. They were on the alert at all times for the sound of whirring blades, but to their good fortune, heard none all morning, and they decided the search must still be to the north.

He called a halt around two o'clock, and making their way inland to a small meadow dotted with numerous evergreens, set up camp for the afternoon.

"I'm sorry, Francine, but we are only stopping for a few hours. No fire this time, just the hardtack again- can you get by with that? The horses desperately need the rest and food, and we really can't afford to stop at all. I know this will be an awfully short nap for you, when you need a good, sound sleep, but we just can't stop for any longer."

Francine was so tired she could hardly stand, but she was nothing if not game. Besides, what choice did they have? If they wanted to avoid capture, they would have to do whatever it took, and it looked like at least for now, they would be a little short of rest.

"I'll be alright, Jesse. Don't worry about me."

"I do worry, but I just don't think I have any choice. We have to lead them this way, and we have to gain on them or we aren't going to make it." He embraced her tenderly, feeling her relax against him.

"Francine, thank you for loving me. My heart is so full at times with the thought of it that I am unable to express all that I feel. It is truly a miracle for me. I love you."

She smiled up at him, and kissed his cheek tenderly. A full beard now covered his rugged face, and she thought he looked quite striking in it. His beard was black and streaked with gray, complimenting his half white eyebrow and eyelashes.

They unpacked and unsaddled the horses, hobbled them in the denser patches of grass under the trees, curled up together with Sammy, and were instantly asleep.

Jesse woke her four hours later, and within twenty minutes they were back in the river, heading south once more.

Chapter 37

They followed the river in this manner for three days, taking turns carrying Sammy at times when the water was too deep, sleeping for only a few hours at a time, and eating only cold food until they were within a couple of miles of Gibson Dam; it was time to head west and then north again.

Coming out of the river for the last time, they rested the horses on the bank for a short while, thankful to be out of the water. Sammy fell on his side with exhaustion and was instantly asleep. At first he had really enjoyed the novelty of the journey through the high country, but now, like the horses and his masters, he was exhausted.

But it seemed Jesse's plan had worked; they had neither seen nor heard a helicopter for the past two days. They had gained some time, but at great expense; the horses were nearly spent, and would need an extended rest very soon. Jesse just hoped he had earned them a big enough lead to give it to them.

They traveled west for several hours, and when daybreak found them, they had secured a campsite that was lush, but very secluded. A small spring trickled out from a clump of rabbit brush, and huge boulders formed an almost natural enclosure. It was secure, and private.

Jesse had a good fire going in short order, and they were soon feasting on fried bread, the last of the bacon, the last can of peaches, and a fabulous cup of strong coffee.

"Ah," Jesse sighed after the first sip, "Nectar of the gods! I don't mind not sleeping, but I sure do mind not having my coffee!" He savored the aroma and the flavor of the hot drink. "I think we can spend at least a day here, Darlin', so you can get a really good rest for a change. The horses are about played out, and if they don't get at least one whole day off, we'll for sure be walking into Canada on our own sore feet."

"Can we afford to stop, though, Jess? Is it safe?" Francine was exhausted, and desperate for sleep and rest, but she was terrified of being caught at the same time.

"I think we've given them the slip, at least for now. No helicopters mean they are still looking north for us. Whoever is tracking us is good, and they will eventually be on our trail again, but I think by pushing as we did, we can take the time to rest now. Besides, like I said, we really don't have any choice in the matter; we have to rest. You have to rest."

Francine ran over to him and gave him a big bear hug. "Oh, thank you, thank you, thank you! I am so tired I could sleep for a week!" At the look he shot her, she quickly reassured him. "I'm okay, Jesse, I really am, but I *am* tired. We all are, I know. Hey, last one to sleep is a rotten egg!"

Laying out their ground sheets, with their blankets on top, they collapsed in each other's arms, tumbling and laughing. Jesse's reaction to this close physical contact with his wife was instantaneous; he couldn't help himself. Whenever he got this close to Francine, he wanted her, and it seemed that conditions and energy had nothing to do with it.

Francine felt his hardness against her, and groaned inwardly. She was so tired! But she loved him, and her hands went immediately to his belt.

"Francie, no, we don't have to do this. You're tired, exhausted in fact. And I'm tired. I guess some parts of my body just haven't gotten the message yet. I can wait, Hon, let's just go to sleep."

"Jess, can you? Do it, I mean?"

He laughed at her naivety. "Francine, I can always do it! Unfortunately, at times. But you're tired. Later, love."

She smiled lovingly at him again, and her hands continued their mission. Then she rolled on top of him, and kissed him deeply, sensuously, and they became lost once more in each other.

***

They camped in that spot for two days, sleeping, eating, making love, and recouping their strength. They had both lost weight, along with the horses and Sammy from the grueling pace and lack of regular meals. Heating spring water in the cooking pot, they were able to enjoy at least a semblance of a hot shower by pouring the warm water over themselves after soaping thoroughly. Francine couldn't remember any real shower feeling any more refreshing to her. Jesse was able to snare two rabbits and a porcupine, and they feasted on fresh meat. Sammy was ecstatic! The horses seemed to spend as much time sleeping as eating, and Sammy slept nearly all the time. The evening of the third day, they packed up and headed northwest once more, deeper into the wilderness.

***

Evan and Samuel had followed the trail east and then south until they hit the river, when suddenly the trail vanished. Samuel crossed the river and began searching for sign first on the east bank, and then backtracked to search below his starting point. Evan did the same on the west side of the river, with no luck. It was as if Jesse and Francine had vanished from the face of the earth. It was obvious the pair had traveled in the river itself for some time, but the question was, had they gone north or south?

Logic told both men that if Jesse was trying to get to Canada, he would head north. Samuel, however, being the tracker that he was and a full-blooded Flathead, had his doubts. What would he do if he were in Jesse's place? He pondered for a while, then decided that if he were Jesse, he would head south, trying to throw his pursuers off the trail. The man was smart, no doubt about it. Yup, that's what he would do all right; he'd go south in the river.

Evan decided that the pair had headed north, and said as much to his tracker.

"We'll head north, Samuel. You take the east side of the river, and I'll take the west. They had to come out of it someplace, and we'll find it. Okay? Let's go."

"Boss, I don't think so; I think they went south to try to throw us off the trail. I think they went south in the river for a very long way, and now they will circle back and head north and west again. If I were him, that's what I would do, for sure."

"But he has a woman with him, so I disagree with you Samuel. He isn't going to keep that woman out in the wilderness any longer than he has to, and that means getting to Canada the fastest way he can. Which means he went north."

Samuel merely shrugged. He got paid by the day, so it was only more money in his pocket. They could travel north for a week, and he was certain they would never run across Jesse's trail; the man had gone south, he was sure of it. But Evan was the boss, and he could take the responsibility for the wrong decision.

The two men traveled the banks of the Sun River for two days before Evan conceded defeat. He was angry, and where before the chase had been only a job to him, now it had become personal. It was as if Jesse had deliberately set out to make a fool of him, and that was one thing Evan couldn't tolerate. Any sympathy he had felt for the fugitive vanished. Oh, he would get Jesse Windchase, all right. And now he didn't much care whether he was brought in alive or dead. The Indian was no longer a man to him; he was prey.

They headed back downstream, searching for the tracks that would betray where the fugitives had exited the river; it took them another four days.

Jesse and Francine had gained the time they so desperately needed; the ruse had worked. Unfortunately, where before they had an impartial tracker after them, now that tracker was angry, and an angry man travels faster and harder with the added provocation.

***

Two days after breaking camp, Francine called Jesse to pull up.

"Jess, that little sorrel gelding is lame. We need to check him out."

A quick inspection revealed the animal had lost a front shoe, and was now limping painfully.

Jesse bowed his head, sorrowful at the loss of another good horse. But there was nothing for it; the pack animal would have to be turned loose. He would never make the trip barefoot like that. If it had been a hind shoe, he might possibly have been able to hang in there, but a horse carries most of its weight on the forehand. Without a shoe, especially carrying a heavy pack, there was just no hope.

"Jess, what is it? A rock?"

"No, Francie, he threw a shoe somewhere back there. He's pretty lame now, and even if he had enough hoof left to tack another shoe onto, I don't have another one in his size. He's the one with the little feet."

"What will we do?" But she knew, deep inside, what they had to do; either put the horse down, or just turn him loose. Either way, they were now going to have to ditch some more supplies.

"Well, we either take him out in the forest and put him down, and hope no one finds him, or we turn him loose. Either way, I think whoever is after us will find him. But he can't keep up, and he can't carry anything from now on. What's your vote Darlin'?"

"Oh Jess, we can't put him down. We just can't! It would be like putting Sammy down! We should just turn him loose." She had dismounted Mesa and walked over to the gelding, cradling the horses' fine boned-head in her hands. Tears filled her eyes at the thought of leaving the animal, which had so gamely traveled with them this far.

"Damn! If I had just packed even one more shoe in his size! I have two more in the aught size, but no double aughts. I'm not sure he has enough foot left to tack a shoe onto anyway though." He sighed deeply. "Oh well, nothing for it. Let's get his pack off and see what we can do without from now on."

There wasn't anything they could do without. They were really down to bare necessities as it was. After careful deliberation, they decided to pitch most of the clothes. They took up the most space, and if they kept the warmest coats and shirts, they would have protection from the coming winter; they could buy more clothes in Canada when they got there. They couldn't spare any of the blankets or what flour and foodstuffs they had left, and they for sure couldn't afford to pitch any of the guns or ammunition. If worse came to worse, the guns and the shells would be the last things to go.

Francine stayed with the remaining four horses, while Jesse led the gelding deep into the woods. He then unpacked the horse, and hid the packsaddle, halter, and bundles of clothing as best he could under brush and rocks. Patting the gelding fondly on the neck, he turned him loose and walked back to where Francine waited sadly for him. The little horse wasn't about to be left behind however, and soon followed, limping badly.

When they mounted and set off again, the gelding tried valiantly to keep up for the next couple of miles, but gradually hunger and pain slowed him, and then he stopped altogether. He whinnied piteously several times as his friends continued down the trail, and then fell silent as his need for grass took over and he settled down to graze contentedly.

Francine shed a few tears, but soon got herself under control. Jesse's jaw was set, and for the next hour he set his face resolutely ahead, willing them to make it to Canada and safety.

They were down to only two saddle horses and two packhorses now. Supplies were only bare necessities; they couldn't afford to lose any more.

***

Sammy was out of dog food. He would have to start sharing the people food, and when Jesse had the time and luck, whatever rabbits could be snared. He didn't dare shoot any game; not knowing for sure where his trackers were, he couldn't take a chance on them possibly hearing a gun shot. But Sammy had to eat, and so did they. With only flour, sugar, and salt left, they would have to be depending on what they could find in the woods, and whatever game Jesse could snare. And it was getting colder every day.

Chapter 38

Evan and Samuel found their camp in the rocks, Evan whistling softly to himself at the genius of the place. It was a great hideout; the perfect campsite with food, shelter, water, and grass.

"How old, Samuel?" He wanted to know, as close as possible, how far ahead their quarry was.

Samuel checked the signs carefully, then deduced as best he could how old the camp was.

"Two days, maybe three, boss. Looks like they were here for a couple of days, at least. They got a good rest, and cooked themselves some fresh meat."

"If we really push, we should catch up to them in a day or two then, right?"

"Should. If they don't take to any more rivers!" He smiled to himself, understanding Evan's embarrassment over the river incident. They would have caught the pair already if Evan hadn't decided to be the "big white man" of the group. Arrogance and stupidity. Samuel was used to the attitude, though. It might be the '70's, but some things didn't seem to change, and the low esteem with which most whites held Indians was one of them. But again, he got paid by the day, so he was just making more money with each mistake Evan made. He would like to be home for the winter, though, so he hoped this wouldn't take too much longer. They rested for a few hours, allowing their animals to rest and eat, napped themselves, and then set out on the trail again. Evan stepped up the pace, determined to narrow Jesse's lead.

***

It was September, and the Aspen had turned their leaves from soft summer green to violent burnished gold. Frost covered the ground each morning, and fall was unmistakable even without the telltale colors of the leaves. Indian paintbrush had donned its vivid red coloring, and deer now sported their thicker winter coats. The flies suddenly vanished, the misery they had caused the poor horses daily finally over. Mountain brome grass was now brown, cured for the winter, dried heads waving in the gentle evening breezes. Snow had already fallen on the mountaintops, sometimes settling below the tree line on the waiting pines with a fine dusting of white powder.

Francine's pregnancy was showing now when she removed her jacket. She was about four months along, and the baby had been moving for about a week. At first, Francine hadn't been sure what she was feeling, since it had been so long since she had felt the light fluttering sensation of movement. There was nothing quite like it, however, and Francine relished those private moments when her baby became more real to her. She wanted to share the joy with Jesse, but was afraid of the added worry it might cause him; if the baby became more real to her with its movement, it would probably do the same for Jesse. She knew he was worried enough as it was, with her being pregnant, the law after them, and winter about to set in. Unwilling to add to his concerns, she decided to wait to share this with Jesse until he could place his hand on her stomach and feel the movement for himself. When the baby was bigger, she would show him, but for now, the joy was to be hers, alone.

***

The trackers didn't make quite the progress they had anticipated that day, but they couldn't be far behind now. The tracks Samuel was following were no more than a few hours old. Tomorrow, the chase should be over. They made camp early, intending to get an early start, and possibly wind this whole thing up by the next afternoon.

***

Jesse had just awoken, and was lying quietly, watching Francine. Lord, but he loved this woman. And she obviously loved him a great deal in return. He couldn't imagine any other female willingly following a man through the Bob Marshall, pregnant, in the fall. She was something else, all right, and he was proud. She was so very much more than he deserved or ever hoped to find. And she was carrying his baby! Watching her sleep, he again became aroused. Damn! He wished sometimes he could just shut things down. But he couldn't seem to get enough of her no matter how often he either chastised or indulged himself. She must think he was just a sex maniac, but he couldn't help himself or his reaction to her. Francine never refused him. He was so blessed! He leaned over her, kissing her eyelids softly.

"Francine, wake up Love."

Coming slowly back to reality, Francine slowly raised her arms over her head and stretched. The action brought her shirt tight against her breasts, now enlarged with her pregnancy, and Jesse couldn't help staring. Francine laughed to herself as she watched him–he was so transparent! It was obvious he wanted her yet again, and the knowledge that he did was enough to ignite her desire for him in return. *"We're just like a couple of teenagers, for heaven's sake!"* she thought whimsically. *"A couple of stupid teenagers."*

Jesse was slowly unbuttoning her shirt when he heard the horse's piercing scream of pure terror. Jumping to his feet, he grabbed the loaded rifle he kept by his side and ran for the horses, terrified of what he might find. Sammy tore ahead of him, barking crazily.

***

A mountain lion was clinging to the haunches of the bay gelding, pulling him down with the sheer weight of his body. A full- grown male, the lion had the advantage; the poor horse was hobbled and unable to run.

Jesse took in the scene before him, aimed, and fired all at the same time. There wasn't time to think, only to act. A bullet slammed into the lion's chest, and the animal sank to his feet, raking the horse all the way from his loins to his hocks. Levering the 30-06, Jesse fired another shot, this time hitting him in the head, and the lion was dead.

Francine ran up behind him just in time to see the lion fall to its side, blood trickling from the wounds. The gelding was standing with his head down, in agony, deep gashes torn in his hindquarters. The horse was done for. If this had happened down at the ranch, it might have been possible to save him, but out here, there was no hope. He would have to be put down, immediately.

Jesse and Francine were both sick. Putting a horse down was right up there with shooting your dog, and they hated it. But there was no choice, it had to be done. Walking over to the injured animal, Jesse talked softly to him, stroking him, then while Francine held her fist to her mouth, he stepped back and shot the horse cleanly between the eyes. It was over in seconds.

Walking back to Francine, Jesse gathered her close and held her tightly as she cried for the horse that had come so far with them. She sobbed softly for several minutes before Jesse held her away from him. Wiping her tears with the back of his rough hands, he wasn't sure how to tell her what must be said.

"Francine, it looks like things have to change a little, now. Those shots, well, I don't know how close the trackers are, but they might have heard them. We have to leave, right away, and I don't think we can take anything but the guns and ammo with us. We have to travel as light and as fast as we can. We'll have to leave your other mare, too. She'll just slow us down. No packs, only what we can carry on our saddle horses. The way I figure it, we have a good ten days ride ahead of us, and it isn't going to be fun. We're heading as straight as we can for the border, now. Are you up for it? We can't even stop to fool around anymore!"

Sniffling, she gazed up at him. Leave everything? Her horse?

"I want to bring Janie."

"We can't, darlin', she'll slow us down too much. We just can't take the chance."

"We can just lead her, can't we? If she's not carrying a pack, she can for sure keep up with us. What difference can that make?"

He thought about it for a moment, and then relented. "Okay. You can bring her along, but without a pack. A halter and lead rope only. We have to really make some time, now. If they heard those shots they could have nearly pinpointed where we are. Let's saddle up and head out."

They didn't bother trying to hide the packsaddle and supplies; with a dead horse and lion lying there, it was pointless. Saddling their horses, they set out, Francine leading her sorrel Appaloosa mare on a loose rope, Sammy in his usual place behind Mesa's hocks. They had two rabbits hanging from Jesse's pommel, snared earlier that afternoon. In the cooler weather, they should keep for a day, so they had food for at least that long.

Jesse turned his face to the north, and they headed straight for Canada.

***

Samuel and Evan were giving their horses a breather when the first two shots echoed loudly through the forest. Their heads snapped up in unison, facing west, trying to pinpoint the origin of the shot.

"What the...?" Evan was startled. Why would Jesse risk being discovered by shooting off his rifle? It didn't make any sense, except for two possibilities; either Jesse didn't have any idea how close they were, or he had run into some big trouble up ahead. He decided it must be trouble, because Jesse wasn't stupid enough to fire a rifle at the risk of being detected unless it was absolutely necessary. He wondered even as he kicked his horse into a trot as the third shot rang out what could possibly have made Jesse shoot.

Samuel, leading the two pack mules, was having difficulty keeping up, and Evan was first on the scene by several minutes. He was sickened at what lay before him. Shaking his head sadly, he dismounted and bent to inspect the lion carcass. He was a big male, probably about four years old, shot once through the chest and once cleanly through the head. The gelding lay directly in front of him, shot neatly between the eyes. Well, now he knew why Jesse had risked firing the rifle; he would have done the same thing rather than watch a horse suffer like that.

Samuel rode up quietly, and dismounting, took in the picture etched in death before him. He too was sickened by what lay before him.

Near the horse lay its packsaddle, and supplies, and over near another tree was another packsaddle, still laden with supplies.

"Boss, they took off with two saddle horses and leading a third, but they left the packs and supplies. They're gonn'a try to really make time, now, traveling light. There's no way we're gonn'a be able to even keep up with them, let alone catch them while we're leading two mules. Horses are faster than mules even without packs, and we haven't got a prayer. Any suggestions now?" He looked around him and shook his head. It would be a shame if the quarry managed to get away from him after all this time. A dirty shame.

Evan was furious. He wasn't going to lose this pair, no way. Not after coming this far. But how to catch up with them now? He thought for a moment, and then made his decision. He didn't much like it, but didn't see that he had any choice in the matter.

"Samuel, I'm going to send you on ahead, without a mule. You follow them and leave me a decent trail, and I'll come along behind with the mules. We're going to need these mules and all they're carrying to make it out of here after we catch up with them, so we can't leave them. Can you do that?"

"Sure, I can do that easy. But what do I do with them when I catch up to them, Mr. Smazick? Just wait for you, or head back, or what?"

"Well, Samuel," he said as he bent to draw in the dirt with his finger, contemplating what he was about to say next. "You find them, and you handcuff them both; I want to have a little talk with Jesse Windchase. He's given us quite a run up here, and he's going to pay for that. But I don't intend to bring him out. I have a feeling that would be impossible; he won't allow that. So, because I don't intend to end up as wolf fodder up here in the Bob, we're going to take care of him first. Her too, if it comes to that. I think we can come up with a believable enough story about what went wrong, and it shouldn't be a problem. But we're bringing bodies out, Samuel, if we bring anything at all. Not people. I've had enough, and I think two murders on Jesse's slate more than warrants the verdict, even if the victims deserved what they got. You got any problems with that, Samuel?"

The Indian thought for a moment, then looked up at Evan. "No, sir. I won't pull any triggers unless I have to, but what you do is your business. You white men have your own ways of doing things, and I'll leave you to it. My job is to find them, that's all, and then back you up if I have to."

"Just so we understand each other, Samuel. Just so we understand each other."

Chapter 39

Jesse and Francine were making time now. Unencumbered by the heavily laden packhorses and spurred on by the threat of apprehension, the pace was easily accelerated. And therein lay the variable in the equation; Samuel was drawing wages, but Jesse and Francine were fighting for their lives. And Samuel still had to follow tracks, slowing him down, while the fugitives simply picked their way and forged ahead. Their lead began to slowly increase once more.

That evening, it snowed. The temperature dropped forty degrees in two hours, not an uncommon occurrence in the high country, but potentially life threatening to anyone unprepared in it. While Jesse and Francine had left the ranch prepared, they now had nothing but the clothes on their backs, and while they had warm coats, they had left most of their clothing with the discarded packs. They could not afford to stop to build a fire; they had to keep moving as long as their horses could still put one foot in front of the other.

The first flakes were truly beautiful, large and soft, and Francine couldn't help but relish the quietness and serenity of the snowfall. But as the time passed, the wind picked up, the snow began to swirl, and the cold began its deadly marrow piercing insinuation.

Francine was numb; Jesse was worried. Not only would the storm be dangerous for Francine, but the snow was also slowing them down- and worst of all- leaving tracks to be easily followed unless the wind picked up and blew them in. But at the same time travel would be increasingly dangerous. They pressed on, heading as straight north as they were able given the terrain.

Within two hours the storm began to truly rage, and Jesse knew they would have to stop. It would be foolhardy to try to continue; visibility was limited and the wind and cold were penetrating. Jesse was shivering with the cold, and he knew that

Francine must be suffering. Pulling off into a clump of trees he dismounted and turned to help Francine.

She was nearly frozen, and her legs refused to obey her commands. Unable to dismount on her own, Jesse had to help her down. He was heartsick at her condition. What had he done to her? How could he have asked her to come with him into this wilderness? How could he have left her behind?

He helped her to a relatively protected area under some big blue spruce trees, and sitting with his back up against one of the largest, he folded her in his arms and began to rock back and forth, doing his best to warm her with his body, talking soothingly all the while. Sammy lay quietly at his side. He wished she had told him how cold she was. He could have stopped sooner! Why hadn't she said something!

"Francine? Love? You okay?" Stupid question, of course she wasn't okay! He cursed silently to himself.

"Jess...I'm fine...just tired. And cold. So cold." She sighed softly against his chest.

Unsnapping his shirt, he slid her hands inside against his ribcage in an effort to warm them with his body heat. He didn't know what to do for her toes, which must be frozen also. He was terrified that the stress might make her lose the baby, and if that happened, he knew he would never forgive himself.

Exhaustion soon overcame her, and she slept soundly, and as she did so, he could feel the heat slowly seeping back into her body. Thank God! he thought, and sent a further silent prayer of thanks heavenward. When he thought she was warm enough to leave for a short period of time, he eased away from her to cut some large branches for a makeshift shelter as protection from the wind. They would be unable to travel until the storm quit. At least he felt safe enough here; the wind had certainly covered their tracks well enough, and nobody would be sneaking up on them in this storm.

After the crude shelter was constructed, he set about building a fire. Without heat, they would probably not survive the night, and when the storm finally did let up, if the skies cleared, the temperature would drop even further. He didn't intend to freeze to death out here! Before settling down for the night, he did set a couple of snares just in case an unwary rabbit might happen by while they slept.

With the shelter's crude protection from the wind and the fire snapping brightly, Jesse lay down and pulled Francine tightly to him.

"Jess?"

"Hush, love. I'm here, and the fire is going good. Everything is going to be okay."

"Jesse, I'm so cold, and so very tired. I'm sorry, Cowboy. Sorry I quit on you."

Tears sprang to Jesse's eyes. "You didn't quit me, hon. You did just fine. Now you go ahead and sleep as long as you want. I'll be right here."

They lay tightly together, spoon fashion, and Francine was instantly asleep. Jesse's mouth twitched in the semblance of an ironic smile; for once his body was behaving itself. He had wondered if it were possible. Kissing her softly on the nape of her neck, he soon joined her in the deep sleep of exhaustion.

Samuel had quit trailing them hours before. Early winter storms were nothing to take lightly, and there was nothing personal for him in this chase. Besides, they weren't far ahead of him now, and he knew it was just a matter of time. He squatted by his own fire, slowly chewing some hardtack, and waited for the storm to pass.

The morning sun blazed through a mesmerizing blue sky and tiny diamonds reflected its rays in a million ways from the fresh snow. A good six inches covered the ground, with deep drifts in places covering secrets beneath. The scene was so brilliant it hurt their eyes to look at it as Jesse and Francine emerged from their forest shelter, ready once more to head north in their desperate flight.

Jesse had managed to snare two rabbits during the night, and they had a feast for breakfast along with Sammy. They cooked everything they had, and any leftovers would taste awfully good by the end of the day. They were off schedule, having traveled by night up until now, but Jesse knew they couldn't afford to wait until nightfall to continue. Whoever was trailing them would have had to stop for the storm also, but like themselves, would be up and moving at first light.

Francine seemed to be back to her old self this morning. Oh, she was still tired, of course, but there seemed to be no permanent ill effects from her ordeal of the day before. Jesse again thanked God for His goodness to them.

While she wasn't joking as much as she had in the past, she had color in her cheeks and a soft smile for him on her lips when she found him gazing quietly at her. Walking over to him, she wrapped her arms tightly around him, and lifted her face for a kiss.

He kissed her tenderly full on the lips, then left soft little nips all over her face and her eyelids.

"Francine, have I told you yet this morning that I love you?"

"No, Jess, you haven't. Does that mean you changed your mind?"

With that smart remark, he hugged her suddenly to himself so tightly that it knocked the breath out of her.

"Never! And don't you ever forget it, woman!"

"Then maybe you had better kiss me again, just so I'm sure. What do you think?"

As he bent his head to kiss her soundly once again, he felt his body reacting to her once more.

"Damn! I just can't help it, hon. I'm sorry."

Francine laughed. "That's okay, Cowboy. I guess I won't be worrying as long as I get that kind of reaction every time I get close to you."

"I don't think we have time this morning, though. Besides, I'm sure that's about the last thing you need right now!"

"Jesse, you astound me, you really do. I just don't know where you get your energy!" And laughing, her hands went to his belt one more time.

"Francine, no, don't."

"Francine, yes, do." She laughed. "We'll make it real quick this morning, what do you say?"

He groaned, and was lost. Again.

***

Fifteen minutes later, they were mounted and heading north, Canada only a two-day ride ahead of them now by Jesse's best calculations.

Chapter 40

It was anticlimactic, really. Not at all what Samuel had expected to happen.

They had been watering their horses in a cold mountain stream, the late afternoon sun warming their backs, when Samuel essentially stumbled onto them. Sammy had missed his arrival, concentrating as he was on quenching his thirst. Jesse and Francine were each holding their horses as they drank loudly, pawing in the water the way horses sometimes do. No one heard his silent approach.

Francine turned first, and a gasp escaped her when she saw the tracker only about fifty feet away. Jesse heard her and spun on his heels, reaching for his pistol as he did so, but he was too late. Samuel rested easily on one hip, a Smith and Wesson .357 pointed carefully at Francine. Sammy came up out of the water, growling.

"Drop the gun, Mr. Windchase. Nice and easy. And call off the dog."

"Sammy, no," Jesse ordered the dog. Then he debated for only a second. With a .357 aimed at Francine, he knew he didn't stand a chance, and he wouldn't consider endangering Francine's life like that. He didn't drop the pistol, but slid it carefully back into its holster.

"Unbuckle the belt and throw it over to your left."

Jesse did as he was instructed. He choked back a sob. They had been so close! So very close! Another day and a half and they would have been home free. *God, how could you desert us now?* Jesse pleaded silently.

Francine was crying now, exhaustion, fatigue, and tension all taking their unavoidable toll. The tears coursed silently down her cheeks, and she turned to Jesse as he gathered her close.

"It's okay, hon. I'm still here. I'm sorry, love. So sorry."

"We were so close, Jess. With that her legs gave out and she sank to her knees, Jesse going down with her, still trying desperately to comfort her.

Samuel stood impassively, letting the moment happen. When the pair finally looked up at him again, he motioned them away from the creek's edge, and they complied, leading the horses.

"Well, now what?" asked Jesse.

"You- over here by me." He motioned to Francine. "Mr. Windchase, you go hobble those horses for now, then come back over here. And don't even think of trying anything if you want to keep your woman safe."

Francine looked first at Jesse, and as he nodded his head slightly, she told Sammy to stay with Jesse, and then walked slowly over to Samuel.

"Turn around, and put your hands behind your back." As she turned, he quickly slapped the handcuffs on her slender wrists. He didn't much like doing that to a woman. Something about cuffing a woman just didn't seem right, but he didn't have much choice in the matter it seemed. He didn't dare leave her at her liberty.

"Mr. Windchase, get to hobbling those horses. And make that dog stay with the horses or I might have to shoot him."

Jesse did as he was told. He didn't have the strength or the will right now to do any arguing. What good would it do? He was caught, and there was no way out. He knew in that instant just how old Chief Joseph must have felt when his run for Canada had failed in much the same way.

He unsaddled and hobbled the horses, told Sammy to stay with them, then walked slowly back to where Francine now sat on the ground, her hands firmly restrained by the cuffs behind her back.

"Over here, cowboy, slowly, and turn around. I'm keeping the gun on the woman, so don't try anything."

Jesse strode over to Samuel, and turning around, presented his back and his hands for the tracker to cuff. Once he was secured, Samuel turned him around to face him.

"Well, I'll be! They didn't tell me."

"Tell you what?"

"They never told me you were blood. They never told me we were tracking a breed like myself."

"Would it have made any difference?" Jesse asked.

"No. A guilty man is a guilty man. I get paid to do my job."

"Now what?"

"Now we wait for the boss. He should catch up with us in a day or two."

"Why don't you let her go? She isn't guilty of anything except following me into this godforsaken wilderness."

"No."

"Can I at least go sit with her?"

Samuel debated that for a moment, then nodded affirmatively. The woman looked too tired to do much of anything. For that matter, they both looked that way. Of course, a person can never tell… But he did wish someone had told him he was tracking another Native American like himself. He would still have taken the job, but they should have told him. He selected a suitable spot, and then set about making camp. They would wait here for Evan to find them; the rest would do them all good.

The sun had melted most of the snow by now, and though the ground was still wet, it was not unpleasant, and Francine was resting quietly when the first pain sliced through like a knife in her lower abdomen. She gasped and drew her knees to her chest with the suddenness of it.

"Jesse!" She called for him in her panic. It was the baby. She was losing the baby. "Oh God, no!" And this time she screamed out as another pain shot through her.

Jesse was on his knees at her side in an instant.

"Francine, what is it?"

"The baby, Jess. The baby. I think I'm losing the baby."

Samuel's head shot up in surprise. The woman was pregnant? He hadn't known that, either.

"You- can you let us loose here? Please?"

"No. You stay as you are."

"Look- what's your name?"

"Samuel Three Irons."

"Samuel, my wife is four months pregnant, and she seems to be going into labor. It's way too early, we've got to do something! Turn us loose for heaven's sake- we aren't going anywhere!"

"No." Samuel walked over to the couple, Francine now sweating profusely, pain racking her body every five minutes. It was obvious that the woman was pregnant, and in danger of going into full labor. He didn't much want a dead baby on his conscience, but he was unsure how to handle this situation.

"Mr. Windchase?"

"Can you please let us loose here? Please!" He stared intently at Samuel, willing him to see their plight.

"Mr. Windchase, do you have honor?"

"Samuel, I do have that."

"Will you pledge to me on your honor that you will not try to escape if I release you both?"

"On my honor, man. Now please!"

"If you try to escape, I will not hesitate to shoot you both, your woman first. Do you understand?"

"On my honor before God we will not try to escape. Good enough for you?"

Samuel, looking deep into Jesse's eyes, knew that the man meant what he said. Jesse would honor his promise. He bent down and unlocked both sets of handcuffs.

Francine moaned as Jesse gathered her close to him and began to rock her once more. She was not going to lose this baby. Not their baby, conceived in such love! Not if there was anything on this earth that Jesse could do to prevent it. But what could he do?

Only one course of action came to mind. If he could get Francine to relax before she was any further along, perhaps this would pass. Jumping up, he told Francine he would be right back, then ran over to gather up all three saddle blankets.

Using one for a pillow and one as a ground sheet, he lay down and pulled Francine full length on top of him. He knew that just being close to him was usually a comfort to her, and with the added warmth of the third blanket on top of her along with his body heat and all weight removed from her abdomen, maybe, just maybe . . .

Samuel knew a moment's hesitation when Jesse took off running, but his doubts were removed when he made up the makeshift bed of saddle blankets. He hoped for their sakes that what they were doing would work. An herbal tea would have done the trick, he knew, but they had no cups or pots to brew some in until Evan got there with the pack mules.

"Francine, love, I want you to try to think about the most beautiful place you know of, the most peaceful place. Rest and calm your mind, and think positive. Relax. Breathe deep. That's it."

"But Jesse! I . . ."

"Francine, relax. For the baby's sake. You can do it. Relax. You have to relax."

She felt the strong beat of Jesse's heart through her shirt against her chest, and she began to relax as he had ordered. She suffered, terrified, through four more severe pains, after which they began to quiet down to one every fifteen minutes or so, and then of lesser intensity. After about two hours, they ceased altogether.

"Sir, what is your name please?" Francine called softly.

"Samuel Three Irons, ma'am."

"Thank you, Mr. Three Irons." And she drifted off, sleeping lightly.

Jesse thanked God again, prayerfully, for His care and watchfulness over his wife. They may have been captured, but she was safe, and the baby was safe once more.

"Mr. Windchase, does your honor still hold?"

"It does, Mr. Three Irons."

"I am taking you at your word, one human being to another. Do you know what I am saying? Even though you are a murderer, I am taking you at your word."

"I do know exactly what you mean. I gave you my word, and my word is good. And for what it's worth, I have never killed anyone in my life, no matter what anyone has told you."

"We will talk later, Mr. Windchase. You and your woman have a pleasant night." He had looked into Jesse Windchase' eyes, and his gut told him this was an honest man. But he would sleep very lightly, with his gun in his hand.

***

Twice during the night, Jesse got up to relieve himself, and to just sit and stare into the darkness. Samuel watched him, his gun ready, but each time Jesse never went far, and always came back to be with his wife. He kept his word to Samuel, and respect for the murderer grew in the tracker's heart and mind. He wasn't sure, if he were Jesse, that he would have stayed, pregnant wife or not, knowing what would be waiting for him back in civilization. He liked to think he was an honorable enough to keep his word, as Jesse was doing, but he just wasn't sure…

Chapter 41

Jesse slept little, his heart and mind deeply troubled. He considered his options, which were few. He could just walk away, and trust that Samuel Three Irons was bluffing and would not shoot Francine. But could he take the chance? What if he was wrong, and Samuel really would do as he had promised? And what were the odds of his successful escape with his pursuers so close?

He reasoned that in fact his chances were actually fairly good. He could just walk away and fade into the forest. He might die there, or he might actually finally make it to Canada. But in reality, it was no choice at all. He could not and would not leave Francine, no matter what was ahead of them. And besides, despite all other considerations, Jesse had given his word, and his word was one thing he honored above all else. He would stay, and whatever was to be, would be.

Francine was heartsick. The depths of her despair seemed boundless, and she saw no hope for her and Jesse's future. How could they have come so far, only to be caught so close to their goal? So close! Another day and half, and they would have been safe, Jesse, Francine, and their baby. And now?

She was terrified that Jesse might be hanged. Even if he got life in prison instead of the death penalty, she would lose him forever. Her baby would have no father, and she would have no husband. She would have little reason to go on living, other than for their baby. Although after the previous afternoon she had her doubts that she would even be able to carry the baby to term given the stress that was now coming upon her. She was beaten and utterly defeated. Deep inside, she harbored a slight hope that Jesse might just walk away on one of his walks to relieve himself. She hoped desperately that he might consider doing just that; yet she knew her love. He did have honor, and she feared that he took giving his word very seriously. If he said he would not try to escape, then he would not. Her heart ached for him, and for herself. Her world had come to an end. Lord, she cried deep in her soul, why didn't you just let me die when Todd was there? Why let me live for- this? I am dead without Jesse anyway- you should have just let me die then!

Sitting up, she hugged her knees to her chest and began a slow, steady rocking motion. Back and forth, back and forth. She was not going to cry, not ever again. For Jesse's sake, she would not cry. She knew he was worried about her, and that her tears would just exacerbate that worry.

Jesse was at her side in an instant. "Francine, are you okay? The baby?"

"I'm fine, Jess. The baby is fine. I just- can't help it."

He stroked her hair, feathering kisses in the wake of his hand. His heart ached for her, but there was little he could do. It was all up to Samuel, and whomever they were waiting for.

Samuel watched the scene before him, trying not to be moved by it, but feeling his heart begin to ache for the pair in spite of himself.

"Mr. Windchase? Is your woman okay? The baby?"

"She's fine, Samuel, just unbearably tired and sad." And he continued his tireless stroking, seeking to somehow ease her pain the only way he knew how.

***

Evan rode into camp that evening, just about dusk. Seeing Jesse and Francine unconfined nearly sent him into a frenzy.

"Samuel- get handcuffs on those people! What are they doing loose!"

"Mr. Smazick, Jesse here gave me his word he would not try to escape, and he has kept his word. He isn't going to take off on us, we can trust him."

"Trust a murderer? I don't hardly think so. Come over here, Mr. Windchase."

Jesse did as he was told, and Evan slapped the handcuffs on his wrists once again.

Gesturing to Francine, he called to her "Now you. Over here."

"Evan, we can let her be. She isn't going anywhere." Samuel thought it was a shame to humiliate these people in this fashion, knowing it wasn't necessary.

"She might try something. Can't take any chances. Over here," he repeated to her.

Francine obediently rose to her feet and came to present herself for the handcuffs. Evan slapped them on none too gently, then spun her around and told her to go take a seat once more.

"Evan, for heaven's sake, she's pregnant! Does she have to be cuffed?" Samuel pleaded one more time.

"Don't try to tell me how to do my job, Samuel. Your job was to find them, my job is to arrest them and bring them out." Turning to Jesse, he barely restrained himself from spitting in the Indian's face. He hated Jesse Windchase; the man had made a fool of him out here in the Bob, and he didn't like being made a fool of. Well, they would just see who would come out of this alive.

It was too late to do much of anything that evening, and besides, Evan was tired from the long day of riding. Tomorrow was soon enough to put his plan into action. There wouldn't be any prisoners coming out of the Bob, or bodies either. Why waste the taxpayer's time and money? The man was guilty as sin, and the state had already spent a fortune hunting him down. No, Jesse Windchase and the woman could just stay up here permanently. He would see to it in the morning.

Jesse could read the blatant hatred in Evan's eyes. He wasn't sure just why it was so, but the fact remained that Evan truly hated him, and it worried Jesse. Often, men who carried that kind of intense feeling within them failed to act rationally in certain circumstances. Jesse began to wonder just how far Evan was willing to go in this case.

Evan was the only one who slept soundly that night. Jesse was worried, Francine was terribly uncomfortable, and Samuel was having a battle with his conscience. He had been prepared to feel nothing towards Jesse and Francine, but after meeting the man, he found he was drawn to him as a result. He harbored a deep resentment that he hadn't been told of Jesse's heritage. True, it wouldn't have mattered as far as his job went, but he still thought someone should have told him. And he began to wonder what else he hadn't been told. Jesse was just too honorable to be guilty of everything he had been accused of. It didn't make sense. Something was missing here, and he determined to find out just what it was. But he sure didn't like the idea of not bringing the pair out alive. He didn't much like it at all.

At first light, Evan and Samuel were up, replenishing the fire, seeing to the stock, and putting the coffee on to boil. Sammy had crept back to be with his mistress during the night, and no one made him leave. Jesse could smell the coffee simmering in the pot, and found himself nearly salivating with the aroma. At least there was to be coffee! He was tired and hungry, and could only imagine how Francine was feeling. However, it soon became evident that the food and coffee were not going to be shared with the prisoners.

Jesse determined not to beg. He thought about it for Francine's sake, but one look at her face told him she was feeling the same way he was. She was not going to beg, either.

Samuel finally spoke up. "Evan, aren't we going to give them some?"

"Nope.'

"Evan!"

Evan looked over at the pair, and through clenched teeth muttered, "No sense to waste it on them. They don't need it."

Jesse barely heard the muffled words, and began to doubt that he had heard correctly. He couldn't have heard what he thought he heard! Evan was not planning on taking them out of here. He wasn't planning on taking them anywhere! My God! he thought. They're going to kill us! His heart broke, not for himself, but for Francine. He couldn't believe they would actually kill a woman, and a totally innocent one at that. Her only crime had been in loving him, and his heart shattered at the thought.

He glanced at Francine's set face, and realized she hadn't heard the muffled comment from Evan. Good. Perhaps he could spare her that knowledge at least until the last moment. For the first time in his life he regretted keeping his given word.

Evan had debated how he was going to accomplish his plan for the past several days. He was going to need a plausible explanation as to why they weren't bringing any bodies out of the Bob, and had finally decided that a probable bear attack was the best answer. They would bring out a few effects, enough to prove that the bodies had actually been found, but when a Grizzly gets done with a person, there often isn't enough left to bring out. They could bring the horses back with them, or just turn them loose. He hadn't decided for sure on that one yet. The dog they would just shoot also. No one would ever be the wiser, and the state would be saved a lengthy trial as well as a lot of money. Seemed just about perfect to him. He could have done it last night, but didn't want his camp disturbed. He would do it just before they left this morning.

Samuel didn't know exactly what Evan had planned, but he did know that Evan certainly meant to carry out his threat. These two people were not coming out of the Bob Marshall alive, if Evan had anything to say about it. Normally, Samuel wouldn't really have cared one way or the other, but in this case….

"Evan, who did Jesse kill, anyway? I never did hear." Samuel hadn't heard, and had never cared enough to ask the circumstances. His job had simply been to track Jesse down.

"Killed and mutilated that cowboy over by Ennis last spring, remember? It was in all the papers. Castrated the man then killed him. Horrible death."

Samuel had seen it in the papers. But he had to hear it from Jesse.

"That right, Mr. Windchase? Did you kill that cowboy?"

Jesse looked Samuel straight in the eye, and then replied, "No sir, I did not. After what he did to Francine I admit I did hunt the man down and castrate him, planned to kill the bastard too, but in the end I couldn't. So I left him. Alive. What happened after that I can't say. But I didn't kill the man." He paused, then added forcefully, "On my honor, Samuel, I did not kill that man."

And Samuel knew in that moment that Jesse was telling him the truth. One human being to another, one Native American to another, one man to another, it was the truth.

"What did he do to Francine?"

Jesse quietly related how he had found Francine in the cabin, how Todd had beaten her nearly to death and left her to die.

Samuel looked long and hard from Jesse to Francine, back again to Jesse, then over to Evan.

"Evan, did you know this story?"

"Yes, I know the story. The foreman told me the whole thing, down at the ranch."

"And you still plan to . . ?"

"Damn right. The man killed his wife years ago, and this is only his word against the evidence. Oh, he killed that man all right. I think two murders are enough evidence for any kind of judgment and verdict.

"Mr. Windchase, did you kill your wife?"

"No, sir, I did not. Again, on my honor, I did not. I went to jail and served ten years for a crime I did not commit."

Evan rose from his place, his face impassive, and walked slowly into the woods. He was gone about ten minutes, and when he returned, his steps were measured, his face set.

"Evan, this will not happen."

"What do you mean, 'this will not happen?' This damn sure *will* happen, right here, right now. Let's get to it and get ourselves out of here."

"No." It was said quietly, but forcefully. There would be no killing up here, not as long as he was alive to stop it. For what that cowboy had done to Francine, he deserved whatever Jesse had done to him. No man should be allowed to treat a woman like that. If Jesse hadn't killed him, it was still justice that he had died somehow. Jesse did not deserve to go back to jail, and he sure as hell didn't deserve to die. Samuel turned his back for a moment, and removing his hat almost in an act of reverence, raised his face to the sky. Praying? He replaced his hat, and when he turned back to Evan, his .357 was aimed straight at his superior.

"No, Evan, it isn't going to happen. These people are going to Canada, just like they planned, and you aren't going to lift a finger to stop them."

Francine's heart began a slow steady throbbing. Could it be possible? Were they really going to make it to Canada after all? Was Samuel going to go against his boss and help them? She was afraid to believe what she was seeing and hearing, afraid to hope.

Jesse had moved as close to her as he could stand. He longed to put his arms around her, to give her whatever comfort he could. He too could hardly take in what he was hearing. Samuel Three Irons was willing to put his life and future on the line for them, and he couldn't remember anyone other than Glen and Francine who had been willing to do that for him ever before. He was overwhelmed.

"Samuel," he began, not wanting to distract the man, but also wanting to voice something to him. "Samuel, are you sure you want to do this? You will become a criminal yourself. Think carefully about what you are doing here."

"Yes, Samuel, think very carefully about what you are doing here. You don't want to go through with this!" Evan couldn't believe what was happening.

"Don't worry, I'm not about to shoot anybody unless I absolutely have to. But these folks are not going anywhere they don't want to go. Not as long as I am able to prevent it. Come over here Jesse, and we'll get those cuffs off."

Jesse was only too happy to do his bidding, and when Samuel had released him, he took the keys and ran to release Francine.

"Jesse?" Francine could scarcely believe what was happening. Was there hope after all?

"Now, you folks load up whatever you need and get out of here. I think Evan and I are just going to set here and rest for a couple of days before we head on down out of this wilderness. Two days give you enough time to make Canada?"

"I think that should just about do it."

"Then git!"

"Samuel?" Jesse held his hand out to the tracker. "Thank you, brother. I won't ever forget you or what you have done for us here."

Samuel grasped Jesse's hand warmly. "You take care of that woman for me. Hear? Now get going!"

With one last long gaze at his new friend, Jesse gathered Francine close to him and started for the horses, Sammy close on their heels. For a moment he thought about taking some of the lawmen's supplies with him, but in the end decided against it. He didn't want theft added to his account, and besides, it didn't matter anymore; he could shoot whatever game they needed on the trail. Two days! That's all the time they needed. They just might make it after all!

Jesse and Francine were saddled and ready to ride in minutes. Without a backward glance, they rode silently into the high forest and disappeared once more.

Chapter 42

Samuel kept Evan handcuffed, hands in front of him for the rest of the day. There was no spoken communication between the two, and Samuel was happy with that. They sipped their camp coffee, and napped during the heat of the afternoon. Samuel figured they could head out the following morning. If he had any trouble with Evan, and if the worst happened and Evan got free, Jesse and Francine had a big enough lead they would easily cross into Canada before Evan could catch up with them. If all went as planned, the two men would simply start riding back toward Helena.

They were awakened around two-thirty that afternoon by the horses, restless, trying to escape their hobbles. Samuel rose to see to them, leaving Evan lying in repose on the ground near the now dead fire. Evan screamed, but the bear was on him before Samuel had any idea a bear was even in the area.

Samuel emptied his .357 in the direction of the huge beast, but he was too late. Before he could grab his rifle, the giant paws had ripped Evan to shreds and dragged him off into the forest.

Samuel shook his head sadly. He would be coming out of the Bob Marshall alone. He thought briefly about going after the bear, but discretion took over. It would be just plain stupid to go after a wounded Grizzly defending his latest meal. No, he would go home alone.

There was no more reason to wait now and Samuel soon broke camp, the mules packed once more. The tracker mounted and gazed once to the north almost wistfully before he reined his horse to the south and headed for home.

***

Sound carries for miles sometimes in the high country, if the lay of the land is just right. The sounds of the pistol shots barely echoed through the mountains, but Jesse heard them. He reined in his horse, puzzling as to what might have gone wrong. He sincerely hoped that Samuel was okay, and that Evan hadn't done anything stupid just to salve his feeble pride. But there was nothing he could do. He owed Samuel their lives, and he wished him well. "Thank you again, my friend," he whispered into the soft breeze.

"Jess?" Francine questioned from behind him.

He swiftly dismounted, dropped the reins and strode back to Francine. "Bend down here, woman!"

She did as requested, and he kissed her long and hard.

"I love you, Francine. I do so love you!"

She kissed him again, then he turned and walked slowly back to his horse, and mounting, continued across the face of the hill, heading north.

***

Shortly after dark the following day, Dennis Murphy was heading home after a long day of fence riding. He was late, and was thinking about the cold supper that probably awaited him at the Lane Ranch cookhouse. Off in the distance, he thought he spotted a movement on the crest of the far hill, and it was dark so he couldn't be sure, but it looked like a couple of riders and a dog heading due north into the vast Canadian night. Moonlight reflected off what seemed to be the ghostly white blanket of an Appaloosa horse. The riders were visible for only a moment, and deciding his eyes must be playing tricks on him, Dennis shook his head and continued on down the trail.

***

Francine Larson and Jesse Windchase were never seen again. It wasn't long before it seemed they had never existed. But every now and then, a Flathead Indian tracker named Samuel

Three Irons would gaze wistfully to the north for extended periods of time, lost in thought. Remembering. Hoping.

About the Author

Mary Stormont writing as Catherine Boyd holds a BS degree in Agricultural Production, Animal Science as well as an Associate degree in Nursing from Rock Valley College in Rockford, IL. She spent thirty-five years living and ranching in Montana in the general area where this novel is set. She was married to a rancher for twelve years, and after her divorce she worked in the area as a general ranch hand and then as a sheepherder near Bridger, MT. After becoming a Registered Nurse, she returned to Montana and worked in small rural hospitals and nursing homes.

She has written and published two pamphlets, *"Choosing a Nursing Home and Living With Your Choice"*, and *"Are You*

Sure? Are You Really Going to Heaven?" which is in its eighth printing.

She has ridden much of the area in the book, with the exception of "the Bob" so the descriptions are pretty accurate. Sixteen Mile Creek is very real. Maudlow is a real town with maybe fifteen people in it, and that's probably stretching it a bit today. It is essentially a ghost town now. Hatfield Mountain is real, and she saw a Grizzly bear there just as Francine did. The mountain lion attack on the horse is based on a real event, however in real life the lion attacked a horse in her neighbor's corral in the middle of the night. His furiously barking dogs alerted him and he was able to drive the lion away with a shotgun. They were able to save the horse with immediate veterinary care, but scars left from the lion's claws never disappeared. The C/6 ranch is an actual ranch, but with a different brand. Catherine worked there for one summer while attending MT State University. C/6 is her personal brand, and was used in the story to protect the ranch's privacy. The appaloosa horses in the story were her personal mounts for many years. Catherine worked as a "night calver" for a rancher for two years, and the calving descriptions are very accurate. Most Montana ranch kids DO go to college, contrary to what many Easterners think! The story is pure fiction, however. She never knew or heard of any woman passing herself off as a cowboy to escape detection.

Made in the USA
Middletown, DE
10 September 2020